Thunderforge Pubs

dpInk

Donna Ink Publications, L.L.C.

SIEGE OF THE SMALL WORLD

Thunderforge Pubs | DonnaInk Publications, L.L.C.

Thunderforge Pubs

United States of America

SIEGE OF THE SMALL WORLD

WRITTEN BY

GERHARD PLENERT

Thunderforge Pubs
Publishers Since 2012
An imprint of DonnaInk Publications, L.L.C.
601 McReynolds Street, Carthage, NC 28327

Thunderforge Pubs

Copyright © 2020 by Dr. Gerhard Plenert.

Library of Congress Cataloging-in-Publications Data.
Name: Plenert, Dr. Gerhard, author.
Title: "The Siege of the Small World" / Dr. Gerhard Plenert

Description: Thunderforge Pubs an imprint of DonnaInk Publications, L.L.C.: *"The Siege of the Small World" is the first book in a fantasy series entitled, "The History of the Small World." This series follows the lives of a group of leprechauns whose world has been disrupted and they go on a challenging and eventful quest to restore harmony.*

Identifiers: ISBN – 13 – 978-1-947704-02-2 (alk. paper); 978-1-947704-09-1 (eBook); 978-1-939425-80-5; Subjects: BISAC: FIC009100 FICTION / Fantasy - Action & Adventure; FIC009040 Collections & Anthologies; FIC009120 Dragons & Mythical Creatures; FIC010000 Fairy Tales, Folk Tales, Legends & Mythology; FIC002000 Action & Adventure. Classification: LCC - PS3600-3626; LCC - PN6120.15-6120.95.

354 p. cm.

Printed in the United States of America
First Edition: 12 11 10 9 8 7 6 5 4 3 2; 2019. All Rights Reserved.
Book design by: Ms. Donna L. Quesinberry.
Book illustrations by: Ms. Felicia Chen and Ms. Aliya Chen.

For more information contact:
DonnaInk Publications, L.L.C.
601 McReynolds St., Carthage, NC 28327
www.donnaink.com

TABLE OF CONTENTS

FOREWORD

By Ar. Perumal N

This is an enlightening series of interesting events which holds the reader captive. The vivid details engage the reader with glimpses of Small World which includes dwarfs, lepelves, elves, gnomes, and leprechauns. The story is a reflection of the challenges of a world where light and truth triumphs narrowly but only when sought by the few good.

It enthralls the imaginative mind, bringing it into a world of fantasy. The journey focuses on enclaves of leprechauns and leads us to culminating heights of tragedy, thrills, deception, snares, and dangers throughout a journey which addicts the reader and leaves them thirsting for more.

I thoroughly enjoyed reading this book and recommend it for people of all ages and interests. This adventure would make a wonderful movie.

Ar Perumal Nagapushnam, Architect
Post Grad Dip Architecture
Selangor, Malaysia

THE SIEGE OF THE SMALL WORLD

by Dr. Gerhard Plenert

2nd Edition

Thunderforge Pubs Imprint

DonnaInk Publications, L.L.C.

www.donnaink.com

PREFACE

THOUGHTS FROM THE AUTHOR

I, Gerhard Plenert, love fantasy. I wanted to write a novel could be enjoyed by young and old alike. That meant it had to be interesting, full of surprises, and engaging enough to captivate the attention of the mature reader. It also had to be filled with creative and interesting characters. But for the younger mind it couldn't be excessively violent. That was what I created here in this first book of a series titled "The History of Small World". I hope that you, the reader, have as much fun reading it as I had in writing it.

ACKNOWLEDGEMENT

WITH GRATITUDE

This book has been many years in the making and there are numerous individuals that need to be recognized. Of primary importance would be my conscience that validated the flow and identified any holes in the plot, Renee Plenert. And, secondarily my publisher, Ms. D. L. Quesinberry, Founder-Chief Execution Officer (CEO) of DonnaInk Publications, L.L.C. through Thunderforge Pubs Imprint from Carthage North Carolina.

I want to give special thanks to my illustrators and artists. The cover design was done by Sammy Lee Benson of Sacramento, California who also did some of the illustrations throughout the book. A couple of the illustrations were also done by my sister Helen Plenert Horiuchi of Carmichael, California. Some illustration touchup work was performed by Stephen Lamar Smith also of Carmichael, California. But I want to give as special, heartfelt thank you to Jonathan Noronha Pushnam who traveled all the way from Selangor, Malaysia to California in order to create the majority of the illustrations that are found throughout this book. He's an incredible artist. Thank you one and all for your incredible help.

My many years of reading fantasy novels on airplanes, as I travelled for work, taught me a lot and I need to share my appreciation to the many fantasy authors that came before me. Their ideas, approach, and style have been an inspiration to me, and I offer my sincere thanks.

Introduction

How it All Began

Many years ago, far too many for anyone to remember, the smaller inhabitants of the outer world became overpowered by their larger brothers. The "bigger ones" (men and giants) wanted more land forcing the "smaller ones" (dwarfs, elves, leprechauns, and lepelves) into increasingly tinier corners of the world. Before long they didn't have enough land to farm, and they were forced to be dependent on the bigger ones. As the legends tell us, the smaller ones found themselves pushed out of the flat lands and into the mountains. Searching the mountains for a new home, a few of the dwarfs were more courageous and entered into tunnels that had heretofore been avoided. Tradition had always told them that the tunnels housed evil spirits. But the courage of the dwarfs allowed them to discover a new world for themselves, a world "underneath." Luckily, they found these tunnels were too small for the bigger ones to enter. But the tunnels easily fit the size of the smaller ones.

As the dwarfs delved deeper and deeper into the tunnels, they found themselves in a new world. The tunnels opened up into an enormous cavern, much bigger than anyone could see across. This new world had mountains, rivers, lakes, and forests. It even had a bright glowing orb somewhere near the ceiling, which simulated the sun. The orb's brightness would cycle, glowing brighter during the day, and going completely dark at night. This world had trees, and grass, and insects. In fact, it looked much the same as the world they had come from on the surface. The dwarfs called their new world Small World.

The adventuresome dwarfs retreated back to the surface to retrieve their dwarf cousins and to bring all of them to this new world. Initially, there was fear at entering the tunnels, but after time it was decided that the dwarfs would all migrate to this new world. They proceeded with the migration hoping to leave everyone else, bigger or smaller behind. But it didn't work out that way. The other smaller ones, the elves, leprechauns, and lepelves had noticed the dwarf migration, and followed suit. Before long the entire smaller population had resettled in this new world. The departure was successfully concealed, and the bigger ones were left with the mystery of never knowing what had happened to any of the smaller ones.

The geography of Small World comprises three major sections, the North Groves, the Central Ranges, and the Southern Plains. The tunnels through which the dwarfs had initially entered Small World was near the south. Over time, Small World developed into what it is today. In their attempt to separate themselves from the other smaller ones, the dwarfs migrated as far away from the entrance to Small World as possible. The dwarfs ended up in the North Groves.

Population growth and migrations built up farms and cities, much the same as in the bigger world, except now everything was built to fit the smaller inhabitants. Three cities were developed in the Southern Plains. The first of these was Gije on the Jove Plateau, which became the land of the elves. A second was Amins on the southern edge of the Amins Grove, which became the land of the leprechauns. The third city was Giter on the northern edge of the Amins Grove, which became the land of the lepelves. The lepelves are a blend of the elves from Gije and the leprechauns from Amins. Being half-breeds and therefore outcastes from each of these communities, they created their own home.

The North Groves became home to the dwarfs and had two cities, Hilebon and Hilebin. The North Groves and the Southern Plains rely heavily on trade between themselves. They exchange fruits, clothing, baskets, and furniture using the Albo Pass over the Central Ranges. Trade was primarily conducted by the dwarfs, since their southern counterparts were less adventuresome and preferred to avoid traveling.

The Albo Pass was the safest route of travel for the dwarfs between the North and the South. An alternate route was the Kilo Pass, but this route involved passage through the dangerous and feared Kabul which was in the middle of the Central Ranges. The only other remaining route was along the Avol River which required a treacherous three hundred leprechaun length ascent at the Sheere Cliffs.

The Albo Pass traveled along the west edge of the Central Ranges and posed no serious dangers. It was the highest of the trails and therefore has the most treacherous weather. This trail also ran along the Lamos, a cliff that was believed to drop off to the center of the world. Many of the Small World inhabitants, particularly dwarfs, allowed curiosity to get the better of them and had tried to scale down into the Lamos to see what they could find, but none had ever returned.

To the east of the Albo Pass was the Kabul ruled by Lord Krakus. Lord Krakus was an old leprechaun wizard of the south who one day, during evil experiments, was engulfed with flames causing burns all over his body. By using his wizardry and pieces of dead animals, he was able to reconstruct a body for himself, but the people of the Small World thought his new body was grotesque. This created fear and their fear of the Lord caused him to flee the populated areas near him in total rejection. This rejection caused the Lord to develop a hatred for all the inhabitants of Small World. In isolation, he established his own land in the wasteland area of the Central Ranges known as the Kabul.

In the Kabul, Lord Krakus vowed to take revenge on the other regions of the Small World. He started by developing three major cities. The city situated furthest north was Morgos, the home of the Magotites. Magotites were maggot-eaten dead animals brought back to life by the Kabul Lord so that he could use them for his evil designs.

The central city in the Kabul was Tragis, on the edge of the Kabul volcano. This volcano contained many tunnels, including the laboratory of Lord Krakus wherein his evil experiments continued. Tragis was also the home of the trolls, the tallest and strongest, but also the ugliest of the Small World creatures. Tragis contained the Kabul Lord's castle which was guarded by the trolls and which controlled all the activity of the Kabul.

The third major city of the Kabul was Gamotz, the home of the gnomes. Gnomes were irresponsible and illogical creatures with bodies of deformed Small World beings. They were the mutated result of a holocaust that occurred in the Upperworld, soon after the "smaller ones" came to Small World. The gnomes were rejected by the inhabitants of Upper-world and, following the Lifefight Wars, found their way to Small World where they found sanctuary in the Kabul. This was where they established their new home.

The Kabul was a region avoided and feared by both the North Groves and the Southern Plains. The reign and fear of Lord Krakus caused contact between the Kabul and the other areas of Small World to stop. And everyone wanted to keep it that way. They wanted to avoid the contact and conflict. But the North Groves and the Southern Plains knew little of the evil designs of the Kabul Lord.

DEDICATION

TO THOSE THAT MATTER

This Book is dedicated to the leader of the
Small World of my life,
Renee Sangray Plenert

My parents George and Ida Plenert
(Who gave me the chance to live in the greatest country.)

And my 8 Kids
(Who mean the world to me.)
And the yet to be Numbered Grandkids
(A process which is beyond my control.)

Who Keep My Life Under Siege!

The Siege of the Small World
THE HISTORY OF THE SMALL WORLD

The Southern Plains became dependent on trade with the North Groves. Each had their own areas of expertise and each had come to rely on the other for their survival. But for some unknown reason this vital trade came to an abrupt halt. The Dwarfs no longer came to the south to trade. Most believed the Dwarfs of the north couldn't be trusted.

What was their game?
Were they trying to starve out the south?
Were they trying to increase the price for their goods?
Where were they?
What game were they playing?

This is an entertaining series of interesting events, which hold the reader captive. The vivid details engage the reader through glimpses of the Small World, which includes dwarfs, hepelves, elves, gnomics, and leprechauns. The story is a reflection of the challenges of a world where light and truth triumphs narrowly but only when sought by the few good.

Ar Perumal Narapishnam, Architect
Post-Grad Dip Architecture
Selangor, Malaysia

The Siege of the Small World

THE HISTORY OF THE SMALL WORLD
Written by
Dr. Gerhard Plexert

SIEGE OF THE

SMALL WORLD

EPIGRAPH

And thus the Lamanites began to increase in riches, and began to trade one with another and wax great, and began to be a cunning and a wise people, as to the wisdom of the world, yea, a very cunning people, delighting in all manner of wickedness and plunder, except it were among their own brethren." (Mosiah 24:7 – The Book of Mormon)

PROLOGUE

A STRUGGLE BEGINS

The Southern Plains became dependent on trade with the North Groves. Each had their own areas of expertise and each had come to rely on the other for their survival. But for some unknown reason this vital trade came to an abrupt halt.

The Dwarfs no longer came to the south to trade. Most believed the Dwarfs of the north couldn't be trusted.

What was their game?

Were they trying to starve out the south?

Were they trying to increase the price for their goods?

Where were they?

What game were they playing?

Chapter One

The Council

After several attempts Amaz was finally successful in quieting the group thereby allowing him to start the meeting. His handsome face showed aged lines of concern. He started the Amins' council session with a fury, "How long can this go on? Why are the dwarfs making us suffer in this way? Are they delaying deliveries? To push up prices?"

Balbot, one of the younger and more outspoken members of the leprechaun council, burst in, "Those dwarfs are a sneaky lot. They are just trying to get the best of us. We all know that. We should go up there and give them a good thrashing and refuse to do business with them in the future."

"Why didn't we go up there sooner?" complained Yanon, the military figurehead of Amins who was the police captain of the city. He wasn't a regular participant at the council sessions, but he had been invited to this day's meeting because police action might be required. "Why have we waited six months before deciding to react to this problem?"

Algo, the elder, spoke up immediately, "Balbot, you are just showing your youth. And Yanon, you know that we expected the dwarfs to show up any time. They have been late before. Let's give them the benefit of the doubt. They've always been good to us in the past. We haven't had trouble with them until now. I'm sure there must be a good reason for this delay. Let's send a committee to the North Groves and see what the dwarfs have to say for themselves."

This was the morning of the council. The Council of Amins was held once every month to discuss problems, pass judgments, and make decisions regarding the development of Amins. They were the governing body of the Amins city-state. This day was a very important morning for the council members, much more so than most meetings which were usually entangled with bureaucracy. The city of Amins had not received shipments from the North Groves for over six months. The people of Amins were becoming emotional. They blamed all their problems on the dwarfs. The baskets, clothing, and food products from the North Groves had become a vital part of the lifeblood of the leprechaun population. They were disturbed that the dwarfs had not come to purchase any of the fruit or furniture the leprechauns produced. Many of the furniture makers had become very hungry and were forced to store large quantities of dwarf-sized furniture that they could not sell to anyone but the dwarfs.

There was tension in the council. It seemed as if everyone was talking at once. The rumblings of the many private conversations echoed through the chambers. The twelve members of the council led by Amaz, the "wise elder", waited in anticipation of Amaz's continuation of the meeting.

The council chambers were inside the immense State Hall. It was a beautiful old hall built by the old ones many ages ago. The "old ones" were the first inhabitants of Small World. They were the first to settle the area and the work they did was still held in high esteem.

The hall had huge windows with colored glass brought in from many parts of Small World. The council members enjoyed speaking in this hall since their high-pitched voices could be heard many times over with the echoes that the hall created. The furniture in the chamber was simple. It contained one over-sized round table with beautifully crafted chairs made from the wood of the rare Karkat tree, a tree that was unique to Small World.

It was a devilish winter morning. It was pouring rain and the streets were muddy. The people were so hampered by the weather that completing their daily chores had become impossible. This had also helped to put everyone into bad spirits.

Amaz stood out from the crowd. He was taller and stronger looking than the others. He had the look of a great intellectual. His appearance gained him the respect of everyone he encountered. Today however, his face looked aged with concern.

Amaz stood up and slapped his hand on the table several times in an attempt to bring the council members and visitors to order. It would be a difficult job to control this unruly group. He knew he must resolve the major issue with the dwarfs immediately or no other business would be possible.

There was a hub of conversation around the table. Strong agreement with Algo was obvious. A committee would have to be formed and sent to the North Grove to establish contact with the dwarfs and to find out why trade had stopped. After allowing a few moments of debate, Amaz had to again slap his hand firmly on the table to bring the council back to order. "How can we send anyone out in this weather? And how can we rightfully ask anyone to go into a possibly dangerous situation?"

Again, the council went into a hub of side conversations. Aver, the furniture maker, yelled out above all the other voices, "We can't wait for the weather. It may be several months before the weather clears. We must send out a committee immediately. I'll go myself if I have to."

Algo, the elder, was calm as he spoke, "We have become too dependent on the dwarfs. They have always handled the transport of our goods back and forth, and leprechauns have rarely needed to make the journey. But, since we're not hearing from the dwarfs, I see no other choice. A committee must go immediately."

Amaz called for a vote and the result was unanimous in favor of sending a committee to the North Groves. Balbot and Yanon grunted that they had tolerated just about enough of the dwarfs. But Amaz was still concerned, for he knew that a more serious decision lay ahead. He asked the question, "Who do we choose for a journey of this type? It should include members from all the southern cities. There should be members from Gije, Giter, and Amins. How do we form this group on such short notice?"

Again, Avre interjected in a boisterous voice, "With or without Gije and Giter, we must go! This problem must be resolved."

But Amaz was insistent, "We've always had good relations with Gije and Giter. We cannot go behind their backs to the North Groves and try to get special treatment. We must try to include representatives from all communities and give them the opportunity to go with us."

Algo was quick to agree with Amaz, "This trip must be a united effort with a show of strength from the Southern Plains if it is to be a success."

Balbot also agreed with this, but for a more hawkish reason. He said, "If a committee must be sent it should be a combined committee. If this confrontation results in a war, they need to help us fight the North Groves."

Amaz called for a vote and it was unanimously decided that a committee would be formed immediately and that this committee would request volunteers from Gije and Giter.

Then Algo spoke up, "Who knows the way to the North Groves? How do we send a committee into an area that may be extremely dangerous without any guides?" For the first time the room became quiet. The answer could be read on everyone's face.

Yanon broke the silence, "There is only one person in the Southern Plains who has ever gone to the North Groves."

Avre burst in, "You can't mean Elasti! He is soon to be wed to Jizeel, the daughter of Amaz. Surely Elasti and Amaz, and of course Jizeel, would disagree to such a journey at this time."

Amaz was thoughtful. He felt heartbroken. In a broken voice he said, "I realize that Jizeel may never forgive me, but I must think of the welfare of the entire town. I see no other alternative." With his voice cracking he turned to the guards and said, "Send for Elasti!"

After the guards had departed to find Elasti, Amaz asked the council members, "Who should accompany Elasti on the trip?" Several suggestions were made and votes were cast. Two companions, Agot and Broch, were selected. Both were lifelong friends of Elasti and the three were very close. The council hoped that their closeness would make the trip somewhat enjoyable for them. Additionally, Agot and Broch were brave young lads, which would hopefully make up for the fact that Elasti was considered a little cowardly.

The guards were able to locate Elasti quickly and he soon arrived. Upon entering the council chambers, he hesitated and, not knowing what was in store for him, spoke up with, "How can I be of service to the great Council of Amins?"

It was the duty of Amaz to explain to Elasti, "You have been selected as one of a party of three to go to the North Groves and meet with the dwarfs. You are to find out why they have not come to trade with us."

Elasti couldn't respond. His mouth gaped wide open. After a few moments he said, "I have only made that journey once with the dwarfs. It is a very long and difficult journey. It involves many nights out in the wilderness. I beg the council to select someone better fit and more capable than I. Please give me a reprieve from going on this trip."

Amaz stated, "Your experience in traveling to the dwarf's home is the very reason why we are forced to select you. You are the only one that knows the way through the Hile Groves. You will make this journey a success."

Elasti continued to plead, "But I am about to be wed. My bride will be heartbroken. You are sending me on a journey from which I may never return." Looking straight at Amaz he said, "How can you do this to me? Don't you accept me as a son-in-law?"

Amaz saw the pain in the eyes of the young boy and said reassureingly, "I look forward to the wedding and the day that I can call you my son. However, we of the council must go beyond personal feelings and consider the wellbeing of the entire city. We must do what is best for Amins. We must find out why trade has ended and restore relations with the dwarfs so that our quality of life will be restored. We have no alter-native. You must be ready to leave tomorrow morning with Agot and Broch to travel up the Albo pass to the North Groves. On your way you must go to Giter and Gije and attempt to recruit others who are willing to journey with you so that there is representation from the other cities."

Elasti said emphatically, "I will not go! The only reason I went the first time was because the dwarfs promised me it would be fun. It was not fun. It was a horrible journey. One that I vowed I would not make again! Now you want me to be part of an expedition of only three people all the way to the North Groves without the shelter of the Dwarf's wagons! I refuse!"

Amaz had to appeal with all his heart, "You will be the hero of Amins. You are the only person here that we can rely on to save us from ruin. Do you not see the carpenters begging to sell their wares? The devastation that has been created in Amins is irreparable if we do not reopen trade with the North Groves immediately."

Elasti was speechless. He knew that his own father, a carpenter and furniture maker by trade had been complaining bitterly about poor sales. He blamed these problems entirely on the dwarfs. How would his family feel if he refused to help them when they needed his help the most? After a long pause he finally said, "I'm not going willingly. This trip scares me!"

CHAPTER TWO

THE JOURNEY BEGINS

The morning was overcast and dreary. The rain had stopped but the ground was still wet and mushy. Their supplies were packed. Elasti, Agot, and Broch were ready to go. All three were young, in their early 20's and they had been childhood friends. Elasti was always the conservative member of the group. Whenever the other two wanted to do something that seemed a little risky, Elasti would always bring them back to their senses.

Agot was the one with the crazy ideas. He was the risk taker. He would be the one who always wanted to know what was over the next hill. And Broch was his shadow. He was the follower tagging behind Agot's leadership. Broch was also the biggest and the strongest of the three. He was the workhorse.

It was very early, before the sun began to shine, and the three met in the street ready for their departure. Amaz and Jizeel joined them to say goodbye. Elasti was doing his best to reassure Jizeel that he would return soon, but he wasn't that sure if he would ever see her again. And she could not hold back the tears.

Amaz wished the three travelers could be spared from having to make this journey but he knew it had to be. He offered them the best of luck and encouraged them onward by saying, "We need your help. We are depending on you to bring back good news from the North Groves. We look forward to when we meet again."

With these words, the three were off! They kept looking back and waving, tears in their eyes. It wasn't long before they rounded the first bend by the Amins groves, and their beautiful city was out of site.

Losing sight of home was all Elasti needed to set him off on a barrage of complaints. "These packs are heavy," he barked. "We have to carry extra supplies because of the wet weather and cold temperatures this time of the year. Why couldn't we wait for nicer weather?"

Leprechauns weren't noted for being enthusiastic travelers. Being out in the cold, wet weather away from home overnight was against their

nature. They were exceptionally short in stature, no more than about a third the size of a man. They were the shortest of the Small World inhabitants, with the lepelves running a close second. They had very little hair on their bodies, not like the dwarfs who were practically covered with hair. Maybe this was what made the leprechauns dread the cold nights outdoors even more. They were a clean looking stately sort of people, dressed in fine clothes and trimmed out neatly with ribbons and sashes around their collars and sleeves. They were also musical, with a heritage rich in folklore, poems, and songs. But this was not a time for singing. Elasti hated the cold, wet outdoors, especially at night. The rain wasn't heavy, but it would build up on the leaves of the trees and walking amongst the trees resulted in rain clumps falling like large sheets of water, causing the travelers to suddenly become drenched.

Elasti was in one of his worst moods, constantly complaining. Agot and Broch put all their effort into trying to calm him as they traveled the south road to Giter. Elasti complained about the weather. He complained about the mud on the roads. He complained about his heavy pack. Most of all he complained about being selected for the journey. "Why did I have to go when I was so close to being married to Jizeel? Why did I have to go when I hate the long dreary journey along the Albo Pass?" He cursed the dwarfs for ever having shown him the location of Hilebon and Hilebin.

Agot tried his best to be understanding. He attempted to assure Elasti that all would go quickly and that soon they would be back at home. He kept talking to Elasti in a soft gentle voice and eventually Elasti was calm. But by the time Agot had Elasti settled down, Broch had been worked into a frenzy. Now Broch was in a sour mood having to listen to all the complaining. "Why were we stupid enough to let ourselves be talked into this journey? They only selected us because we could be easily intimidated," he complained. And so, it went, all day long for the first day, Elasti and Broch continually setting each other off with their complaining.

As evening came and darkness started to settle in, the leprechauns decided to set up camp. The South Road was separated slightly from the Amins Groves and the trees were becoming fewer and smaller. It was now easier for the threesome to find a flat patch of grass for their tents. The grass would make their bedding softer. Elasti set to work immediately gathering sticks together for a fire. The wood was wet, and it took some time before Elasti had a successful fire blazing. In the meantime, Agot and Broch had the tents set up. The warmth of the fire and the soft, comfortable looking sleeping bags in the tents softened the tempers of the three travelers. It wasn't long before all three of them were huddled around the fire trying to dry off the dampness.

The three sat silently staring into the blaze. Each had his own thoughts about the journey they were about to make. Each had his own hesitations and fears, but each knew that they must go forward with their travels. Eventually Agot broke the silence with a song:

Far to the West,
We know of a place,

Where all who have entered have died.
The Lamos has no bottom,
Its top looks the same,
Don't go there unless you can fly.
I knew of a brave lad,
Who too soon met his fate,
Now his ghost screams to all who walk by.
"Away from this place,
Don't climb in with me,
Your bride won't be the first to have cried."

Then Agot asked Elasti, "Have you seen the Lamos?"

"Yes, when I traveled north with the dwarfs, and you will be seeing it as well," Elasti answered.

"What's it like?" Agot continued.

"It's like nothing I have ever seen before," Elasti responded. "It's like looking down and seeing up at the same time. It's like seeing nothing. It made me feel so dizzy I could only look at it for a very short time."

"Will we have to go near it?" asked Agot. "It scares me."

"Not unless you want to," said Elasti teasingly. The glare that he received from Agot was all the answer he needed. "We'll be seeing it from a distance. You don't need to go any closer unless you want to."

"The song says that you can climb down into the Lamos. How is that possible?" asked Broch.

Elasti shrugged his shoulders, "I was told that the edge of the Lamos was soft like a riverbank and that you could get enough footing to climb down into it. I never saw the side because I refused to get close enough to look down into it."

The conversation ended and each of the leprechauns was left to his own thoughts. Agot, who loved books, had brought a couple of his favorites. He pulled one out and started to page through it as if he were investigating it. "Do you only read the pictures?" teased Broch as he watched.

"My father gave me this book for the trip," responded Agot, unruffled by Broch's remark. "It's about the Avoli River. It describes how it gouges deep into the earth as it moves on toward the Lamos. It has only a few pictures. Would you like to have a look?" He reached out to hand the book to Broch.

Broch took the book and paged through it. "The Avoli River is different from the Avol River," remarked Elasti. "It's much larger, deeper, and scarier. The water moves so fast it feels like it's trying to suck you in. As far as I'm concerned, crossing over the Avoli River is one of the worst parts of the trip north." Broch held the book out to Elasti as if to hand it to him. Without taking the book and yawning Elasti said, "You can look at your book. I'm going to bed. It's been a long day."

"Me too," agreed Broch as he handed the book back to Agot. "We have another long day tomorrow." Broch and Elasti were soon snoring with that squeaky sort of snore that only a leprechaun can make.

Agot had different plans. Now that his friends were asleep, he dug freely into their packs and removed all of their pants. Then he proceeded

to hide them in a bush nearby after which he also crawled into his sleep-
ng bag.

The night did everyone good. The drizzle seemed to have stopped
just for them. They all got a good night's rest. Agot and Broch's complaining had settled down considerably and they had resigned
themselves to the journey. They were ready to tolerate whatever lay
ahead.

"Let's get going," said Broch as he started to assemble his pack.
"The sooner we get this trip over with, the sooner we get back home."

"My pack!" shouted Elasti. "Someone's been in my pack. My pants
are missing."

"It must have been one of those pants-grabbing gibbons," suggested
Agot.

"Pants-grabbing gibbons don't exist, but pants-grabbing Agot's
do!" retorted Elasti. "What did you do with my pants?"

Just then Broch realized that he had also been vandalized. "It looks
like you aren't the only one that has had his pants grabbed," he said.

Agot had made sure that he was fully dressed by this time so that
his companions couldn't retaliate against him. "Why do you accuse me
of taking your pants?" he questioned. "I can't wear more than one pair
at a time." Broch and Elasti started to approach Agot. Their looks
seemed to indicate they weren't amused about the turn of events.

Agot grabbed his pack and took off running down the road toward
Giter but Elasti was not weighed down by his pack and caught up with
Agot quickly. Elasti dove at Agot's feet and grabbed him around the
ankles, causing him to trip and fall. "I give in! I give in!" Agot giggled.
"Your pants are in the bushes next to our camp."

Elasti, feeling he was not dressed appropriately to argue hurried
back to the bushes and quickly got dressed. Agot couldn't control
himself and burst out laughing as he watched Broch run after Elasti so
they could both draw their pants out of the bushes.

"These pants are damp and cold," complained Elasti. "Just wait
until tonight. You'll get your dues." Elasti and Broch quickly finished
their packing and the three were off. Agot occasionally burst into
laughter as he reflected on his little caper.

The journey from Amins to Giter took three days. There was very
little rainfall during the rest of the trip, only a few sprinkles during the
second night when the three were all safely tucked away in their tents.
However, the weather had become a little colder than had been
expected.

Agot was careful to keep all his belongings tucked away safely
inside his tent at night. He knew that his friends would be on the
lookout to trap him.

In the afternoon of the third day the three arrived in Giter. As they
entered the city lepelves gathered around the three leprechauns to find
out why they had journeyed so far. When the three travelers tried to
explain the reason for their journey the people of Giter made rude
comments about how ridiculous the whole plan was. The people of
Giter were not interested in hearing the details of the leprechauns'

plans. They didn't trust the leprechauns because they knew the leprechauns harbored a prejudice against lepelves. Additionally, the lepelves had always disliked the dwarfs who they considered a "chubby" and "hairy little lot" and "very sneaky too."

"Why should we waste our time going to the North Groves to see dwarfs?" the people complained. "We can live just fine without them." The lepelves weren't as dependent on the trade with the dwarfs as the leprechauns had become.

The government in Giter was a kingdom. The palace of Giter was in the center of town and to the left of the main street of the city. As the three approached it they stopped at the palace gate to ask the palace guards if it would be possible to gain an audience with the king.

"What for?" asked one of the guards who appeared to be the head of the watch. "The king doesn't just let any passerby drop in on him without a good reason, especially foreigners." Leprechauns were easily distinguishable from lepelves, not so much by their bodily appearance, although they were a little smaller, but by their clothes and their accents. Lepelves looked sloppier and more rugged. They tended to be dirtier and had none of the frills and ribbons that was an integral part of the dress of the leprechauns. The conversational style of the lepelves also gave the impression of being rugged. They gave their r's and t's more emphasis resulting in an angrier tone to their speech.

"We have an urgent message from the Council of Amins for your king," Elasti pleaded. "We have been sent here from Amins in order to give this message to him. Please let us meet with him!"

"The king would have my head if I came to him with a fool request like that. If you want to meet with him, make an appointment with him like everyone else. Right now, his appointments are set for the next two weeks at least. Get lost! You can get yourself a room at the tavern down the street if you want."

As they started to walk away from the palace, some of the town's people who had been watching the entire episode, yelled at them, "We told you so!"

The threesome was quite angry at this point. But they weren't sure what to do. After another hour of ridicule, Elasti became upset with the whole affair. It was apparent to him that arguing would get them nowhere. It would be impossible to find anyone in Giter who would go along on their journey and be an asset on the trip.

Just then, without saying a word, Agot pointed down a side street and the other two leprechauns turned their head to look in that direction. There, walking between a couple of the buildings was a dwarf and a gnome. "I thought lepelves didn't want anything to do with dwarfs," commented Agot. "And where did the gnome come from?"

"The king of Giter doesn't know what goes on outside of his own town," Agot barked. "Let's get out of here quickly before we get mixed up in some kind of trouble. Let's go on without lepelves. I didn't want to travel with them anyway. They would probably just complain every time they had to help."

"Let's go on! Something's just not right here." Elasti agreed. Broch was quick to make it unanimous. So, the three went quickly through Giter and left the town without bothering to stop at the tavern or anywhere else.

CHAPTER THREE

HEADING NORTH

They continued along the South Road toward the Albo Pass. The journey from Giter to Gije would take five additional days. The weather grew wet again and the muddy road became difficult to travel as the three journeyed up the foothills into the highlands that bordered the great Lamos. During the fourth day of travel the three arrived at the Avol River. The Avol was the romantic river of the Southern Plains where many a folk story about bravery and romance evolved. It was a wide, slow-moving river that was crossed by the use of a pull boat, a barge that was connected to each shore by a rope. Although the weather was overcast and somewhat gloomy the three speechlessly enjoyed the scenery as they crossed the river.

After the crossing the three set up camp. It wasn't quite dark yet, but the thought of camping near this beautiful spot along the Avol appealed to the travelers. As they were staking their tent, Broch went over to help Elasti. "Are you ready?" Broch whispered.

"Let's do it," Elasti whispered his response. "Let's split up and go from each side."

Agot hadn't noticed the activity between his two friends. He was too busy setting up his tent to realize that they were coming towards him. Suddenly Broch and Elasti grabbed Agot from each side. Agot screamed and kicked as the captors dragged him off. Agot realized that the two were after revenge. He could only guess what they had in store for him.

Agot soon realized what it was. They were dragging him back towards the river. He screamed and kicked but he knew that unless he could somehow break away from them, he was destined to take a bath fully dressed.

As they arrived at the edge of the river Broch and Elasti gave Agot a hard push. Agot tried to hold his balance but his foot hit a rock which tripped him. Splash!!! He fell face first into the water. Broch and Elasti laughed so hard they fell to the grass and rolled on the ground holding their sides.

"I haven't seen anything so funny in years," Broch chuckled.

"That was definitely worth the bruises we received while trying to drag him down there," Elasti cackled as they slowly returned to camp. "He'll think twice before he makes us spend a day in damp pants again."

Agot coughed as he came out of the water. "You nearly drowned me," he yelled. But the two just laughed all the louder.

Near the end of the fifth day of their travels they journeyed by the Kilo Pass. This was an old seldom traveled route that led to the North Groves. However, this pass was rarely traveled due to the legends of the evil tragedies that happened to those who journeyed this way. So seldom was this route traveled that weeds and bushes were beginning to grow over the trail. In places it was hard to find the path. "I'm sure glad we're not taking that route," commented Broch. "I would hate to travel through the Kabul."

Shortly thereafter they again bedded down for the night and the following morning they passed the second cutoff to the Kilo pass. It wasn't long before the leprechauns were journeying over the Avoli River Bridge. This would be the first of two times that they would have to travel over an Avoli bridge on their way to the North Groves.

The Avol River, that the travelers had crossed earlier, ran southwest and emptied into Alica Lake. This lake was drained by the Avoli River which ran northwest out of the lake and cut deep through the Lamos Mountains emptying into the bottomless Lamos. Similar to how the Avol River was connected with mythological things of beauty, the Avoli River with its bottomless ending carried with its legends of treachery, danger, and evil.

The bridge over the Avoli River was high out of the water, about 20 leprechauns high and the rushing waters could be seen far below. The three travelers were quick to scurry across the bridge and were happy to plant their feet on the solid ground of the other side. They didn't dare to look over the side of the bridge for fear that something terrible might happen to them. It wasn't that they were afraid of heights; it was just that hanging so high over this treacherous river made them feel very uncomfortable. If they were to somehow end up in the river, they would fall over the endless waterfall at the end of the river and would never be seen again. There was something mysterious and eerie about this river whose waters fell away and disappeared.

Once on the other side they felt braver and looked back at the river. They saw it churning and bubbling as if it were being boiled. Big bubbles formed on the top of the water, and they would occasionally pop and spray water out in all directions. It seemed fearsome.

"I don't think I could ever get used to traveling over that river," commented Elasti as he stared down into the canyon from the top of the western cliff. "It gives me a feeling that I'm no longer in control of myself, like something bad might happen at any moment."

"I know what you mean," commented Agot. He stayed further away from the edge than the other two. He saw no sense in getting too close. "I feel that way too. Let's get out of here fast."

It was on this, another wet and dreary day of their travels, that they started to get close to the Albo Pass. Elasti once again began to get discouraged about the trip. "Why should we waste our time going to Gije to talk to the elves?" he complained. "We'll probably get the same hassle that we got in Giter. I say we go on to the Albo Pass and save ourselves the three or four days we would waste by going to Gije."

"But Amaz directed us to get someone from each of the two cities," Agot replied fearfully. "We won't be as effective with the dwarfs if we don't. They'll just think that the leprechauns are the only ones complaining and that we're too small to be bothered with. At least if the elves come with us the dwarfs will know that all of the Southern Plains is in an uproar. Besides, there's safety in numbers just in case we have problems during our travels."

Broch retorted, "I agree with Elasti! Why waste our time with a bunch of elves? Let's go on toward the North Groves and get this thing over with so we can get home. I'm sick and tired of stomping around in the mud. It makes my feet feel twice as heavy."

"It's getting dark anyway," said Elasti, "let's make camp and sleep on it and take a vote tomorrow." All three agreed and camp was quickly prepared.

In the middle of the night Elasti heard a loud grunting. Then he heard something that sounded like a scream followed by crying. He jumped up and out of his tent quickly. He stood before his tent listening, trying to identify the source of the sounds. It was coming from Agot's tent. He yelled Agot's name in order to wake him. Since that didn't work, he went into Agot's tent and gave him a shake. After several shakes Agot suddenly sat up and screamed, scaring Elasti half out of his wits. This also woke Broch up too, who then came running over to join them.

"What's going on?" Broch asked Elasti.

Agot, trying to calm everyone explained, "I just had a bad dream. I was being chased by grotesque creatures who were trying to grab me and eat me. They looked like they were creatures made from the dead parts of animals. Some kind of manmade creatures. It was horrible!"

"Sounds like magotites from Kabul," explained Broch.

Elasti joined in, "That's exactly what they sound like. How grotesque."

After a slight pause Agot continued, "I'm better now. Go back to bed. I'll be alright."

"Are you sure?" asked Broch.

"I'm fine," responded Agot, rather embarrassed. "I'll see you in the morning."

The rest of the night was peaceful. The following morning a quick vote was cast, two against one and, after journeying another half a day the three turned north on the Albo Pass, not traveling to Gije.

The three adventurers started climbing high into the Lamos Mountains. It was the middle of the eighth day of their journey. The three were hiking up the Albo Pass when they came upon the second bridge crossing the Avoli River. This was one of the most beautiful and scenic areas in all of the Small World. At this bridge the Avoli Crevice was four-hundred leprechauns deep. At this point the river had now cut deep wide canyons through the ranges as it rushed by under the bridge and spilled deep into the Lamos, never to be seen again.

As the three quickly crossed the bridge they were mystified by the beauty that surrounded them. The trees reached high into the sky, so high that their tops could hardly be seen through the mists that clouded the day. Their majesty seemed to rule over the wide abyss of the river. Branches could only be seen near the tops of the trees and moss was thick on the bark making the whole forest appear green. The thick under-growth of ferns and bushes kept the ground from being seen anywhere but on the trail itself. It was as though the whole forest had been beautifully painted. The sides of the crevice were also covered with growth and only in the river and in the sky above could another color be seen. The river was white with turbulence, and the noise of the crashing water echoed in the canyon.

This was the first time that Agot and Broch had seen this sight and they became engrossed in it. They stood on the far side of the bridge watching the river rush by underneath. It was hard to understand how something so beautiful could have such an evil reputation.

It was fitting that the rain had stopped for such an occasion. The sun was shining and was desperately trying to break through the mist in order to give the weary travelers still another dimension of beauty. As this feeling surrounded them, the three comrades were speechless. It was as though they had met their match; as though they had reached the bounds where heaven met hell. Here in one setting was sheer beauty and the destructive evil of the river.

"Somehow this river looks different than I remember it'" Elasti said as he broke the silence. "This time I see its beauty and at the same time I feel a danger surrounding us. I just can't explain it." The others were silent. It was a though Elasti had spoken for all of them. Ignoring the danger, they felt, the three sat down, allowing this strange, mysterious power to engulf them.

As the three pulled themselves out of their mystifying trance and stood up again to continue their journey they could see the thick forests that lay ahead. They could also see that their route would take them higher and higher into the mountainous ranges. The journey from this point on would get colder, steeper, and more rugged.

The three continued their climb following the Albo Pass. The road climbed high as they entered the Central Ranges and the forests contin-ued to grow thicker around them. It soon became difficult to see the sky.

The Albo trail was a very old trail. It became difficult to see the ground because of all the moss and ferns that grew in along the trail. The trees had been cleared from the trail long ago which, in spite of its lack of use in recent months, left the route very distinct.

Suddenly Broch SCREAMED in anguish! Elasti and Agot turned quickly in shocked surprise only to see their friend slowly fall to the ground beside them with an arrow deep in his heart. Time suddenly seemed to slow down dramatically. To Agot and Elasti everything seemed to move in slow motion as they jumped down next to Broch to

help him. But it was too late. Broch was dead. Their quiet world which had moments earlier been filled with serenity had suddenly become horror. Heaven had become hell. The two remaining travelers were in total shock as they knelt next to Broch. What had happened? Who had done this? Why did this happen? What should they do? Numerous questions raced through their minds. But before either of them could search around for answers; before they could even look up at each other; Agot was also hit by an arrow. He also fell face down on the trail with a hard thump, an arrow planted deeply in his neck.

After this second strike Elasti knew he had to respond, and he reacted quickly. He didn't take time to check if Agot had been killed. He already knew the answer. He leaped up dropping his pack and supplies and leaving them behind so he could run faster. He quickly surged into a nearby grove.

His world continued to move in slow motion. He could see an arrow coming towards him and he almost felt like he could reach out and catch it as the arrow came whizzing toward him. He could sense the arrow zip by his head, narrowly missing him by just fingers.

Elasti became panicky. As he crashed through the undergrowth bushes, he only knew that if he did not continue running, he would soon meet the same fate as his friends. He continued to charge forward in a straight line until he could run no more. Where could he hide? He searched around him for options. The undergrowth had gotten thicker as he ran deeper and deeper into the grove. He quickly found a thick cluster of bushes and scrambled inside.

What had just happened? Who was this deadly hidden enemy that had just killed his two traveling companions? Where was he? Dozens of questions zipped through his mind. He continued to feel as if life was in slow motion which allowed him more time to think. But he couldn't come up with any answers.

Elasti could not comprehend the senseless killing of his two friends. But he knew he had to hide out and keep quiet to make sure he had avoided the same fate. There he lay listening to hear if anyone was following him but all he could hear was the very loud beating of his heart. It beat so hard in his ears that he was afraid that the enemy would hear it. And this made him even more terrified.

The relaxed, calm lifestyle that a leprechaun was familiar with was completely disconnected from these senseless killings. He could not comprehend that this type of cruelty could exist in his familiar and secure world. He had previously never feared for his life. He was never in a situation where he could die any minute.

His mind flashed back to a time a couple of years earlier when he had gotten stuck high up in that old Balkwood tree. He got himself into many similar situations where he feared possible injury, but never had he felt as though he might be killed at any moment by some unknown evil. Now that he was sitting quietly, he had time to think, but thinking made it worse. Terror and shock engulfed him so powerfully that it took several hours before his heart quit racing. It took that long before he was sufficiently relaxed to where he could even think of what he should do next. By then it was dark.

His fears refused to let him move from the bushes. He lay there in his uncomfortable position with sticks piercing his back and side. But he felt he must be as still as possible. And he had to endure the discomfort all night long. He waited for the morning light praying silently to his God that he would somehow be able to sneak back to the Southern Plains.

Surprisingly Elasti felt no hate for the council that had sent him on this trip. His only feeling was that wanted to be back in their council chambers to warn them of the dangers. The loss of his friends' lives suddenly seemed more important to him than the loss of his own life. Fear was now turning to grief as he thought about his companions. Tears welled up in his eyes as he promised himself that they would not have died in vain. Grief surrounded him as his tears dripped off the end of his chin and dropped on his lap.

Elasti started feeling as though a new force was beginning to overtake him, a force that focused on a higher need. A force that had no room for his earlier cowardly behavior. He had run away when his friends needed him, and he felt stupid. But at the same time, he knew that he really did not have a choice. His friends were dead and staying behind would have surely ended up with him dying as well.

As he continued his thought process Elasti suddenly feared for the lives of his whole village. Were these attackers going there next? Was his village going to be the next to be struck dead? He had to warn them quickly.

He tried to determine who the attackers could be. The only explanation he could think of was that the dwarfs were trying to conquer the South. They had previously seemed like such a nice folk the last time he was with them. Now he had to warn the Council of Amins that the dwarfs were invading. The dwarfs must have been plotting to conquer the Southern Plains all along. That must have been why they eagerly engaged in trade with the South. It was all part of the plan so that they could learn more about the three southern cities. Once the South had become dependent on their trade, they would stop the trade in order to weaken the South, and then commence their attack. Elasti knew that the South could not survive against an attack for very long. They were not prepared to do battle.

As he planned his next steps Elasti realized his mistake. When he feared for his life and ran from the trail, he hadn't paid any attention to the direction in which he was running. He had run west, toward the Lamos. "How stupid!" he thought to himself. "If I would have run the other direction, I could have worked my way along the Avoli River back to the South Road. Now I've got to head back across the Albo Pass because that bridge is the only way for me to cross the river." How could he possibly get back across the Avoli River without being seen on the bridge? His dilemma troubled his mind and kept him awake all night long and now morning was starting to dawn.

Elasti slowly poked his head out of the brush that he had been hiding in. He hadn't heard anything all night and felt confident that no one had pursued him. He carefully selected a large tree close by and clambered up to see if he could spot his attackers. He carefully and with deep concentration looked in every direction. There was nothing to be seen. He decided to start heading south toward the Avoli River. He knew he could not return east back to the Albo Pass. He was certain that he would be spotted. The Avoli River would have to be his guide and maybe he could journey along it and, if possible, find another way to cross it there-by avoiding the bridge that he and his companions had used before. That was his only hope. But it was a slim one. His attackers would be sure to realize that he would need to cross that bridge and they undoubtedly would be guarding it carefully.

Shortly after midday he arrived at the river and started to work his way east-ward along its edge. This time the river no longer appeared beautiful. Now it was a threat, a barrier between him and his only hope for survival on the other side. Getting back to his home and safety required that he cross over this river, and that meant crossing the bridge.

He continued on his journey along the river's edge. Occasionally he would climb a tree to see if he could spot any dwarfs, who he still assumed were his attackers. After a few hours he was finally able to see the bridge off in the distance. Not surprisingly he had found no other way of crossing. The bridge was his only possible route. He would certainly be spotted if he tried to climb down the sides of the sheer canyon walls to the river. Even if he did succeed at getting down, once at the bottom, crossing the swift moving rapids would be futile; the Avoli River was too wild and vicious. The treacherous current made it impossible to cross and it was very wide, far too wide for Elasti to try to swim. He undoubtedly would be dragged into the Lamos before he made it across.

He thought of building some type of structure to forge the river, but he soon realized that a raft was also a foolish option considering the rapid movement of the water. It would most likely end up sending him into the depths of the Lamos. And there was no way he could ever build himself a bridge out of logs. Getting long logs down into the gorge would be impossible for him to do by himself. Felling trees would also be very noisy. And then positioning them there would be impossible. He felt as though he could not risk the noise. Elasti was desperate. He could not think of another plan. Using the bridge, he had come over was the only feasible option.

He again climbed up a large tree. At first, he could spot no one. Per-haps, if he was lucky, he could rush across the bridge without being noticed. Luckily, just as he was about to climb down from his lookout, he suddenly discovered way off in the distance what must surely have been his attackers. To his amazement they weren't dwarfs. He saw what he was sure must be gnomes. The mere presence of gnomes outside of the Kabul was unheard of. And now he had seen them twice. Once in Giter and now here on the Albo Pass. The only way gnomes would leave the security of their home in Gamotz was if they were forced to. Somehow these gnomes had been driven from the Kabul or they were sent out from there on a mission. But why would they journey over the Albo Pass? The Kilo Pass would be more convenient for them to use. What was their purpose here? And why would gnomes kill his two friends for what seemed like no reason at all? Discovering the gnomes raised more questions than it answered.

Elasti felt stupid about his accusations against the dwarfs. He realized that his prejudices had gotten the better of him. Now he realized that perhaps the dwarfs had come down to trade with the South and were also killed by the gnomes, just like his two friends had been. Maybe the dwarfs were thinking the same about the southerners. Maybe they thought the leprechauns had been the killers of the dwarfs who had been sent to conduct trade. He realized he should have trusted the dwarfs. They were always good to him and his people.

He slowly and quietly climbed down from the tree that he was on and selected another tree closer to the gnomes hoping to get a better view. Climbing up this new tree he noticed that the gnomes had set up camp just short of the bridge. He realized it would be impossible to cross the bridge without being spotted. The gnome camp was strategically located to keep anyone else from the Southern Plains from crossing over into the Central Ranges. He also knew that they were watching for him, anticipating that he would try to cross the bridge back to the south. He studied the camp, hoping for some inspiration telling him what he should do next, but nothing came to his mind.

Elasti climbed down from the tree and found himself a secure hiding spot in a dense clump of bushes where he could sit and think. One thing was sure. There was nothing he could do in the daylight. Maybe, if he waited until the gnomes were sleeping, he could quietly cross the bridge. It would be night and he hoped the darkness would shield him. He sat in the brush and waited.

Unfortunately, as night fell, Elasti's hopes also to fell. The gnomes had built an enormous fire that lit up the entire area. The gnomes could easily see across the entire bridge. Again, Elasti felt that his situation was hopeless. He wanted to cry. The only thing that stopped him was his fear of making the least bit of noise and alarming the gnomes of his presence. He began thinking about his beautiful Jizeel. Had he seen her for the last time? He was beginning to think that there was no hope that he would ever return to his beloved home in Amins. He sat in frustration, blankly staring at a squirrel scurrying on the ground as he said a prayer, hoping that maybe he would receive some inspiration.

Suddenly it happened. Inspiration had struck as he watched the squirrel scurry up a tree and hang onto a branch. The squirrel didn't run on the top of the branch, it clung on underneath. This gave Elasti an idea! If he could not risk going over the bridge, would it be possible to go under the bridge? Could he sneak down the embankment and under the bridge, and then crawl up into the bridge structure and cross the river by going along under the bridge like the squirrel? He didn't know if his idea would work, but at last he had an idea, and with an idea he had hope. He carefully hurried out of the brush and over to the embankment to see if his idea would work. If it was to work, it would have to work at night. The darkness would help to conceal him as he crawled down the embankment. The bright fire north of the Avoli River would not light up the north canyon wall. He would be able to hide in the shadows without be-ing detected by the gnomes.

He was going to try. He was going to crawl down the embankment about ten leprechauns' distance, and crawl along the edge of the cliff until he was under the bridge. Then he would crawl up under the bridge and into its structure to see if his idea was possible. In his excitement, anxious to get over the edge of the embankment, Elasti stepped on and broke a dried branch that had fallen from a tree. The break made a loud crack, loud enough to attract the attention of the gnomes. Suddenly he was gripped by fear. What should he do now?

Three gnomes came running over to the area of the noise. They stood right in the spot where Elasti had broken the branch and looked around on all sides. One of the gnomes stood out from the other two because of the hat he wore. It was filled with badges and symbols. He appeared to be a leader of some sort since the other two gnomes did not wear hats. "It must have been an animal," the gnome leader said.

But another gnome said, "Animals don't make that much noise."

Fearing that the gnomes would look over the embankment, Elasti had quickly scrambled up a tree just seconds before the gnomes arrived. He was sitting in a tree only a leprechaun's length above their heads. He could feel his heart beating and felt as though the noise of his heart was so loud that the gnomes must surely be able to hear it. What would happen to him if they found him? Obviously, he knew the answer. The dwarfs had told him how gnomes tortured their victims in grotesque ways. What kind of torture would they choose for him? Or maybe, if he was lucky, they would just shoot him with an arrow like they did his friends, and it would be over with quickly without much pain.

Luckily, the gnome leader, feeling as though he had been challenged by his companions, came back with, "Do you see anything?" His two companions both denied seeing any sign of a leprechaun, so the gnome leader said, "Let's go back. This is a waste of time. If anyone tries to go over that bridge, we'll see him! We'll just wait for him. We better hurry or we'll miss out on our share of dinner. I called dibs on the upper thigh of one of those leprechauns and I don't want anyone taking it first." The three gnomes gave another look around the area, grunted and walked away. They had looked every direction but up.

From the conversation between the gnomes Elasti realized that his two friends had become the main course for their dinner feast. He felt devastated. It was bad enough to think of his leprechaun friends being killed, but now they were going to be eaten as well. Elasti felt like screaming. He felt like charging into the camp and killing every gnome there. But fortunately, his more rational mind took over. He knew that any crazy moves would result in him being part of the feast as well.

And then who would warn his friends back home? He knew he had to keep a level head. He had to get back to Amins.

Elasti stayed up in the tree a good hour after the gnomes had given up their search. He wanted to make sure that there were no stragglers who stayed behind. Then he slowly came down the tree and carefully followed his plan. He crawled over to the edge of the steep river embankment.

He went so slowly that it took a long time for him to get to the edge. Once he was there, he strained hard to see if there was any way to crawl under the bridge but, even with the bright firelight of the gnome camp the shadow that was cast by the bridge had made it too dark to see if the bridge had any structure underneath. The brightness of the fire blinded him from seeing into the darkness. He realized that he would have to go ahead with his plan to crawl under the bridge hoping the shadows that hid the underside of the bridge would also hide him as he crawled along the side of the cliff.

As Elasti was scheming and planning his escape he happened to look a little closer at the large fire the gnomes had built. He noticed something cooking over the fire. He was disgusted by what he saw. It looked like his friends had been tied to a spit over the fire and were slowly being rotated and cooked. The sight raised a revolution deep inside of him and he immediately became weak. He felt as though he temporarily passed out. Suddenly and uncontrollably he vomited.

He looked again hoping it wasn't true. But it sure looked like their bodies were hanging over the fire. Elasti looked away. He couldn't bear to think of his best friends in this way. He crawled away from his vomit and made his way over the edge of the embankment.

Elasti trembled as he said a prayer and carefully began to lower himself down the side of the dark embankment. It was a difficult climb. His eyes were still blinded from the firelight and it was difficult to find his footing. He still felt a little weak from the surge of emotion that he had felt when he saw his friends cooking over the fire. The embankment was steep and muddy and occasionally he slipped and made small sounds. But fortunately, these sounds weren't noticeable over the noise of the gnomes.

Once down the side he started to work his way slowly along the inside of the embankment. He constantly looked up expecting to find a gnome head peering down at him. What would he do? He couldn't bear the thought of ending up over that fire like his friends. Maybe he would just jump. Falling off into the river and then into the Lamos had to be a better end then being captured by gnomes.

Fear of imminent death caused thoughts to whiz through his mind. How he wished he could relive so many things in his life. He would be a lot nicer and more helpful to people and not always so selfish. If only he could make it to the under-side of the bridge and then safely to the other side. He vowed he would change his life forever. Little did he realize that because of his experiences during this last week his life had already been transformed.

The journey to the bridge was very slow. It took Elasti almost two hours, but it seemed like an eternity. The voices of the gnomes became louder and more threatening as he went. Finally, his eyes had become adjusted to the darkness and he was able to make out where the bridge was located. When he finally arrived under the bridge his heart leapt for joy. Luck was on his side. There was indeed a structure under the bridge that he could crawl on.

By this time, he was so close to the gnome camp that their voices had become quite loud. It was scary to think that just over the edge of the embankment was a large gnome camp filled with creatures that would enjoy cutting him up and adding him to their dinner plate.

The structure under the bridge became a sanctuary for him. He crawled up into the structure and sat there for a few moments trying to get himself calmed. The adrenaline rush that he was feeling had made him jittery. He had never felt so scared in his life. Adding to that was the fact that this was his second night without sleep causing his knees and hands to shake with weariness. He would need to regain some energy for the crawl to the other side. He kept trying to reassure himself that the gnomes would never find him as long as he stayed quiet. But these re-assurances lacked faith.

He started to work his way up into the structure of the bridge. Not surprisingly, it was wet and slippery. Any mistaken footing causing a slip would result in his falling into the Avoll River. And, if he didn't fall, the noise would surely notify the gnomes of his presence, which was an even less desirable prospect. The thought of being captured chilled him.

He did occasionally lose his footing but only slightly. He would always quickly recover, but each time his heart beat a little bit stronger. He was forced to go very slowly, and it took him several hours to slowly and cautiously work his way across. Just as he neared the opposite bank daylight was breaking.

He knew he had to hurry. He became tense and the pressure caused his head to pound. He gradually crawled down off the bridge structure onto the embankment on the other side. He looked around trying to find a concealed place to climb to the top. He spotted a way that he thought would keep him from being spotted. The bank at this point seemed to be grown in with sufficient brush. And the brush would give stability to the embankment which would help him climb to the top.

He was exhausted having lost the whole night's sleep, but he knew he had to go on. He could not rest for fear of falling asleep. He went ahead, his body throbbing with weariness and his heart pounding with fright.

Slowly and cautiously he inched along the embankment to the spot he had chosen for the climb to the top. Would the gnomes see him? He dared not look across at their camp, superstitiously thinking that if he didn't look at them then they wouldn't notice him. He feared that the gnomes would see him looking their way. He felt safer pretending that they just didn't exist.

Crawling along the embankment was scary. The cliff was steep and slippery. But he knew he had to move fast before the morning dawn made him too visible. Eventually he made it to the place where he thought he could crawl up without being seen by the gnomes. He crawled through the brush toward the top of the cliff. As he crawled, he realized that the cover of the brush wasn't much protection. There were lots of open spots that weren't fully covered. He wondered how he could prevent himself from being spotted in the encroaching morning light.

He got closer and closer to the top. Inch by inch he crawled upward. The excitement of getting over the top was mounting and he couldn't control himself any longer. He started to move a little quicker. His excitement at reaching the top, assuming somehow that it meant he would now be safe, caused him to become careless.

He was less than a leprechaun length from the top when he sprang up. How could he be so stupid? He had jumped into in full view and was scrambling at full speed up the last portion of the embankment and over the top. What had gotten into him? The pressure had been more than he could stand, and he had lost control. What would happen now?

Suddenly he heard the running of gnome feet on the bridge. He also heard gnomes yelling as they came rushing across the bridge after him. He saw a gnome arrow fall harmlessly to the ground some distance to the side of him. They were after him, and he knew that the only thing he could do was run. Run he did, as if the whole survival of the Southern Plains depended upon his speed, which it did.

Elasti ran like he had never run before, away from any trail and into the woods ahead of him east of the Albo Pass. He kept running and running for a while in one direction, then in another, deeper and deeper into the forest. He ran for what seemed to be hours before he dared to look behind. When he finally wrestled up enough courage to look, the gnomes were nowhere to be seen.

He decided the gnomes must not have been close enough behind him to keep track of where he had run to. But, from what he had heard, they were excellent trackers. Remembering how the gnomes didn't think to look up into a tree earlier, he chose a high tree and began to climb. He found his view restricted by the dense forest, but he decided to rest in the tree until he felt it was safe to go on.

It was uncomfortable. His eyes wanted to shut, and his mind kept telling them to stay open. His head hurt, his chest hurt, and his legs hurt. Now that he was sitting, he felt as though he had been overcome by some immense encompassing power that had totally drained him. But he knew he had to go on.

He waited several hours. Still there was no sign of the gnomes. He concluded that they must have given up the chase. Slowly getting down he continued forging his way homeward. He headed south in the direction he thought the South Road must run. He knew that he had to find the road so that he could find and cross the second bridge across the Avoli River. Much to his surprise it wasn't long before he discovered that he was well on his way towards it. He discovered that in fleeing from the gnomes he must have run much further than he realized.

CHAPTER FOUR

RETURNING

lastivom traveled off to the side of the road staying a good distance from it so that he wouldn't be noticed, yet always keeping the road in sight so that he wouldn't lose his way. He had two more rivers to cross, the second Avoli River crossing and the Avol River crossing. As soon as he had made these crossings, he would be comfortably close to Amins, assuming that the gnomes had given up the chase. But first he must rest. He found a heavily overgrown thicket of bushes that was out of sight of the main road. He found that he had absolutely no energy, but he struggled to get to sleep because of the high adrenaline rushes of the day.

As he lay on the ground, he became aware of the slightest movement or noise around him. The fear of being found caused him to jump at the slightest sound of a bird or a squirrel. Suddenly he was startled by a large shadow passing over him. At first, he feared the gnomes creeping up behind him. But the shadow didn't stop. It kept moving right past him. Then he noticed an eagle flying far above him. The eagle was so quiet and so well hidden by the trees that, if not for the shadow, it would have gone unnoticed. This was an unusual sight. Eagles were rare in Small World and were considered to be an omen. What could the presence of this eagle mean?

Elasti had lost all track of time. His weariness mixed with his grief over the loss of his friends and his uncertainty about the gnomes left him conflicted. What were the gnomes after? And, now the presence of the eagle left him confused. He didn't understand what it all meant, and he was even more uncertain what his role in all of this would be. He began to wish that it had been him that had suffered the fate of the gnome's arrow rather than one of his dearly loved friends. How would he be able to tell their parents of the tragedy that had befallen them?

Hours had passed. Before he realized it, night had again fallen. He had made very little headway. Staying off the trail had made travel extremely slow. And he knew that traveling at night would be foolish.

He would surely get lost, and if not lost, probably captured by the gnomes because of the noise he would make. He had to stay hidden in a clump of damp bushes until the following morning while his fears tormented him most of the night.

It was morning and Elasti had gotten very little sleep but at least he felt a bit rested. He forced himself to his feet and began to press on. It was late afternoon before he arrived at the first river crossing. He quietly climbed a tree close to the road to see if anyone was in view. He saw no one however he noticed the eagle was still circling overhead. It seemed to have been following him all day. He decided to run for it. He got down from the tree and took off running like a dart. He ran with all his might until he arrived safely on the other side of the bridge. Nothing happened. No gnomes could be heard. There wasn't even the sound of a squirrel. He kept running until he was back up in the woods some distance south of the road. Then he finally felt safe once again.

Shortly after crossing the Avoli River, night began to close in, and he decided to find another well hidden place to rest. Losing his equipment during his first encounter with the gnomes was now starting to make his journey difficult. He made his bed out of the leaves and twigs that were available, but they weren't much comfort.

Elasti was finally starting to feel more secure. If the gnomes were on his trail, he would have met up with them at the bridge. He felt that he might finally be able to sleep. He was very tired, not having slept for three nights. He curled up and it wasn't long before Elasti lapsed into a well-deserved deep sleep.

As luck would have it, it started to rain. But even with the rain falling on his face, Elasti slept on. It wasn't long before puddles formed, and he lay in the mud. Still Elasti slept on. The entire gnome army couldn't have awakened him.

When he finally awoke, the sun was high overhead. He felt as though he had slept for days. He was wet but refreshed. He was ready to continue on in his journey. He took off, again staying slightly to the south of the South Road. He was determined to make it back to Amins as quickly as possible. He decided he would not go through Giter because he didn't want the lepelves to have the pleasure of ridiculing his misfortune. He owed them no explanations or warnings. Additionally, having seen a gnome and dwarf there when he passed through previously added to his suspicions. Why would they befriend an obvious enemy? Regardless, his loyalty was to his own people. He would go directly to Amins.

He had mixed feelings. He was delighted to have regained his sleep, but at the same time he had wasted daylight by sleeping so long. At least he was able to travel faster as a result of his rest.

The day was uneventful. There were no gnomes, and the eagle that persisted on staying overhead began to be more of a familiar companion than a dangerous threat. His concern about being followed had left him.

As he made camp for the evening, he felt safe. He selected his location carefully making sure it was well hidden. This night there was no heavy rain, only a strong mist, which did not keep him from a deep slumber. He awoke in the morning thoroughly refreshed and eager to see his journey to completion.

It was several hours before he came to the pull boat that crossed the Avol River. He felt more confident this time at being out in the open during the river crossing. He was sure that the gnomes had not come this far. He ran out onto the road and jumped onto the barge. He pushed himself off immediately and started his journey across the river. Once out on the river he felt even better. Surely now the gnomes couldn't reach him. Even if they tried to pull the barge back to shore with the tie rope that was attached to it, Elasti would simply jump into the river and swim the rest of the way. He felt extremely confident in himself as he pulled his way across.

He saw a shadow moving across the water. At first it gave him a start. Without looking up he already knew what it was. His eyes glanced skyward, as if he was hoping the inevitable would not be there when he looked, but it was. There, in the sky was that same eagle. Having the eagle follow him for a few days had been tolerable, but now its persistence started to concern him. Questions started rolling through his mind. Was it the same eagle? It had to be. There weren't that many eagles in Small World for him to have encountered several different ones in the last few days. Why was this eagle following him? What did it mean? Was it a good omen or a bad omen? Elasti was worried. He had so many questions and no answers.

When he finally reached the other side of the river, he hurriedly tied the pull boat up so that it couldn't be pulled back, and he ran until he was back in the woods. He felt safe. The gnomes would never catch him now. He was on home ground. It would be a straight trip through the Amins Groves and on to Amins. Elasti walked on as fast as he could.

The woods were thinner now. The trees were smaller and quite often he would encounter open grassy areas. Every time he walked out into one of these open areas he would look skyward to see if the eagle was still with him. And each time the eagle would be there.

Elasti could barely see the Amins Groves when night started to fall. He decided to stop and rest before entering the groves. Although he felt he knew the groves well, he decided he would most likely have trouble guiding himself without the light of the sun. He set up camp and settled in. Sleep came easy since he was still very tired.

Suddenly Elasti was awake. He was struggling, fighting and kicking. He was captured. He was a prisoner in some sort of bag. He continued to struggle and fight within the confines of the bag when he realized that he must be lying on the ground. The end of the bag must be open because he could feel that his feet were free. He kicked and crawled toward the opening at the end of the bag. He was out. He was free. But it was still dark. There wasn't anyone around. What had happened? Then it hit him. He was dreaming. Yet, it seemed so real. It was as if the whole episode had really happened. He could remember being captured and stuffed into a bag. He listened. It was silent. Perspiration soaked his clothes. It had been a nightmare.

Elasti was thankful that it was just a dream. Now he began to confuse himself about his experiences since leaving Amins. Did he really go up the Albo Pass? Were his two best friends really dead? He sat down and tried to recount the events of the past few days to determine what was real and what wasn't. Then he looked up at the moon and, almost as if it was planned, he received his answer. The eagle could clearly be seen, high in the night sky crossing the face of the moon, telling him that everything that had happened to him was real.

Elasti became frightened anew when he realized that it was all true. His friends were dead, and gnomes were after him. He had just experienced a bad dream, but all the rest was very real. All the rest of what was happening was the real nightmare. Then he recalled how Agot had also suffered a frightful dream the night before he was killed. Was the dream that Elasti had just received another prediction of the future? Was the eagle that circled a spy from the gnomes? Elasti was asking himself questions that did not seem to have answers.

Elasti was working himself into a frenzy. The night, the eagle, his nightmare, and the many unanswered questions just made it worse. He was starting to shiver. At first, he thought it was just the cold night air, but he realized he didn't shiver like this on any other nights. He was scared. He didn't want to wake up in the morning a prisoner of the gnomes as his dream predicted. He had endured too much and made it too close to Amins to be captured now. He knew he wouldn't be able to sleep anymore; his fears had taken care of any possibility of rest. He decided to go on.

He would not stop until he arrived home. He journeyed straight into the Amins Groves and headed directly towards Amins. Most leprechauns and lepelves would have been afraid to enter the Amins Groves at night but this had been his favorite playground as a boy. He didn't have any trouble finding his way. As time slipped away, he pressed ahead faster and faster. The sky was clear with a full moon which was a pleasant change after the previous night's rain. The moonlight made traveling easy.

Morning came and Elasti began to regain some of his earlier confidence. He became overwhelmed with a feeling of relief at not being captured. The warmth of the morning sun made him confident of a successful arrival to his hometown. He started singing loudly in an attempt to fill his mind with pleasant thoughts. It was not that he had for-gotten his lost friends. He would never forget them, but by being able to warn his people he would make sure that their lives were not lost in vain. This would give his people the time they needed in order to prepare themselves for the probable attack by the gnomes.

He was confident that the council would be able to find some solution to the gnomes. Things would somehow work out and soon life would be returned to normal. So, he sang:

Praise to the rainbow,
Praise to its God;
He will protect us,
As long as we are strong.

Praise to His power,
He helped me win again;
He saves us from the floods,
And the mud.

Elasti pressed on. The eagle was still in the sky overhead, but by this time the leprechaun had become so confident of his success that the eagle's presence did not bother him anymore. He pushed forward.

The excitement of arriving home would not allow him to rest. He forced himself to push ahead. It was now late afternoon and starting to get dark when Elasti finally saw his home, the city of Amins off in the distance. His troubles would soon be at an end, or so he thought. He looked toward the sky to see his companion. The eagle was nowhere to be found.

CHAPTER FIVE

THE EMERGENCY COUNCIL SESSION

Elastivom found himself lying in his own bed. He could not remember how he got there. He only remembered running through the forest and entering his home city and then all went blank. Exhaustion had overwhelmed him.

With a good night's rest in his own bed, he felt ready to go out and discuss what he had learned. He needed to share the news about his fellow companions. He began to get up when his father, an abnormally tall leprechaun, burst into the room shouting, "You must hurry! The Council is waiting for you. They need to know what has happened to you, Agot, and Broch. Get dressed quickly and come with me to the council chambers!"

Elasti suddenly flashed back to reality. The terrible news about his friends would upset the whole city. How would they react? Would he be blamed for their deaths? Whatever the outcome, he knew he had to face the Council.

His father left the room and Elasti did as he was told, he dressed quickly and went to meet his father so that they could walk together to the council chambers. His father didn't press him for any news, he could see that Elasti was very troubled, and Elasti would be forced to share his experiences soon enough.

His father was also a member of the Council, but much less boisterous than many of the others. He was considered more of a thinker than a talker. Even though he was not pressed by his father, Elasti felt like sharing the news of the disaster as they walked towards the chambers. He explained what had befallen his two friends. He relayed the story of their tragic deaths. Elasti's father was heartsick to think of how the families of Agot and Broch would react. They would soon learn the fate of their sons.

It was a mild, wintery day. The sun was out, and the rain had stopped, but the streets were still muddy. Many of the town people shouted greet-ings to Elasti as he walked by. Some were friendly; others only showed concern because Agot and Broch were not with him. All were curious. They wondered what had caused Elasti to return alone. But they knew better than to stop his progress by asking him questions.

Elasti didn't take time to chat. His father hurried him along to the council chambers. When Elasti finally entered the chambers, he found that all the members were seated and waiting. Members of the council could see by his expression that the news would not be good.

Amaz, as always, started the session, "Come forward Elasti and stand at the table. Your news is the only business we have before the council. Please explain what has happened to you, Broch, and Agot." Elasti was shaking. He could see concern in the eyes of the council, and occasion-ally blaming looks that hinted that he had abandoned his companions. He could also see that the parents of Agot and Broch had been allowed to attend the council session, and they sat in anxious anticipation of the dreadful news that he would share.

Why had he fought for his life, only to come back to these searching, blaming eyes? What had he expected? Had he expected to be greeted as a hero? He didn't deserve these cold stares from his own people. He didn't even want to go on this journey to begin with. Now he felt like he was going to be blamed for the disaster that had occurred.

Elasti bowed his head as though he was about to utter a humble pray-er. "Agot and Broch are both dead," he said, feeling it was best to get the worst of the news over with immediately. Agot's mother scream-ed out with pain and began to sob. She was near hysteria and had to be helped from the room. The other three parents were stunned and speech-less. They feared the worst but had not expected anything this bad. Tears of emotion soon filled the chambers.

Amaz let the dreadful news sink in. He knew how he would have felt, had he lost his only son. It was after quite some time before he felt the meeting could go on. "Continue Elasti, but first tell us how they died. Was it an accident?"

"No. They were brutally murdered." Again pain, anguish, and tears flowed from the parents, and also several of the members of the council.

Quickly Balbot jumped up and said, "I knew it! Those dwarfs are out to get us! Now they have killed two of our people! We must attack the North Groves immediately!"

Amaz could see that this council session would get out of control quickly if he didn't take a strong lead in it immediately. He gave Balbot a very stern stare and said, "Sit down! We will not have any more outbursts like that." Then he looked at Elasti and said, "Please continue and explain their deaths."

Elasti was shook up by Balbot's outburst. "It wasn't the dwarfs. I did-n't see any dwarfs when we were attacked."

"Then who was it?" asked Amaz.

"Gnomes! They must have come from Gamotz. We were ambushed. We were traveling along unaware that they were even around. All three of us had arrows shot at us and we didn't see anyone. The gnomes attacked us at the Albo Pass, just past the Avoli River. They caught us by complete surprise. Agot and Broch died instantly before they even knew what hit them. I just barely escaped. I even had to risk my life to sneak back just to find out who had done the killing."

"Gnomes!" said Algo. "How could that be possible? They wouldn't dare cross into the Southern Plains."

"But they haven't crossed into the Southern Plains," said Elasti. "They've cut off all the central ranges from Kabul to the Lamos. There is no way to get to the North Groves."

Amaz cut in, "All right, let's hear the whole story Elasti. Take it from the beginning when you left Amins up until you return last night. Please, don't leave out any of the details."

Elasti slowly relived the journey to the Albo Pass for the council. He told about how in Giter they had been severely rebuffed and how they had decided not to wait to see the king but to go on to Gije. He mentioned how they saw the dwarf and gnome on a side street and how he wondered what the connection was between Giter and gnomes and dwarfs. He explained how the threesome later decided not to go to Gije either. He told about the journey across the Avoli River and the sudden attack. He told about his efforts to sneak back across the river. And how he had to cross underneath the bridge. And how he was chased by the gnomes.

When Elasti had finished reliving his journey to the council, members of the council were allowed to ask questions. The first question was, "Why didn't you take a representative from Giter or Gije with you? No wonder you lost the lives of Agot and Broch. Surely if only one representative from each of the cities had gone with these two lives would have been saved."

The wise Abree spoke up immediately. "Do not blame Elasti for not having taken representatives with. The only result would have been that more lives could have been lost. A party of ten would have been no more successful than a party of three against as many gnomes as Elasti describes. I agree it was a mistake not to try to convince the people of Giter to participate in the journey. It was also a mistake not to go to Gije, but the result would not have been any different. How many unnecessary lives would still have been wasted? Let's not take out our grief on Elasti. Let's be thankful that at least he was able to return safely. Without his being able to warn us of the pending threat, all the lives of Amins might have been lost. At least now we can prepare. Let us all thank Elasti for his brave and courageous return. I'm not sure any of the rest of us could have been as ingenious."

Several of the council members expressed their thanks.

Amaz spoke up, "What's done is done. Let's plan our future. What can we do now?"

Amir spoke up sternly, "I fear a much bigger doom. I fear the possibility that the Kabul Lord will not stop at controlling the Central Ranges. I believe that he is preparing for an attack on the Southern Plains. He may already have attacked the North Groves. He may even be sitting in Gije. And we may be next."

During all this talk, Elasti was very downhearted. This was the first time that he had come to realize that having bypassed Gije and Giter may have cost the lives of his two friends. He heard no more of the conversation of the council members but withdrew totally. He was very upset with himself. He recalled that it had been his idea not to try to get representatives from either of the other two cities. The responsibility of his friends' deaths weighed heavily on him.

Balbot jumped up, "Why so much discussion? The solution is obvious. We must attack immediately. We can't allow the gnomes to cross into the Southern Plains."

Amaz returned, "Not so quickly Balbot. We can't go charging into a situation without making sure that we will be successful. We're not prepared for a war, and it sounds like the gnomes are."

The council was awestricken. The entire chamber was totally silent for several minutes. Algo finally broke the silence, "What do we do now? How can we conquer a bloodthirsty hoard of the size Elasti described? We do not have the weapons, the trained soldiers or the abilities. We are not trained warriors. We have only a very small group of police. This is an impossible situation! Generations ago our people escaped the outer world so they could survive in peace in Small World. And now we're in the same situation all over again. Where are we going to run to this time?"

Amaz spoke, "It is apparent that on our own, Amins is helpless. We must rally the support of Giter and Gije. Even with their support our combined army won't match up to that of the gnomes. We are forced to get in touch with the North Groves in hopes that the dwarfs will join us in this conflict. They know how to use weapons and we need their experience."

Avre, the wise, spoke up at this point, "We need more than just the dwarfs' help if we are to challenge the forces of the Kabul. We must get the support of the Wizard of Havinis."

The entire council looked at one another and started grumbling among themselves. Balbot spoke up, "How do we know the Wizard of Havinis really exists? No one we know has ever seen him. Maybe he is only a legend. He has not been seen by anyone in Small World for at least two hundred years."

Avir responded, "There is only one way to attract the attention of the Wizard of Havinis, if he exists. We must cross the swords of power."

Amaz spoke up, "We only have one of the swords, and the dwarfs of the North Groves have the other."

Avir responded, "Then we have no choice but to contact the dwarfs in the North Groves, not merely for their support, but for their sword."

Amaz retorted, "If we are to take this action we must move quickly. We cannot delay or the gnomes will be all over the Southern Plains before we have a chance to protect ourselves."

Avir, the wise, spoke up again, "I beg the council to listen to a suggestion. We have amongst us in Amins a wise man of old. This wise man is Bananot." At this many began to jeer and laugh at Avir, so much so that Amaz had to quiet the council. Bananot was considered the fool of the city because he was obsessed with his magic tricks and his isolated hermitlike activities. He avoided contact with the citizens as much as possible. His strange behavior caused the children of the city to fear him as though he were something evil.

Avir continued, "Don't laugh! Bananot is a very wise man. If you remember many years ago, he predicted that just this type of attack would occur, and we all laughed at him then. He predicted that the Kabul would take over all of the Central Ranges and disrupt the contact between the North and the South regions. Again, we all laughed and said that the Kabul Lord would not dare try to do such a thing. Now we find that he is doing exactly that. If we had not been so proud and had listened to him before, maybe we would not be in this situation now. We have only our own arrogance to blame for the deaths that have occurred, nothing else." Avir's speech made the council members think. Were they really personally responsible for the two deaths?

Avir went on, "I warn you now that it is time, we listen to Bananot and see what he has to say."

The council was stunned into understanding but not convinced. They believed Avir's idea of contacting Bananot was a long shot. But Amaz, being a wise man, sent for Bananot immediately.

Discussions about Bananot continued and soon all agreed that it would be wise to at least hear what he had to say. What did they have to lose? Bananot was called for and soon he arrived. He was immediately escorted into the council chambers, and Amaz addressed him, "We now see that your prediction about the attempted takeover by the Kabul has come to pass. We wish to know more about your predictions for Amins. Will Amins be affected by the Kabul Lord, and if so, how much time do we have?"

Bananot was very surprised by the council's sudden interest in his opinion. He enjoyed the situation tremendously and took advantage of it by going into a long-detailed discussion about how he had come to the conclusions of his prediction. Amaz did his best to hurry the old man along, "Please tell us what we need to know. What can we do about the present situation with the Kabul? What will the results be?"

Bananot spoke, "I cannot give you specifics. All I know is what was stated of old. The saying was passed verbally down through many generations and is now recorded on the scrolls of old. It goes; 'The Kabul will rise and leave its bounds. It will be but one year after the war before the Small World will reach a state of stability once again. United move to victory or divided to defeat.'"

Balbot burst out, "But what does that mean?"

Bananot continued, "The state of stability may mean the defeat of the Kabul, or it may mean domination by the Kabul. That fate is left up to us. We determine it by our unity or division, but this we know for sure; the Kabul left its bounds over five months ago when communication with the dwarfs was disrupted. This means that we have less than seven months in order to conquer or be conquered. Soon the Kabul will be crossing the Avoli River and entering the Southern Plains."

The council was in shock. Discussions broke out between the various council members. No one found grounds to challenge Bananot's conclusions. Amaz turned to the Old leprechaun and asked, "How can we of Amins change the tide of what is happening? We are but a small city with very few warriors."

Bananot was quick to respond, "We must pull the forces of the entire South together along with those of all the North if we are to stand a chance against the Kabul. In addition, you must call upon the powers of the Wizard of Havinis in order to unite and rally these combined forces. The Wizard of Havinis will have the answers."

But Amaz protested, "But the North and especially the South are not warrior tribes. How will we be able to contact the North with the Central Ranges cut off to us?"

But Bananot insisted, "Only united do we have a chance against the forces of the Kabul. The trip North must be made, but the scrolls do not tell us how."

Amaz spoke up, "The Kabul is very clever. They cut off our contact with the north in order to divide us and destroy our joint efforts. The Kabul Lord must also know the teachings of the scrolls and about the swords of power. By breaking off contact between the North and the South, he has stopped any chance for the two swords to be crossed."

Albo spoke out, "Our only choice is to form a committee and send them to the North Groves. This committee should be composed of a small group of our best warriors, perhaps no more than ten who must attempt to go to the North Groves by a route other than the Albo Pass."

Extensive discussions continued. No longer was the credibility of Bananot challenged. It was better to prepare for the worst, assuming that Bananot was correct, and to later find out that he was wrong than to arrogantly assume he was wrong and wish later that they had listened to his advice. Plans had to be made.

They realized that since the Kabul Lord was also a wizard, he would do anything in his power to stop the crossing of the swords. Unfortunately, it was impossible to know if Krakus, the Kabul Lord had already attacked Hilebin, the home of the Princess of the Northland and the place where the North Sword was kept.

Amaz spoke, "We know from Elasti that the Albo pass cannot be traveled. That only leaves us with three other possible routes. The first being through the center of the Kabul, which if the Kabul is preparing for war seems too dangerous to attempt. The second would be to travel along the east side of the Kabul through the Central Ranges along the Avol River."

Elasti, although not a member of the council, had to speak up, "The Sheere Cliffs are impossible to scale. The dwarfs have told me many tales about those who have attempted the climb and died. The only way to get to the top of those cliffs is to go around them by going into the east end of the Kabul and coming very close to the homeland of the gnomes. This route would place us on the open plains near their home and we couldn't help being noticed by them. Going through the western mountains of the Kabul would be safer, but still very dangerous."

No one disputed Elasti's comments; he had more insight into the difficulty of the Sheere Cliffs than anyone else. Amaz continued, "This leaves us with the last choice which Elasti was referring to, which is to travel to the North Groves along the Kilo Pass."

This time Avir spoke up, "The Kilo Pass also goes through the Kabul and leg-end claims it contains many other dangers that are unknown."

Amaz responded, "We also have a very important additional consideration and that is time. The Kilo Pass, having once been a trail that was regularly traveled, will most likely be an easier route than any other way."

Elasti added, "The Kilo Pass travels through the western mountains of the Kabul which is heavily wooded. This would offer the best cover of any of the three options. I would not anticipate that the gnomes would expect any of us to be foolish enough to enter that region of the Kabul. I would not expect any guards along that trail."

Balbot raised another question, "Why have the dwarfs not come down the Kilo Pass and contacted us? Surely, they must have realized what is going on. Why did they not try to make contact?"

Avre responded, "Perhaps they have already been conquered. Or perhaps they have tried to come but have been unsuccessful. Perhaps this same fate also awaits us. Either way we must take the initiative and act now."

After a slight delay Elasti spoke up again, "Then that only leaves us with one choice. The Kilo Pass is the most direct, quickest and safest route to the North Groves."

The council held a vote and it was decided that the Kilo Pass would have to be the acceptable route. The southern representatives would have to use this route during their journey northward.

Amaz spoke, "Now the question arises, who should be on this committee?"

Elasti jumped up, "I must go on this mission."

The father of Elasti was stunned. Hadn't he already suffered enough? Amaz also looked at him in surprise, "But you were so hesitant on the last journey. Why are you volunteering to go on a journey that is guaranteed to be more dangerous?"

Elasti's response was simple. "It is not for me but for my friends that I must go. If I can help in any way, then they will not have died in vain."

Amaz responded, "You do not need to feel any guilt over your friends' deaths. You did all you could. Do not let guilt force you into something you will regret."

Elasti insisted, "I must go on this journey! I am the only one that knows the way through the Hile Groves once we arrive in the North. It is important that I go along on this journey for that reason alone."

Amaz could not argue the point. In his heart he had hoped that Elasti would go along on this expedition for exactly that reason. But he had not expected him to be quite this enthusiastic or insistent. "I agree that Elasti should go along on this journey. His knowledge and experience in a trip to the North Groves can make the difference between success and failure."

"Are there any suggestions for the other members who should be included in this committee?"

Many names were discussed, and many individuals were suggested. Finally, a team of nine was decided on. This team would include seven of the best from Amins, plus at least one representative from each of the cities of Giter and Gije.

Amaz then stated, "We cannot force any of these leprechauns to go on this journey. We must have them all brought before the council and they must each be given the opportunity to accept or reject this mission."

Amaz requested that each of those selected be brought to the council chambers in precisely two hours' time. He also asked Elasti to return at that time since he was going to be one of the members of the committee. He then called a recess.

CHAPTER SIX

THE COMMITTEE

It had been a long day. The mud was thickly caked on their shoes as they stomped through the Amins Grove heading for their home in Amins. On his back Hasko carried several small rabbits that he had shot earlier in the day with his bow. Next to him his friend Hiztin carried fifteen birds that he had successfully captured. Hasko and Hiztin had been hunting together for many years starting as childhood friends. They made a good team working together to acquire food for their city of Amins. They were 12 years old, one year older than Elasti who had just finished his schooling.

Hasko was a scout. He skillfully led them through the Amins Groves while Hiztin was one of the finest bowmen in the Southern Plains. Together they had never come home empty handed and always took pride in showing off their catch.

They were still a couple miles from home when they could see someone running along an old deer trail hailing them, "Ahoy Hasko and Hiztin, is that you?"

Hasko yelled back, "Yes. What brings you after us?"

"I was sent by the council to fetch the two of you. You are to meet the council at their chambers one hour from now. You must hurry!"

Hasko and Hiztin looked at one another confused. What could possibly be so urgent? By now the messenger had caught up to them, and they questioned him, "Why have we been summoned to the council?"

The messenger responded, "I have no idea. All I know is that you are to be there and that it is very urgent. The council has been meeting since early this morning. Everyone thinks it has something to do with Agot and Broch's deaths and with Elasti's return last night."

Hiztin was startled, "Agot and Broch are dead? How is that possible? What happened to them?" Although neither Hiztin nor Hasko were ever close friends with either of the two, their deaths were shocking news. Death by old age was normal and acceptable, but death because someone

was killed was disruptive to the status quo. Amins was too small a town for the death of any of its citizens to go unnoticed.

"All I know is that they were murdered, but I wasn't allowed to stick around long enough to get the whole story. Now let's hurry up and get back. I want to get the rest of the story of what happened." Hasko and Hiztin were in their grubby hunting clothes which was caked with mud. They had to hurry in order to have enough time to get cleaned up before they went in front of the council.

"Well then we better get going!" Hasko said to the messenger. As they began to walk at an accelerated pace, he turned to Hiztin, "What do you think this is all about?"

"I don't know but I have a feeling it isn't going to be good."

As Hasko and Hiztin hurried along the trail they talked to one another about the intentions of the council. Had war been declared on the dwarfs and had the two of them been selected to be soldiers? They enjoyed hunting for food, but killing dwarfs was an entirely different matter. They weren't sure they would be ready for such an assignment.

Jesves was not one of the prettier girls of the city. She had always been considered boyish and competed effectively with the boys in hunting, shooting and running. She was able to compete with the best of them, but she had one ability that no other leprechaun in the Southern Plains had. She had an incredible sense of direction, even in the dark. Many times, she would be sent to retrieve a group of lost hunters safely back to their homes. She was a quiet girl, about 13 years old, who didn't have many friends and wasn't interested in getting any. She liked her life as a loner.

Because of her uncanny abilities, it came as no surprise that the council might called for her to discuss the trip to the North Groves. But when the messenger arrived at her small home at the north end of town and asked Jesves to come to the council meeting she was very fearful. She had a reputation of getting into trouble. Her initial reaction was one of fear that one of her latest exploits had been discovered and that she was going to be reprimanded for her carelessness.

When asked to come to the meeting she was confused. "You can't tell me why I've been called?" she asked inquisitively.

"I'm sorry but I wasn't given the chance to learn much about what occurred in the council meeting today. I think it has something to do with the sudden return of Elasti without Agot and Broch"

"That's it," she thought to herself. "The two got lost and they want me to go out and find them. I wonder where they got lost at. They should have had enough time to make it all the way to the Albo Pass by now. It should be fun going up there to find them. I'm sure glad it hasn't got anything to do with something I've done wrong."

Then Jesves asked, "When do I have to be at the council chambers?"

"You have about one hour and a half before they reconvene."

"Thanks, I'll be there," she returned. She bid the messenger farewell. She had been working on her garden and she was dirty. Her long brown hair was unkempt and the clothes she was wearing was sloppy and ragged. An invitation to come before the council was important to her. She wanted to make a good impression to compensate for the numerous times she was reprimanded by the same group. She rushed in her house to take a bath and get cleaned up.

The military forces of the Southern Plains, or so they were called, had always been very small and were more of a token assembly of boy scouts and police than a real force. The leader of these troops was a tall and powerful leprechaun, about 30 years old, named Yanon. Yanon was self-taught from some of the old books of the Lifefight Wars and had practiced as best he could with his little army. About once a year he would get together with Gilbon, his counterpart in Giter, who had a force about twice Yanon's size, and they would set up training skirmishes. Yanon always took his leadership position very seriously and therefore was considered the best military leader in the Southern Plains. His associates had a great deal of respect for him. If a military encounter ever did occur, he would have no problem rallying support from his troops and all the citizens of the city of Amins.

Yanon was out on a practice skirmish. He was about an hour's walk south of Amins in the grassy plains, when the messenger from the council arrived to inform him that his presence had been requested at the council meeting. At first, he protested. He was enjoying his skirmish and wanted to finish out the session. "I can't leave everything I'm doing and just go running off. Who will provide the leadership to finish the practice session we are in the middle of?" he raged.

"I don't know," replied the messenger, "but the deaths of Agot and Broch have the council very worried, and I think they want your help."

"What?" Yanon was shocked. "Agot and Broch have been killed? How?"

"Elasti made it back, but barely. He almost lost his life in the process. Apparently Agot and Broch were murdered somehow. I don't know any details. I overheard most of what I know, but I understand it has something to do with the Kabul."

"Impossible! Elasti, Agot, and Broch were traveling along the Albo Pass. How did they come into contact with the Kabul? This doesn't make any sense."

"Please hurry! We don't want to be late. Several others have been called and they are all supposed to meet back at the council chambers in

one hour." Yanon knew that he must go immediately. He abruptly can-
celled the remainder of the day's events and left with the messenger for
the city.

He was asleep out in a grass lawn in front of his home near the
western end of town. This seemed like a funny place to find the strongest
man in all the Small World, but Bydola enjoyed his afternoon rests. If
you were to pass by his home at this time of the day that's where you
would be sure to find him. Bydola enjoyed his afternoon naps after
working hard at the rock mines south of town. His workday started much
earlier than most. He was responsible for making sure that everything
was operational. His day normally began before sunrise.

He didn't have an exceptionally good-looking face, but his size and
strength caused all the ladies to take notice of him. The hard work he
engaged in caused him to appear much older than his age of 22 years.
He liked it that way. He was a loner and wasn't interested in having
friends. Those friends that he did have knew better than to disturb him
during his afternoon rest. So, he was very irritated when the messenger
from the council woke him up.

The unfortunate messenger hesitated about fifteen minutes before he
was able to build up enough courage to awake him. Bydola looked large
and powerful laying there on the grass asleep. His size brought fear into
the messenger. But eventually the messenger worked up enough courage
and shook the big leprechaun as best he could.

As Bydola rose, he cursed, adding to the messenger's fear. "What's
the big idea?"

"The council has called an urgent session and they want you to meet
with them."

"What do they want?!" Bydola blasted.

"I don't know," said the messenger, "but they said it was urgent. I
must have you back there within an hour."

"And just how do you expect to get me back there?" Bydola was in
a grouchy temperamental mood, the way he always was when he woke
up. "What could be so dang important," Bydola said, "to wake a fellow
up in the middle of his rest? Isn't anything sacred anymore?!"

"I'm sure the council realized that you were resting. I'm sure they
wouldn't have awakened you if it wasn't extremely urgent. They called
for several individuals to meet with them."

Bydola was starting to come to his senses and he became concerned.
Had he done something wrong? Has there been a problem at the rock
mine? His mood softened and he spoke to the messenger in a normal
voice, realizing that it wasn't the messenger's fault that he had to be
wakened.

"You said it will be about an hour before they reconvene right?" he
asked.

"That's right," the messenger returned.

"All right, let me get a little cleaned up and I'll get there on time."

Obydon's house was near the center of town, near the council chambers. Amaz knocked on the door of his son's home and yelled out, "Obydon, are you home?" He decided to go and fetch him personally rather than send a messenger.

The response came back from a lady inside the house, "He's round back," she yelled.

"Thanks," responded Amaz who recognized the voice of his son's wife.

In Amins, the leadership of the council had always been an inherited position, not because of any formal decree, or written law, but because certain families were considered to possess leadership qualities and therefore, they were considered "naturals" for the position. This was the way Amaz had received his leadership position. His father had also held that position. And his son Obydon would be the next to hold this position of authority. At the age of 18 Obydon was still too young to be seated on the council, but his time would soon come when he would have to start learning the ways of the leaders. The remaining members of the council were elected representatives of the community at large and they all had an equal voice.

Amaz walked around the small clay block house. The homes in Amins were simple, not excessively elaborate like those of the elves. The only decorations that could be found were the flower boxes that outlined the porches and trimmed the windows. The roofs were also made of a thin clay tile, hardened so as not to allow rain to enter. The cracks between the tiles were plastered with mud so that the cold was not able to leak through.

The insides of the houses were also plain. Most homes contained only three or four rooms, sufficient to make living comfortable and not much more. Leprechauns loved the outdoor life and during the daytime they typically had as little roof covering them as possible. So Amaz was not surprised to hear that Obydon was not in the house.

Amaz stepped around the side of the house admiring the flowers as he went. It wasn't long before he spotted Obydon and called out to him, "Obydon, you must come with me. We must go to the council chambers."

"Why today? I'm not of age yet to be seated in the council. I was hoping to still get this firewood cut and put away."

Amaz looked solemn as he explained, "We have grave news about the messengers that were sent to the North Groves. They were attacked and Agot and Broch have been killed."

"Is Elasti safe?" interrupted Obydon. He knew how much the marriage meant to his sister Jizeel.

"He is weary but quite safe," responded Amaz. Then he went on to explain that the three had been completely overtaken by forces from the Kabul. "We've decided that we must take another route to the North Groves so that the North and the South can be united in a force against the Kabul."

Obydon was skeptical, "Are you sure this is a wise decision? You know that none of our people are trained warriors. Even our so-called police militia knows little more than how to catch a burglar."

But Amaz responded, "I'm afraid we have no choice. The taking of the Albo Pass is surely not the ultimate objective of Lord Krakus. He wants revenge for the humiliation her received when he lost the Lifefight wars. We must send a committee to the North Groves and this committee must carry with it the sword of power from the South so that it can be crossed with the one from the North. Only then do we stand the chance of driving the Kabul forces out of our lands."

"This will be an extremely dangerous journey. How are you planning to get to the North?" questioned Obydon.

"The only route possible is the Kilo Pass," responded Amaz sadly. "The Albo Pass does not seem feasible since it is heavily guarded, but we are hoping that Lord Krakus will consider the Kilo Pass too dangerous for us to travel on and therefore will not be guarding it."

"I pity the poor souls that will have to travel along that route," Obydon thought out loud. "I hope you have not selected Elasti to have to suffer this journey again."

"Yes, it will be a very dangerous journey," Amaz stated. His head was bowed down toward the ground. He could not bear to look into the face of his son knowing what was in store for him, so he said, "Come, let us hurry to the council chambers."

As they started to walk toward the chambers Obydon asked, "Have you found anyone willing to take on this great risk?"

Amaz couldn't bear to answer and said simply, "It's too early to tell."

CHAPTER SEVEN

THE PARTING

The council had reconvened and standing at the foot of the council table before the council members were the seven perspective members of the expedition. There was Hasko, the best scout in all of the Amins groves, with his friend Hiztin the best bowman in all of Amins. There was also Jesves with her amazing sense of direction, Yanon the figurehead military policeman of the city, and Bydola the rock miner. But it was the last two of the seven that concerned Amaz the most, Obydon his only son and Elasti, who had already suffered so much, and who would once again be delaying his wedding plans.

Not until now did Amaz realize how much his family would become personally involved in this decision to contact the North Groves. Amaz, being the head of the council, opened the meeting with an explanation to the seven perspective travelers, "I'm sure that you all have questions about why you were summoned here. By now you are starting to understand the situation we are facing. Let me summarize it again for you. The Kabul has killed two of our most beloved citizens and has taken over the Albo Pass. But what is worse is that we fear that this is not the limit of their invasion. We believe that this move is simply an attempt to cut off contact between the North and the South. Krakus surely knows that if the swords of the North and South are not united, he stands a better chance of conquering and dominating the whole of Small World. We believe that his ultimate goal is to gain total control and to seek revenge for losing the Lifefight wars.

"The council has decided that it is our duty to travel to the other cities of the south and warn them. It is also our duty to journey to the north and warn the dwarfs. At the same time, we must take the sword of the south to the north so that the great Wizard Havinis can be contacted in hopes that he can help us out of our dilemma without any more bloodshed.

"The council has tried to select the best possible leprechauns for this expedition. You all have special talents that would benefit this expedition. I feel confident that you understand the urgency with which we must act.

"We have selected a team of seven individuals for this journey and I'm sure you have already guessed you are the seven we have chosen."

Most of the party was not as surprised at the announcement. But Obydon's mouth dropped open in shock. "Could this really be happening to me?" he thought.

Amaz continued, "I do not want anyone to go on this journey that isn't committed to its success. Therefore, even though you were selected for this journey we want you to consider carefully what we are asking of you, and then, if you agree with our decision, we would like you to volunteer for the expedition."

"While you are thinking about the big decision you are about to make, I would like Elasti to replay the explanation of his journey to the Albo Pass for your benefit." Elasti walked to the front of the group and proceeded to tell his story. The process took about fifteen minutes, and when he had finished, he returned to his position next to his companions.

For a few moments the room was deadly silent. Amaz broke the silence by turning to Elasti, who was already committed and asked, "Elasti, will you go?"

Without hesitation Elasti stepped forward and exclaimed, "I am dedicated to the success of this expedition. At night my dreams are filled with the blood of my dead friends crying out to me for revenge. No one can keep me away."

With this kind of dedication from the one individual who had suffered the most, Amaz knew that getting the commitment of the rest of the members of the group would be much easier. He turned to Yanon, who he was also confident would not refuse him and asked, "Will you go?"

Yanon responded affirmatively, "When do we get started?"

Hasko, Hiztin, and Jesves, each gave their agreement in turn. Each agreed that this expedition was necessary, and each was willing to share their skills for the safety of their city.

But when it became Bydola's turn, he was not as quick to agree. "I would be a fool if I didn't express my doubts about the success of this mission but I also feel that I could never forgive myself if I refused to go and someone else was to get hurt because of my hesitations. Therefore, I must go on this expedition."

Then it was time for Amaz to question his son Obydon. He feared that this may be too much for him, but he knew he must ask, "Will you go my son?"

Obydon answered like a true politician, playing the role of his father's son, "The safety of Amins is in my hands. How can I possibly say no?"

Tears could be seen around the eyes of Amaz as he said, "I know how hard this is for each of you. Today you have made me proud."

"Yanon, I will expect you to be the leader of the expedition. The well-being of the Southern Plains is in your hands. Now let us discuss further how we plan to carry out this dangerous mission. Take a seat around the table and we will proceed to lay out our plans."

As the newly pledged members of the expedition found places to sit around the council table Amaz sketched a drawing of the Southern Plains. "We will divide the seven of you into two groups," he started. "One group will travel to Giter to meet with the king of that city. This group will try to get someone from Giter to join our expedition. We need a show of strength when we meet the Northern Plains. We need to show that the Southern Plains are united against the Kabul.

"The lepelves are not easily convinced and will not readily agree to go on this mission. It is for this reason that I feel Yanon must go there because he is a good speaker and also because he has military contacts in that city. There are lepelves who trust and respect him. Elasti also needs to go there so that he can tell his dreadful story.

"Obydon, you will also go to Giter and your role will be that of sword carrier and the representative of the Amins council. The fourth member of this group will be Bydola, whose strength will be invaluable in solving the problems of this group.

"After acquiring the support of Giter, you are to travel to the Tako Ruins just a short way up the Kilo Pass where you are to wait until the second expedition arrives. Once the two separate expeditions have re-grouped you are all to head up the Kilo Pass to the home of the dwarfs.

"Ilasko, Hiztin, and Jesves, you are to go to Gije and attempt to achieve the same goal. The elves have always been very helpful, and you should have no trouble in recruiting their support. You must make your journey as quickly as possible and that is why we suggest you take the old back road to the Jove Plateau. It has been many years since this road has been traveled, but because of the urgency of the mission it is your best route. That is why we have selected Jesves for this part of the journey. Her unique sense of direction will be invaluable in those parts of the trip where finding the overgrown road can become difficult.

"We place all our trust in you. We will await the crossing of the swords. We know you will not be able to communicate with us, but we are confident you will be successful. Now go home to prepare and get a good night's rest. Your journey starts early in the morning. We will all be out to see you off."

Each of the council members gave their best wishes and a word of farewell.

Amaz entered his private office adjoining council chambers. It was a connecting room to the general chambers where the council had just met. He closed the door behind him and latched it with the three locks. He walked over to the windows and closed the blinds on each of them, thereby darkening the room. He proceeded over to one of the many bookcases that lined the walls, reached under one of the shelves, and released a lever that allowed the bookcase to slide easily away from the wall like a great door.

Being the head of the council gave him responsibility for all community belongings. Among these belongs was a collection of the old weapons that had been used in the Lifefight Wars. Never did he dream that the weapons of his ancestors would need to be brought back to life. In all the city of Amins, only Yanon was familiar with the use of a sword and only he carried one. For him it was more of a showpiece than a weapon. He trained with it on occasion, but never with the serious intent of doing anyone harm. In his role as police officer and military leader he used it to scare children who misbehaved.

In this secret chamber of city belongings was also the revered Southern Sword. This was a sword of power and it had once been instrumental in the defeat of the gnomes. It was during the Lifefight Wars that the gnomes had tried to overpower Small World. It was this sword and the Northern Sword together that finally gave the inhabitants of Small World victory over their attackers of the Jove Plateau, but not before the great city of Tako had been devastated. Now the remaining residents of Small World lived primarily in the North Groves and the Southern Plains.

The two swords would once again be forced into battle against those enemies that had caused the original forging of the swords. It was the Wizard of Havinis who originally forged these swords. He had given one to the leprechauns and one to the dwarfs. According to legend, if Small World was ever in need of the wizard, they have but to cross the two swords together in order for him to return.

Amins lit a candle and proceeded behind the bookcase. He slowly descended the stairs leading down to the underground chambers. At the bottom of the stairs was a small circular hallway which contained seven doorways leading to seven rooms. Amaz was familiar with these chambers and moved directly to the first door. He entered the room and spent about ten minutes there. He then left this room and went on to the second door.

Upon entering the second room he found the collection of weapons that he had sought. He selected five swords and six knives, the best he could find. He departed from this room and left the weapons out in the hall to be retrieved later. He then went to the third room which housed the treasures of Amins. There in the center of the room encased handle down into a large stone pillar, stood the Southern Sword, the blade pointing perfectly erect.

Amaz walked over to the sword and touched the blade. It felt frozen, as though it was made of ice. Legend had told him never to remove the sword unless it was needed. Its removal would cause it to be activated. He never understood how a sword could be activated but he was now going to find out.

He tried to remove the sword by pulling on it, but it wouldn't budge. He crawled up on the stone slab and attempted to pull the sword up by the blade. The sword was too sharp, and it cut his hand. He reached for the handle of the sword where there was just enough of it showing out of the top of the pillar for him to grab hold, and he pulled upward. The sword was quickly released from the pillar as if it had never resisted his previous efforts. The release was so sudden that it caused Amaz to fall over backwards, right off the top of the pillar. He landed on the ground with a thud.

"Rats!" he cursed, rubbing the arm that he landed on. Then he noticed the sword that he was holding. It had begun to shine. It glowed with a yellow brilliance. There was a jewel in the center of the handle, a green jewel which emitted strange amber light. He stood up trying to get his composure. He was about to lay the sword on top of the pillar so that he could brush himself off, when he noticed that the pillar on which the sword had been stuck had sealed itself of its wound. In the place where the sword had been standing was a green jewel identical to the one in the handle of the sword. This jewel emitted the same light that could be seen shining from the jewel in the sword.

He brushed himself off and reached for the sword. This time he found it to be rather warm to touch. It was as though the light of the sword radiated in harmony with the light on the pillar. He picked up the sword and now found it to be very light, much lighter than the other swords he had left in the hall outside.

Retrieving the sword, he exited the room, collected the other swords and knives from the hall and proceeded up the stairs. Having passed through the bookcase doorway he laid the newly acquired arsenal on his desk and proceeded to close the secret access to the private chambers.

The morning was misty causing it to be chilly. The sun had not yet begun to rise, but there was enough light to see a thick layer of clouds in the sky. The weather fit the mood. No one looked forward to the day's events, but everyone knew it had to be.

Most of the residents of Amins were out on the streets. This was the most exciting thing that had happened in the city for as long as most people could remember. It was unusual that anyone would leave the city even for a short time, but to send seven of its citizens off to the North Groves with unknown dangers lurking ahead was very much out of the ordinary for this normally quiet community.

The travelers were finishing their preparations, their bags were packed, and they were saying their final goodbyes. Obydon held his wife tight. Fear could be seen in her eyes. She was concerned for his safety and hoped for a quick return. She also knew that this journey had to be. But she wasn't sure why her husband had to be the one to go.

"Be really careful," she told Obydon, "you're all I've got. I need you back in one piece."

"Don't worry," he tried to assure her. "I have every intention of returning back quickly and safely. I'll miss you terribly. Don't forget me while I'm gone. Don't start looking for a replacement for me!"

"Don't be funny," she scolded. "I need you. I only wish I could have gone with you on this little expedition. If only I had been better than everyone else at something, like hunting, shooting or scouting then perhaps they would have selected me to go along. You can bet I'll be ready next time." Obydon wasn't sure what she meant by that, but he wasn't going to pursue it now.

"Don't get carried away," Obydon scolded. "I can just see you spending the next year driving everyone crazy with a new over energetic image. Just enjoy being yourself. I like you just the way you are."

"You'll see," she answered.

Elasti was with Jizeel. "I nearly lost you once," she sobbed, "why do I have to risk you again? My father could have found someone else. Why do you have to go?"

"I could never live with myself if I didn't go," responded Elasti. "After seeing what happened to my friends, I must do everything in my power to make sure their deaths aren't in vain. I owe it to them and to their memory to help this expedition in every way that I can. Please try to understand. I would much rather be with you safely here at home, but I would never be able to live with myself if anyone else got hurt and I could have prevented it."

"I do understand," she tried to assure him even though in her mind she didn't agree. "It's just that I'm being selfish with you. I'm so close to having you all to myself and I'm just not willing to risk you to something none of us understand. But I know you have to go, and I respect you for it. Please take care of yourself and hurry back."

"You can bet on it. And while I'm at it, I'll bring you home a little surprise from the North Grove," he responded, not really sure what that surprise would be.

"How about a pair of those carved earrings that the dwarfs make," Jizeel suggested. "That would be a perfect wedding present."

"We'll see," responded Elasti, happy to see her cheered up.

Bydola, Hasko, Hiztin, Yanon, and Jesves were all giving similar goodbyes to friends and loved ones. It was a sad day, but it was also an exciting day.

Amaz called the travelers together. "It's time for you to set out on your journey. Speaking for the council, and all the citizens of Amins, we thank you for your bravery. We are all proud that you would risk your very lives for the protection of our beautiful city. Please be careful and hurry back to us."

Amaz continued, "Before you depart, I must turn the Southern Sword over for safe keeping. Obydon, I present you with the sword and ask you to remember that this sword represents our only hope. I know that each of you will guard it with your lives."

The crowd was hushed. Most of the citizens in the city had never seen the sword, and this opportunity to view it generated awe. Obydon stepped forward and accepted the sword from his father. It shone with a brilliance that defied the gloominess of the day. It didn't seem to need the sun for its brilliance. It seemed to be able to generate its own light.

"Thank you for your trust," responded Obydon. "I pledge to do my best to make this expedition a success."

Yanon stepped forward, "As leader I speak for all of us. We promise to keep you, the citizens of Amins, in the forefront of our minds. We promise not to let the evil of Kabul touch our beautiful city any more than it already has with the loss of our two friends."

A cheer went up from the crowd. Everyone knew that this promise was more hope and well-wishing than anyone had the power to carry out, but it made the crowd happy to hear the words.

Each of the travelers was then given swords and knives which they fastened on to their belts. "I hope you never have to use these," said Amaz as he handed them out, "but it's better to have them and not use them than to need them and not have them." The passing out of the swords brought a stark realization of the potential dangers that lay ahead for every one of the travelers. What had they gotten themselves into?

"You better get going now," Amaz said. "Don't ever forget that the love of the people of Amins will always be with you."

Final goodbyes were said, and the two parties were off each in their different directions. Yanon, Obydon, Bydola, and Elasti headed northeast along the South Road toward Giter. Hasko, Hiztin, and Jesves took off in a southwesterly direction, leaving town from the opposite end.

Children ran after both parties, filled with excitement and asking lots of silly questions like, "Are you going to kill any gnomes." It cheered the two parties to see the delight and the eye for adventure that inspired the children's comments. Many of the youngsters followed for quite a distance out of town before finally being sent back to Amins.

CHAPTER EIGHT

THE ROAD TO GIJE

"Well we're off," Hasko started the conversation trying to break some of the chill of the morning by getting everyone talking. "I guess you know why they picked us to go to Gije, don't you?"

"Probably because they were afraid that your big mouth would blow it for them in Giter," was Hiztin's joking response. Hasko and Hiztin often kidded each other. It gave them a way of releasing some of their mild irritations without being overly offensive about it.

"Are you referring to my eloquent speech? They could have used me in Giter. But, as I was saying before I was so rudely interrupted, do you know why they selected us for this journey?" He was specifically speaking to Jesves this time pretending to ignore Hiztin.

"No, I don't," replied Jesves. Jesves wasn't used to the closeness that Hasko and Hiztin felt. The three had lived together in the same city all their lives but their paths had seldom crossed.

"They always pick their best men, errrr, best individuals, to do the toughest jobs. Don't you agree, Hastle?" Hasko responded. "Hastle" was a nickname Hasko used for Hiztin when they were picking at each other.

The conversation wasn't constructive, but it managed to keep everyone amused. The heavy mist of the morning turned into a mild but steady drizzle by noon. The sky was still overcast which left the group somewhat moody in spite of Hasko's efforts to cheer them up.

They decided not to stop for lunch. They wanted to get as far as possible that day, so they ate as they walked. The path that they followed along the old southern washed-out road was starting to show signs of age. It had become quite grown over in areas, and occasionally the grass was so thick that the path couldn't be seen at all. When the trail seemed to disappear, the group would simply continue on in the same direction and eventually the trail would reappear.

"I'm sure glad you ended up as part of our team," Hasko said to Jesves. "You've done an excellent job of keeping us on the trail. Without your help we probably would have gotten lost several times." Hasko was trying to get Jesves to talk more but she wasn't one for a lot of words. She liked being a loner. She was comfortable with silence.

"Boy that's the truth!" Hiztin interjected. "Hasko gets lost going from his front door to his living room. Maybe some of your sense of direction will rub off on him." Hiztin was again teasing Hasko. In reality Hasko was considered the best scout in Amins. He was able to spot the tracks of animals when anyone else would have given up hope.

"I don't really know what it is that helps me get around," Jesves said apologetically. "I just do what 'feels' right and it always seems to work out."

The group continued on until shortly after sunset. They made camp by first starting a fire that allowed them to get dried off. Then, by the light of the fire, they cooked supper and set up their tents.

"How many days walk do you think it will be before we arrive at the base of the Jove Plateau?" asked Hiztin. He knew that once they arrived at edge of the plateau, they would have to climb up the side of the cliff to get to its top. "I hope the climb isn't too tough."

"If we keep moving at the pace, we moved today we should get there the day after tomorrow," responded Hasko. "I sure hope this rain stops soon. It's making the traveling uncomfortable." All three of the travelers had become thoroughly soaked during the day's travels. "What do you think, Jesves, will we be able to keep up this pace."

"It looks promising so far," she responded. "I think we will be crossing through part of the Amins Groves soon and that may slow us up a little."

The three crawled into their sleeping bags and it wasn't long before they were asleep. Their small tents did an effective job of keeping the rain out and they slept quite comfortably.

The morning found them with weather that had changed for the worse. The rain had gotten more intense. It was still not a driving rain just a steady heavy rain that would keep them soaked and uncomfortable for most of the day.

"Rise and shine," bellowed Hiztin. He was the first to get up and he was already rebuilding the fire and making preparations for breakfast. "Let's get the show on the road!" Making a fire in the rain was tricky but years of experience had given Hiztin the knowledge and ability to build a fire under just about any condition.

"Can't we just cancel the day today and stay in bed," complained Hasko. "I'm not really in the mood to slop around in this rain. Why don't you two go on ahead and I'll catch up with you later."

"Quit your complaining and get up," Hiztin responded.

Jesves climbed out of her tent. She didn't feel excited about getting up either, but when she saw that Hiztin had already busied himself making breakfast she felt guilty and got up quickly to help.

"Call me when breakfast is ready." Hasko lazily responded.

Hasko's laziness didn't disturb Hiztin. The two had grown very close and Hiztin knew that there would be plenty of times when Hasko would do him favors in return. In spite of his criticism, he enjoyed occasionally catering to his friend.

It wasn't long before breakfast was ready and Hasko could no longer find any excuses. The three ate breakfast, broke camp and proceeded to extinguish the fire, which didn't take much effort in the rain.

The rain had made traveling worse than they at first anticipated. Many parts of the path were filled with water puddles and had become very muddy. Often the travelers were forced to journey along the side of the path in the thick grass which slowed them down even more.

They traveled on, fighting the mud and the rain until nearly noon, when the rain finally subsided to a slow drizzle. Traveling had become easier again, but it still wasn't comfortable. They decided to stop for lunch and make another warm fire thereby giving themselves a chance to dry out. They hoped that the heavy rain had ended for good and that soon the drizzle would be gone also.

After lunch they were off again, working their way toward the Jove Plateau. The spirits of the travelers had improved and Hiztin began singing:

We are the marchers,
One, Two, Three;
We journey further,
Than you can see;
No one can keep up,
With our quick pace;
We will march bravely,
To meet our fate.

"Can't you sing something a little more positive," complained Hasko. "I'm not real excited about meeting my 'fate'. I plan to stick around for a while yet."

"Can you think of a better song?" responded Hiztin, slightly annoyed. "At least I'm singing. All you're doing is griping." Hiztin started the song up again and this time Hasko joined in. After a few bars, Jesves also caught the spirit of the song and soon all three were marching and singing along as though they didn't have a care in the world.

The terrain started to get brushy. Small bushes started to appear along the side of the road and occasionally there was even one on the roadway. For a while these bushes were no more than a small annoyance that they simply walked around. But after a while the bushes got so thick that the three would get scratched up when they tried to bust their way through.

It became apparent that if they were going to continue on this route, they would have to start hacking their way through the thicket. The three took turns using their swords to beat a path.

"I hope this is the only thing I'll ever have to use this sword for," thought Jesves out loud, as she fought her way through a thick clump of the brush. They were now entering the area where the path traveled through the Amins Groves. The brush would often wrap itself around trees allowing it to hold firm. The trees also gave the brush the opportunity to grow higher, and often the travelers would end up tunneling their way through a clump of brush.

The mist had let up and the travelers were starting to feel dry. But even with the improved weather they were uncertain if they would make it to the Jove Plateau the next day.

The brush and grass had become thicker and higher as they hacked their way along the pass. "Woopsssss!" yelled Jesves who was currently in the lead as she suddenly came to a stop. Hiztin who was right behind her didn't stop fast enough and ran into her. She fell to the ground scrambling to grab onto the brush next to her. Hiztin saw what had caused Jesves to stop so suddenly. They had come upon a ravine that was at least 25 leprechauns deep and 15 leprechauns wide. By running into Jesves he had caused her to slip on the muddy edge of the ravine. A section of the muddy edge had broken away under her weight and now she dangled over the edge, hanging on to the brush for dear life.

Hiztin quickly grabbed a hold of Jesves' hand and pulled her back up on the embankment. "Sorry about that," he said apologetically.

"It's alright," she responded. "That ravine came up awfully fast. I'm sorry about stopping so quickly but it was quite a surprise. The brush kept me from seeing it ahead of time."

By now Hasko had wormed his way up to the edge of the ravine and was looking over the side. "This must have gotten washed out by a flood or something. It sure looks deep. Worse than that, it looks awfully muddy."

"It will take us a good day to climb down the side of this ravine and back up the other side," said Jesves. "I wonder if it's worth it. Once we've accomplished this task, we may find another ravine just like it further down the road. Maybe we should cut off north and go around Alica Lake and catch the South Road to Gije. We'll end up wasting too much time if we try to fight our way through ravines like this."

"I'm not sure which will take longer," returned Hasko. "We may also find the same ravines and problems when we're trying to work our way north. We're probably better off sticking with the route we planned and making the best of it. Hopefully, this will be the only ravine we'll encounter."

"That's pretty optimistic," she returned. "I still think we might be better off heading north."

While the discussion was going on between Hasko and Jesves, Hiztin was busy analyzing the ravine, as was always his nature. He pulled one of his precious steel arrows out of his quiver and tied one end of a cord to it. He took aim on a large tree on the other side and let the arrow fly. It struck solidly into the side of the tree. He pulled the cord tight and saw that his arrow was firmly implanted in the tree. He took the other end of the cord and tied it firmly to a tree on his end of the ravine, making sure that the cord was taut.

"What do you think you're going to do with that cord?" asked Hasko noticing Hiztin's activities. "You can't climb across the ravine on that, it's not strong enough. It will break for sure."

"I couldn't use a rope, or it would have been too heavy for the arrow," explained Hiztin. "This cord will work out just fine. Besides, I wasn't planning to try to get across on that cord. I was planning on having 'you' crawl across on that cord!"

"Fat chance of that!" burst out Hasko. "You must really think I'm crazy!"

"You're lighter than me and so you're the logical choice. Besides, if the arrow pulls out, you'll just end up falling back over to this side of the ravine. Hold on to the cord tightly and pull yourself back up. It's easy. Give it a try."

"You're crazy if you think I'm going to risk my neck on some fool idea like that!" Hasko responded. The two argued back and forth for quite a while, with no one seeming to be getting the upper edge.

Jesves thought about what Hiztin had done. Maybe it would work. But why not pick the lightest person of all to make the attempt. She should be the first to go across.

Leaving Hasko and Hiztin arguing she went over to the cord and hand-over-hand worked her way across to the other side. The cord and the arrow held firmly. She made it across with no difficulty. It took nearly ten minutes to get across, but the two were so busy arguing the entire time that they didn't notice.

"Hey!" she yelled, trying to get the attention of her two companions. No response. It was as if they didn't even hear her. "HEY!" she yelled again, much louder. Still no response. "Great," she thought. "They are too busy arguing to even hear me."

She picked up a rock and threw it at the two. The rock hit Hiztin squarely on the shoulder. "Ow! Why'd you do that? What's the big idea?" He was so angry that he initially didn't even notice that she was on the other side of the ravine. The rock had hurt his shoulder and that was all that concerned him at the moment.

"Look where she is!" said Hasko, realizing what had transpired. "She's over on the other side."

Hiztin's facial expression changed from anger to surprise. His idea had worked. They would be able to get across using his method. "Untie the cord from the arrow," he yelled to Jesves, "and I'll untie my end also. Then retie it firmly around the tree and I'll retire mine."

Jesves was excited and acted as if she knew exactly what to do. Hiztin retied the cord at his end and then tied the end of a second cord around Hasko's waist and told him to proceed across. Hasko hesitated, but the thought of being outdone by a girl got the better of him and he proceeded to brave it across.

Once on the other side, Hiztin used the second cord to pass their packs across, by tying one pack at a time to the middle of the cord. Then Hasko pulled the cord across to the other side. Soon everything had been successfully transported to the other side except Hiztin.

Hiztin grabbed a hold of the cord and started to work his way across. Everything seemed to proceed as it should when suddenly there was a slip in the cord at Hasko's end of the ravine. "Help!" yelled Hiztin. Hasko and Jesves saw what was happening. The cord was starting to unravel causing Hiztin to drop. Hasko and Jesves quickly grabbed onto the cord and held on tight.

"Hurry across!" yelled Hasko. "I'm not sure how long I can hold on!" Hiztin didn't need to be told twice. He started hand-over-handing it across the rest of the ravine as quickly as he could. He was almost there, only two or three more swings in order to be safely on the other side, when the cord broke, right in front of where Hasko was holding it.

"Oh no," whispered Hasko, as he watched Hiztin, still clinging to the cord disappear down the side of the ravine. He was afraid to go to the edge and look. He slumped down to the ground where he was and put his face into his hands. "What have I done?"

Jesves was about to try to console him, when they heard a faint "Help!"

"What was that," said Hasko as he jumped up. "Did you hear that?" He rushed to the edge of the ravine.

There, clinging to a bush on their side of the ravine, not more than two leprechauns down the side, was Hiztin, hanging on for dear life. "Throw me a rope!"

Quickly Hasko grabbed a rope, tied it to a tree, and threw it over the edge of the cliff. Hiztin grabbed the rope and pulled himself up. Simultaneously, Hasko pulled the rope up to help Hiztin come over the top a little quicker. Soon he was over the side of the cliff. "I thought you were going to leave me down there," Hiztin said, but that was about all he was able to say before Hasko grabbed him and gave him a big hug while tears flowed out of his eyes.

"I've never been so happy to see you in my life," Hasko told Hiztin through his sobs. "I thought you were a goner."

All three of them sat down. They deserved a rest after all the excitement. It was more than any of them could handle in one day.

High above their heads, in the top of a tree, unnoticed by any of them, sat an eagle. He seemed to be resting as well. He had enjoyed watching the adventures of the three travelers, and now he seemed to smile. He stood up on his perch, spread his magnificent wings, and flew away.

Hasko, Hiztin, and Jesves didn't wait too long. They knew that they had to get on with their travels. After their short break they got up to continue on with their travels. Frustratingly they realized that the brush on this side of the ravine was nearly as thick as the brush they had just gone through on the other side. At the edge of the ravine where they were there wasn't much more than standing room. They started to hack their way through the brush to get away from the ravine. They took turns so that no one would get too tired.

"I guess we're committed to taking this route now that we're on this side of the ravine," said Hasko. "There doesn't seem to be any reasonable way of getting back." No one disagreed as they plowed ahead through the thicket.

It wasn't long before the sun had set and the travelers started to scout for a place to spend the night, but no clearing could be found. They ended up cutting their own clearing in the brush.

Legend told that within the Amins Groves it was dangerous to start fires. The groves hated fires and protected their trees from them. They weren't sure exactly how the groves prevented fires, but they decided not to take the risk. The three decided that this meal would have to be a cold one and they began preparations for dinner.

As they sat around eating Hasko began to review the day's events. "You had a close one today didn't you Hastle. I sure hope you don't plan any more of your antics for tomorrow."

"It sure isn't anything that interests me," he responded. "I'm just glad to have lived through it."

"We're glad you're alright too," said Jesves. "Actually, you had a pretty good idea with your arrow and cord." Hiztin blushed. He wasn't very good at taking compliments from girls, even if they were tomboyish girls. He suddenly felt a feeling of warmth, closeness, and appreciation toward her. "We should have used it to pull a rope across and then you two could have come across on the rope. Then the cord wouldn't have broken. All three of us going across on the same cord became too much weight."

Hiztin didn't say anything. He didn't know quite what to say or how to say it, so he decided he'd better change the subject. "How close are we to the Quali Swamps?"

"Not very close according to my understanding," responded Hasko. "It's quite a bit north of where we'll be traveling. Does that bother you?"

"I've just heard so much about the swamp rats," Hiztin returned. Rats weren't his favorite creatures. He hated them and the thought of encountering rats in the swamps, especially rats that were reported to be killers, made him shiver.

Hasko was aware of Hiztin's fears and decided to play on them. "Those rats haven't been known to kill anyone for quite some time. They're probably pretty tame by now. Maybe we should catch some and bring them home for pets."

"Don't be crazy!" returned Hiztin, knowing that Hasko was trying to irritate him.

Jesves caught on to Hasko's little game and started up her own little line of antagonism. She had become very comfortable with her fellow travelers during the past couple days, and she now felt that she could join in on some of the wordplay. "I've heard that some groups of the rats have escaped from the Quali Swamps and have traveled quite some distance. There was a story about a lepelf that was caught by a hoard of these rats close to Alica Lake. All that the rats left were bones, and even they had been licked clean."

"Really?" asked Hiztin taking the bait and falling into her trap.

"Yes, and they're supposed to be about a half a leprechaun tall," added Hasko. "They're big and mean."

Hiztin didn't know what to believe. He was sorry he'd ever brought up the subject. Now he would probably have nightmares about the rats.

Jesves, seeing Hiztin's insecurities, decided to let him off the hook. "There aren't any rats in the Quali Swamp. That's just an old legend.

How could rats live in the water? Don't worry about them. Besides, we won't be passing very close to the swamps."

That was enough for Hiztin. He quickly finished eating and crawled into his sleeping sack. He fell asleep quickly in spite of the disturbing discussion. He had experienced an extremely exhausting day.

The weather was nice on this the third morning of their travels, much nicer than the previous couple days. It was still overcast, but the rain and mist had stopped, and the three travelers were excited about the weather change. They had hoped for a nice dry day. They still had the thick brush to contend with, but the improvement in the weather gave them hope that they would make better progress.

They ate breakfast, broke camp and finished their last leg through the groves. After leaving the groves their speed improved significantly. They were able to travel faster because the brush had thinned out and they no longer had to contend with it. Blazing a path through the short grasses and occasional small bushes was a lot easier than trying to tunnel through the large brush. They traveled on for several hours again taking turns at battling the scrub.

Crash! Hiztin, who was trailing the party, fell to the ground.

"What's the matter clumsy?" asked Hasko, turning around to see what happened. "Did you trip?"

"No!" returned Hiztin as he tried to get up. "Something pushed me."

"Sure, thing Hastle," criticized Hasko. "A birdie came down and pushed you, right?"

"No, something pushed me!" Hiztin insisted looking around to see if he could see anyone.

"I didn't see anything," commented Jesves as she looked back at Hiztin.

"You guys don't have to believe me if you don't want to but I felt something push me. It almost felt as though whatever it was ran into me accidently. I know when I've been bumped."

"Look," said Jesves, spotting the back of Hiztin's leg, "the back of your leg is all muddy. How did the back of your leg get that muddy when you fell down face first?"

"I don't know," said Hiztin, reaching down to feel the back of his leg. "This is a strange mud. It's very fresh and slimy. We haven't traveled through this type of mud recently. Whatever bumped me left its mark."

"Look behind you," continued Jesves in her observations. "There are footprints, muddy footprints, just like the mud on your pants. Some muddy slimy something bumped into you. Then it ran off in this direction," she said pointing off to the side of the trail. "This creature must have been short enough to fit under these branches. This is strange. What kind of creature would leave a trail of mud?"

"I've never heard of such a thing," said Hasko skeptically. "Whoever heard of mud creatures?" But the existence of the footprints could not be denied.

They continued on without any further encounters but Hiztin constantly kept looking over his shoulder. He was determined to catch this creature in the act if it attacked him again.

Lunch was eaten on the run without stopping to rest. They wanted to make up some of the lost time they had experienced when fighting the dense brush. It had now thinned out and the three travelers could occasionally plow through without having to hack their way. Often, they could easily make out the trail under their feet in the thicket. They could actually see their way without utilizing Jesves's sense of direction. Additionally, this gave them the assurance that they were still on the right track.

Occasionally scattered trees appeared. Not a lot, but the travelers noticed in the distance that they would soon be encountering another grove. Occasionally they would also encounter an excessively thick clump of brush. And as they were approaching this new grove of trees, they encountered one of these very dense brushy areas.

It was Jesves' turn to be in the lead again and as she hacked at the brush she suddenly yelled out, "Whoooa! Hold on!"

"What's the problem?" asked Hasko who was right behind her.

"Take a look!"

There before them lay a mire. It was dark and somewhat spooky. There were no bushes in the swamp and the trees were bare all the way to the very top. There at the top was a layer of branches and leaves. It was as if the trees were trying to reach out of the swamp as far as possible in order to hang on to just a little of their existence. The tops of the trees looked like green umbrellas, blocking out nearly all the sunlight.

The muddy slop seemed about a half a leprechaun deep. They determined this because fallen tree trunks could be seen scattered around lying in the mire. The swamp was barren, with the exception of the fallen trees. The brush had stopped right at the edge of the swamp as if it was afraid to extend any further.

"What are we going to do now?" asked Hiztin. "You promised me that we weren't going to encounter the Quali Swamp. Why did you trick me?"

"We weren't trying to trick you," responded Hasko. "I didn't expect to see these swamps. I've got no interest in being this close to them. The same flood that caused the ravine must have also caused the expansion of the swamps. You can't blame me for something I can't control."

"Well what are we going to do now?" Hiztin repeated his question fearing the answer.

"We can't go around it," replied Jesves. "That may take days. We don't have any idea how big this swamp is. And we'll have to fight this brush the whole way. We're also not going to lose time by going back home."

"And we can't climb on the back of a bird and fly," suggested Hasko sarcastically. "That doesn't leave us with a lot of choices."

"Forgeeeet it!" yelled Hiztin. "No way am I going any closer to that swamp. Have a nice trip and I'll see you when you come back."

"I think we can make it fairly easily," suggested Jesves. "We could use those fallen trees that are laying down in the swamp and where there isn't any tree, we could cut one down and use it to walk on. If we're careful we could walk all the way across the swamp and not even get wet."

"You can do it just fine but you're doing it without me!" insisted Hiztin.

"Hastle, we already told you once that there's no such thing as swamp rats," said Hasko comfortingly thinking he knew what was bothering Hiztin. "What you see, this mud and muck is the only danger we'll encounter going through here. It'll be easy."

"Fat chance! You just better get comfortable with the thought that you're doing it without me."

"What do you intend to do if you stay behind?" questioned Hasko. "Do you really think you're going to get out of here some other way?"

"Read my lips; 'N' 'O'. I'm not going across!"

As the two were arguing Jesves had set out planning her way across the swamp. She quickly felled the first thin tree and was walking out on it to see what type of a trail she could make for herself. She assumed the role as the leader of the swamp crossing by virtue of her ability to lead them in the right direction. As she walked across the logs, Hasko whispered to Hiztin, "What's the matter with you. Are you going to let a girl outdo you? She's not half as scared as you are. Be a leprechaun! Get your act together and get a move on!"

Hiztin was stunned. He had forgotten that Jesves was a girl and was embarrassed but at the same time he was also mad at Hasko for having come up with a way to convince him to go. How awful. He was going to get tricked into going across this swamp and his pride wouldn't let him back out. "Are you sure there aren't any rats in there?" he asked, trying to make himself feel better rather than actually needing to be convinced.

"Of course not," responded Hasko, proud of himself that he had weakened Hiztin. "Would I lie to you?"

By this time Jesves had made it back. "Are you two ready?" she asked.

"I think so," replied Hasko, smiling at his companion. Hiztin wouldn't respond.

Jesves took a rope and tied it around the waist of each of the travelers. "We'll use this rope to pull anyone out that falls in," commented Jesves. She would be in the lead, Hasko second, and Hiztin took the rear, hoping that he would be safer on the end.

They were off. Movement was slow. They had to be extremely careful. The logs were slimy having been in the dark for so long. It would be very easy for the travelers to lose their footing.

There was a strange quiet in the swamp. No birds could be heard. There were no mosquitoes, or bugs of any kind that were common around stagnant pools. It was as though all life had ceased to exist, all but the trees which grew as if they were trying to escape to the sky.

The three felt that they were pretty lucky. Only occasionally was it necessary to fell a tree. And felling a tree created quite a splash, so it was something they tried to avoid. Fortunately, there seemed to be enough logs lying around to allow them to move freely, jumping from one to another as they went along.

Jesves was confident that she knew where she was going in spite of the difficulties. Traveling in a straight line was impossible, and seeing the sun was also not possible. She moved with ease in the direction she felt was right, selecting logs that headed her in the correct general direction.

Splash! Hasko had gotten a little too confident causing him to become carelessness. He slipped and fell into the murky mess, nearly pulling his two companions in with him because of the rope tied between them.

"You klutz!" scolded Hiztin angrily as he flapped his arms wildly trying to regain his balance.

"Do you think I tried to fall in?" asked Hasko in irritation. He reached his hand toward Hiztin, "Here, help me get out." Hasko had managed to get himself covered from head to foot with the slimy sludge.

Jesves and Hiztin tried to pull him out of the mess, one pulling on each hand. But the slipperiness of the mud caused the hand-hold between Jesves and Hasko to slip. Plop! Hasko was back in the mud, but this time, since Hiztin still had a hold of Hasko's hand, he flew in as well; headfirst, right behind him.

Jesves couldn't control herself and burst out laughing. As Hiztin came to the surface of the mire he was furious, and her laughter irritated him even more. He found it difficult to control his anger. He grabbed the rope that was connected to Jesves and yanked her hard. She fell into the mess as well.

"Terrific!" mumbled Jesves as she tried to get her footing in the mud. "Now we all look like slobs. I hope you're proud of yourself Hiztin!"

This time it was Hasko's turn to lose control. He couldn't help himself. The image of the three travelers all splashing around in the swamp mud made him laugh loudly. Hiztin could see that Jesves was only mildly angry with him and so he too started laughing. It wasn't long before all three of the travelers were behaving like children, splashing slush at each other and laughing their heads off. The humor and gaiety of the occasion made them forget they were on a dangerous mission.

"Next time we feel like splashing around in the water, we should pick some place a little cleaner," Jesves complained. "It's going to take me a month to get this slime out of my hair." Jesves had long pretty hair, when she let it down. She usually kept it rolled up in a bun on the top of her head and kept it tucked under a hat, so it wasn't very noticeable. But now her hat had been knocked off and her hair was out. Her hair fell beautifully down to her waist.

"Guess we'll all just have to shave our heads," joked Hasko.

"That may be fine for you, but it won't work out so well for me. I've spent all my life growing this hair, and I plan to keep it!"

The fun was over. The three had to get back to their travels. They climbed out of the mess, pushing and pulling each other until all three were back on the thick log. The wetness of their shoes now made them extra slippery and they had to be even more careful than before.

They moved forward for a couple hours, carefully stepping from one log to the next. Occasionally one of the three would slip off the log and fall into the mess, but they soon became masters at pulling each other out using the ropes. The previous episode, where all three of them fell in the slop at the same time was not repeated.

They moved along silently. It took all their concentration just to keep their footing. Then they heard it" "Beeeewaaareee offf theee Rrrrr-aaaakerrrr!" The voice wasn't much louder than a whisper.

"What was that?" asked Jesves, her eyes getting big.

"I don't know," responded Hasko. "It wasn't loud enough for me to make it out."

Then they heard it again, a little louder than previously, "Beeee-waaareee offf theee Rrrrraaaakerrrr!"

"There it was again," added Hiztin. "It sounded like it said to beware of something."

"I've heard legends about the dead of the Quali Swamps." It was Jesves that spoke up. "The legends say that the souls of those that die here are stranded here forever and seek after the soul of any who pass through here. But I always thought it was just a kid's story my mother told me in order to keep me close to home."

"Beeeewaaareee offf theee Rrrrraaaakerrrr!" The voice was getting louder and could be understood plainly.

"Where's that sound coming from?" questioned Hasko. "It seems to be coming from all directions at once."

"Let's get out of here!" squealed Hiztin. "This is too spooky for me." The three started to move.

The voice didn't stop. It just grew louder. Every few minutes they would hear, "Beeeewaaareee offf theee Rrrrraaaakerrrr!" It didn't seem to come from anywhere. It was everywhere.

There was an abundance of logs now, enough so that they hadn't felled a tree for at least an hour. They guessed that it must be because they were nearing the center of the swamp. They journeyed on, hoping to soon find the other side of the swamp.

Plop! Something big had fallen into the water. The three looked at each other as if to ask, "Did you do that?"

All three shrugged their shoulders. They looked around and saw nothing. Then Hasko suggested, "It must have been something falling off a tree." They continued, but no sooner had they gone three more steps when once again they heard a "plop!"

"What is that?" questioned Hiztin. No one answered. They all just looked around, hoping to see the source.

Plop! They heard it again but saw nothing. It was dark and dingy, but enough light made it through the tops of the trees so that they could make out most of what surrounded them. Plop! Plop! Plop! Three more times, in rapid succession.

"This is driving me nuts!" complained Hiztin. "What is that?" Again no one answered. No one had an answer.

"Beeeewaaareee offf theee Rrrrraaaakerrrr!" That strange voice could be heard again.

"Do you think the "plops" are related to the Raker?" asked Hiztin in a worried voice.

Then Jesves spotted the source of the noises. "Look," she said in a fearful whisper. She was pointing down the length of the log back behind Hiztin who was still bringing up the rear. All eyes quickly turned to look in the direction she was pointing.

"Rats!" yelled Hiztin, as he took two quick steps toward Hasko. "You told me there weren't going to be any rats!"

"I honestly didn't expect to see any rats," responded Hasko. "I was convinced that was just an old legend."

The rats moved slowly toward Hiztin. At first there were only two, then three, then five. The group of rats grew in number. It was as if they were waiting for others to arrive so that they would have enough of a force to attack.

Plop! Plop! Plop! Plop! Plop! The rats could be seen jumping off the trees around them into the water. Hundreds of rats!

On the log in front of Jesves, rats could be seen climbing up as well. Rats were massing towards the three from both ends of the log as if they were preparing for a big battle. Or maybe just a tasty meal.

The rats were huge, about the size of Hiztin's upper thigh. Their heads were hairy. They had so much hair that the only thing that could be seen was the tip of their nose poking out from the front of the mass of hair. The rest of their body was bare and slimy. Their legs were short and stubby. They had a tail that curled up like a pig.

Suddenly a rat tried to climb up on the log right at Hasko's feet. He gave the rat a kick on the nose and it fell back into the water with a "screech!" This seemed to incite the other rats. They all started a high-pitched shriek as though each of them had just been kicked in the nose. They looked and acted as though they were ready to attack.

The three leprechauns drew their swords and prepared for the battle. Hiztin and Jesves each faced in the direction of their expected onslaught, and Hasko waited to take on any rats that might break through from either direction.

"Beeeewaaareee offf theee Rrrrraaaakerrrr!"

"Enough already. We've already found your rats. That voice gives me the creeps," complained Hiztin to no one in particular. Then he added, talking to the rats, "Come on you ugly slobs, let's get this over with!"

They didn't seem to listen or care. They just seemed to continue their preparations for attack.

"Don't rush them," returned Hasko, "they'll get around to us soon enough!"

Another rat tried to crawl up between Hiztin and Jesves. This time Hasko wasn't as kind as previously and he poked his sword into the rat's side. The rat squawked with anguish. Upon hearing this sound the other rats jumped into action. Rats came at Jesves and Hiztin from each end of the log; hundreds of rats. The two stabbed, hacked, hit and poked killing dozens of the rats but the flow of rats seemed endless. Hiztin and Jesves battled for about an hour and were getting tired. Hasko wanted to help but he wouldn't have been able to get past either of them on the log without knocking them into the water, and this was one time he didn't want to end up in the water.

So Hasko stood and helplessly watched. Occasionally a rat would try to crawl up on the log behind Hiztin or Jesves, but Hasko would quickly kill it. He watched the battle intensely, so intensely that one time while he was preoccupied with the battle a rat had crawled up and came up behind him. The rat took a big chomp into the back of Hasko's foot. Luckily his boot was thick enough to take the bite, but the surprise of being bit made him jump. This jump made him slip and he fell down onto the log in a sitting position straddling the log with one foot going into the water on each side of the log.

As soon as his foot hit the water, the rat that had clamped onto his boot went completely under the water and had to quickly let go of its hold. It swam to the surface so it could breathe. But he was right next to Hasko's leg and this scared Hasko. He could see the nose of the rat pushed right against his leg and he tried to pull his leg out of the water, but his quick movement almost knocked him into the water on the other side of the log. He had to be more careful or he would be in the water and at the mercy of the rats.

But then he made an interesting observation. The rat next to his leg didn't bite him. It swam around behind him and proceeded to try to get on the log. The rat wouldn't open its mouth and bite him while it was in the water.

He whirled around and gave the rat a quick whack with his sword and knocked it back into the water. Then he stuck his boot at the rat and kicked it. It tried to swim away. He poked it and again it tried to avoid him. The rat would not bite him if he was in the water.

"Well, I'm not doing much good here anyway. I may as well give it a try," said Hasko as he threw both legs over to the same side of the log and proceeded to slide off the log into the muddy water.

Hiztin and Jesves gave him a quick glance as if to say, "Have you gone mad?" but they couldn't pay much attention to him, they were too busy in their own battles.

Hasko went up to another rat that was swimming in the murk and poked it, testing to make sure that his theory was right. The same thing happened. The rat simply turned and swam away.

He watched his friends and realized that they were too busy to hold a conversation. He also saw that they were growing very tired and that if he didn't do something soon, they would surely be bitten. So, he pulled both ends of the rope at once.

Splash! Both of them hit the water at once, leaving their attackers behind. "Have you gone mad?" yelled Hiztin as he fought for air.

Hasko held Jesves's arm until she could get her footing. "I've discovered that the rats won't bite us in the water. They won't open their mouths in this murky mess. They won't bite until they're on top of the log. Just watch." He proceeded to demonstrate how poking a rat would only make it move away rather than attack.

"If we stay in the water we'll be safe, as long as we don't allow the rats to climb up on us and as long as we don't go to close to anything that the rats can stand on or jump on us from."

"You're a genius," smiled Jesves. "When I first saw you jump in the water, I thought you had lost your mind. But now I see that it was pure bravery. I was starting to worry about how long I would be able to hold out against those rats. The flow of them seemed endless." Hasko blushed at the compliment. He was no better at handling them than Hiztin.

The three kept a lookout in each direction, making sure that no rat got too close. The rats on the log just stood there and watched as if they were expecting the leprechauns to return to the log any minute so that the battle could be continued.

"Beeeewaaareee offf theee Rrrrraaaakerrrr!"

"Not again!" complained Hiztin. "We already figured out how to defeat your Raker," he yelled out as if he thought the voice could hear him.

"The Rrrrraaaakerrrr is yettttt to beeeeee!" responded the voice as if it heard Hiztin's yell.

"The voice heard me!" remarked Hiztin fearfully. "What's going on? It sounds like our troubles aren't over yet." Then he yelled again hoping the voice would respond, "What is a Raker?"

"The Rrrrraaaakerrrr is yettttt to beeeeee!"

"That voice didn't hear you," responded Hasko as he looked around to see if any rats were approaching. "It just seemed like it a moment ago."

"I don't like this business of 'The Raker is yet to be'," commented Jesves. "It sounds like there's more trouble ahead."

"Before we worry about the trouble that's ahead, let's get out of the trouble that we're in now," said Hasko. "Let's get the heck out of here!"

The three started moving, following Jesves' lead. Hiztin kept a lookout behind for rats, while Hasko watched the sides. Footing was difficult. Often a foot would get stuck in the mud or on a root and they would have to get it unstuck. Or someone would trip over a branch that was hidden under the water's surface. But the rats seemed to have met their match. They swarmed behind the travelers, always keeping their distance so that Hiztin couldn't reach them with his sword.

The three splashed on for about an hour. Occasionally they would have to climb over a log that blocked their path. They would do this one at a time, while the other two kept the rats away. It wasn't a major obstacle, it just slowed down progress.

Soon the rats seemed to give up. They dwindled in numbers until none could be seen.

"Beeeewaaareee offf theee Rrrrraaaakerrrr!"

"Well we seem to have gotten rid of the rats," commented Jesves. "Now if we could just get rid of that voice."

"The Rrrrraaaakerrrr is yettttt to beeeeee!"

They plopped ahead, slopping in the mud and fighting their way closer and closer to shore. Another hour went by. The strange voice could still be heard, but it was getting fainter and fainter all the time.

"Look!" yelled Jesves pointing straight in front of her.

"Look at what?" asked Hasko, before he noticed what she was pointing at.

"Oh my gosh!" Hiztin responded. Straight out in front of them, in the direction they were moving but still some distance away was brush, the same type of brush that they were fighting their way through when they arrived at the swamp. They could also see light shining on the brush, as though the sun was finally able to break through.

"It looks like we made it. I never thought those bushes would look so good."

"Yipeeee!" shouted Hasko, and the others joined in a wild round of cheering. They started moving as fast as they could in the sludge. They had forgotten all about the rats. Even the grime didn't bother them now. They just wanted to get to those bushes off in the distance.

The travelers thought they were finally alone. The rats were gone and by now the voice had died out and was no longer around to haunt them.

Off to the right of them, quite some distance away something rose slowly out of the water. It was hairy and big, much bigger than the trunk of a tree. As it rose all that could be seen was the hair, falling around the mound that looked like a small hill. It moved upwards until it was about two leprechauns out of the water. Then it stopped.

The threesome froze in their steps. They couldn't move fast anyway, but this sight had filled them with fear and they just stood there. For several moments nothing happened. Then suddenly two lights appeared; purple lights centered on the one side of the mound as if they were two eyes. The lights shone for several moments; steady and unblinking. Then, just as suddenly as they came on, they went out, and slowly the mound started to sink. It disappeared back into the murky sludge from where it came. After a few moments it was gone. The threesome seemed not to be noticed by whatever it was.

The three excited travelers started moving as quickly as they could. They started rushing to get to what they hoped was the edge of the swamp.

Suddenly as if to give one final loud plea, the hidden voice rang out, "Beeeewaaareee offf theee Rrrrraaaakerrrr!"

"I thought we were rid of that voice," commented Jesves. "This must be one last attempt to drive us crazy."

After several moments they heard, "The Rrrrraaaakerrrr is yettttt to beeeeee!" And then after several more moments came the plea, "Hellllllllp Meeeeeeeee. Hellllllllp Meeeeeeeee," repeated over and over again, louder and louder, until it seemed as though their eardrums would bust.

The three ran faster and faster, occasionally one of them would slip but still they wouldn't stop. It was hard to tell if they were running towards the edge of the swamp or away from the voice. "Hellllllllp Meeeeeeeee." Then suddenly the voice stopped. Everything was dead silent. The three leprechauns had stopped also. The suddenness of the way the voice had ended its plea puzzled them. It was as though a final end had been put to whatever was crying for help.

They went on, not quite as quickly as they had been moving before, but still fast enough to cause an occasional slip. And then they made it. They had reached the brush. They could see that they had indeed reached the edge of the swamp. Delight showed on the faces of each of them. They quickly employed their swords and began to chop their way through the brush. It wasn't long before all three of them were safely out of the swamps, and back on dry ground. They sat down and rested. The excitement of having safely made it across the swamp had worn them out, and now all they could do was relax. They stank but felt good at the same time.

Hiztin threw himself back and lay down on a pile of sticks. It wasn't the most comfortable bed he had ever made for himself, but it was a relief from the hours of excruciating travel through the swamps. At this point he didn't care; it felt good just to be back on dry ground. He thought about the journey across the swamps, and especially about the rats. "They promised me that there wouldn't be any rats," he thought to himself. "Now I'll probably have nightmares for a month about them." He felt angry and irritated, but he didn't say anything. He knew it wasn't their fault. They didn't enjoy the rats any more than he did. He decided to try and forget about the whole episode.

Jesves sighed. She sat down, bowed her head, and said a silent prayer to the favorite god of the leprechauns, the God of the Rainbow. The prayer calmed her down enough to where she could again think straight. Something bothered her. Would she be able to find her way back to the trail? She was fairly confident about the direction in which they were traveling but did the trail also continue in the same direction. "Probably not," she thought out loud. "It wouldn't have continued in a straight line for so long. It probably bowed south to avoid the swamp. I sure hope I can put us back on the right path."

Hasko didn't care about anything. He had made it across with his companions and he was safe. He thought about Jesves's comment about him being a genius, and he was proud. He thought he was hot stuff, and he loved it. Without him they would have never made it. The rest of this trip has to be a breeze after this swamp ordeal. Even the Kabul itself couldn't be any worse.

After a half an hour of total, exasperated silence, the calm had to be broken. "The sun's almost set and we probably only have about a half hour of daylight left," commented Hiztin. "Let's get a little further away from this swamp before it gets too dark."

"I'll go for that," commented Jesves. "I'd just as soon get as far away from here as possible. I'd also like to find some clean water so that I can get washed off, especially my hair. I feel awful."

Hasko and Hiztin had almost forgotten about the grime that covered them. They were too busy in their thoughts. But now, at the mention of it by Jesves they felt dirty and also desired to find some water where they could get cleaned off. With a great deal of effort, the three got up. Hasko claimed that he owed it to his friends the rat killers, Hiztin and Jesves, to be the first to take a turn at beating a path through the bush, and his two companions didn't argue. They were off.

It wasn't long before the worst of the brush was over, and travel became a little faster. Occasionally they were able to walk through the brush without hacking at all but there would still be the occasional thick clump.

Soon it was dark. They decided to make camp at the next clearing but there was no next clearing. In fact, there hadn't been any clearings since they had gotten out of the swamp. The decision was made that they couldn't put off making camp any longer, and so they would have to create their own clearing. They hacked away at the short undergrowth bushes until they had a spot big enough to setup camp.

"I'm awfully disappointed that we weren't able to find any water for a bath," observed Jesves. "I won't sleep in my tent tonight. The stink is more than I could handle in an enclosed space. Maybe, if I'm lucky it'll rain tonight, and I'll get cleaned in my sleep."

They made a fire with the twigs they had hacked down. Then they proceeded to collect damp leaves and use them to wash their face and hands as best they could. The insides of their waterproof packs hadn't been affected by the dunking in the swamp. The bedding and other clothes were dry and clean. They changed clothes so they could at least feel and smell a little cleaner, and then they made and ate dinner. As usual, Hasko took charge of most of the meal preparations.

"This is the best meal I've eaten in a long time," joked Hasko, "especially since it's the only meal we've eaten today." He was hoping for another compliment from Jesves, but it didn't come.

Conversation was thin. They were all very tired and soon they were tucked away in their beds and asleep.

"Owww! What's the big idea?" yelled Hiztin, waking the others with a start. The fire had gone out and it was dark. The cloud cover hid the light of the stars. He could see nothing.

"What are you yelling about?" complained Hasko. "Don't tell me you're dreaming about rats."

"Someone stepped on my face, someone in their bare, muddy feet. They smashed my face and got it all muddy."

"Oh, you're dreaming. Go back to sleep!"

"No, I'm not. Jesves," Hiztin yelled, "did you step on my face?"

"Nope! Take Hasko's advice and go back to sleep."

"Yeah Hastle," Hasko complained, "next time dream a little quieter."

"Ouch!" This time it was Jesves who let out the yell. "What is it?" questioned Hasko.

"My feet just got stepped on," she returned. "Someone is walking around in our camp."

Suddenly all three of them were quiet. They listened intently trying to discover the intruder. They heard nothing.

"Look over there, high up in the trees, back in the direction where we came from," Hiztin whispered. "Do you see those two purple lights?"

"I see the lights, but what could they be?" questioned Jesves. "The closest tree was back at the swamps. There wasn't any tree back where those lights are."

"That's strange," whispered Hasko. "It sure looks like eyes. But how could eyes shine like that? And what has purple eyes? If that is a creature, it must be enormous. No bird could hold still in midair like that."

Then suddenly as if someone had hit a switch, the two lights went out, both exactly at the same time. The three lay stunned and quiet. They couldn't understand what was happening around them.

Hasko got up quietly and went over to the fire pit. He felt around until he had collected some of the sticks that weren't totally burned and used them to rekindle the fire. Soon, with the help of Jesves and Hiztin, a large fire was blazing but they could see no one. They looked around to see if they could find any sign of a visitor.

"Look here!" Jesves yelled. "Muddy footprints on my sleeping sack. In fact, there are muddy footprints all over the place. Aren't these the same type of footprints that we saw the time that Hiztin got knocked over?"

"They sure are," Hiztin agreed. "They're too small to be our footprints. I wonder what made them."

"Look here," Hasko yelled. "Someone's been in my backpack. It's been opened and there's mud all over it."

They were stunned. What could possibly have been here to visit them? And what could have walked through the bushes so quietly that it didn't even break a twig? And what was the origin of the purple lights? They could see nothing over in the direction where they had seen the lights, no tree, no bird, nothing.

They built the fire up as large as they could, hoping that it would keep their visitors away and they tried to go back to sleep, but it was no use. There were too many unanswered questions for them to trust the night. After about a half an hour Hasko suggested that they take turns staying up and keeping watch. The other two quickly agreed. At least now each one of them would at least be able to get some sleep.

Hasko took the first watch. He sat close to the fire hoping it would keep him safe. The night was very quiet. Suddenly he heard the flapping of wings over his head. It scared him and made him jump. He looked up and saw nothing. He sat down again and waited quietly hoping the remainder of the night would be uneventful.

Hasko would occasionally take a sweeping look around the camp in all directions to see if he could spot anything. It was during one of these sweeps that he again spotted the purple lights, or at least he thought he did. When he spotted them, they immediately went out. He looked to see if he could find a tree or an animal off in that direction, but it was too dark to make anything out, even with the fire going strong. He superstitiously assumed that the lights went out because he looked in that direction, so he tried to take quick peeks over in the direction occasionally trying to catch the lights on, but he didn't have any luck. He just didn't time it right, or maybe there really weren't any lights after all.

The three leprechauns had decided to take a two-hour watch each, and Hasko's watch was about over. He got up to go over and try to wake Hiztin when suddenly seemingly out of nowhere a big muddy blob about half his height ran full speed into his side. He was so stunned that it knocked him over. The muddy blob changed directions and disappeared into the darkness. Hasko sat on the ground dazed, trying to interpret what had just happened.

He started to stand up again. He wasn't completely in an upright position, when another muddy blob tried to run him down, missed him, and ran past him and again just as quickly disappeared. "This isn't for real," he thought. "What are these creatures?"

The third time it happened he was ready. He started to get up again very slowly waiting and watching for whatever it was that kept attacking and sure enough he was almost in an upright position when it came. The creature ran directly into Hasko. Hasko had steadied himself for the impact, and when the creature bounced into him, he grabbed at it but what he grabbed was mud. He ended up not getting any grip and the creature easily slipped away.

But Hasko was not prepared to encounter a second creature which plowed into him from behind and down he went. "Well I guess if they want me on the ground I'll stay on the ground," Hasko concluded. And he sat there and waited to see what would happen next.

He had gotten a better look at the creatures this time. They were structured like humans, but they didn't have the same features as humans. They had what appeared to be a head, arms, and legs, all attached to a body, but they didn't have any visible eyes, nose, mouth, ears, or fingers. They were able to see where they were going because they always seemed to know where Hasko was, but how they found their way around was difficult to determine.

Suddenly as he sat there and watched, one of these creatures stepped out of the shadows and stood there, as if it was looking him over. It stood there staring at Hasko for a good five minutes.

Then, much to the surprise of Hasko, it spoke. Its speech was garbled but distinguishable. "We muidivengers. Watch you pass Raker. You hero. Raker scare. We help. Show trail. Tomorrow. Now sleep. We watch. No talk us. No hear. Now sleep. We stay away. Fire too hot. Now sleep." The muidivenger disappeared back into the darkness.

"What's the deal?" said Hasko to himself, realizing that the muidivengers couldn't hear him. "Am I supposed to trust you guys after you dug around in my pack? I'm not too sure I believe you." Hasko did not trust what he had seen.

He decided to let Hiztin take his turn at the watch. He crawled over to his side and awoke him. When he explained about the muidivengers Hiztin's eyes got big. "You mean you really saw one of them?" he asked.

"You'll be seeing them yourself soon enough," Hasko answered.

Hiztin was excited. "It sure would be nice to run across friendly creatures for a change," he commented.

Hasko crawled into his sack and watched to see what would happen. Hiztin walked around, trying to spot one of the creatures. Hasko had intentionally not warned him the creatures ran into him and before long Hiztin found himself knocked over and sitting on the ground. He barely got a look at the creature, but he realized he had seen what Hasko had described. He started to get up and again he was run down. Hasko was watching the events and was having trouble keeping from laughing. Soon Hiztin got the message. Don't get up. He crawled over to the fire and sat with his back to it waiting for the creatures to reappear.

About one hour into Hiztin's watch, he still hadn't had a solid look at one of the creatures. He was debating whether it would be worth getting up again in order to see the creatures when suddenly off in the distance he saw the mysterious lights. They were the same purple lights he had seen earlier. He strained his eyes to see better but he couldn't make anything out. Even with the fire going it was just too dark off in the distance.

Then, when he least expected it, out stepped one of the muidivengers. Apparently, it had noticed Hiztin's curiosity. "That Raker," the muidivenger said.

"Raker?" repeated Hiztin. "What is a Raker supposed to be?"

"No talk us. No hear. Now sleep." The muidivenger swiftly disappeared.

Hiztin realized that the muidivengers couldn't understand him so questioning them would be fruitless. "Raker?" he wondered to himself.

The rest of Hiztin's watch was uneventful. He went to Jesves and woke her so she could take a turn at the watch. He warned her about the idiosyncrasies of the muidivengers and went crawling off to sleep.

Jesves sat by the fire, warming herself and thinking. She said another prayer, thanking her Rainbow God that he had found a way for her to get back on the right trail. Now she wouldn't have to worry about the rest of the journey. She stayed by the fire during her whole watch, never moving except to throw a few sticks on it. She enjoyed the opportunity to think. It made her relax.

It wasn't long before daybreak, and the entire camp came to life. Jesves had prepared breakfast as her companions tried to force themselves to get up. They ate quickly. They were eager to get going and arrive at the Jove Plateau and hopefully find some water with which to wash themselves.

Just as they had their packs prepared and the fire extinguished a muidivenger appeared. "Follow," it said as it scurried off.

Follow they did, as best they could. They still had to fight the brush. The muidivenger was able to move right through it somehow. It had to constantly wait for the leprechauns.

"I'm not totally sure this guy is leading us in the right direction," suggested Jesves, "unless the trail made quite a directional change from where it was going before."

"What do you suggest?" asked Hiztin.

"I guess we trust him and follow him. It still seems to be our best option."

They continued on. Suddenly they arrived at a small mound, thickly covered with brush. The muidivenger lead them around to the side of the mound where they found a tunnel entrance exposed. "Home. You slow. This faster," it said pointing to the tunnel.

"These creatures are strange," whispered Hiztin. "I thought he was facing us, but now he's pointing like he's facing the other direction."

"Hastle, this guy wants us to trust him," Hasko said with a worried scorn. "He wants us to go into that tunnel. I don't like the idea."

"Do we have a choice? Seems to me that if he thinks it's faster, we ought to give it a try."

"I'd like to go as well," Jesves said. "This creature fascinates me and I'm curious about its tunnel."

"I guess I've been out voted," Hasko complained. He addressed the muidivenger as if he thought it could hear him and pointed into the tunnel. "Lead the way."

The muidivenger took off into the tunnel and the three cautiously followed. The tunnel wasn't designed for leprechauns. As small as they were, they still had to bend their heads in order to keep from scraping the top of the tunnel. And they felt as though they were constantly walking through the mud trail left by the muidivenger. At first, they went downward for what seemed to be quite a long time. Then abruptly the tunnel leveled out.

Small orange lights were placed all along the sides of the tunnel on the walls. They looked like rocks about the size of a thumb that seemed to glow. Hasko was looking at one curiously and the muidivenger guide tried to explain, "Creator make."

That explanation didn't seem to help much. Who was 'Creator' and how could he make rocks glow?

There were numerous sides tunnels off of the main tunnel that they were traveling in. Often, they would encounter a muidivenger busily scurrying in and out of the tunnels as if their work had urgency about it. Often a muidivenger would bump into one of the threesome. It felt like the muidivengers all moved as some previously defined rhythm. It was as if the leprechauns were out of step with this unexplained rhythm and were walking where they shouldn't be.

One side tunnel appeared to be the entrance to a larger tunnel, and they noticed tiny muidivengers no larger than about one-third the size of their guide. These tiny creatures were peeking out at them as if they had never seen a leprechaun before. When the little ones realized that they had been noticed they turned around and scurried back into their chamber and hid.

"Must have been children," observed Hiztin.

"They were cute little guys, weren't they?" commented Jesves. She continued, "We could really get lost bad in this maze of tunnels down here. I'm sure glad we have a guide, or we could end up spending the rest of our lives here."

Suddenly their guide took a turn down one of the side tunnels that headed off toward the right. This tunnel seemed to be another main tunnel with many small side tunnels branching off. The three and their guide had traveled in the tunnels for several hours when suddenly this new tunnel started heading up and they could see the light at the end of the tunnel. Hasko whispered a sigh of relief. He was beginning to think he would be lost in this tunnel maze forever.

They ascended the exit quickly and found themselves outside in the bright daylight. The sky was still overcast, but bright compared to the darkness of the tunnel. They were blinded temporarily until their eyes adjusted to the light, but the sudden brightness didn't seem to affect the muidivenger. He continued moving ahead at full speed.

Coming out of the tunnel, Hasko complained, "It sure is nice to be able to stand up straight again. I was starting to develop a permanent humped back."

After their eyes had adjusted, they were able to evaluate their location. The area where they found themselves was still brushy but not as dense as previously. There were also occasional trees. Off in the distance toward the west they could make out the cliff leading to the Jove Plateau.

"He's lead us almost to the very edge of the Jove Plateau," Jesves said. "He's saved us hours with this detour through the tunnel. Now I understand why he seemed to be leading us in the wrong direction earlier. He was routing us toward his tunnel shortcut. Hurry he's waiting for us. We better get going if we're gonna let him lead us to the trail."

Their guide had gone quite a distance ahead but when he noticed the leprechauns weren't keeping up with him, he stopped. The three scrambled through the bushes after him.

When they started to get close to the muidivenger it took off again and they had to struggle to keep up. "Isn't it amazing how that creature can walk through those branches without even noticing it but when they run into us, they are solid," Hiztin observed.

"Maybe you're just too fat for them," teased Hasko. "Maybe that's why they run into us. They just expect to be able to go right through us like everything else but there's something about us that won't let them go through."

"Those creatures ran into me intentionally last night," commented Hiztin. "They knew they were going to knock me over. There's something more to this bumping business than meets the eye."

"I think you're right Hiztin," commented Jesves. "There's a lot more to these creatures than meets the eye. I wonder what they mean by the 'Creator'. And how about those glowing stones? I don't understand how that works. It's too bad they can't hear us. It would be nice to have them explain a few things."

They came upon a small stream that seemed to flow from the direction of the cliffs toward the swamp. "Water!" observed Jesves with excitement. "Clean water!"

But the muidivenger continued ahead as if nothing had happened. "We can't stop now, or this guy may not finish our guided tour," claimed Hasko. "At least we know there is clean water here and hopefully we'll find more in the near future."

"He can wait long enough for me to get a drink and clean my face," she observed. She knelt down to take a drink and splashed some water over her face. The other two couldn't resist the temptation to do the same. It felt nice after having been covered with a thick layer of grime for nearly a day.

The muidivenger had stopped a little way ahead and was waiting for them again. They crossed the stream by walking on the same log that the muidivenger had used and they were off again following him in hopes of finding the lost trail. They had only gone another dozen steps when they found themselves back on what seemed to be the same trail that they had left behind on the other side of the swamps.

"Go," directed the muidivenger pointing in the direction of the cliff.

"Thank you," said Jesves to the muidivenger as she bowed low in hopes that he might understand her gesture. No expression was recognizable, so it was hard to tell how he reacted.

The muidivenger turned and disappeared back in the direction from which they had come. They watched him until he was out of sight in the distance. "That sure was a strange little creature," commented Hiztin. "He just appeared when we needed help and disappeared again just as quickly."

"I'm sure glad he decided to help us," commented Jesves. "This trail is quite a bit off the route that we were taking. It would have taken us quite a while to find it again. Now I'll tell you what I'm going to do next."

"I'll bet I can guess," commented Hiztin as if his thoughts were united with hers. "That stream wasn't that far back, and it sure felt cool and refreshing. A nice bath sure sounds good."

"You read my mind perfectly," responded Jesves as she started to walk back towards the stream.

All three were quick to jump into the stream. Jesves choose a place a little way up stream and out of sight of her companions. At first all three just sat in the water enjoying the feeling of cleanness that flowed over them. Then they proceeded to scrub themselves down. They washed the clothes that they had muddied in the swamp on the previous day. Also, the clothes they were wearing on the current day had to be cleaned as well because the smell of the swamp was on their bodies. And the mud that the muidivengers had deposited on them during the day left an odor that they wanted to get rid of.

High up in a tree above them no one noticed the eagle that sat quietly watching.

After their baths they had lunch and started out again heading for the cliffs. They quickly found their way back to the trail and headed off in the direction of the Jove Plateau. The old trail was much easier to follow. Even with the slight overgrowth that existed, there was still less brush to contend with than previously when they were off the trail. It only took about two more hours of travel before they arrived at the base of the cliffs.

Looking up Hasko complained, "I didn't expect this cliff to be quite this steep or quite so high. Didn't they tell us that there would be a rope ladder hanging over the side and that all we would have to do is climb it to the top."

"Look up there," commented Hiztin. He could see the remnants of the rope ladder hanging about two thirds of the way up the cliff. "It looks as though the rope ladder wasn't able to handle the weather over the years."

"Hiztin, you showed us how to get across the ravine, and Jesves you lead us through the swamps, I guess it is my turn to lead us up this cliff. I'll climb up to the top and lower you a rope over the side. Then all three of us won't have to endanger our lives by trying to climb this cliff."

"Great idea," Hiztin agreed. He knew that Hasko was a much better climber than he was, and the thought of this high and steep climb wasn't something he looked forward to.

Hasko left most of his baggage behind, taking only those ropes and tools with him that would help him on the climb. The climb was slow and difficult. Often Hasko would find the need to retrace his steps and try alternative routes. The climb became frustrating and discouraging. Hasko started to talk to himself, giving himself a pep talk and telling himself that he had to make it to the top. He was not about to travel back through those swamps. Occasionally his talking turned to swearing when he lost his footing in the looseness of the dirt, or when a bush that he was clinging to pulled out in his hand, but he pushed on.

At one point, when he was changing the direction of his climb he suddenly slipped and slid several leprechauns back down the side of the cliff. He quickly laid himself flat and straddled his legs looking for something to grab. Eventually his slide was stopped by a small bush, but not before he was scratched, bruised, and very dirty. He pushed on because he knew his friends were counting on him.

At the bottom of the cliff, Hiztin and Jesves sat down in a small patch of grass a slight distance from the cliff so they could observe Hasko's efforts. They started talking about their recent experiences and about their homes. It was as though they were trying to forget their frustrations and trials.

"You know, we've been living in the same town together all our lives," Jesves observed, "and we have hardly ever said 'Hi' to each other. Don't you find that a little strange?"

"There are lots of leprechauns in Amins who have never been introduced to each other," he responded. "It's not that we're an unfriendly town, it's just that people don't talk much unless they have something to say."

"But once you get them started talking it's tough to get them to stop," Jesves added.

Hiztin wondered if she was talking about Hasko or himself. He continued, "What kinds of things do you like to do to keep yourself entertained?"

"Go on hikes through the Quali Swamps and through muidivenger tunnels," she remarked sarcastically showing a smile on her face. She proceeded to talk about her existence in Amins, about what she liked and disliked, and about what her hobbies were. She enjoyed having Hiztin show interest in her. It wasn't long before she became quite personal telling Hiztin her little secrets and prejudices.

Hasko's climb to the top took several hours, which gave them plenty of time to talk. Hiztin was amazed at how much the two of them thought alike. He started to feel a special closeness to Jesves and told her how much he enjoyed the similarity. Hiztin was thankful for Hasko's efforts, not so much for the work he was doing but for the time that allowed himself and Jesves to talk. The hours the two of them spent together he started to have feelings for Jesves that he wasn't ready to interpret or understand, but it felt nice.

Slowly a swarm of hopls, which were small one-legged birds about the size of a fist, passed where the two of them sat. The birds were incredibly agile, and their one leg didn't seem to hinder their abilities. These birds had somehow lost their left leg in their evolutionary process, but it didn't seem to slow them down. They managed just fine on one leg but their hopping movement along the ground made them humorous to watch. The birds traveled in swarms of several hundred, so when they passed by, some of them hopping and some flying, their movement made quite a bit of noise. They also had an interesting communication system worked out making certain sounds that allowed them to be able to communicate information to the rest of the flock. The sounds were a combination of squawks, scratches, pecks, and peeps. The squawks were quite distinguishable and by watching the birds Jesves and Hasko were soon able to figure out which squawks meant food, water in puddles, danger from thorns, and so on. They even seemed to give a squawk for the presence of Hiztin and Jesves that warned the others to stay away.

Hiztin and Jesves became totally fascinated with these birds. They had never seen quite so many at one time, nor had the birds ever ventured quite so close to them. These birds had not learned to be afraid of leprechauns. Soon they hopped off, continuing in their adventures looking for food.

Hiztin and Jesves became so enthralled with their new found friendship, the stories that they were telling each other, and with watching the birds that they had forgotten completely about Hasko, who had finished struggling and fighting his way up the cliff. He was standing up on the top yelling, screaming, and jumping up and down trying to attract their attention without success. He was now resorting to throwing rocks, small ones and then larger ones over the side hoping the two would notice him.

Hasko was afraid to throw the stones too close to his companions for fear that he might seriously injure one of them. Unfortunately, the rocks could not be heard over the fuss of the birds. Hasko became furious. How was he going to attract their attention? He sat down and looked around him. Then he got an idea. Maybe, if they couldn't hear the rocks, they would be able to see a bush. He went and uprooted a small nearby bush and heaved it over the side.

"Crash!" the bush smashed against the ground causing a cloud of dust and scaring the birds into hysteria. Hiztin jumped up and looked upward. Fear flushed through him. He remembered Hasko and wondered if something happened to him? He looked up and saw Hasko standing at the top of the cliff waving his hands. Jesves also looked and noticed with excitement that the climb had been successful.

Hasko started pointing down, as if he was trying to attract their attention to something. The two tried to follow his pointing and then they noticed his concern. Hasko had tied his rope to a tree at the top of the cliff and had thrown it over the side, and there it hung, the end of it about one-third of the way up the side of the cliff. His rope was too short.

"Either he forgot the second rope or else he misjudged the height of the cliff," commented Jesves. "Now what? We can't climb up to the rope, it's hanging too far out and away from the cliff and we can't expect Hasko to come back down for the other rope. I guess we'll just have to climb up there too."

"But how are we going to get all our packs up the side of that cliff?"

Jesves continued, "Maybe only one of us should go back up there with the second rope and the other should stay down here with the packs."

Hiztin didn't like that idea either. He had seen how much trouble Hasko had with the climb. It would be more difficult for him. Teasingly Hiztin waved to Hasko to come back down and get the other rope. Hasko made gestures that indicated he wasn't at all interested in that idea. He was lucky to make it up there the first time.

Then Hiztin got inspired. He realized he couldn't communicate with Hasko over the sound of the birds, so he wrote out a note explaining his idea and tied it around one of his swifter arrows. He fired the arrow into the air at Hasko, hoping it would get enough range to make it to the top of the cliff.

The arrow didn't make it, it was just short of its mark, but it stuck into the embankment only half a leprechaun from the upper edge. Hasko moved the rope over to where the arrow had planted itself and climbed down far enough to retrieve it. After climbing back over the side, he unraveled the note and discovered Hiztin's intentions. He pulled the entire length of rope back up to the top of the cliff and proceeded to tie a large loop at its end. Then he lowered the rope back over the side.

At the bottom Hiztin was preparing another of his steel arrows. He had tied a thin cord to the arrow and was waiting for the rope to be lowered once again. Jesves, seeing that Hiztin was busy on some scheme, stood back to watch for the results.

With the rope lowered, Hiztin took his arrow and fired at the loop. The first arrow fell short. He had hoped it would go through the loop but there wasn't enough power behind it to get it high enough with the drag of the cord. Jesves, seeing what he was doing ran to retrieve his arrow for him.

He tried again. This time a slight breeze caused the rope to move just slightly out of the way of the arrow and once again the arrow fell to the ground. Hiztin was encouraged. That shot would have been on target if not for the breeze.

He tried again. This time he was on target and the arrow slid through the loop. When the cord came into contact with the rope, the arrow stopped suddenly with a jerk and fell. Hiztin pulled back on the cord until the arrow came into contact with the loop. The arrow had now turned itself sideways and it acted as a brace against the loop.

"Yippee!" Jesves yelled. "You're a genius, Hiztin." Hiztin blushed.

Hasko was jumping and waving on the top of the cliff.

Hiztin waved to Hasko, and Hasko started to pull the rope back up over the side of the cliff. Hiztin quickly tied the rope that he had in his pack to the end of the cord and Hasko soon had both ropes and the cord on the top of the cliff.

Hasko removed the cord and tied the two ropes together tightly. He then lowered the ropes over the side and the end of the second rope hit the ground loudly at the bottom of the cliff. Now there was plenty of rope to spare.

Hiztin and Jesves proceeded to tie their packs to the end of the rope and Hasko pulled them to the top of the cliff, one at a time. After all the baggage had arrived at the top Jesves and Hiztin proceeded to climb the rope to the top.

Once on the top the three greeted each other happily. They enjoyed a bit of a victory celebration for having made it to the top of the plateau which, in their minds meant they would successfully make it to Gije. They were thankful that the three of them were selected for this expedition. All three had been vital to its success.

The top of the plateau was quite different in appearance from the valley below. There were only occasional trees and bushes. The majority of the plateau was covered with thick grass about half the height of the leprechauns.

The view from the top was fantastic. They could see all the way back to the Quali Swamp which they recognized by the clustered sea of top-heavy trees. They could see the hopls down below them, still moving slowly in their strange rhythmic sort of way.

The travelers retrieved their ropes and repacked them. The sun was just setting, and they realized that they had spent the majority of the afternoon accomplishing the climb. Hasko was dirty and tired and was ready to rest. They decided to journey only slightly further that day and then find the best place to camp. It wasn't long before a site was chosen, and camp was made.

Atop a tree, an eagle sat watching and it seemed to smile.

CHAPTER NINE

ON THE PLATEAU

The night was uneventful for Hasko and Jesves, especially when compared with their previous night's encounter with the muidi-vengers. The rest left them in good spirits and physically recovered.

Hiztin didn't seem to sleep as well as the other two but it wasn't the cliff or the ravine or even the swamp rats that caused his restlessness; it was Jesves. The time he had spent with her at the bottom of the ravine had brought new meaning to the word misery. He couldn't sleep and he was uncomfortable, but he didn't know why. He went over their conversation in his mind, over and over again. It wasn't as though either of them had said anything upsetting. In fact, the entire conversation had been very enjoyable. He kept reminding himself how she had told him he was a genius. But he just didn't understand why that should keep him from sleeping. He had never felt that way before. Breakfast was made, but Hiztin didn't feel much like eating.

After breakfast the first order of the day was to once again locate the trail. Jesves scouted the area in the vicinity where the old rope ladder ended and quickly picked up the direction in which they should be heading.

The morning hours of the journey were uneventful. The three travelers admired the serene, calm feeling that the area gave them. There were soft rolling hills and grassy fields speckled with yellow, white, and purple flowers. It left the travelers hushed with awe as they admired the scenery. It was so drastically different from what they had encountered the last couple days.

Hiztin decided he had to talk to Hasko about his feelings for Jesves. Hasko had been his lifelong friend. Maybe he could help explain the situation. The first opportunity he had to get Hasko alone, he would discuss these new feelings with him. Surely in Gije he would get the opportunity. Or perhaps tonight when Jesves was asleep.

They stopped and rested for lunch but Hiztin still had no appetite.

Hasko had noticed his lack of appetite and commented on it. "What's the matter? You usually eat like a horse. You're not going to be able to keep up with us if you don't eat right."

"I'm all right," Hiztin responded. He spent most of the time trying to sneak peeks at Jesves without being noticed.

The afternoon brought them a surprise. They were journeying along making good time when suddenly the trail disappeared. The grass suddenly came up to their chins. It squared off like a wall. The trail just stopped. It was abrupt and very strange.

Traveling became difficult. Fighting their way through the tall grass meant they couldn't move as fast as they were moving previously. It was still better than the bushes they fought through earlier in their travels. They had hoped the trail would hold out all the way to Gije.

"Did we make a wrong turn somewhere?" asked Hasko.

"No way. Jesves knows where she's going," interjected Hiztin defensively. He suddenly felt it was his duty to protect Jesves.

"This grass will cause another delay," commented Jesves giving Hiztin a curious look because of his reaction to Hasko's comment, "but I'm sure we're going in the right general direction." There wasn't much they could do but go forward. The tall grass persisted for the remainder of the day's journey. No sign of the trail reappeared.

It was about half an hour after sunset when the three encountered a small clearing where the grass was only about knee high. They decided that this would be a perfect place to set up camp for the night. They made a fire and quickly ate dinner. Hiztin, having skipped the two previous meals and having walked all day had finally become very hungry. He ate considerably more than his fellow companions.

The three decided not to set up their tents. Although it had been a cloudy day there didn't seem to be any threat of rain, and the night air felt good.

The night once again left Hiztin unable to go to sleep. He lay in his sack watching Jesves sleeping. After he was sure that Jesves had been asleep for at least an hour he climbed out of his sack and went over to where Hasko was sleeping. He put his hand over Hasko's mouth and shook him gently. Hasko woke with a jerk, looking at Hiztin with fear wondering if there was some kind of danger.

"Be really quiet, Hasko," Hiztin whispered. "I need to talk to you."

"In the middle of the night?" questioned Hasko, looking at him as though he had gone mad.

"I don't want Jesves to hear our conversation."

"Well, what do you want?"

"Not here, let's walk a little way, just in case she wakes up."

"You've got to be kidding," Hasko was starting to get irritated.

"Please, this is important," Hiztin pleaded.

Hasko got up and walked with Hiztin out of earshot of Jesves. "Alright, what's the big urgency?"

Hiztin tried to explain what he was feeling. He discussed how he couldn't eat or sleep and how he wanted to spend time with Jesves alone.

Hasko was surprised. He had always been close to Hiztin. They had shared everything. They had grown up together, gone through school together, and last year when it was finally time to leave their parent's home, they even built themselves a house together where they now lived. How could Hiztin possibly not want him around? He felt jealous. "Are you trying to tell me you don't want me around you anymore?"

"Not at all," Hiztin protested. "You've always been and always will be my best friend. I'm just trying to explain this strange feeling so you can help me do something about it. What can I do?"

"You've never been in love before have you?" Hasko asked Hiztin.

"No."

"Well, I hear that love kinda messes up your mind. Sorta like when we used to chew on a little pollo weed. Is that what you feel?" asked Hasko, wondering if Hiztin had become a little lightheaded.

"Oh no!" declared Hiztin. "This is much worse!"

Suddenly they heard a loud scream, coming from the direction of the camp. They turned quickly and ran back, only to find Jesves scrambling up a tree, followed by four werewolves. They could identify the creatures as werewolves because werewolves didn't have tails. They are humans who were poisoned with werewolf venom causing them to turn into tailless wolves at night.

In what remained of the light of their fire they could see blood flowing from Jesves's leg. The werewolves stood at the base of the tree and barked up at her. She found herself a branch, sat down on it, and yelled for help.

Hiztin was frantic. Seeing Jesves in danger was more than he could handle. He grabbed a stick and ran after the wolves forgetting about his own safety. He started beating on the wolves, but to his dismay they did not run. Instead, two of them turned around and started to attack him. It was all he could do to keep the wolves at stick's length.

Hasko, seeing the predicament searched for his sword but remembered that all the weapons had been stacked under the tree where Jesves had taken refuge. He decided to grab a stick as well and assist Hiztin.

The two, wielding their sticks, were able to keep the wolves at a distance, but they soon realized that their strategy wouldn't work much longer. They had to do something to get rid of the werewolves. They didn't want to spend the rest of the night waving a stick at them.

Then Hasko got an idea. He told Hiztin to keep fighting off the attacking wolves. He ran over to the fire and grabbed two hot and still burning sticks and handed one to Hiztin. With the flaming sticks they poked at the wolves who yelped as the red-hot ember enflamed their fur and scorched their hide. They kept striking back and soon the air reeked with the stink of burnt hair and flesh.

Hasko made a heroic effort to stab one of the wolves in the eye with the hot ember. After several attempts he finally succeeded, and the pain was too much for the werewolf. It took off running and howling in pain.

The other werewolves, seeing the anguish of their companion decided to give up the battle and follow. Soon all the werewolves had departed.

Hasko and Hiztin ran over to Jesves's sanctuary. They helped her down noticing that she had become very weak from the loss of blood. They helped her over to her bed sack and Hiztin quickly went to work trying to stop the flow of blood. "How did you manage to escape?" he asked her.

Jesves explained, "I was awakened when I heard them trying to rip open our food bag and so I decided to try and get to our weapons and chase them off. Unfortunately, they noticed me running to the tree and came after me before I was able to get to the weapons. All I could think of doing was to scramble up that tree. But I didn't make it before one of the wolves had taken a bite out of my leg. Now I've been poisoned with the werewolf venom. I'm going to end up like them." She started to sob.

"No," insisted Hasko. "It takes 24 hours for the venom to take control of your blood stream. We'll have to get you to Gije before then so that we can get help. I'm sure they'll have a cure."

"Absolutely," insisted Hiztin, his heart in a frustrated flutter, "We'll get going as soon as I get you bandaged."

"Not so quickly," insisted Hasko, "We can't be more than a half days journey away. Let's get a couple hours rest before we start off. We're going to have to carry Jesves all the way. If we let her walk her heart will beat quicker and the venom will spread faster. You go to sleep first," Hasko demanded. "You're short on sleep anyway."

Hiztin protested, but he soon saw it was of no avail. He finished working on Jesves's leg, made her as comfortable as possible and proceeded to crawl into his sack. By now Hiztin had become so tired that even thoughts of Jesves and the adrenaline of the excitement with the werewolf encounter couldn't keep him awake. He was soon snoring loudly.

Hasko built up the fire and added a couple extra small fires around the edge of the camp so that their camp was surrounded by fires. He retrieved the weapons and waited, anticipating another attack from the werewolves. But the attack never came.

Hasko let Hiztin get several hours rest, realizing that his friend hadn't slept well the previous night. He prepared the packs tying them together in such a way that Hiztin would be able to carry them all. Then he awoke Hiztin and Jesves and told them it was time to head out.

The light of the day was barely visible, but Hasko knew that it was enough light to keep the werewolves away. He now understood why the elves had decided to not use the back road any longer. The danger from the werewolves was too great and there was no way that the complete journey across the plateau could be made in one day. Using the back road would require them to spend the night, and anyone using that route would be attacked.

The three started out with Hiztin carrying the packs and Hasko carrying Jesves on his back. They had to rest often because their loads were heavy. Occasionally they would trade off. The differences in the two loads placed different pressures on their bodies and they noticed that by trading off they were capable of traveling farther without stopping to rest.

The tall grass also slowed their efforts considerably. It was hard enough packing heavy loads, but to have to fight the high grass as well during the entire journey caused them to be exhausted in just a couple hours.

Jesves noticed the strain and insisted, "This is too much for you two. I can't let you bear the full burden of my problem. I'm going to walk for a little while and give you a rest."

"No!" insisted Hiztin.

"Yes!" returned Jesves. "I am in just as much danger if this journey takes too long as I will be by straining myself too much. If you two would go first and press the grass down for me as much as possible, I'll walk slowly behind you. And if I drop behind don't worry. I'll catch up again when the grass slows you down. Now let's get going."

Both Hasko and Hiztin saw the logic of her reasoning. They split the packs between the two of them and proceeded to go to work on the grass. Jesves followed behind slowly.

After traveling for another hour, they were suddenly rewarded. The high grass came to a sudden end and the three found themselves in an open valley filled with grass no more than knee high and topped with flowers of all varieties and colors.

"We must be getting close to Gije now," commented Hasko. "I've heard that the fields around it were colorful and beautiful, but I never imagined anything quite as beautiful as this."

They could see the Gije Groves off to the right of them. They hadn't noticed them before because of the high grass. They knew that if they followed along the west side of the groves, they would run directly into Gije. They were excited to realize that they would soon arrive at their destination.

They convinced Jesves to allow them to carry her again for a while now that they didn't have to contend with the tall grass. The two traveled on carrying their loads. Ahead of them they could see a section of the Gije Groves reaching out from the main body of the groves. They decided to circle around these trees and stay on the west side of the woods. As they started to come around the bend of the trees, they encountered the path that they had lost in the thick grasses.

After a few more minutes they had worked their way completely around the cluster of trees and they saw the most magnificent sight that they had ever encountered. There before them, only a short distance away stood the grand elfin city of Gije. The city was enclosed all around with a wall and at each of the six corners of the wall was a magnificent spiraling tower. In the center of the city the palace could be seen reaching high above the perimeter walls. The city was encircled with a moat and on the west side an entrance was visible.

The fortifications around the city were constructed during the Life-fight Wars in order to protect against the invading hoards and it was at these very walls that the gnomes met their final defeat. From here they were driven back to the Kabul, where they have since been allowed to live in peace. But now, under the perversion of the Kabul Lord Krakus, descendants of these very same gnomes may again be battling at these walls.

Farmers could be seen working in the fields that surrounded the city. Several of them noticed the three travelers and realized that they must be in trouble since Jesves was being carried. The farmers quickly took one of the wagons lead by a strong mihorse and headed over to help them. A mihorse was a four-legged animal whose shoulders come to about the height of an elf's shoulders. It was the strongest of the domesticated animals in all of Small World and was primarily used for farm work.

"How goes it you three?
We're here to help thee," one of the elves called out. Elves have a musical language which sings and rhymes. Leprechauns found Elvin speech fascinating and enjoyed listening to it.

"We need help," responded Hasko who considered himself the spokesman of the three, "Jesves has been bitten by a werewolf and if we don't get her help fast, we'll lose her."

"We know your plight,
We've got help that's right," that same elf responded.
"All aboard, let's ride,
To a doctor's side."

The elves helped Jesves aboard the wagon. Hasko and Hiztin threw their packs aboard and climbed on themselves. The wagon wasn't large enough to hold all the leprechauns and the elves so one of the elves led the mihorse while his two Elvin friends walked beside the wagon.

"Do you really come,
By the back path?
No one's gone that way,
Since we lost Gath.
He had gone that way,
Just to find food;
When a werewolf bite,
Made him turn cruel," it was the second elf that was doing the talking. He seemed both fascinated and concerned about their journey.

"We have traveled from Amins using the back trail," explained Hasko. "We have an urgent message for your Lord about a serious threat that exists for all of the Southern Plains. We traveled the back road because we thought it was shorter, but we have encountered so many dangers that we now realize it was foolish. The most important thing now is to get Jesves to a doctor. Can you help us with that?"

"Of course, we'll help,
That's why we're here;
We'll do our best,
To bring you cheer," commented the second elf.
"The safe recovery of your friend,
Is guaranteed given time to mend," interjected the first.
"We'll set a meeting,
With the Lord Gimans;
He'll want you to tell,

What all this means.
So, tell us now,
Why you made this trip;
Our curiosity will make us flip," the second elf requested.

"It was recommended that we address the Lord first and allow him to express his thoughts on the danger to Gije rather than we getting everyone unnecessarily concerned," commented Hasko. "I'm sorry. I'm not trying to be rude since you have been so kind to help us out. But you'll have to wait until he makes his announcement. Please tell us your names. We haven't been introduced yet."

"I am Gione,
Gido is this one," spoke the first elf pointing at the second.

"Geday leads the mihorse,
He'll take us the best course."

Hasko introduced himself and his two companions. They were now nearing the city walls, it would be only a few more minutes before they were safely within the city and Jesves would be able to receive help. Gido ran ahead to make appropriate preparations for their arrival.

The remainder of the conversation evolved around an explanation of the journey that they had just made from Amins and of all the dangers and trials they had encountered. The elves were fascinated at their bravery.

The mihorse and cart had arrived at the bridge that gave entrance to the city. As it clomped over the wooden bridge the leprechauns received their first glance of the inside of the city. Its buildings were magnificent, with oval windows and roofs that were peaked upwards at the ends. There were lots of flower boxes, just like in Amins. The city was spotlessly clean, even more so than Amins. The leprechauns were enchanted. They had never seen anything quite so magnificent. It was almost magical.

"This bridge we cross,
Goes up every night;
To stop attacks,
Werewolves come to fight," Gido explained. Without the bridge the werewolves would be forced to swim the moat and climb the walls in order to gain entrance to the city. This was impossible for the wolves, so the city was safe.

Unknown to any of the travelers an eagle sat atop one of the towers near the entrance to the city and watched the travelers enter the city. The eagle seemed to smile.

Upon entering the city, they found the streets lined with elves waiting to greet them. They were cheered as though they had won a major battle. "What's all the excitement?" asked Hiztin.

"This is the first,
That trail has been cursed," commented Gione.

"No one would dare,
The back trail to bare."

Geday led the horse down the main street and then took a turn down a side path between two houses. After passing several homes he stopped

at a door that was decorated with a drawing of a pan of blood. "This must
be the doctor," Hiztin commented.

"Your thought is quick,
This is doctor for sick," Gione commented.

Just then Gido walked out of the doctor's office with a stately older
elf at his side.

"This is doc Erock,
He wants her in quick;
If we don't act now,
She'll be awfully sick," stressed Gido with concern.

They helped Jesves out of the wagon and into the doctor's waiting
room. Jesves had become very weak. She was limp and didn't seem to
recognize what was going on around her. They immediately passed into
a back hallway which appeared to lead to a collection of small rooms,
many of which had occupants. The doctor guided them directly into a
room that had been prepared for Jesves. They laid Jesves on the bed and
the doctor proceeded to chase everyone out of the room and close the
door.

"This doctor don't like,
When we watch what he do;
But he's the best,
I guarantee you,"
Gido commented. Then he continued,

"I have a place,
For you to stay;
Please follow me,
I'll show the way."

Gido led Hasko and Hiztin down another side street and brought
them to a large tavern. Again, the elves of the city waved and cheered,
delighted with the new arrivals.

"I talked to the Lord,
He says here you'll stay;
You should eat and rest,
Then come see him today.
I'll return in two hours,
If it's all right with you;
And take you to him,
So your task you can do."

"Thank you for your hospitality," commented Hasko. "Won't you
stay and eat with us?"

"Back to the fields,
I must make haste;
And pick up my tools,
Then time we can waste."

Gido gave his farewell. Gione and Geday had already left for the
fields with the wagon and Gido hurried after them.

Inside the tavern, Hasko and Hiztin found a table arranged and a
meal prepared and waiting for them. They were delighted at the hospitality of the elves. When they tried to pay for the meal they were refused,

being told that the Lord had ordered their care and payment would not be accepted. They were shown to their room where, to their delight, they found beds and a bathtub, already filled with warm water.

"I feel like I've died and gone to rainbow heaven," commented Hasko. "This place is magnificent."

"If only Jesves wasn't going through this torture," commented Hiztin worriedly. "I hope they can help her."

"Don't worry about her. She'll be all right."

The two took baths and jumped into their beds, and within minutes they were both asleep.

A knock on the door made Hiztin jump out of bed as though he were ready to battle the werewolves or rats he was dreaming about. He was still jumpy from the events of the previous days.

Hasko was not quite as dramatic, but the knock was also a rude awakening from his peaceful sleep. "Who's there?" he yelled.

"Gione and Gido here,
It's time to go;
The Lord is anxious,
He wants to know," came the voice of Gido.

"Just a second, we'll be right out," returned Hasko. "We just need to get dressed."

Hiztin sat down on the bed with a look of relief on his face.

"You're still jumpy. Hurry up," observed Hasko. "We've got to get a move on."

Hiztin lazily got off the bed and proceeded to get dressed. "The rest sure felt good."

As they left their room, they found their new friends waiting for them. Hiztin questioned them about Jesves.

"We've talked to the doctor,
Recover she will;
But she cannot journey,
For two days still.
You can go visit,
But first we must see;
The Lord and his council,
And learn what will be."

The four left the tavern and walked down the main road toward the tall palace in the center of the city. This was the one that they had noticed sticking high above the walls of the city as they approached it earlier in the day. Gido was giving them a tour as they walked along explaining the various buildings and sites.

"We have no hungry,
We have no poor;
We share all goods,
From a general store.
Whoever needs,
May freely get;
But he who wastes,
Works more for it."

The leprechauns were fascinated at how different this city was from their home in Amins. It was walled like a fortress, yet it was filled with elaborately designed buildings and fountains. And the idea of sharing everything seemed very strange to them.

It wasn't long before they arrived at the palace. They were taken directly to the council chambers, where they found the Lord and his councilors waiting for them. The chambers were elaborately designed, filled with colorful ornaments, statues, and pictures. In the center was an oval table, and at one end of it sat a stately elderly elf, with graying hair.

Hiztin and Hasko were given seats at the other end of the table, directly opposite the lord. This was the place of honor for guests or anyone who had business before the council. They found it interesting that the Lord used a different style of poetry than his subjects. They wondered if this had something to do with his rank, or if it was just a personal preference.

Gione and Gido took their places at the table, which surprised Hiztin and Hasko. Most of the members of the council were elderly, about 50 years old, but Gione and Gido couldn't have been more than 28. "I hadn't realized that our new friends were so important," whispered Hasko. "I had mistaken them to be ordinary farmers."

"We welcome you,
You've come a long way,
My name is Gimans,
I am the Lord;
You are leprechauns,
Your names are Hiztin and Hasko,
You've risked much,
Please be welcome."

Hasko again took the lead as self-acclaimed spokesman. "Thank you for your kindness and hospitality. You have been exceedingly generous. We wish we were on a pleasure trip. Unfortunately, we were forced to make this journey with unpleasant tidings."

"We realize the danger,
For your friend we are sad,
Please tell us your tidings;
Your story we must hear,
Your friend is recovering quickly,
We thank you for your risk."

"Let me start at the beginning." Hasko proceeded to tell the story of their loss of trade and the irritation and difficulty that this had brought upon the citizens of Amins. He explained the first mission that Elasti, Agot, and Broch undertook to go to the North Groves using the Albo Pass, and how they had encountered gnomes. He explained how Agot and Broch had been killed and how Elasti ran for his life back to Amins.

Hasko discussed the decision of the Amins Council to send a second expedition to the North Groves in order to cross the Southern Sword with the Northern Sword and how it was felt that representatives of Giter and Gije should accompany this expedition. One group had gone to Giter to recruit help and their group was chosen to come to Gije. He explained their journey to Gije via the back road and discussed all the difficulties they had encountered.

"We feel that there is the danger of Gije being attacked first since this is the place of final defeat last time during the Lifefight War," he continued. "We think that the Kabul's strategy might be that if they can overpower this elfin city then the rest of the Southern Plains will not pose much of a challenge. Therefore, we have come for two purposes. One to warn you of the pending danger so you can prepare yourselves, and second to request ambassadors from Gije that will join us in our attempt to journey to the North Groves."

With this Hasko fell silent. He had made his request, now it was up to the council and the Lord to make their decision.

At first it was silent, and then a discussion erupted amongst the members of the council. In Gije the council members debated all decisions without the Lord taking part in the debates. He remained an observer in the proceedings. Once the debate has concluded, the Lord would make his decision and all citizens of the city would abide by it whether or not they agreed with one another during the debate.

Fortunately for the leprechauns the debate that took place centered more on how they should proceed rather than if they should proceed. All members agreed that something must be done.

Considerations for the protection of the city, for the raising of a military force, and for the selection of representatives to travel to the North were discussed. Finally, after about three hours of debate, the council fell silent as the Lord Gimans arose;

"This will be done,
The policing force will recruit an army,
The army will be trained,
Our stores will be checked;
Our food and weapons will be inspected,
Our strongest warriors will be readied,
The police chief will become the military leader,
We must begin.
We'll go the North Groves,
We must keep our leaders here,
We'll send one of our best bowmen,
And a representative of the council;
We'll send Gido,
Along with Gijivure,
The rest will stay to protect the city,
Prepare Gido and Gijivure to go.
We thank you for your bravery,
Please accept our hospitality during your wait;
Wait for your friend under our care,
Your heroism praises us all."

The council was adjourned. Hiztin and Hasko were excited. Their journey to Gije had been a success. They had warned Gije and had received the town's support. Now it was time for the Lord to announce to his people what had happened and what was proposed. A bell in the

steeple above the palace was chimed calling for a gathering of the citizens of the city. Gimans asked Hasko if he would once again tell his story for the benefit of the townspeople and he readily agreed. Within a half hour all the people had gathered. Gimans introduced Hasko and Hiztin to the citizens from a second story balcony in the palace, and then asked Hasko to tell his story. Hasko repeated the same story that he had told the council. Then Gimans proceeded to detail out the defense of the city including what he expected the citizens to do in order to prepare for this defense. After explaining the city plans, he proceeded to explain the journey to the North Groves and that two representatives of Gije had been selected for the journey. He didn't specify names because Gijivure had not yet been contacted about his part. At the conclusion of this general meeting Gimans asked the elves of the city to give thanks to the brave heroes who ventured to help them. The townspeople let out a loud cheer, giving Hasko and Hiztin the feeling that all their trials had been worth the effort.

Now Hasko and Hiztin had only to wait for Jesves. Two days wait wouldn't be all that bad here in Gije. They felt they deserved the rest after what they had gone through.

On their way back to the tavern Hiztin requested to go see Jesves. He wanted to make sure she was improving satisfactorily. The doctor reported that the venom had not spread as badly as at first anticipated. He informed them that she would recover fine, but that it would definitely be the day after tomorrow before she would be able to do any kind of traveling. He allowed them to peek into her room, but he would not let them disturb her because she was sleeping soundly.

When Hiztin saw her laying there he felt a pang. He wanted to go over to her side and hold her and maybe even kiss her cheek, but his pride wouldn't let him. He decided that his companions would make fun of him if he did that. Besides, Jesves probably wouldn't appreciate it anyway.

It was already past supper time when Hasko, Hiztin, and Gido arrived back at the tavern. Gione and Gimans had gone to find Gijivure to tell him the news and to help him prepare for his journey. They planned to meet together later in the tavern with Gijivure and introduce him to his new traveling companions. Then they would all be able to discuss the journey they were about to make.

The tavern was packed with the local citizens, all interested in hearing the details surrounding the proceedings of the afternoon. They were eager to meet Hasko and Hiztin and to give their personal thanks. Hasko and Hiztin were honored guests and enjoyed their role.

Soon after their arrival in the tavern, they were joined by Gimans, Gione, and Gijivure. Gijivure was a tall elf, taller than the rest of his people. This made him nearly twice as tall as the leprechauns. He had a pleasant personality. He had a jolly cheerful attitude and showed no discomfort at being chosen for the journey. He was about 15 years of age, three years older than Hasko and Hiztin. His youth made the leperchauns feel even more comfortable with him.

A private room was requested where the six would be able to have dinner together and discuss the details of the planned journey. The distraction and questions of the curiosity seekers was keeping the team from making plans. The room was quickly arranged, and they found themselves seated around a table in one of the guest rooms. Dinner was readily prepared and the six enjoyed each other's company in a very relaxed environment.

After dinner they continued to discuss the journey to the North. The danger of the Albo Pass and the plan to travel the Kilo Pass was discussed. All agreed that it seemed to be the best choice even though it was dangerous and could have many unknown perils.

It had become rather late and, in spite of their afternoon rest, Hasko and Hiztin were very tired. Gimans, realizing their condition, suggested they continue the discussion the next evening. They were going to be there another couple days and there was no reason to try to get everything planned out in one evening. All agreed and they adjourned.

The next day started rather late. Hasko and Hiztin saw no reason to get up early so they took their time waking up. As they were getting dressed Hiztin felt he needed to continue the conversation that he had started with Hasko two nights earlier. "Do you really think I'm in love with her?" he asked.

"Not this again," bellowed Hasko, throwing up his arms as a sign of disgust. "How should I know if you're in love? I don't think you're in love because you haven't known her long enough to be in love with her. But from what I've seen of love, I could never make any sense of it anyway." Hasko was a little jealous over Hiztin's interest in Jesves. Hasko had never been in love, or at least he never thought he was, and so he couldn't understand what made Jesves so important to Hiztin.

Hiztin could see by Hasko's attitude that this discussion would get him nowhere. He decided to drop the subject and he would have to try and decide for himself whether he was in love or not.

When the two finally went out for breakfast, Gione was waiting for them.

"I'll take you around,
We'll see what is found;
We'll check on Jesves,
And pack up a feast."

They enjoyed breakfast together. They learned that Gimans was busy starting the city preparations, while Gido and Gijivure were preparing for their journey. They were hoping to depart on the following day. Hopefully Jesves would be well enough. They all planned to get together again that evening for supper to discuss any final arrangements.

The day was spent sightseeing and learning about the culture of the beautiful people of Gije. Hasko and Hiztin enjoyed learning as much as they could about this interesting lifestyle.

Several times during the day they checked in on Jesves. Once in the early afternoon she was awake, and they were able to talk to her. She was in great spirits. She even got out of bed and walked around some, indicating that she had recovered miraculously. "Doctor Erock keeps me

drugged. He says that his drug allows my body to concentrate on killing the venom, but it means that I spend almost all my time sleeping."

Just then the doctor walked in. He indicated that she was doing an excellent job of defeating the poison and that it looked as though she would most likely be able to start traveling tomorrow if they would promise not to push her too much. This made everyone happy. They all wanted to get going to the North Groves so that they would be able to return home again as soon as possible and defend their homelands.

Hasko and Hiztin explained the previous day's events to Jesves. They told her about the council meeting and about the decisions that had been made. They described how an explanation was given to the people and about their dinner meeting the previous night. They described the two new companions to her. They told her how supportive the people of Gije had been.

Hiztin sat close to Jesves the whole time, sometimes holding her hand, sometimes brushing the hair away from her forehead. He wanted her to be well and to be able to join them in touring the city. But it was more important that she recover as completely as possible before they set out again on their travels.

That evening the same six, Hasko, Hiztin, Gione, Gido, Gimans, and Gijivure, met together for dinner. After a very enjoyable meal, Gimans started the discussion.

"Last night I sent out scouts,
They inspected the Albo Pass,
They went to the Avoli River,
They saw the gnomes on the other side;
The gnomes hadn't come across the bridge,
The Avoli River is still the border,
They're guarding the Albo Pass,
The scouts returned safely an hour ago."

"This means that we should be safe following the South Road to the Tako Ruins," commented Hiztin. "It also means that the gnomes haven't started their attack as we feared they might. Perhaps they aren't ready yet. Perhaps they still want to increase their numbers before they attack."

"We think so also,
They're just not ready,
But the attack will come,
This gives us time to prepare;
Preparations must be made quickly,
Their attack could come within two days,
They may be arriving any time,
We think alike in our preparations."

Gimans had checked on the gnomes in order to see how serious the threat really was. He was glad to find out that they had not advanced, but he showed lines of concern on his face indicating that he knew this battle was inevitable.

The discussions continued for several hours. Nearing the end of their conversation Gido slipped out to go and check on the condition of Jesves one last time. When he returned, he reported:

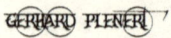

"Jesves is well,
The doc says go North;
The morning is fine,
For us to march forth."

They cheered the good news. A morning departure would allow them the opportunity for a full day of travel. The meeting ended so that final personal preparations could be made.

CHAPTER TEN

THE ROAD TO GITER

The expedition of four leprechauns headed north from Amins along the South Road. They knew very little of the dangers that lay before them. They had very little preparation for this type of journey either mentally or physically. Each of them realized that they had to be the ones to carry out this journey because they were the best and the most experienced in the city.

Yanon had taken the lead. He walked as though he was determined to make the journey a success and his manner gave the impression that he knew exactly what he was doing. But in his mind the wheels of thought were desperately turning. He hadn't thought much past Giter. He knew how difficult it would be to convince the citizens of the city that the expedition north had merit. Its citizens were isolationists. They didn't trust anyone, not the dwarfs, nor the leprechauns, nor often even themselves. They lived in constant fear of being taken advantage of especially by the "sneaky" leprechauns.

The king of the city feared the citizens of his own city. He lived in paranoia that everyone was after his throne. He kept control of all business enterprises and all schools. The businesses were run by his direction. He would dictate what would be done and when. In the schools the children were indoctrinated with a "love your king" dogma that treated the king as a god to the point where the children reported on their parents if any comments were made contrary to the king's doctrine. All citizens, male or female, were kept working six days a week. This kept the children under the influence of the king for all but a few hours every evening and Sundays during which the king kept everyone busy with required festivals and indoctrination meetings.

Even Yanon's friends in the police forces of the city were only working associates. No one had any decision-making power. It would be difficult to convince them of the danger. To further complicate the expedition a request for an envoy from the city would surely require an

audience before the king himself who was very vocal about his dislike of the leprechauns.

In many ways Yanon had hopes that he would fail to get someone to accompany them from Giter. Anyone that came with from that city would surely be more trouble than he was worth. The lepelves had developed an apathy that left them only concerned about themselves and the here and now. This would conflict with the personalities of the leperchauns. Yanon felt there was very little hope that this expedition would include someone from this city. But Amaz had directed him to try so he knew he must.

Elasti and Obydon walked together, following behind Yanon. The two were nearly brothers-in-law; that was if Elasti could only stay in Amins long enough to get married. Elasti had thoughts of Jizeel. When he thought about her, he felt a little stupid at insisting that he come with on this expedition. Maybe he had let his emotions get the best of him causing him to make a rash and foolish decision. But in his heart, he knew he had to do this for his friends, Agot and Broch. He knew they were in a better place in the rainbow with god. But they had meant too much to him for him to forget them now.

Obydon was deep in thought as well. He felt honored to be the carrier of the sword. This was the first time a major responsibility had been laid upon his shoulders that would affect the welfare of the entire city of Amins. He worried about his abilities. Would he be worthy of the honor and duty that had been given him? He wasn't sure. But refusal was beyond consideration if he was to be the future Head of the Council of Amins. He had a big burden to carry if he was to follow in the footsteps of his father. He knew he must do his best, no; he must do better than his best. He must succeed. He must conquer any trials that were placed before him and he must prove himself as the future leader of his people.

Bydola brought up the rear. He appeared to walk slowly in comparison to the others. His large stature gave the impression that he had more strength than his three friends put together. He enjoyed being called on this expedition. It gave him the feeling of importance. He always thought that the other citizens of the city had little respect for him. His being needed for this journey gave him a new respectability. He felt recognized and appreciated, and he vowed to himself that he would do his best.

The morning was quiet since all four of the travelers were deep in thought, each concerned with his own expectations. The weather was drizzly, and the darkness of the clouds seemed to indicate a high likelyhood of rain. The road was muddy and in spots there were water puddles that the travelers had to walk around. Traveling became more tiresome as the mud caked their shoes, but they journeyed on, not stopping for lunch. They snacked as they walked and decided to save their big meal for later on in the evening when they had a nice fire to warm and dry themselves by.

The journey to Giter would take two days. The first night would be spent outside in the rain, but the second night would hopefully find them under a roof in that city.

As the afternoon drug on Yanon started to discuss the difficulties that they might encounter when in Giter and also during the rest of the journey. He stressed the importance of getting everyone sword trained and ready for possible dangers they would encounter. He also emphasized the need for unity amongst themselves while they were in Giter. The lepelves would try to disrupt this unity by separating them and asking them searching questions. They would behave suspicious and would look for hidden meanings or reasons for the journey. "We must maintain our unity at all cost. If they find any weakness, they may go so far as to accuse us of conspiracy and attempt to imprison us," he stressed.

This brought everyone to the realization that there were dangers they would encounter before they engaged any gnomes. Their first danger already existed in arriving in Giter. "Bydola," Yanon continued. "I would like you to journey through the city and camp on the other side, waiting for us there where the road continues toward the north. If we don't appear within two days, go straight back to Amins through the Amins Groves and report the problem. Do not come back into Giter."

Bydola nodded in recognition. He had no interest in putting up with those fool lepelves anyways. This would give him the opportunity to avoid meeting with the king.

As the foursome journeyed on, they continued their strategy discussions. Yanon would contact his friends in the city and see if they would arrange for a meeting with the king. Then Elasti would make the first appeal to the king by telling his story of the first expedition. Yanon would explain the urgency of the current mission and appeal to the king for support. If the appeal was taken lightly, Obydon would show his sword, thereby showing that the city of Amins was serious about the risk to its safety and that they had made a commitment to this expedition.

The discussions made the day go faster. It wasn't long before the sun had set, and it was time to find a place to bed down for the night. Although they expected heavy rains they never came. The mist had made the travelers damp and a large fire was built where they could dry themselves. Dinner was cooked and all four of them ate hungrily having only snacked for lunch. It wasn't long before they were all bedded down in their tents for the night.

Then night brought heavy rains. It poured down so hard that the ground couldn't absorb the water quickly enough. Soon puddles were building up in some of the depressions.

The four friends were fast asleep. They noticed very little of the storm other than maybe being awaken by an occasional clap of thunder. But each clap didn't last long and wasn't enough to cause them to open their eyes.

Elasti was dreaming of his new wife. In his dreams he had just been married and they were in their new home in Amins. He was in the scrub tub taking a bath when suddenly he slipped and went under the water. He was struggling to sit up but couldn't. He could feel the water over his face, and he felt as though he was suffocating. Suddenly he sat up and yelled, "Help Me! Help Me!"

Suddenly Elasti was awakened, being dragged and shaken. Yanon was pulling him out of a puddle of water. Elasti was submerged in rainwater and in his struggles and with his yelling he had alerted Yanon and the rest of the team. They arrived just in time to pull him free. When Elasti was fully awake he felt stupid. He felt childish. "I'm so sorry," he kept apologizing to his three friends. "I guess the dream woke me up."

"It wasn't just the dream," Yanon assured him. "You were actually under water. Your tent was in a low spot and the rainwater had built up to the point where you were drowning. It's a good thing that you woke up or we would have really had a problem. I'm glad your dream made you scream."

Reassured Elasti gratefully thanked his companions. Then they all went to work together to relocate his tent to higher ground. But Elasti was embarrassed. He went off by himself and hibernated. He just wanted to be alone for a little while. His emotions about being married, and about nearly drowning had overwhelmed him. He felt foolish. And he wanted to think.

Obydon, Bydola, and Yanon, all soaked because of their little adven ture with Elasti, migrated over to the fire. They built up the fire and sat there trying to warm and dry themselves. They beckoned Elasti to join them, but he waved them off.

Elasti continued to stay off at a distance for about an hour. He was feeling foolish about his decision to be by himself, especially since his friends kept encouraging him to come over and join them. He was just about to give in when he saw something move out of the corner of his eye near the center of the woods. He looked around and tried to spot what he had seen, but to no avail. He couldn't see a thing. "Now my mind was playing tricks on me, all because of these foolish fears," he scolded himself.

Then he saw it again. This time it was clearer. Something had defin itely moved off in the distance, but it was closer now. He tried to find it but again he was unsuccessful. He watched for a few more minutes off in the same direction. Then suddenly he saw it clearly and he realized why he hadn't seen it before. It blended in so nicely and was the same color as the trees. It was a bear. A big bear and it didn't look friendly.

"Bear!" Elasti yelled at the top of his lungs.

"Where?" Bydola asked, jumping up. "I can't see anything." The brightness of the fire had blinded him from the dark.

"Coming your way. Hurry! Run!" Elasti responded with a panicked voice.

Just then there was a crashing of fallen twigs and branches and the bear was plainly visible, charging at the attendants of the fire. Elasti's screaming must have spooked the bear. Obydon, Bydola, and Yanon scrambled. Each charged towards a different tree in the groves. They scrambled up their respective trees as quickly as possible. Because each of the three ran towards a different tree, the bear was temporarily confused. He stopped the chase and watched the three of them. He had difficulty deciding which to chase. The delay gave the threesome enough time to get into a tree. The bear decided to pursue Bydola and quickly chased after him. But he was too late. Bydola had scampered high enough into the tree to avoid capture.

Obydon would have been a better chase for the bear. He struggled and slipped several times, but eventually made it up into the tree himself. Elasti had also found a tree and sat on a branch that was high enough to avoid the bear. The bear was frustrated by his unsuccessful chase. Unobserved by the four leprechauns, who were mostly concerned about staying in their respective trees, the bear slowly and quietly meandered away.

Eventually the four each found that they had comfortably positioned themselves on branches in their trees. Then, without warning three thumps were simultaneously heard. "Ouch!" yelled Bydola. He had fallen out of the tree and had landed with a thump on the ground right on the hilt of his sword. The back side of his leg would surely be bruised the next day.

At the same time there was suddenly a large splash from a soaked branch. By now fire was blotted out. But the fallen threesome only noticed that they had fallen out of the tree. Only Elasti noticed that the fire had been extinguished.

"You can say that again," added Yanon to Bydola's comment, who had also fallen out of his tree. His landing was also not very graceful and resulted in him twisting his wrist. He felt pain with every movement and knew that this injury would cause him considerable inconvenience during their travels.

"What's going on?" complained Obydon. "It was as if the branch I was sitting on just disappeared out from under me." His injuries weren't quite as severe as those of the other two, but his pride hurt the most. "And where's that bear," he continued with concern, being surprised at its sudden disappearance and disinterest in him. "It just seems to have disappeared."

"That's what I thought happened too," commented Yanon. "My branch just wasn't there anymore. But I thought I was dreaming. How could a branch disappear out from under you?"

"That makes three of us. I thought I was sitting comfortably and securely on the branch and then my branch disappeared too," added Bydola.

"Now maybe you'll believe me," interjected Elasti sarcastically. He was still sitting comfortably in his tree.

"What do you mean?" asked Obydon.

"We were warned that the trees in this forest are alive. Remember how I told you they wouldn't let us build a fire, but you didn't listen to me. Now the fire's been put out and the trees won't let you sit in them because you insisted on building up a big fire. They're mad at you."

The others thought for a minute. Was it possible that Elasti had been right all along? It sounded ridiculous. Trees that wouldn't let anyone sit on their branches? Trees that put out fires?

"Then how do you explain the bear?" questioned Yanon defensively.

"The bear was just sent to scare you away from the fire so that it could be put out. The trees don't like to hurt anyone seriously. They had to get rid of you first in order to snuff the fire. That's why the bear's gone now. He wasn't needed anymore. Besides, why didn't they throw me out of the tree? They only threw you three and isn't it strange that all three of you fell at the same time. There's no doubt in my mind that there's more life in these trees than you think."

"I'm convinced," concluded Obydon. "Now that we've made these trees mad, we better get the heck out of here. I don't want to run into any more bears."

Yanon and Bydola were silent. They didn't want to concede defeat yet, but they didn't want to continue arguing. What Elasti said did make sense. They each decided in their own minds that they wouldn't make any more fires in the Amins Groves, just in case.

Elasti descended from the tree he had been perched on and the four packed up their camps and began to leave the forest. Yanon, Obydon, and Bydola now felt very uncomfortable there.

During the encounter with the Amins Groves trees the rain had let up considerably. Finally, the ground had a chance to soak up some of the water. The puddles had slowly become smaller.

"Let's not try to set up camp again tonight," commented Yanon. "The ground's too damp to build a good fire and the tress will just put it out anyway. And we'll just make a bigger mess of our tents if we try to pitch them here. Why don't we travel on? The sun will be up in a couple of hours anyway. We'll let the sun dry things out and hopefully there won't be any more rain. Then we'll take a rest break for lunch and try to catch up on some of our sleep during that break."

"I agree with that," commented Bydola, "the excitement has taken all the sleep out of me anyway and I don't feel like lying around in the mud. But you're going to have to go slow. This bruise on my leg is going to keep me limping for a while."

The travelers set out north. The road was still covered with water in many places, so they were often forced to travel along the side of the road. This caused them to walk in rain soaked, knee-high grass. Their pants became even more drenched. Between the mud caked shoes and the drenched pant legs, traveling was uncomfortable and slow.

They pressed on. Bydola's leg started to hurt him more and more all the time. His pain slowed the party down, but Bydola insisted that they should get as far as they could during the morning and then give his leg a good rest in the afternoon. "After all," he claimed, "it wasn't broken, only badly bruised."

It wasn't long before the sun rose and occasionally it broke through the clouds. The warmth of the sun, even though there was very little of it, felt good. The ground continued to dry up. The puddles of water seemed to disappear. But the mud continued to be a nuisance and slowed their progress.

The morning seemed to drag on forever. On several occasions Elasti put in his bid for an early lunch. It wasn't so much that he was tired, he just felt miserable and he wanted a nice warm fire and a chance to change into some warmer dryer clothes.

At first Yanon simply ignored his request but when Bydola also voted for a rest because of the pain in his leg Yanon took notice of the need for a break. He felt that maybe he was trying to push them a little too hard. Bydola had been very patient with his injury. When Yanon came upon a clearing that seemed as though it had stayed above the heavy drenching of the rains, he decided to call a rest break and allowed the travelers to build a big fire staying as far away from the groves as possible.

With the fire going it wasn't long before all the travelers were dried off and warm. They ate a hearty meal. Then Elasti and Bydola decided to take a nap. Obydon and Yanon leaned back against a rock feeling that sleeping would just make them feel even more tired when it came time to start walking again. But it didn't work. Soon they were both dozing, and it was three hours later when Yanon finally came back to life.

They lost about four hours that afternoon. Yanon realized that the prospect of them arriving in Giter before nightfall looked dim. He proceeded to awake all the travelers hoping that they would still be able to get in three or four more hours of walking before they bedded down for the night. They packed up their supplies, extinguished the fire, and set out down the road toward Giter.

Yanon's wrist still hurt him badly but, other than having to be careful with it when he handled his pack, it didn't keep him from pushing ahead in his travels. It already felt a little better than it had during the morning and he felt sure that it would be completely usable again by the next day.

It was well after sunset before they decided to make camp. The cloud cover had broken up slightly. The light from the moon and stars allowed them to travel a little further into the night. Using the best estimate that Elasti could come up with, they still had about three hours of travel before they would arrive in Giter.

They made camp. The night looked as though they wouldn't have the same experience with the rain that they had encountered previously but they wisely pitched their tents on the tops of whatever mounds of dirt they could find, just in case.

The next morning the sky was almost clear. The sun caused the travelers to feel warm and comfortable again. The night had passed without incident, and they were ready to set off for the last leg of their journey to Giter.

About three hours into their travels they could see the city rising over the horizon off in the distance. They knew they would be within the confines of the city walls within a half an hour. Bydola was extremely happy to finally lay eyes on the city. His leg had felt pretty good when they started out in the morning but after three hours of travel it again gave him considerable pain. He looked forward to the chance to give it a rest.

Yanon proceeded to brief each of the travelers on their roles. Bydola would proceed through the city as planned and make camp on the far side. Obydon and Elasti would get rooms at the local tavern for the three of them, while Yanon tried to arrange an audience with the king. Each felt that he knew what was expected of them and hopefully they could be done with their activities in the city as quickly as possible.

Giter wasn't an elaborate city. In fact, it was quite plain. There were no walls surrounding it and it was composed only of houses. There was one main road through the city and all buildings were located on either side of this main thoroughfare including the palace.

Surprisingly to the four travelers, the king's palace didn't stand in stately attention over the rest of the houses. It was taller than the rest of the buildings but only about twice as tall making it two stories instead of one. Its appearance did not command the respect of passersby.

The palace had guards posted all around it. This also seemed strange to the leprechauns who would have expected the guards to be guarding the city rather than the palace. There was only one entrance to the palace, which was heavily guarded, just like the rest of the palace. There were no windows on the first floor. The few windows that existed were all on the second floor.

As they walked by the palace entrance, they could see a large center courtyard through the open doors. The courtyard had gardens and fountains, in sharp contrast to the rough appearance of the rest of the buildings in the city where there were no flowers to beautify the dwellings, and the streets were cluttered with wagons, carts, and garbage. It was obvious that the residents of the city had very little pride in their city and in the overall appearance.

"I've always been told that lepelves were lazy," whispered Bydola to Elasti, "but I never figured it would be quite this bad."

"You haven't seen anything yet," returned Yanon who had overheard the comment. "Wait till you see the inside of the tavern. That's a real dump."

"I can't understand why people would want to live like this when they don't have to."

"Culture," was Elasti's response, "they were brought up this way and they don't know any better."

Bydola could only shrug his shoulders.

Shortly after passing the palace, they found themselves in front of the tavern. It was now time for the four to separate. After bidding their farewells, Bydola continued towards the west end of the city. Yanon headed off for the home of his friend where he hoped to arrange for a conversation. He hoped that his friend may be able to help him with his mission. Possibly this friend would be the one accompanying the travelers on the journey to the North Groves. He hoped the two of them would be able to get together later that evening in the tavern.

"It's just like he said," Obydon commented, referring to Yanon. "It is hard to believe that anyone could enjoy living like this." The floors of the tavern were littered and dirty. A disorderly chaos prevailed throughout the room.

They went over to the bar and asked the bar attendant about arranging for a room for the night. "What do you want a room for?" asked the rude tavern keeper.

"We're interested in spending the night here in the city," Elasti commented attempting not to reveal any more than necessary.

"Well that doesn't tell me anything," was the barkeeper's response. "Besides I don't take care of rooms. I serve drinks and that's all. If you want a room, you'll have to talk to the tavern owner and he's busy."

"When would be a good time to meet him?" Obydon asked, trying to avoid raising the temper of the tavern keeper.

"When he's done eating! He's sitting over there," the attendant pointed in the direction of the front window, where a heavyset lepelf was busy stuffing himself with a plate full of greens. "Let me warn you. He doesn't like outsiders any more than I do."

"Thanks for the help." Amis tried to stay friendly realizing that future situations might occur where he would need the help of this bartender. "How do we order a meal?"

"You sit your backside down and grab one of the ugly waitresses you see flopping around here. I keep hoping for a waitress that would be worth grabbing but it doesn't look like I'm ever gonna see that happen."

"Thanks again," Elasti responded, as he started to walk away from the bar.

"Hey," the bartender let out a loud cry showing his irritation with Elasti and Obydon. "Information isn't free around here. Pay up or I'll come over there and take it out of your hide."

Elasti went back and gave him a menial tip for his information.

"I don't believe this place," commented Obydon. "No wonder you wanted to get out of this city as soon as possible. I would have preferred going with Bydola and sleeping out in the rain, rather than receiving this rude treatment."

Elasti selected a table close to the owner of the tavern. This would allow him to start a conversation with him if he should ever take a breath between bites.

Getting fed without waiting all day to be served required grabbing a waitress. The grab became very literal. The waitresses moved at their own speed. It took over half an hour before the travelers successfully got the attention of one of the two ladies serving the tables. They managed to order soup and bread and after another half hour they finally received their food order. Unfortunately, it was cold by then.

While they were getting ready to eat their meal, they suddenly noticed a small vibration. "That was scary. What was that?" commented Obydon in a nervous tone.

"It must be a Giterquake," returned Elasti. "I've heard about them before but have never experienced one." Looking around the room he said, "No one else seems to have noticed it. They must all be used to these vibrations."

The quaking continued to grow stronger. "Shouldn't we leave the building?" questioned Elasti.

"Nobody else seems to be worried about it," responded Obydon, not wanting to overreact to the Giterquake. He didn't want to give the lep-elves any reason to ridicule him and so he suppressed his fear.

Then suddenly and unexplainably the quaking stopped. Elasti and Obydon looked at each other questioningly realizing that neither had any answers. They decided to forget the incident as if it never happened.

Shortly after the two received their meal the tavern owner, who was still sitting at the table next to them, signaled the completion of his meal with a loud belch. Elasti took this opportunity to ask him about a room, "Sir. We are interested in a room for the night. Is there something available that we can rent."

"Why'd you call me 'Sir'?" the tavern owner responded. "Do you think that by calling me 'Sir' you'll get the room cheaper? Well no chance. You'll pay just as much as everyone else. Maybe even a little more because you're dumb enough to call me 'Sir'."

"Sorry," said Elasti. "I meant no offense. I was only interested in a room for the night."

"What are you foreigners doing here anyways? Are you spies or something? We don't like spies around here, and we like foreigners even less. What do you want here anyway?"

"We're only passing through and we need a room for the night. Do you have a room for three leprechauns?"

"Three? I only see two of you. Where's the third? You hiding some-one? I knew you were spies. Where's your partner?" By now the loud voice of the owner had attracted the attention of the entire tavern. Several individuals had gotten up out of their chairs and were standing close by to see what would transpire. Others just sat in their chairs and listened with amusement.

"Our partner will be joining us shortly. He went to visit a friend."

"Nobody in Giter is friends with spies. You trying to tell me you spies got friends here in Giter? No way."

Elasti was getting frustrated. "This fool is starting to irritate me," he whispered to Obydon.

"Look," Elasti started, no longer trying to hide his irritation. "We aren't spies. We're only passing through. There are three of us and we need a room for three. Are you going to give us one or aren't you?"

"Listen buster," the owner showed his anger. "Nobody talks to me like that. If you want a room, you better shape up. There's no reason to get obnoxious with me. I've been taking good care of you as it is."

Elasti was about to tell the tavern owner to "keep his room" feeling that it would be more desirable to sleep outside than to have to tolerate any more abuse. Obydon realizing that Elasti had met his limit quickly jumped in, "We meant no offense. We're just tired after the long journey. Couldn't you please arrange a room for us for the night?"

"Well, I guess since you put it like that," the owner said, recovering his pride. Then he yelled at a young boy, "Give them the key to the room at the end of the hall." Looking back at Obydon he said, "That room will hold the three of you nicely. You better learn to control your friend there," he said pointing to Elasti. "His mouth is going to end up getting

him in trouble. By the way, I want payment in advance for that room. You pay for it when you pay for your meal before you get your key. Got it?"

"Yes, thank you," was Obydon's reply hoping to terminate the conversation as quickly as possible.

The tavern owner got up and left the front room heading for the kitchen. The rest of the people in the room returned to their normal state of affairs.

"I hope everything that we do in this city doesn't turn out to be as difficult as getting a room or a meal," whispered Elasti sarcastically. "If this keeps up, I think I'll join Bydola."

"Don't go yet," returned Obydon, "I'm thinking of joining you."

The two finished their meal quickly. They felt uncomfortable sitting in a room full of lepelves who spent most of their time staring and snickering.

They paid for their meal and for the room and were given the key to the room by a young boy who turned out to be the son of the tavern owner. The boy seemed almost apologetic when he gave them the key. His behavior seemed out of character for the rest of the lepelves. His attitude confused them and left them wondering what the boy was apologetic about.

The two went to their newly rented room, only to find it in the same disarray as everything else in the city. There was litter on the floor and the beds were in disarray. They decided that the first thing they would need to do was to clean it up and organize it a little. They decided to stay in the room for the rest of the day only venturing out if they had no choice. They would much rather stay cooped up in a dumpy room than to be tormented.

Bydola had continued traveling through town on the South Road heading out of town. His limp had gotten pretty bad. He was tempted to rest with his companions in the tavern for a little while but decided not to and continued on, planning to make camp at the first convenient spot that he encountered outside of town.

Being alone left him a little scared. He decided that he would feel safer hidden away in the Amins Groves then he would in Giter or on the main road in spite of what had happened two nights ago with the trees. The difference in the atmosphere of this city as opposed to his hometown of Amins, and the unfriendly lepelves, bothered him greatly. He felt extremely unsafe and uncomfortable. He had never encountered an unfamiliar culture before, at least not in the situation where he was the minority, and this had given him a mild case of culture shock.

As he passed a small group of children, a cry went out, "Look at the fat little leprechaun. I'll bet if we trip him, he'll roll all the way to Amins." The children were just teasing and meant nothing serious by their remarks, but Bydola was not accustomed to such disrespectful behavior, and it disturbed him greatly. He kept quiet and decided to ignore them. He knew he couldn't take his frustrations out on these children, especially not if Yanon was going to succeed in getting the king to help in the expedition, so he ignored the children and continued on his way.

He was relieved when he finally passed what he thought was the last house of the city. He felt like continuing to walk for the rest of the day in spite of his limping leg just to get as far away from this city as possible. But he knew that this wasn't what he was instructed to do so he hobbled on for another half an hour and found a clearing next to a small pond. This was the perfect place to camp. Clean water to take a bath, and a soft grassy floor on which to pitch his tent. He was positive he would enjoy camping out here for the next two days.

In two days, his friends had promised to join him again. Two days wasn't long. That amount of time would give his injured leg plenty of opportunity to heal, maybe not completely but at least to the point where it wouldn't give him as much pain anymore. He would also be able to recover from the loss of sleep he had experienced during the past two nights.

"Staying out here will be a lot nicer than having to stay in that dreadful city," he thought to himself. Then he thought about the cruel children that he had encountered. It made him feel sad along with all the other frustrations of his travels and tears welled up in his eyes, and he started to cry.

Unnoticed by him, high atop a tree, far above his head, an eagle sat and watched.

Yanon left his companions and headed south down a small alley between two houses. He knew right where to go. He had been at the home of Gilbon many times. Gilbon was the military leader of Giter, responsible for the guards at the palace which were the police that kept the peace. He had a small army of about 20 men. The army was seldom used, only when the king felt he should demonstrate his power by parading the troops up and down the main street of Giter.

Yanon met with Gilbon annually just to stay in touch. It was a tradition that had been established and which existed since the Lifefight Wars. Originally it included the elves as well. But many years ago, the then king of Giter had been very rude and insulting to the visiting elves and the elves haven't been a part of the annual meeting since.

Yanon went directly to Gilbon's house and knocked on the door.

"Who's there?" a voice from inside the house bellowed loudly.

"Yanon from Amins is here to see Gilbon."

"You're a little early this year," it was Gilbon talking as he opened the door. "We're not supposed to get together for several months yet.

Come in Yanon, what brings you so far from home?" Gilbon put out his hand for Yanon to shake.

Yanon took his hand and entered the house. "I come here on urgent business. A threat exists to the Southern Plains, and I have been instructed to explain this threat to your king in hopes that he might see fit to allow us to work together for the safety of the South."

"What is this great threat?" questioned Gilbon sounding unconvinced.

Yanon knew he must say as little as possible. Amaz had instructed him to reveal very little until he was before the king. Then he should tell his whole tale. In this way the pride of the king would not be hurt. "We fear a threat from the Kabul. I have brought two companions with me who wish to tell their story to the king. Can you arrange for me to see him?"

"Krakus of the Kabul wouldn't dare attack us. He knows he's no match for us. That's why he went to the Kabul in the first place. You're going to have to be mighty convincing in order for the king to take your news seriously."

"We have been instructed by our Council of Amins to tell this story to the king and this we must do. Won't you please help us in setting up a meeting with him?"

"I'll give it a try but I'm not going to make you any promises," Gilbon remarked. "Before we go to the palace, won't you sit down and eat with us? It's nearly lunch time. Then you can tell me all about this Kabul nonsense."

Yanon accepted the lunch invitation, but he knew he must avoid the story of Elasti's journey. He spent his time telling the story of what had happened in the Amins Groves and how they had barely escaped with their lives. Yanon tended to exaggerate slightly in an attempt to make the story more interesting to his audience.

During their meal they felt a vibration, slow at first, and then it grew stronger until the glasses were jumping around on the table. This lasted about five minutes, and then suddenly just when it seemed that the quaking would become too violent for the dishes to be able to stay on the table, the shaking stopped.

"Giterquake," Gilbon explained.

"They usually don't get that violent, do they?" questioned Yanon. Gilbon uncaringly shrugged his shoulders and continued eating.

When they were through eating Gilbon offered Yanon some of his lepelf after-dinner ale which was hard to decline, but Yanon knew he had to. He had tasted that ale once too often and it left him with very little control of his senses. The lepelf ale was just too strong for a leprechaun even of his stature. Yanon realized that Gilbon was trying to learn more about the threat from the Kabul by using the help of the ale and this made it all the more important for Yanon to avoid tasting it.

After lunch, their conversation made very little progress for either individual. Gilbon wanted to learn more about the Kabul and Yanon wanted him to go to the king and arrange the meeting. Both individuals ended up frustrated and irritated. Eventually, Yanon decided that the only way he was going to get Gilbon to make the request before the king was if he walked him over to the palace himself.

After a bit of coaxing Yanon successfully got Gilbon to stand up and the two proceeded out the door and down the street toward the palace. Gilbon explained, "You won't be able to come onto the palace grounds with me unless the king gives his direct permission. Leprechauns are foreigners and he doesn't trust foreigners. He thinks you're all spies, so you'll have to wait out here for me. I'll go in and talk to him and let you know what he says."

Yanon responded with, "Don't forget to stress that we're envoys sent directly from the Council of Amins to give him this message. Hopefully that will convince him of the importance of our message."

Gilbon left Yanon out in the street. Yanon didn't mind being left alone in Giter. He had done it many times before. The cultural difference between Giter and Amins was not as shocking to him as it was for his companions. He strolled up and down the street staying close by but trying his best to pass the time.

"So, he thinks we're going to be attacked, does he? It doesn't surprise me. Those leprechauns never had much sense anyways." The voice was that of Gorbot, King of the lepelf kingdom of Giter. He was seated in his dreaming room, a room he had specially designed for himself. It was lavishly painted on all the walls and on the ceiling with elaborate colors and designs. The king enjoyed this room because it helped him to relax and to forget the many problems that existed in Giter. He became tired of his citizens hounding him. Didn't they realize how good they had it? Couldn't they just leave him alone?

Before him stood Gilbon, "I tried to get as much information out of him as I could, but apparently the Amins Council has given him strict orders not to tell his story to anyone but you."

"Well, I don't like those sneaky foreigners just popping in here and expect ng me to jump at their every whim. Eventually I'll see them just to satisfy my curiosity but I'm going to do it at my convenience not theirs. You tell your leprechaun friend that I'm busy with affairs of state and that I won't be able to meet with him until tomorrow or maybe the next day. You also tell him that I'll only give him a half an hour so he should get everything he's going to say done in that amount of time. I don't want him wasting my whole day with his nonsense. Do you hear me?"

"I understand sire. I will relay your message," answered Gilbon.

The king instructed, "You come back tomorrow about noon and we'll see when we can get together with these leprechauns."

"I'll return then," said Gilbon as he bowed, more out of fear than out of respect. Gilbon left the room and proceeded to leave the palace.

"Guard!" Gorbot bellowed out. A guard, who was standing outside of the door to his room, entered. "Get me Giterod!" The guard bowed in understanding and left to fill the request of his king.

"The king says maybe tomorrow around noon. He says he's busy with affairs of state and he won't be able to see you till then. It's best if we wait and I'll check with him around noon tomorrow." Gilbon was talking to Yanon out in the street. Gilbon was afraid to tell Yanon what he really thought of the king's reaction because he feared retaliation. He had an important job and he was able to keep that job by playing a proper role in the politics of Giter. He would not lose that position now especially not for a leprechaun.

Yanon was disappointed. They would have to sit around and waste one whole day. "Thank you for your help. I probably should get back to my friends at the tavern and see how they're getting along. Can I meet you again tomorrow for lunch at the tavern, and then we'll go to the palace to see about a meeting?"

"I'd be delighted," responded Gilbon. "I'll meet you for an early lunch. I'm looking forward to meeting your friends to hear their story."

Yanon and Gilbon walked back to the tavern together. Yanon again expressed his disappointment at the king's lack of interest. Gilbon remained apologetic for the king emphasizing how busy he was but Yanon knew better.

At the door of the tavern the two separated with Yanon entering the tavern and Gilbon returning to his home to continue his work for the day.

The tavern wasn't new territory to Yanon, he had been here before. He was familiar with its' rough nature and its' rowdy clientele. He noticed a young boy cleaning off one of the tables and after approaching the boy he asked about Obydon and Elasti. Without stopping his work, the boy responded that they were given the room at the end of the hall.

Yanon proceeded toward the room that the boy directed him to and found his friends there lying on their beds resting. "We won't be able to meet with the king until tomorrow afternoon. He's trying to show off his status by making us wait. This is a nuisance. Now we'll have to sit around killing time." Yanon's irritation was apparent.

"How stupid!" Elasti was exasperated. He recounted the experience that he and Obydon had tolerated in the tavern. "We won't get out of this town soon enough to suit me."

Yanon knew that this delay wasn't necessary but there was nothing he could do about it. "We'll have to go to Bydola and tell him of this delay so that he doesn't become concerned about us." He jumped on his bed, folded his arms, and soon drifted off in his thoughts.

"We have some visitors in our town, some leprechauns." It was King Garbot talking to Giterod, the king's personal guard and servant who had just arrived to the dreaming room. The king continued, "I don't trust leprechauns. I want you to find out as much as you can about them. Gilbon was here earlier and he can probably tell you a few things he's learned. They're probably staying at the tavern. Go over there and find out what the lepelves in the tavern think of these foreigners. Hurry!"

"Sire your wish is my command." Giterod bowed as he responded. "Should I see about any souvenirs they may have that we could add to our treasury? I can have a look through their belongings when they're not around. I'm sure there's a few things we can find that would be of inter-est."

"No. I'm going to have an audience with them in a day or so. Let me find out what they have that would be of interest first before you alert them and cause them to be more careful. I'll let you know when you can check into their belongings. Now go and learn as much as you can about their real motive for being here."

"Yes sire," Giterod said as he bowed and left the room. Giterod played the role of the king's private spy and the king often used him to handle his secret inquiries, especially when the possibility for gain existed.

Evening approached and Yanon, Elasti, and Obydon got hungry for supper. But only Yanon was willing to venture outside of the room to retrieve his meal. "Tell you what I'll do for you two. I'll go out and have them deliver our meal to our room," Yanon suggested. "How's that sound?"

"Great," responded Obydon, "can you see about them getting it to us while it's still warm?"

"Now you're asking for too much," commented Yanon jokingly.

He left the room and soon found one of the waitresses for the tavern. "We'd like to order our meals and we'd like them delivered to our rooms. Could you bring us some stew and bread?"

"We don't deliver no meals to no rooms," she blurted out. "Are your kind too good to eat with the rest of us grubby common folk out here in the tavern? If you are, you deserve to starve!" She walked away and continued rambling on about how big an insult this was to the lepelves that this miserable leprechaun thought he was too good to eat with them.

Yanon couldn't get in another word, and soon gave up the verbal contest. Dejected and hungry he returned to the room to report that the three of them would have to venture out into the tavern if they planned to eat a warm supper. Otherwise, they would have to be satisfied with the cold food in their packs.

Cold food started to sound pretty good, when suddenly there was a knock on the door. Yanon opened the door and found a young boy standing there. It was the same boy that had directed him to this room earlier.

The boy carried a tray and on the tray was a large bowl of stew, three small bowls, and a loaf of bread, three spoons, and a knife. "I overheard you talking to the waitress. She doesn't really mean what she says. Everybody here is good people they just get a little scared sometimes 'cause they don't understand strangers. Here," and he pushed the tray toward Yanon. The boy was very nervous and wanted to get away as quickly as possible.

Yanon, having taken a liking to this boy who seemed concerned about them, asked, "What's your name?"

"Gabrona. I better get back to work. My father won't like it if he sees me here talking with you. I better go now."

"Don't be so nervous. We won't hurt you. We appreciate your kindness. Here, let me pay you." Yanon handed some money to the boy who quickly stuffed it into his pocket without even looking at it.

Money in the Southern Plains consisted of a lump of geld, a metal that was very rare. This form of payment was very seldom used. Most payment was done by some form of barter such as a chair for a chicken, and so on. But when traveling to Giter, chairs and chickens weren't convenient to carry for exchange, so the geld was used.

"I'll be back in about an hour to pick up the dishes," he said as he hurried off.

"Isn't that the same boy who gave us the key to the room," Obydon asked Elasti. Elasti nodded in agreement. "He must be the son of that miserable grouch who runs this place."

Yanon placed the tray on the small table that was in the center of the room, and the three of them enjoyed their feast.

Later that evening Gabrona returned to pick up the dishes and the tray. "Thank you for having been so generous earlier in your payment. If I can do anything else to help you, please let me know." He left with the tray and the empty dishes.

The three hibernated in the room for the rest of the evening and soon they started dozing off to sleep.

Bydola felt very alone. He knew that he was the first person to travel on this part of the South Road since Elasti and his party had traveled there a few days earlier. He enjoyed the lonely peacefulness of the forest. He could hear birds singing in the trees, and by looking across to the other side of the small pond where he was camped, he could see lots of yellow flowers. The setting was the most beautiful he had ever seen in his life. He felt no hesitation or fear when he undressed, climbed up on a large bolder, and dove off into the clear water of the pond for a swim.

He opened his eyes under water in order to see how far he was from the bottom, but he could see nothing. It was as though he had gone blind. In fear he hurriedly paddled his way toward the surface. As soon as his head broke the surface of the water, he was able to see clearly everything that surrounded him. He looked into the water and saw nothing. His body seemed to end at the very surface of the water. He could see reflections of the parts of himself that were above the water, and reflections of the trees around the lake, but he could see nothing that was in the lake.

He moved his hand in and out of the water to test his senses. He couldn't believe what he was seeing. The part of his hand that was under the water would totally disappear. He stuck his head back under the water. Again, it was totally black. Light could not penetrate the surface of the water, it simply reflected at the top.

At first it was a small vibration, too small for Bydola to notice in the water but the land around him started to shake. The violence of the vibration increased and soon Bydola noticed the ever-increasing waves on the pond. They were soon about an arms height and were causing quite a bit of splashing. It was becoming hard to see because of the water splashing in his eyes.

He looked around him and noticed the trees swaying. At first, he was surprised but as the violence of the vibrations continued, he started to become scared. What was going on around him? He had heard of Giterquakes, but this experience made them seem very violent. He thought that when a Giterquake hit it would just be a slight vibration for a few minutes, and then it would end. But this was longer, much longer, and with a lot more violence.

Waves continued to slash against him. He couldn't decide what to do. Would he be safer on land, or was he safer in the water, away from the trees? The trees were whipping back and forth and occasionally branches would fall off and hit the ground.

Suddenly, before he had a chance to decide whether he should stay or go, something grabbed his foot. He was being pulled out toward the center of the pond. With all his strength he tried to counteract the force that had control of him, but he was helpless against the pull of whatever had a hold of his foot. He did his best trying to hop along when he touched the ground attempting to maintain his balance, but he was slowly and helplessly being pulled out toward the center of the pond.

The pond became deeper and deeper. Soon it reached shoulder height and he knew that he would not be able to maintain his balance much longer. The waves splashed up in his face. Finally, he slipped and went under. He fought to recover enough balance for just one more breath of fresh air, but it was too late. Whatever it was that had a hold of his foot was dragging him deeper and deeper down into the pond. It seemed as though there was no bottom. He continued being pulled deeper and deeper. He could feel the pressure of the increased water depth. He was being pulled down so quickly that his ears popped. He felt like he was being pulled to the very center of the earth.

Suddenly and in a very unusual and inexplicable way he fell out of the water and onto the dry ground of some underground tunnel. Whatever had previously held on to his leg had now let go of it. The water that he fell out of seemed to have a lower barrier. It just stopped similar to how it stops at the top of the lake. But this was the bottom. It didn't make sense. The water would not go below this arbitrary barrier.

He looked up and could see the water resting above his head looking much the same as if it were the surface of the little pond.

The pool of water was about an arm's length in circumference and it gave him an eerie feeling to see what he knew must be the water from the entire pond floating above his head. He couldn't identify anything that held the water in place.

His foot had strangely been released by whatever creature was pulling him down. He had never seen his captor. Other than being wet and the ringing in his ears that came from the buildup of water pressure he was unharmed.

He looked around and found himself in a small muddy tunnel. This tunnel had little lights along the walls sitting on rocks that stuck out from the edge of the tunnel. These lights glowed orange and gave off a light that made everything appear to have an orange tint.

He stood up and found the tunnel to be too low for him to stand fully upright. He would have to stoop over to walk through them. He reached out and picked up one of the orange lights and found them to be surprisingly cold. This seemed strange to him because he had always associated light with warmth or heat, but these lights were cold. To further confuse him they were rocks of some type that seemed to glow. He returned the rock to its perch.

He looked at the water above his head. It appeared as though he was looking into a puddle of water upside down. It gave him such a confused feeling that he wasn't sure if it was the water that was upside down or him. He reached into the water and found it similar to the pond above, as soon as his hand went into the water, his hand would disappear.

He splashed in the water and found it rippled much the same as any puddle of water that he was used to except it was upside down, and the splashes he made in the water fell up instead of down. He soon became so fascinated with the water that he found himself playing with it. He didn't notice the two small creatures watching him. After a while he looked down and noticed them standing there. Their presence startled him, and he jumped.

"Follow," one of the creatures said in a low raspy vibrating voice. Bydola could identify no distinguishable features such as a mouth from which the sound could have originated. The creatures looked like a glob of mud with arms and legs, but not much else.

The creatures started to move away from Bydola and headed down the tunnel. "Why have you captured . . ." Bydola started to question them but was suddenly interrupted in midsentence.

"No talk. We no hear," was the response.

Bydola felt frustrated. Where was he? What was he doing here? Then, as if the creatures had understood his thoughts, they said, "Mirror Pond have Water Quist. Water Quist bring you here."

"What's a quist?" Bydola asked not really expecting an answer since they couldn't understand him.

Bydola realized something strange. He wasn't limping. Just before he had jumped into the pond his leg was hurting so bad, he could hardly walk. But now he felt no pain at all. He reached down and rubbed his leg where he expected to find his bruise but felt nothing. How had he been healed? Questions where pounding in his head.

Then the creatures continued their explanation, "You follow us. We bring you to Creator."

CHAPTER ELEVEN

THE CREATOR

Morning arrived in Giter with few surprises. Elasti and Obydon sent Yanon for food and he successfully returned with a tray of assorted goodies. "How should we spend the morning?" Yanon asked. "One of the things we'll have to do this morning is visit Bydola and inform him that this business with the king is going to take longer than we anticipated. But we don't all need to go along for that. Beyond that, what should we do?"

"There are only two choices that suit me," commented Elasti, "either we stay in this room or we spend the morning with Bydola. I have no interest in getting involved with lepelves."

The three leprechauns ate their meal quickly and decided to set out together for Bydola's camp. As they walked out of the front door of the tavern, Yanon returned the empty food tray to the tavern owner's son.

While they were walking toward the west end of town, Yanon thought he saw Gilbon off in the distance, but he wasn't sure because whoever he saw mysteriously slipped behind a house. Yanon didn't comment on the event because it didn't seem important at the time.

Soon they were out of town. They headed west down the South Road hoping they would quickly encounter Bydola's camp. They had traveled about fifteen minutes when Yanon commented, "I should have known that Bydola would get as far away from Giter as possible. I should have made sure he stayed closer. We'll probably end up walking half the way to the Kilo Pass."

They continued on, and it wasn't until another ten minutes had passed before they spotted Mirror Pond along the left side of the road. "That looks like a perfect place to set up camp," commented Obydon, pointing to a clearing by the pond. "I think I see Bydola's pack on the little knoll there."

"Yes, I think you're right," added Amins, "But where's Bydola?"

"Let's go look."

The three walked over to where Bydola's pack had been spotted and looked around. Bydola was nowhere to be seen. His clothes were lying by the edge of the pond. "I wonder where he went. I can't see him anywhere," commented Obydon.

"He couldn't have gone too far if he left his clothes lying at the edge of the pond," thought Yanon out loud. "Maybe he went for a swim."

"What bothers me is that he didn't set up his tent for the night," commented Elasti. "It's still packed together into his pack. There doesn't seem to be any sign of him having spent the night here, there's no fire and not even a sleeping bag laid out. I hope nothing has happened to him."

The three decided to build a fire for Bydola. They planned to wait an hour or two. Surely, he would show up by then. Yanon and Obydon worked on the fire. Elasti decided to take a stroll around the pond to see if he could find any sign of Bydola. By the time he had made it all the way around the pond an hour had passed and when he returned, the fire was blazing. Elasti expressed his concern, "I didn't see any sign of him coming out of the pond, anywhere. I can see footsteps going toward the pond close to where his clothes are, but I can't find any sign of his departure. If he drowned, we should be able to see him floating on the surface of the pond. I don't see anything."

"I'll bet he just laid himself down in those flowers over there and fell asleep," commented Obydon." You know how he likes his naps. You probably just missed his exit because of the grass that's grown in so thick over there." He pointed toward the other side of the pond, where a field of yellow flowers could be seen.

Elasti shook his head in disagreement, but he didn't argue because the thought of something serious having happened to Bydola scared him and he didn't want to generate that same fear in the other two.

The hours passed by and it was getting into the third hour of their wait. They still saw no sign of Bydola. The three travelers had to get back to Giter for their noon appointment with the king, so they scribbled a note telling him about their delays and attached it to his pack.

The walk back to Giter was quiet. Bydola had been gone for so long and he still had not set up camp. They were all worried.

Back in Giter they headed directly for the tavern. Gilbon should be arriving soon to have lunch with them before they went to the palace. As they entered Gabrona waved at them trying to get their attention. He walked over to them swiftly and held a slip of paper toward them. "Gilbon was here earlier and asked me to give you this. He said he won't be able to meet you for lunch."

"I hope nothing's gone wrong," commented Yanon with concern as he reached for the note. He read the note out loud for his friends to hear. "The king has called a goose hunting expedition for this morning and I had to go with. I'll contact you when I return," sighed Gilbon.

"You mean he just took off on us?" blurted Elasti in a voice filled with irritation, forgetting that Gabrona was still standing close by. "These lepelves have no respect for anyone."

"Yes, we do," responded Gabrona defensively, "the king's got important things he has to do."

"Yeah, like goose hunting," returned Elasti.

"What's the problem?" The tavern owner noticed the conversation between the leprechauns and his son and came over to find out what was going on.

"We were scheduled to meet with the king this afternoon and we just found out he took off on a wild goose chase." It was Yanon talking.

"Don't tell me he's out running around in the fields again." The tavern keeper was outraged. "This is crazy. Nobody in the whole city even likes geese, yet our fearless leader insists on running out after them."

"Why do you feel nobody likes geese?" questioned Elasti.

"You know that little pond next to the palace," the tavern owner continued, "well there are three geese in that pond, and nobody in the whole city has bothered to catch them and eat them. That tells me that nobody likes geese." Elasti and Obydon looked at each other in surprise. "Add to that geese don't even fly through here for another two months. He just does this every time he wants to get away from that naggy wife of his. Last time he did this he was gone for three weeks with two thirds of our police force gone with him. Crime in the city was outrageous. But why am I telling you foreign spies this? You'll just end up using it against me."

"Do you know any way for us to catch up with the king?" Yanon asked.

"Sure, I do," the tavern owner responded, "my son Gabrona can take you there. For the right price. But he won't be able to go until tomorrow morning. I need him around here today."

"What do you consider the right price?" asked Yanon. After some negotiation, a price was settled on, but it was impossible to get the tavern owner to allow them to leave that same day. They would leave the next morning at daybreak.

Giterod, the king's aid sat quietly in a corner of the tavern sipping on a mug of ale as he listened intently to the conversation. As the discussion ended and the leprechauns headed off to their room he got up and hurried out of the tavern.

"Who's this Creator?" Bydola asked, forgetting that the creatures he was following couldn't hear him. He desperately tried to keep up with the mud creatures.

"We muidivengers. We help Creator."

Bydola gave up trying to get sensible information out of the creatures. He decided to wait until he met this Creator and hoped that he would be able to get an explanation of what had happened.

They arrived at a larger tunnel that was higher and much wider and turned left. Bydola was now able to stand up straight and he could walk with ease. The journey continued for another half hour. They passed many side tunnels leading off in all directions. It was as though Bydola had encountered an entire city of underground tunnel dwellings, and he felt as though he was walking down the main street of the city. Often other muidivengers would appear busily walking in and out of tunnels as if their mad activity all had some purpose.

They arrived at a tunnel with a very large opening, larger than any they had encountered previously. The opening to this tunnel was even wider than the tunnel they were currently in. Upon entering Bydola noticed that the room was almost an exact circle. It made Bydola feel as though he had entered into a ball. It seemed as if he was standing at the bottom of this enormous ball.

The muidivengers immediately bowed down to the floor paying homage to what appeared to be a large, cubic, polished rock that was floating and slowly spinning in the center of this cylindrical tunnel. This rock wasn't being suspended by anything noticeable to Bydola.

The tunnel was enormous, so much so that Bydola was at least three leprechauns away from the spinning rock. Its surfaces were smooth with no decorations. The only discernible blemish in the entire structure was the entrance through which he had just come.

The smoothly polished rock glowed in an orange light that filled the entire room. This was the same rock light that lit the tunnels he had walked through previously but the brightness of this new rock was so strong that the entire room shone even brighter than he had ever seen the sunshine. But it was a strange mysterious light. He could look directly at the light and not have his vision affected. He was stunned. Was this rock supposed to be the Creator?

"Rise my friends and leave me alone with him," came what sounded like a calm, gentle, elderly voice. The voice seemed to emanate from all directions of the tunnel at once, but Bydola guessed that it must have come from the rock and then echoed throughout the tunnel. The muidivengers reacted as if they were somehow able to understand this Creator. They rose off the ground and left the room. They closed the door behind them. With the door closed Bydola could find no outline of the door to mar the inner surface of the tunnel. It was as if the door had never existed.

Bydola found it difficult to form words. He had so much he wanted to ask but found himself too captivated to talk.

"You need me," spoke the Creator. "You hope to defeat the Kabul, yet you know little of what you risk. Krakus has found power by aligning with the root of all evil. I am proud of the leprechauns in what they are attempting. I am proud of their strength. Unfortunately, the power of evil needs more than merely high-spirited and strong-willed leprechauns for it to be defeated. I have selected you to be my prophet and to wield the power of balance and equity. I will give to you the Protee. The Protee is the power to offset evil with good. Do you accept this power?"

"I'm not sure what you're asking me," started Bydola but then the Creator cut in with an explanation.

"The Protee is the power to suppress the influence of the spiritual evil one. By suppressing this influence, you will be left with only needing to contend with mortal enemies not spiritual ones. Once this offset is achieved, the residents of Small World will stand a chance against Krakus. They will have the power that will give them a chance for success.

"I have selected you to carry this power because only you have the physical strength to endure this power within you. You must wield it with care. You will learn how to use it as you need it. However, I give you little knowledge you don't already have. I only open your eyes to it! Are you ready to receive this power?"

"I'm not sure. But if one of the leprechauns must have it in order to defeat Krakus, it may as well be me. Before I go, let me ask you a question."

"Speak."

Bydola reacted in typical leprechaun style, "If you're the Creator, and if you have all this power, why do you need me at all? Why don't you just go and defeat the Kabul and let us leprechauns return to our homes in safety?"

The Creator gave a brief explanation, "I cannot destroy the free agency of anyone. I cannot force anyone's direction. But I can see that in the future Krakus will be pursuing evil, and that he will be flooding Small World with evil alliances and even though I cannot interfere with his freedom of choice to do so I can instill a force of good into someone such as yourself, in order to offset that evil, but only if you are willing to take on this force of good which is the Protee. You will understand this and much more once the power has been instilled in you. Are you willing to take this power upon you?"

"Yes," Bydola still wasn't sure what he was getting into, but he didn't dare say no if this Protee was critical for the welfare of the world he loved.

"Go now, the muidivengers will place you in a chamber where you will sleep for many days. During this time, you will be trained. Your mind will be filled with enlightenment and intelligence. You must have this intelligence in order to wield the power of Protee wisely. At the end of this time you will be blessed with the power." The voice fell silent and the brightness in the room seemed to dim a little. Bydola felt as though the Creator was leaving him even though he hadn't seen him, only heard him speak.

Slowly the tunnel door again opened. As Bydola left the room he found the muidivengers waiting for him. They led him off to a small chamber that contained only a bed. It reminded him of a tomb. He entered and as instructed he started to lie down on the bed. Then he noticed the muidivengers closing off the entrance by rolling a large rock in front of it which made it very dark. This gave him an eerie, confined feeling. He began to lie down and as soon as his head hit the surface of the rock, all sense of awareness was gone.

Outside, high above mirror pond, at the very top of a tree an eagle sat and waited for the return of Bydola.

The day had come to an end and it was dark outside. Obydon and Elasti had taken up their usual hibernation in their room, trying to avoid contact with the lepelves. Yanon had left earlier journeying back to Bydola's camp in order to update him on their activities. He was just returning to the room, "I'm worried about Bydola. The note we left him was still hanging on his bag just the way we left it and there was no sign of him anywhere. Everything was just as we left it. I walked around the pond like you did Elasti and found nothing."

"I don't see where we have any other choice but to trust that he's alright," Obydon tried to assure his worried friends. "He's big enough to take care of himself. By saying that you saw no sign of him, you're also saying that you saw no sign of trouble. We have no choice but to assume that he's safe."

"That might be easy for you to say," threw in Elasti, "but his disappearing like this and our not knowing what has happened to him worries me a lot."

"While you were gone, I got an idea on how we might attract the attention of the king." Obydon was trying to get their minds off the gloomy subject of Bydola's disappearance.

"What's this bright idea of yours?" asked Elasti.

"We know that the king is hunting for geese. And we know that there are three geese in the pond next to the palace. What if we helped the king find his goose?"

"Yeah, then we can help the king cook his goose, and if we're lucky maybe we'll even get to eat some of it too," added Elasti.

"So, what are you suggesting we do," asked Yanon, "kidnap the royal goose?"

"Obviously!"

It wasn't long before Yanon and Obydon were hiding in the bushes at the edge of the royal pond just to the side of the palace. They were using this opportunity to look out over the pond for any sign of the geese. Elasti had stayed behind. Three leprechauns weren't needed for this little expedition, and someone should stay at the tavern in the event that news of the king arrived.

"Do you see anything?" Yanon whispered.

"Not a thing. It's too dark," Obydon responded.

"Shush. There's a guard over there by the side of the palace." Yanon pointed in the direction he wanted Obydon to look.

"I see him, but I don't see any geese." Then Obydon said in a quiet but excited voice, "I spoke too soon. Here comes one now swimming right close to us." The two were perched on the edge of the pond about a half leprechaun up off the surface of the water. The area was thick with bushes. He quickly grabbed onto a cluster of bush branches and tried to hang out over the pond, hoping he would go unnoticed by both the goose and the guard. He hung there in ambush waiting to grab the goose as it swam by.

Unfortunately, the branches he had selected to grab a hold of had long been dead and by now were rotted and weak. Before he realized his mistake, the branches broke, and he plunged headfirst into the pond still clinging desperately to the branch that was now falling into the water with him. He splashed around in the water making quite a fuss trying to regain his composure and at the same time keep from drowning.

"Quiet down," whispered Yanon, "are you trying to wake up the whole palace?"

"I can't swim!" blurted Obydon frantically.

Yanon slid down the embankment and into the water to retrieve Obydon hoping by some miracle the guard wouldn't take notice of the fuss. After dragging him to shore the two quickly scurried back to their hiding places behind the bush. They looked for the guard. They had lost sight of him in all the excitement.

Then suddenly a voice not more than two leprechauns away from them blurted, "Was that you making all that fuss, you silly goose." It was dark and the two hadn't seen the guard who had come around to investigate the cause of the ruckus. Luckily just then the goose that they had tried to catch was splashing in the water close to shore. It was still frantic over Obydon's sudden entry into the pond.

"Quit making all that noise," the guard continued, "you scared the heck out of me." Yanon and Obydon didn't move. They were even afraid to breathe for fear the guard would hear them. Then the guard turned and walked back around the pond toward the palace.

Yanon and Bydola breathed a sigh of relief. Just then they noticed a second goose swimming close to the bush where they were hiding. "You stay here and keep quiet," Yanon whispered to Obydon as he crawled around the side of the bush.

Obydon could see very little of what Yanon was doing when suddenly he heard a goose squawk followed by silence. Yanon came rushing by. "Hurry up! Let's go!" he whispered as he hastily tried to get as far away from the pond as possible.

Obydon was right behind. "What'd you do? Kill it?"

"I'm trying to hold his beak shut, but he gave me a good bite. Let's just get back to our room before anyone asks us any questions."

The two tried to stay off the main road so that they wouldn't be noticed with their goose. They went around to the back side of the tavern and knocked on the window of their room.

Elasti opened the window. He had been waiting for them. He had prepared a small piece of cord with which to tie the beak shut and he had a blanket with which to wrap the bird so that it could be kept as quiet as possible.

Yanon and Obydon also climbed in through the window. They didn't want to go through the tavern soaking wet. When Elasti saw them, he asked them what had happened. After hearing the story, he burst out laughing unable to control himself.

It was the morning of the fifth day since Yanon, Obydon, and Elasti had left their homes in Amins. They were getting prepared to start on their journey to find the king when a knock on their door startled them. Yanon opened the door and found Gabrona standing there, "Are you ready?" he asked.

"You bet!" Yanon was surprised to find a lepelf as eager as Gabrona. He anticipated having to go and drag him out of bed but here he was ready to get going.

Gabrona was still a youngster, only about nine years old, but he had taken on an important role in the operation of the tavern. He took care of the rooms, cleaned the tables, and did any of the other work that no one else was willing to do. Unfortunately, his father found it necessary to keep the boy out of school in order to do all these chores and this meant that he would probably never be anything more than a tavern keeper himself.

"I've packed a sack of food for us so we can eat breakfast and lunch without stopping," Gabrona commented.

"That's a great idea," Obydon remarked. "Thanks a lot!"

They kept the goose a secret. They realized they would eventually have to share this secret with Gabrona, but they would delay this eventuality until the very last minute. They had packed the poor creature into Yanon's backpack. It had lost most of its energy to fight long ago, having resigned itself to its plight.

They finished their preparations and were off. They left the tavern by a back door and headed north, in the direction of Kolak Falls. "The king likes the falls. He always goes up in that direction, and often he'll spend weeks just sitting at the bottom of the falls enjoying the scenery."

"Kolak Falls!" interjected Yanon. "That's at least two days travel from here. I didn't realize we'd have to travel that far."

"Don't worry," commented Gabrona, "the king moves slowly. He doesn't rush anything. He only travels a few hours each day. My guess is we'll catch up with him early this afternoon. He'll already have set up camp."

"I sure hope so," returned Yanon.

The lepelves had developed an abundance of superstitions about the Amins Groves. They avoided them as much as possible. Hunting expeditions of this type were always directed to the north of Giter where the lepelves felt safer. Traveling through these grassy fields wasn't as easy as traveling along the South Road but the knee-high grass didn't hamper their progress significantly. Often, they would find a hunter's trail which allowed them to move swiftly.

"What's this all about?" asked Gabrona. "Why do you three have to see the king so badly?"

"We think that the Kabul is going to attack and so we're trying to warn your king so that he can prepare the lepelves for any possible danger." Elasti was trying to explain the situation without giving away any of the details.

"Does the king know the reason why you're here?" asked Gabrona.

"I don't know."

"I'm sure he does," interjected Yanon. "I told Gilbon about our fears and I'm sure he would have passed that news on to the king."

"I don't understand," continued Gabrona, "why are you having so much trouble getting a chance to see him? He should be eager to hear your story."

"We're not sure," returned Yanon, "unless it's because he's afraid of getting the people worked up."

Gabrona was left in thought. He knew that the leprechauns wouldn't be able to answer his questions about the king's lack of interest. He would have to get them answered for himself.

The day drug on. The foursome had been traveling four hours when they encountered what appeared to have been a large campsite. "This is where they spent the night last night," Gabrona commented. "We're halfway there. Let's move a little faster so we can catch them by early afternoon."

Gabrona was able to walk faster than the other three. Lepelves were slightly taller which gave them a longer stride. To Gabrona it felt as if the leprechauns were barely crawling. He tried to encourage them on as much as possible.

Traveling would be easier now. Having successfully found the first camp of the king the foursome were now able to follow the trail his group had left. The grass was beaten down and they now knew exactly in what direction to travel in order to catch up with the hunting party.

They journeyed on eating lunch as they continued to travel, staying in hot pursuit of the king and his party. It was shortly after they had traveled a total of about ten hours, when in the distance they saw what they were sure was smoke. "We've found them," yelled Gabrona cheerfully jumping in the air to show his excitement. "Now I'll leave you three leprechauns and head back home."

"What?" Yanon was surprised at this announcement. "You're not going to help us get an audience with the king?"

"That wasn't part of the plan," declared Gabrona. "I was just going to show you where he was."

"That's not what we paid you for. We paid you to get us to the king. All you've done is to show us his smoke."

Gabrona was confused. His father had instructed him to return home after sighting the king's camp. Which was right? Should he stay or should he go? Then the idea struck him that by staying he might be able to find answers to some of the questions that had been bothering him. "Alright. I'll stay long enough to get you a meeting with the king. But then I've got to get going."

The four continued on toward the smoke of the camp. Soon they recognized the camp. It was made up of at least twenty lepelves. As they approached the camp, they noticed a large tent decorated lavishly in the center of the camp. By its appearance it had to be the tent of the king.

"Halt, who goes there?" It was one of the guards at the perimeter of the camp yelling out to the little party.

"It's Gabrona, the tavern keeper's son, and the three visitors from Amins," responded Gabrona.

"You can come ahead but the foreigners have to wait," returned the guard.

Gabrona proceeded toward the guard. He explained why he was there and asked if he could talk to the king about meeting with the leprechauns. The guard granted him permission to enter the camp, but the leprechauns would have to wait outside the camp until the king gave his approval allowing them to enter.

Gabrona was brought into the king's tent. The interior of the tent was even more lavish than the exterior. The floors were lined with furs and rugs and a wooden throne was placed near the back of the tent. "Sire, you have a visitor who came to us from Giter." The introduction was made by a guard.

The king was sitting on this throne talking to Giterod when the interruption occurred. "What brings you all the way out here chasing after me?" he asked Gabrona.

"Three leprechauns have paid me to bring them out here. They desperately want an audience with you. They say it's very important and that the Kabul is going to attack."

"That's absurd! They're just trying to scare us for some hidden purpose. I just haven't figured out what it is yet."

Gabrona was stunned. How could the king take the safety of his people so lightly? This was too important for him to ignore. "Please Sire," pleaded Gabrona, "I think they're serious about the attack. They're going to follow you to the Kolak Falls and back again if that's what it takes in order for them to get an audience with you."

"Oh alright! Alright," puffed the king. "If there's no other way to get rid of them, I guess I'll have to see them." Then turning to the guard, he said, "Guard, bring the leprechauns here."

The king then turned to Giterod and whispered, so that Gabrona couldn't hear, "Get out of sight, but not so far that you can't hear what's going on. I may need you later."

Giterod bowed and left the tent. Within a few minutes the guard returned with Yanon, Obydon, and Elasti. They were presented before the king and he gruffly asked, "What do you three want? You've been pestering me for two days now and I'm getting tired of it."

"Your Honor," Yanon started, but then the king interrupted.

"I'm not a 'Your Honor', I'm a 'Sire'!" the king barked.

"Sorry Sire," Yanon tried again. "We have been sent to you by the Council of Amins to report distressing news." With that Yanon told of the efforts for the first expedition and of how Elasti had been sent out. Then Elasti proceeded to relate his story detailing the events that had happened to him on the Albo Pass.

The king acted bored and disinterested but Yanon picked up the conversation after Elasti had finished, "We have come to Giter for two purposes. First, we were sent to warn you of the pending danger in hopes that your people might prepare your city for the eventual threat. And second, we came to ask for your support on our second expedition to the North Groves."

"This is crazy,'" blurted the king. "If Lord Krakus was going to attack us, why didn't he come straight down from the Kabul and do it? Why fool around with the Albo Pass?"

"We don't know what his plans are," returned Yanon, "but why would he capture the Albo Pass if not to divide the North and the South. We believe he intends to disrupt that unity for some purpose, and we believe it is to weaken us so he can gain his ultimate revenge."

"Those fool leprechauns that went up the Albo Pass got what they deserved. They've got no business poking their noses in where they don't belong. Heading north was a fool idea."

Elasti became flushed. Saying that his friends' deaths were stupid and that they simply got what they deserved was more than he could handle. He was about to verbally tear into the king when Yanon put his hand on his shoulder and addressed the king further, "The loss of those leprechauns may end up saving your hide. We should show respect for their deaths."

The king was undaunted. "Why are you bothering us with this?" he questioned. "Why not go to Gije and get the help of the elves. They're dumb enough to go along with your fool plan."

"We feel that Giter may well be the first city in the Southern Plains to be attacked. That is why we feel you need to make preparations. Also, we have sent a party to Gije via the back road. They should be arriving there soon, and we have hopes that they will gain support from the elves as well."

"Now I know you're crazy," blurted the king waving his arms and throwing his head back in an attempt to add emphasis to his statement. "Even the elves aren't fool enough to go along the back road because of all the werewolves. Yet you send leprechauns down the back road to Gije. You must all be insane."

Yanon, Elasti, and Obydon stared at each other. Was this true? Had Hasko, Hiztin, and Jesves been sent on a suicide mission with a risk of werewolves in the area? No one amongst the leprechauns seemed to know anything about werewolves. This was a complete surprise. Fear swelled up in each of their minds. "Is this true?" questioned Elasti. "Are there really werewolves along the back road?"

"Why do you think the elves quit traveling that road?" asked the king. "Of course, there are werewolves on the back road. You won't be seeing those guys again. I'll tell you what I think. I think you three are planning something. I'm not sure why but you're trying to get the lepelves of Giter all excited over nothing because of some scheme of yours. What are you up to anyway?"

But Elasti was skeptical. Why aren't the gnomes afraid of the werewolves? Why were they able to successfully control the pass between the north and the south for all this time with no problem? But before he could speak up Yanon jumped in.

"Sire," Yanon was desperate. He had to resort to his last appeal. "We have brought evidence of our sincerity. We have brought the Southern Sword which we plan to unite with the Northern Sword." Then he turned to Obydon, "Show him the sword."

Obydon pulled the sword from it sheathe. He had the handle wrapped up so that the elegance of the sword's handle could not be seen. He unwrapped it and displayed the sword in its full glory. Once deprived of its cover, the sword was again surrounded with a bright yellow glow.

"Wow!" gasped Gabrona when he saw the sword.

The king's mouth fell open in surprise. "Is that really the Southern Sword?" he questioned finding it hard to believe that Amaz would allow it out of his control.

Obydon walked over to the king and showed him the jewels in its handle. "I can't believe your council would risk this treasure on something as foolish as an expedition to the North Groves." He was especially impressed with the green jewel in its handle and the amber light it emitted.

"Does this demonstrate our sincerity in what we are planning to do?" questioned Yanon.

"AII this demonstrates is your foolishness!" returned the king. "Dwarfs are an ugly sort. They are fat slobs that I would rather not deal with. It was a welcome event to me when they quit coming through Giter to plague us with the garbage they were trying to sell. Why would you trust them with the Southern Sword? They'll just end up stealing it from you."

Yanon continued, "There's more at stake here than just dwarfs. The safety of the South is being threatened with invasion. Will you help us?"

"Let me think about it. Come back tomorrow and I'll let you know," was the king's response.

The three leprechauns thanked the king for listening to them and promised that they would return in the morning. Obydon wrapped up the sword and returned it to its protective case.

As they walked away, Elasti shared his thoughts with his companions. "I saw a dwarf in the city the last time I was here. As the three of us were leaving the city, we saw what I know was a dwarf and what looked like it might have been a gnome down one of the side alleys. Then they suddenly disappeared. I'm not sure what all that means. The king is playing games with us. He's the one with an agenda, and I have no idea what it is."

"I agree," replied Yanon. "But I also have no idea what it all means."

Elasti continued, "I'm also concerned about the werewolves. Why didn't we know about the werewolves?"

"It's been so long since anyone has traveled that way," commented Yanon sympathetically, "I guess no one remembered the dangers." Elasti was concerned. The whole reason for his coming along on this journey was to prevent harm to anyone else. Were his three companions in danger?

"I wish there was some way we could warn Bydola and the party coming with the elves that there may be werewolves in the area," thought Obydon out loud. Unfortunately, each of the three realized they were helpless. All they could do was hope and pray for their safety.

Elasti added to their torture by commenting, "I've been wondering what has happened to Bydola. I hope he hasn't encountered the gnomes or now the werewolves."

Yanon felt stupid. Had he sent Bydola to his doom by sending him down the South Road alone? "No. I don't think that's right," he continued his thoughts out loud. "If it was gnomes, they would have taken his pack or at least dug through it. I didn't notice any footprints except Bydola's and ours. I don't think his disappearance has anything to do with the gnomes or werewolves for that matter."

This comforted Elasti slightly, but he continued, "I'll be glad when we get back to his camp and find him."

Gabrona had been carefully listening to all the conversations of the day. He thought Yanon, Elasti, and Obydon had been very convincing about the pending danger. Yet the king treated the news with contempt. Gabrona had decided in his mind that he would wait till morning to see how the king would respond. He couldn't understand how the king could remain so neutral about the threat posed to Giter? He would see what happened and then report the results of the meeting to his father. "I'll be spending the evening here with you guys if you don't mind," he commented to the three leprechauns.

"Sure. That's fine," Yanon returned. "Then you can help us get an audience with the king in the morning."

Gabrona felt a little braver. Obydon's Sword of the South had been bothering him and now he felt he could ask. "Would you mind if I held the Southern Sword? I've never seen anything that magnificent in my life."

"Of course," commented Obydon, and he pulled the sword out of its sheathe and unwrapped it. He handed the sword to Gabrona and the boy held it as if it were a fragile baby. He stared at it and studied it in wonderment and awe. He had never experienced such magnificence and beauty in a sword.

After a few moments he handed it back to Obydon. "Thank you."

Yanon saw the need to liven everyone's spirits and attempted to change the mood of the group by involving them in some activities. "Now that you've got your sword out let's do a little training. Obydon, since we have the rest of the evening to waste, perhaps we should start our sword training." The threat to Hasko, Hiztin, Jesves, and Bydola had made Yanon suddenly aware that his group might also be in some danger.

"I'll go for that," commented Elasti. "I was hoping we would get the chance to do some training soon. I want to be as prepared as possible if we're going to run into gnomes and werewolves."

Yanon walked over to an open, grassy area and Obydon and Elasti followed.

By the light of the campfire Yanon proceeded to teach them the battle stance and how they should defend themselves with the sword. Then he demonstrated some forms of attack. Obydon and Elasti practiced these for several hours. "You two are quick learners," Yanon complemented proudly. "Let's try a skirmish. Elasti, you face me and try your defense and attack moves."

Elasti was hesitant but he knew that Yanon was not out to hurt him and so he proceeded. Gabrona watched intently, paying close attention as though this knowledge might be vital to him some day.

Then Yanon turned to Obydon and asked him to do the same. They started. At first the skirmish was just a battle of avoidance and no contact was made. Obydon felt as though something wasn't right. This swordplay had some innate danger in it that he couldn't identify. perhaps he was just afraid of damaging the Southern Sword in some way. "Attack me," Yanon insisted, and Obydon did. His sword came down toward Yanon's head and Yanon moved his sword into position to meet the blow.

A spark of bright light flashed from the point where the two swords touched. It was as though lightning had struck at the very point where the two swords met. Yanon fell to the ground as if all the life had suddenly been taken from him. Obydon stood stunned. He had felt a strong surge of power emanate through the sword, but it seemed as though the source of that power originated from the very depths of his soul. The experience left him as stunned as it did Yanon.

Elasti ran to the side of Yanon. He was still breathing but it was as if he had fainted. He noticed that Yanon's sword had been scarred black at the point where the two swords had impacted. "What did you do to him?" Elasti asked Obydon.

"I don't know what happened. It was as though the sword suddenly surged with power. It took over for me." Obydon knelt down beside Yanon to see if there was anything he could do to help.

"We better get him back to camp and make him comfortable," commented Elasti. "Hopefully he'll recover soon."

The two attempted to pick him up but as they tried to move him, he let out a loud groan. Quickly they laid him back on the ground and just then he opened his eyes. "What happened?" Yanon questioned Obydon.

"The Southern Sword has some strange power in it, and it took over for me. It was as if it stung your sword with a bolt of lightning."

"Well we're not going to use that sword for practice anymore." Yanon tried to sit up but his strength had been drained. He fell back to the ground in a heap. "I think I'll just lay here and rest for a while till I get my strength back."

The remainder of the evening was uneventful. Obydon and Elasti made dinner, and about the time they were finishing their cooking Yanon came to join them. He still felt weak, but he was strong enough to walk around. Then they rested and chatted about the events of the evening including the strange power of the sword. Soon after that they went to bed.

Yanon couldn't fall asleep quite as quickly as his companions. He spent several hours wondering what he should do if the expedition from Gije didn't arrive as anticipated at the Tako Ruins. Should he go to Gije and look for them. Or should he head north without them? And what if King Gorbot refuses his request of aid? Then there would only be four to head to the North Groves. And if they couldn't find Bydola there would only be three left. What chance would three have against a hoard of gnomes? He had to make it North but the chances of making it looked slimmer all the time.

Bydola was lost. He was in a maze of some type, a maze of tunnels. He had been working his way through these tunnels for what seemed like several hours. He knew that he had to make the correct turns, or he would never be able to escape. Fortunately, correct turns seemed to be high-lighted by successively brighter tunnels whereas wrong turns seemed to grow darker. But he never knew if his decision was right or wrong until he had committed himself by entering the next tunnel.

He had come to the intersection of four tunnels, all of which looked dark and forbidding. But he knew that the direction he had just left behind him didn't contain the exit he needed. He looked down the first tunnel, but it just didn't 'feel' right. The second one felt a lot better. He started to enter it but suddenly as he crossed the threshold of the tunnel, he found himself in what appeared to be a tunnel with whirling light. At first it gave him a dizzying, nauseating feeling but slowly he became accustomed to the circular motion. He walked forward and found it curious that the intensity of the light would continually increase the further he went into the tunnel. The light was an orange light much like the one he encountered when he was with the Creator. And its intensity didn't seem to affect his eyes.

He went on slowly. The spinning stopped having an effect on him. He was becoming obsessed with the intensity of the light hoping to be able to find its source. He moved on. Slowly he could see an image starting to form in the distance in front of him. It appeared to be the image of a man, but he wasn't sure. He continued forward and the light became brighter. His anticipation of what he was about to encounter caused his heart to beat wildly. The excitement became unbearable.

Then he heard a voice, "Abogidyide, Abogidyide". It seemed to be calling out to someone, but he was the only one there.

"I'm Bydola," he responded.

"Abogidyide," the voice repeated. It appeared to be the image in the distance calling out to him. "Abogidyide, Abogidyide," it repeated over and over again.

"I'm Bydola!" Bydola responded with insistence. He couldn't understand why he was being called by this strange name.

Suddenly Bydola's eyes opened. He had been asleep, and something had awakened him. He felt bewildered and frustrated. He was bewildered because the experience seemed so real, yet he was frustrated because he was not allowed to see it to its conclusion. He was not allowed to meet the image at the end of the tunnel. He felt cheated somehow, yet he also knew that the reason he was not allowed to approach this image any closer was because he was not yet ready for the experience. He was not yet ready to be in the presence of a light quite that bright.

Bydola was still lying on the slab where he had been put to sleep. The stone door to his tomb was still in place. An orange rock had been placed on a small ledge above his head and the light from this rock gave the chamber a bright orange tint.

He felt different somehow. He wasn't quite sure how. It was as if the experience in the maze had fulfilled him somehow. He felt older but also wiser and more knowledgeable. He felt as though he could sense human-like feeling in the walls that surrounded him as though life itself projected out from them. His head felt light and yet filled to the point of explosion with a new knowledge. He couldn't identify that knowledge, but its presence was unmistakable.

Suddenly the stone door started to roll away from the entrance of the chamber. Two muidivengers stood at the entrance to greet him. "Creator wants you. Come."

"How can I refuse an invitation like that?" he asked himself. The Creator and his importance took on a new meaning to him. He felt a respect and a love for this Creator though he knew not why. He followed the creatures back to the chamber where he had encountered the Creator before. This time when the muidivengers bowed, so did Bydola. He was overcome by the love that flowed from the Creator's presence.

"I see the change that has come over you is good," the Creator began. "Now you are filled with a knowledge of good and evil which will come forth in you when it is needed. You will be able to discern sickness and health and good and evil. From this knowledge you will be able to keep your companions on the true and correct road.

"I give to you two more gifts. The first is the Staff of Protee. With this staff you are given the power to expel evil from your presence." Suddenly a staff, slightly taller than he was, and about the thickness of his wrist appeared in front of him. He reached out and took a hold of it as though it had been an old companion of his.

"I also give you the gift of light." Suddenly one of the orange rocks appeared in front of him. He reached for it and received it as it miraculously drifted into his hand. He studied it for a few moments, turning it over and over as if he was looking for some opening. He came to the conclusion that it was just a rock that happened to glow. He placed it in his pocket as though he was totally familiar and comfortable with its power. Then the Creator came forth with a warning, "Use this power wisely or else it will be taken from you!"

The Creator continued, "The danger that exists in Small World is not just that of the Kabul. The real danger lies in the dark alliance with evil which Krakus has made. Look deeper for the truth in all you do. You will be my spokesman and my eyes for all events that are to come. I warn you again. If the power, you possess is not used wisely it will diminish within you. I give you one more command. Tell no one of what you have experienced here. It is beyond their comprehension and understanding. They will mock you and I will not be mocked. I will not allow the mockery of what is bright, right and good. Go now. Return to your world. Take care and be assured that my light and presence will always be with you."

Bydola bowed once again when the muidivengers bowed. A tear came to his eyes as he left the chamber. It was as though he were leaving his best friend. Somehow, he felt a closeness, as if he had known the Creator all his life. But he had only met him today.

He followed the muidivengers slowly back towards the bottom of mirror pond.

Chapter Twelve

GITEROD

It was the middle of the night and scattered clouds filled the sky. The stars gave off enough light for Giterod to barely make out where he was going. He walked silently and carefully toward the leprechaun camp. He hadn't actually ever seen the Southern Sword, but from all the fuss that the king was making about it, he knew it must be extraordinary.

He was now close enough to their camp that he was able to make out each of the leprechauns and Gabrona. He could also see two swords stacked near the center of camp and guessed that it was highly unlikely that either of these could be the Southern Sword. Not even leprechauns would be foolish enough to leave something so valuable exposed. He looked around to see if he could find a third sword. He found nothing. He thought that maybe one of the leprechauns would be sleeping with the sword, but he couldn't spot the sword next to any of them. There seemed to be no hope. He couldn't find it anywhere.

He decided to step into the center of camp to see if just by some crazy chance one of the two swords that was laying there was indeed the one, he was after. As he did so a small twig hidden under the grass snapped. It wasn't a loud sound; no louder than the chirp of the crickets, but it gave him a start. He looked around to see if anyone had moved. One of the leprechauns turned in this sleep but the rest of the camp lay silent as if the snap had gone unheard.

Giterod stooped down to take a closer look at the swords but could find nothing unusual about either of them. He knew that the handle of the Southern Sword was jewel studded, and neither of these swords fit that description.

"What do you want?" a loud voice blurted out behind him. Giterod jumped up and turned around quickly. He tried to cover his face with his hands so that he wouldn't be recognized. "Is this what you're looking for?"

It was the Southern Sword pointing straight up at his chest and being held by the leprechaun that had stirred earlier. Even in the dim light of the night, the sword shone a magnificent yellow. Giterod couldn't allow himself to be captured or even recognized. He turned away from the sword and started running. As he left the camp, he heard other voices stirring. Giterod ran as though all of the Kabul were coming after him. He headed towards the densest area of the grasses hoping to use the grass to lose any pursuers. He ran for at least fifteen minutes before he felt brave enough to look behind him. He was not being followed.

Now came the hard part. He would have to go back to King Gorbot and inform him that he had failed to get the sword. He circled around the side of the king's camp and entered the camp at a spot where he wouldn't be noticed. He proceeded directly to the king's tent. He knew that the king would be waiting up for news of his conquest.

Upon entering the tent, he found the king laying down and resting on his furs. "Did you get it?" the king asked with excitement.

"No. One of the leprechauns was pretending to sleep on it and when I tried to get it away from him the other leprechauns came after me with their swords. They were lying in ambush to get me." Giterod felt the need to make his failure sound more believable. "I was forced to flee for my life."

"You fool. I should never have trusted you. Did anyone recognize you?" asked the king.

"I don't think so. It was pretty dark, and everything happened so quickly."

The king instructed, "Here's what I want you to do so that you can recover from your blunder. Tomorrow those fool foreigners will come back to ask me to send an envoy from Giter to accompany them to the North Groves. You're to go with them. You're going to be that envoy and you're not to come back to Giter without that sword, do you understand me?"

"Yes sire," answered Giterod.

"Now get out of here and let me get some sleep," barked the king.

The sun was just creeping up into the sky when Obydon, Yanon, Gabrona, and Elasti started to get up. "I wish we would have gotten a better look at our visitor last night," commented Yanon.

"It was too dark to make out his face clearly even with the light generated by the sword, but by his clothes it was easy to tell he was a lepelf." Obydon was defensive about his failure to recognize the thief.

"We better report this to the king." Gabrona was concerned with the possibility that a lepelf would try to steal something so vital to the South. "I'm sure he'll want to punish whoever did this."

No one replied. They all believed the king could care less about the thief. "*In fact*," Yanon thought, "*the king's the only one who saw the sword. He's probably involved in the attempted theft.*" Yanon kept these thoughts to himself. He didn't want Gabrona upset at him just yet.

"Gabrona, as soon as you've eaten breakfast, I want you to go and see about our meeting with the king." Yanon was in a hurry to get going. He had spent a great deal of time trying to come up with counter plans in the event that any or all of Hasko, Hiztin, Jesves, and Bydola were lost. He could not let this expedition fail. He felt that staying with the lepelves any longer was just a waste of time. He would leave right after meeting with the king with or without his support.

Gabrona was also excited about finding out what the king had decided to do. He had fantasies of himself being declared a royal messenger to the North. That would make him feel really important to his friends. Gabrona gulped down his food and rushed off toward the king's camp.

Elasti had developed a parental concern for Gabrona during the time he had known him. "He's not like the rest of those lepelves. He's a nice kind. He deserves a better father than the one he got stuck with. Don't you think?"

"What are you going to do," asked Obydon jokingly, "adopt him? I'm not sure Jizeel will like that idea."

"I just think the kid deserves better, that's all," replied Elasti.

Breakfast discussions continued centered on either Gabrona or the events of the previous night. Obydon found himself deep in thought as well. He had a dream the previous night about how he should be the leader of this expedition, not Yanon. Yanon was just a policeman while Obydon was heir to the head of the council. Jealousy and resentment slowly started to build up in him when he remembered his father's words, "This will be an excellent opportunity for you to learn to lead. Remember, the best leader is one who knows best how to serve others. Leadership is serving others." This comment brought Obydon to the realization that maybe he wasn't fit to lead since he resented his role in serving. He must become a worthy leader and follower, or he might never be granted his seat on the council.

It wasn't long before Gabrona returned with a sour look on his face and gave his report to the team, "The king's taken off. He's sitting out in the fields somewhere waiting for a goose to fly by. The guard says the king doesn't like to be disturbed when he's on one of his early morning hunts and that he'll probably return in a couple hours. But he wasn't exactly sure how long it would take. I can't believe the king is so unconcerned about this danger to Giter. He must know something we don't know."

"Goose hunting!" blurted Obydon. "We forgot all about our goose. That poor devil has been packed away for two nights and a day. I wonder if he's still alive." Obydon started to unpack the goose while Elasti tried to explain their plan to Gabrona. He was concerned that Gabrona might not see the humor of the situation.

"You're going to give the king one of the royal geese to shoot at?" Gabrona was surprised. "That's the most sensible thing I've heard in a long time. Maybe then the king will come back to camp and we can get on with more serious business."

"I'll tell you what I'd like to do with that royal goose," Elasti started.

"Stop that Elasti," Obydon interrupted, "watch what you're saying." Obydon gave a nod toward Gabrona. Elasti took the hint and restrained himself from further comment.

"Do you have any idea where the king is?" Yanon asked Gabrona.

"I'm pretty sure we can find him. I know what direction he went."

The four set off, the goose still wrapped up and tucked away under Obydon's arm. They tried to walk as quietly as possible, refraining from talking. It wasn't long before they encountered the hideout of the king. The noise that emanated from there made it easy to find. "Apparently the king is on more of an ale hunt than a goose hunt by the sound of it," whispered Elasti sarcastically. "That group sounds like they're pretty well liquored up."

"That's putting it mildly," commented Yanon. "If we let this poor goose go, those clowns probably won't even see it."

"Oh well, we've come this far. Let's get it over with." Obydon was getting tired of carting the goose around and was quite happy to get rid of it. He unwrapped the goose and found it to be quite alive and frantic about escaping. It clawed scratched and flapped desperately trying to get away. Obydon untied its beak and let it belch out a squawk that immediately brought silence to the king's ale party. He continued to let the goose squawk a few more times just to make sure that it had gained the attention of the party. He didn't want the king looking into his bottle of ale instead of into the sky. Then Obydon threw the goose up in the air, and it immediately took off.

"Goose! Goose!" Almost immediately arrows began flying. The leprechauns and Gabrona had to duck low into the grass in order to avoid being hit by a stray arrow.

"We've shot the goose!" someone yelled. Yanon looked up in time to see the goose coming down with an arrow through its neck. "Let's go get it." A loud cheer could be heard from the king's hunting group.

Yanon whispered, "Hurry. Let's get out of here. They're going to come looking for the nest and if they catch us here there's going to be more than one goose cooked tonight."

Luckily the flight of the goose had taken the leprechauns out of the line of fire and the king's party went off searching in a different direction. "I'm not going to do that again," whispered Obydon. "That was dangerous. We nearly got shot!"

"If it gets the king back to his camp quicker it was worth it," commented Yanon who was eager to leave for the Tako Ruins.

"I'm not so sure it was worth it," returned Obydon.

After they had gotten out of earshot of the hunting party Gabrona started snickering. "That was funny. I wonder what they're going to do with that goose now that they've got it. No one wants to eat it anyway. And if they recognize that it's one of the royal geese there's really going to be some excitement back at the camp." His laughing made the others see the humor in the situation. They all got a good hearty laugh out of the situation.

"How do they decide which one of those arrows shot the goose anyway?" Yanon asked Gabrona.

"The king always gets credit for the kill no matter whose arrow makes the hit. And if two arrow's hit, they just say that someone got in a lucky shot. There was one occasion where the king was too drunk to shoot but he still got credit for it, even though he didn't fire an arrow."

Back at the leprechaun camp Yanon asked Gabrona to return to the king's camp and await his arrival. He wanted Gabrona to arrange for a meeting as soon as possible.

Gabrona departed immediately. He looked forward to seeing the eyes of the hunters when they returned with their prize.

The king did not return as quickly as was hoped. Gabrona found himself waiting about two hours in the king's camp before the king finally made his appearance.

The return of the king was noisy and excited. "I got a goose!" the king yelled out with excitement to the surprise and amazement of everyone in the camp. Everyone was sure that this hunting expedition was just another ale drinking party. No one truly expected the king to return with a goose. Cheers rang out throughout the camp. Everyone pretended to be pleased.

Gabrona decided to wait until some of the excitement had died down before he approached the king about the meeting. After the king had settled down in his tent, Gabrona approached him. "Sire."

"Yes. What do you want? Can't you see I'm busy? I just got a goose?"

"Yes sire, I heard," Gabrona found it very difficult to keep from laughing, "but I was hoping that you might be able to meet with the leprechauns again this morning."

"Oh yes that silly business about the Kabul. All right go get the fools."

"Thank you, sire." Gabrona turned and left the king's tent in order to fetch the threesome.

It was only a few minutes and Gabrona was back again with Yanon, Obydon, and Elasti. This time Yanon started the conversation. "Sire, have you come to a decision about sending lepelf representatives to accompany us on our journey to the North Groves?"

"Yes, yes," he replied impatiently. Then he turned to a guard standing close by, "Guard, go fetch Giterod."

Yanon continued in the guard's absence, "Have you considered strengthening your city in the event of an attack?"

"Don't worry about Giter. Everything's under control. We know how to take care of ourselves. We don't need any of your help."

Just then Giterod entered the tent and the king addressed him. "Giterod, I want you to go with these leprechauns to the North Groves to talk to the fool dwarfs. If you see anything that looks like Giter is going to get attacked I want, you to get back to me as quickly as possible and report it. Do you understand?"

"Yes sire," Giterod bowed in understanding.

Then the king addressed Yanon. "This is Giterod. He's my best warrior. You take good care of him and I don't want any funny stuff going on. He knows how to take care of himself. He's under my command, not yours. If he doesn't like what he sees he is to return to me immediately. Do you understand?"

"We understand," returned Yanon, intentionally forgetting the formlity of referring to the king as "Sire".

"Enough talk of this defense business. You worry about you and I'll worry about Giter. Now get lost;" barked the king.

Yanon, Elasti, Obydon, Gabrona, and Giterod departed from the king's tent. "When do you plan to get started?" Giterod asked.

"Within an hour," Yanon replied. "Can you be ready?"

"That's rushing me, but I'll do my best. I'll meet you out by your camp when I'm ready," responded Giterod.

Giterod was taller than most lepelves, standing a good head taller than the leprechauns. He was thin, but muscular, and expressed an attitude of arrogance. His personality seemed to fit well to the king. Being only 22 years old he was assigned menial tasks, but he gave many the impression that he was being molded to become the next king.

Giterod went off to pack while the other four headed toward the camp they had set up for the previous night. Gabrona would head back to the tavern while the leprechauns broke camp and headed out to the west end of town where they would wait for Giterod.

"I could almost swear that that guy looked just like the guy who tried to rob us last night," Obydon commented.

"No way," interjected Gabrona, "not Giterod. He's one of the king's most trusted warriors. Everyone in Giter knows about him. He wouldn't do anything like that."

The party quickly returned to their camp. The leprechauns had already packed up all their belongings and had prepared themselves for departure. "It's too bad we're leaving so late in the day. I had hoped that we might be able to get away sooner. Now we won't get to Giter till tomorrow morning. We'll have to make camp again tonight."

Since they were packed and ready to go, they practiced swordplay avoiding the use of the Southern Sword because of their previous experience with it. Once they tired of this they sat down and made plans for their trip to the North Groves. They discussed their concerns about Hasko, Hiztin, Jesves, and Bydola. They discussed what to do about any possible encounters with the gnomes which was difficult to do because only Elasti had ever seen a gnome. And at the time he didn't stick around long enough to get a close look.

Gabrona found all this talk of adventure and mystery exciting. He was thrilled to be involved in the schemes and plans that would bring the expedition to the North Groves and possibly result in the defeat of the Kabul Lord. He longed to join them, but he knew that his father would never allow him to leave the tavern. He was needed too badly.

Hours had passed by and Giterod had still not made his appearance. "Gabrona, would you mind going into that camp one more time to get Giterod for us?" Yanon asked.

"Sure," was his response, and he left for the kings' camp.

It didn't take him long to find Giterod. He was standing in the middle of the camp discussing what the king was having him do when Gabrona approached him. "They're waiting for you," Gabrona started to say.

"So, what! Let them wait. I'm not going to rush for leprechauns," responded Giterod.

"Please hurry. We're not going to get very far today as it is."

"All right. All right." Giterod said his last farewells and headed for the leprechaun camp with Gabrona at his side. "Do you trust these foreigners?" Giterod questioned.

"They seem nice enough."

"They always 'seem' nice, but I'll bet they don't like me?" Giterod was trying to learn from Gabrona if anything had been said that would tie him to the attempted burglary the previous night.

"They like you fine," returned Gabrona, somewhat surprised at the statement. "They just left a friend behind west of Giter and they're trying to get going so that they can get back to him. They're worried about him."

"Well I haven't heard one good thing about leprechauns. They're stubby, chubby and snobbish, and I'd just as soon do without them," replied Giterod.

Gabrona had always looked up to the king and to his military heroes of which Giterod was one. But this kind of talk didn't fit with the fearless hero image that he had always had of these individuals. In his mind the king's avoidance of the problem with the Kabul bordered on foolishness.

Somehow, he must warn the people of Giter about the pending danger if the king wasn't going to do it. He was the only one who had heard the story told by the leprechauns and therefore he must repeat it for the benefit of the people. But would they laugh at him just like the king laughed at Yanon? Somehow in spite of the potential ridicule he felt an obligation worthy of the risk.

When the two lepelves arrived at the leprechaun camp everything was read and the five of them set off for Giter. They planned to journey to Giter first, since Yanon, Elasti, and Obydon had left some of their belongings there at the tavern. Giterod also had a few additional things he wanted to get for the journey including a change of clothes. Gabrona felt he had to return home to warn his people.

Although Giterod was a lepelf which made his stature taller and his stride longer he needed to be prodded continually. He moved at his own pace, without any regard for the others. He considered the whole trip a nuisance. He knew the further they traveled, the further he would have to journey back after he gained possession of the sword.

They were only able to travel about four hours before the sun set. "Let's go for at least another hour before we stop," suggested Yanon. "We're barely halfway to Giter."

"I've had enough," complained Giterod. "The king doesn't expect me to travel any more than this each day and that's all the further I'm traveling."

"Isn't this going to be great fun," whispered Elasti to Obydon, not expecting anyone to hear.

"What's the problem with you?" Giterod barked out at Elasti in an agitated voice. "You don't like how I travel?"

Elasti didn't bother to answer. He knew that anything he said would just irritate the lepelf more.

"Aren't you going to answer me? What's the matter, ain't I good enough for you?" Giterod gave the impression that he was interested in fighting Elasti. He made it sound as if he had been mortally ridiculed.

"Drop it," Yanon interjected. "We're not going to have any of that nonsense on this trip. We've got enough troubles without you two getting at each other's throats."

Yanon saw the hopelessness of the situation. Giterod had forced him to decide to camp here for the night. "Alright, let's make camp," he announced in disgust.

Elasti felt like screaming, *"Don't give in to that twerp!"* but he thought better of it and held his tongue.

Yanon planned to make up for the early camping break by starting out early in the morning. He hoped that Giterod would be excited enough about returning home during the day that he would allow the party to get an early start.

Yanon also felt the need to protect the camp from intruders, so that the previous night's experience would not be repeated. "We're going to keep watch tonight. We'll take turns. Who would like to go first?"

"I'll take the first watch," Giterod interjected quickly hoping to get at the sword and take off as soon as possible.

Yanon was puzzled. Giterod didn't want to travel anymore because he was tired, yet suddenly he was interested in taking the first watch. Yanon had anticipated that Giterod would refuse to take any watch, but this surprising reaction left him totally unprepared. "Alright, you've got the first watch," Yanon conceded hesitantly. Yanon proceeded to assign the remaining watches. In the back of his mind the doubt remained; why had Giterod wanted the first watch so badly?

They made a fire, cooked and ate their dinner. It wasn't long before they had all fallen asleep, all but Giterod and Yanon. Giterod was hoping that he would have the opportunity to take the sword quickly and be off with it leaving everyone else asleep. It would then be several hours before they noticed their loss and by then he would be safely back under the protection of the king and his guards.

Yanon resisted going to sleep because he was bothered. Obydon's comment about Giterod looking similar to the burglar had popped back into his mind and it seemed to coincide with Giterod's interest in keeping the first watch. Yanon did his best to appear asleep but he kept watch on Giterod the whole time. If Giterod was indeed the thief, it would be better they find out about it now before they trusted him with too much. He could do the expedition serious harm.

Giterod found his hopes frustrated. Obydon slept on the sword thereby refusing the lepelf access to it without disturbing him. Giterod realized that the only way he would be able to get access to the sword was by killing Obydon, but this was something he was not yet prepared to do. He sat down, leaned against a log and thought about his plight. His thoughts became so intense that before he realized it, he was also asleep.

Yanon watched Giterod carefully. He noticed how closely he watched Obydon, and soon Yanon became convinced that Giterod indeed was the thief. He decided not to inform the others about his convictions until he had proof. He continued reflecting on how he would catch Giterod in the act until finally weariness overcame him and he dozed off to sleep.

"Giterod!" Obydon barked with excitement, "why didn't you wake me up?"

Giterod woke up with a start. "I must have fallen asleep!" He gave no indication of being apologetic and even acted irritated at Obydon for disturbing him.

"You wanted the first watch, and then you just fell asleep. What's the big idea?"

"Don't get so excited. Nothing happened, did it? So, calm down and quit getting so ruffled," was Giterod's response.

Obydon was stunned. "It's time you realize that you've got to become an active participant in this expedition, not just an observer. So far you've done nothing but slow us down and complain."

"Listen!" Giterod came back sounding even more irritated and still a little sleepy. "I'm here because the king wants me to keep an eye on you guys, not to be your slave. I'm not going to let you leprechauns bully me into anything. I'll move at my own good speed."

Obydon's frustration was getting him nowhere. He realized that he couldn't convince Giterod to help by yelling at him, so he dropped the issue hoping that maybe Giterod would develop the desire to help on his own. Obydon proceeded to prepare breakfast and Yanon, Gabrona, and Elasti, who were awaken by all the excitement, started to get up.

The four were nearly finished with their meal before Giterod made any attempt to join them. Then he asked, "Where's my breakfast?"

"Do you really expect me to serve you when you refuse to help out?" questioned Obydon. "You make your own breakfast!"

Giterod went back to where he was sitting, sat himself down, folded his arms, and began to sulk. Yanon, feeling sorry for him got up and offered him some of his own food. "No thanks!" was Giterod's arrogant gruff response. "You foreigners think you're too good for me. I don't want any of your junk. I'd rather starve!"

Gabrona felt embarrassed and confused. He felt as though he was obligated to take sides with Giterod since he was a lepelf, but he found it difficult to reconcile such foolish and childish behavior. Giterod's behavior made him feel as though he should apologize to the others on behalf of all lepelves. He decided that the best thing for him to do was to stay out of the situation completely and demonstrate by his actions that all lepelves were not like Giterod.

After breakfast the leprechauns and Gabrona were quick to pack up their sacks and prepared to leave. Giterod, who was still in a huff, took his time with his preparations. He wasn't going to give in even a little bit. He was going to delay this expedition as much as possible. The thing that irritated him the most was that he had fallen asleep and had not taken advantage of the opportunity to get the sword. Now he would have to travel even further and longer before he could get back to the king's camp.

The others waited with patience and irritation until Giterod was finally ready and then they set off for Giter. They followed the trail that had been made earlier during the journey north to find the hunting party. Retracing over the same path made travel easier and quicker in spite of the slow speed at which Giterod traveled.

It was shortly before noon when they arrived at the tavern in Giter. "I've got to go home and make some preparations," Giterod explained. He hoped to be able to delay the expedition until nightfall, thereby forcing them to spend the night in the city.

"We'll meet you here at the tavern in an hour," returned Yanon fully intending to spend about two hours. He thought that if he told Giterod one hour he'd surely be ready in twice that time. Maybe he could outwit the arrogant lepelf.

Giterod departed without responding. Yanon, Elasti, and Obydon entered the tavern with Gabrona and immediately encountered the tavern owner. "It's about time you four got back. Where the heck have you been so long? I need Gabrona to work here at the tavern. I can't have him strolling all over the countryside with you when he's needed here! This will cost you more."

"We're sorry for the delay," began Yanon but Gabrona interrupted.

"It's not their fault," Gabrona explained. "They were delayed by the king for the dumbest reasons." He felt as though he was exceeding his normal boldness by interfering with his father's reprimand, but he had become friends with the leprechauns, and he felt the need to defend them. He remembered all the unnecessary delays caused by Giterod and the king.

"Well, hurry up and get to work!" Gabrona's father barked at Gabrona. He decided not to push the issue any further. He was familiar with the way the king was.

"We'd like to stay for a quick lunch and then we'll be leaving," commented Yanon.

"Do what you want," returned the tavern owner as he turned and walked away.

The three leprechauns sat down for lunch feeling brave enough to eat in the tavern since this would be their last meal in Giter. The service took a long time but eventually they got some stew and bread which they hurriedly ate. Then they went to their room to pack up the remain-

der of their belongings and to await the return of Giterod. They laid back and relaxed, enjoying the opportunity to rest.

Over two hours had gone by since Giterod had gone and there was still no sign of him. "He's trying to delay us again," commented Elasti. "Now I know how that goose felt when it was being dragged along unwillingly to the king's camp. I feel like we're being dragged along by Giterod's whims. I don't like it!"

"I think you're right, but I can't understand why," returned Obydon.

"I think I know why but I can't prove it." Yanon decided to reveal his thoughts. "I don't think he intends to go with us on our expedition to the North Groves. I think he's after Obydon's sword and he hopes to steal it from us. So, the further we travel before he steals it, the longer he will be forced to travel when he has to return home again."

"That explains why he wanted the first watch so badly last night," Obydon thought out loud. "He was hoping for a chance to get the sword then. It's a good thing I was sleeping on it."

"I wonder how desperate he is to get the sword," Yanon continued. "Maybe sleeping on it frustrated his plans last night, but he may not let that stop him in the future."

"What do you mean?" questioned Elasti.

"If Obydon keeps sleeping on the sword, Giterod may be forced to either hit Obydon over the head or kill him in order to be able to get at the sword."

"You don't really think Giterod would go to such extremes to get it do you?" questioned Elasti.

"I'm just saying I'd rather not find out the hard way. The way he was sent with us by the king was strange. At first the king didn't want anyone to go with us and then he suddenly wanted Giterod to go along. It's very suspicious. I have to wonder if the king isn't behind this little scheme to steal the sword. I've been thinking about some way to test my theory and I think I've finally come up with a way. Let's see if this test proves my theory that Giterod is just after the sword and is not interested in helping us at all."

"What is this test you have planned?" Obydon was curious.

"Let's leave him behind. If he was told to steal the sword or even if he wants it for himself, he'll catch up with us. But if he really doesn't intend to come with us to the North Groves he'll use our departure as a good excuse to get out of the journey. I don't think we'll be disappointed if he never shows up again and if he does, we'll know that we better watch him closely. If he suddenly does show up and becomes real friendly, I think we can safely conclude from his sudden shift in attitude that he has pressure from the king to get the sword."

"I'll go for that idea," added Obydon. "It sounds perfect. Let's get out of here. I'm sick and tired of this town and of Giterod's complaining."

"How far are we going to go before we wait for him?" questioned Elasti.

"How about the North Groves?" interjected Obydon sarcastically.

"I thought we'd go as far as Bydola's camp," added Yanon ignoring Obydon's comment.

The three departed leaving a message with Gabrona that they had decided to go on ahead and that if Giterod wanted to join them he would have to catch up with them. Gabrona smiled at the turn of events. He was glad that they had taken a stand against Giterod's arrogance. In his mind he wished them the best of luck, knowing full well that they might never return to Giter.

Elasti, Obydon, and Yanon left town by the West exit and headed toward Bydola's camp. They had seen no sign of Giterod, which pleased them. They wanted to see if he would indeed follow them. If nothing else, they would at least be letting him know that they were not interested in anymore of his delays.

As they approached Bydola's camp from a distance they noticed a few squirrels and birds fighting over the food in his pack. With the exception of these little creatures the camp was exactly as they had left it earlier. Even their note was still attached to the pack.

"What could possibly have happened to him," questioned Yanon. "He wasn't robbed, or his valuables wouldn't be here. He couldn't have drowned, or his body would be floating on the water. How could he have just disappeared like this?"

The three started to scout around, looking for any sign of what might have happened to Bydola. They searched the grasses, the bushes, and the few trees that were in the area. The only tracks they could find were their own. They were puzzled and bewildered.

They were still searching, looking for some type of sign of Bydola when suddenly everything shook. The ground shook and the trees in the area swayed. Even the grass shook. The water rippled. It felt a lot like the Giterquake that they had felt in Giter during their stay there a few days back. But it wasn't as strong a quake and it didn't last very long.

The leprechauns started to look at each other in wonder when Elasti suddenly cried out, "Look!" He was pointing toward the center of the pond.

All eyes turned quickly in the direction in which Elasti was pointing. Walking slowly toward them out from the center of the pond was Bydola. All that could be seen was his head but as he walked in their direction toward shore the water must have become shallower because he slowly rose further and further up out of it.

Bydola held a blank, dazed expression on his face as if he was totally unaware of what was going on around him. His eyes looked forward, and he moved as though he were extremely tired and had aged immensely. His movements were robotic.

"Bydola what's happened to you?" Elasti yelled out, hoping for some response. Bydola gave no sign of recognition. He continued his slow, obsessed pace forward.

"Bydola," this time it was Obydon yelling out, hoping for some response. Bydola remained blank. They noticed the staff he was carrying and wondered what it meant. He had almost reached the shore when the three came running toward him. They feared that something dreadful had happened to him; something that none of them had ever experienced before. It was as though something had destroyed his very essence; his very soul.

As they moved closer, they noticed a light, a faint orange light that seemed to envelop him. It was as though the light emanated from inside of him; from his presence. They stopped short of grabbing him observing the light and trying to identify it. They were lost for words not knowing how to explain or how to react to this strange situation. Elasti seemed to fall into his own confused trance as he stared at Bydola, his mouth hanging open in total disbelief.

Bydola came out of the water and continued his straight march approaching his friends on shore. They noticed tears swelling and flowing from his eyes. His eyes were red as though he had been crying for hours. His head was slightly bowed down which had previously prevented them from noticing these tears. But now everyone was aware of them. This sight shocked them even more. Bydola wasn't the type of person to get emotional and his tears seemed so out of character.

Yanon reached forward to touch Bydola and comfort him but no sooner did his hand touch Bydola on the shoulder when Bydola collapsed to the ground. All strength seemed to have suddenly been drained out of him as he lay there in a heap with his eyes closed and his body limp. Elasti ran and grabbed Bydola's sleeping sack and brought it over to where he lay. The three rolled him over onto the bag and then tried to make him as comfortable as possible. They hoped that his loss of consciousness was only temporary.

"What do you think has happened to him?" questioned Elasti.

"I have no idea," responded Yanon. "I guess we'll just have to wait for him to tell us. We'll have to wait till he comes around so we can talk to him."

The sun was starting to set. It had been a good five hours since Giterod had separated himself from the leprechaun party claiming to get some materials together for the long journey. He smiled at himself thinking how easy it had been to delay the expedition. He was just entering the tavern as he proudly mused at himself thinking that he would excuse his delay by claiming a sickness in his family.

Upon entering the tavern, he looked around and saw no sign of his traveling companions. He decided that they must be hiding out in their room and that he would just sit down at one of the tables and act as though he had been waiting for them for quite some time.

Several minutes passed and Giterod had ordered some ale planning to enjoy his wait when Gabrona spotted him. "They left hours ago," Gabrona informed him. "They waited two and a half hours for you and gave up. They said that if you wanted to go on the expedition with them you will have to catch up."

"What! They just left me behind?" Giterod was furious. His big plans to get the sword and to delay the expedition had failed. "Those stupid twerps. How could they do this to me? The king ordered them to take me with. Wait till I catch up with them. I'll teach them to be rude to our king!"

"I guess they didn't feel obligated to listen to our king," replied Gabrona.

This comment from Gabrona startled Giterod. He expected Gabrona to be more supportive and not so outspoken. "Well I'll teach them how to treat our king!" He pounded his fist on the table, got up and stomped out the front door.

Giterod was outraged. How could these leprechauns be so rude? Now he would have to rush to be able to catch up with them. He couldn't stay behind, or the king would throw him in prison for not obeying his orders to bring back the sword. He had to catch up and try to gain their trust in order to get another opportunity to grab the sword. He would have to be a little more tolerant of their demands; and maybe even helpful. He decided that if he let them think that they won then they maybe they wouldn't be so careful with the sword thereby giving him a better chance to steal it.

Giterod rushed out of town walking as fast as he could in an attempt to catch up with the leprechauns. Gabrona watched him go and smiled. It served him right to be treated that way. Maybe this would teach him a little respect for the leprechauns.

After traveling half an hour it had become dark and Giterod become concerned about catching up with the leprechauns. Luckily Giterod noticed a campfire burning off in the distance. Having seen the fire, his hopes were instantly raised. Had he arrived at their camp?

As he came closer to the camp, he could make out three individuals sitting around the fire. From the distance they appeared to be the leperchauns. Perhaps all wasn't lost. Catching up with the leprechauns turned out to be easier than he had at first thought.

"Hey," Giterod yelled out.

One of the leprechauns stood up and yelled back, "Is that you Giterod?"

Giterod knew he had to gain their friendship if he was to get the chance to snatch the sword. "Yes. How are you doing? Sorry I was late. I had a sickness in my family."

Elasti and Obydon looked at each other in silent communication as if they both understood what the return of Giterod and his sudden friendliness meant. "I'm glad you were able to catch up with us," returned Yanon.

Giterod had gotten close enough to hear them without yelling. Yanon continued, "We arrived at the camp of our friend Bydola who was waiting for us outside the city and upon our arrival he fell unconscious. He has been that way ever since. We are hoping he will recover by morning. Have you ever seen an orange light, like the one that surrounds him?"

"Let me see," commented Giterod as he approached Bydola. "Boy that's strange. I've never seen anything like that before."

"When we arrived, he was walking out of that pond and when he reached shore he simply collapsed."

"What pond?" asked Giterod in astonishment, looking around frantically. The darkness had hidden the pond from view.

"That pond," returned Yanon, pointing in the appropriate direction.

"That's mirror pond," explained Giterod, finally recognizing where he was. "You say he was in that pond? There's a water quist in there. Legend has it that no one has ever escaped that pond alive. In fact, there are those that believe that the water quist will even come out of the water if it gets hungry enough." Giterod looked more than concerned, he was frantic. He started to move around the campfire to the side furthest away from the pond.

"Then you don't have any idea what has happened to him?" questioned Yanon again.

"Nope! We better get away from here. This place isn't safe."

"We shouldn't move Bydola without knowing more about his sickness," continued Yanon. "Maybe if we stay here, we'll get the opportunity to learn about this quist and be able to help Bydola. What is a water quist anyway? Do you know anything about it?" The question was directed to Giterod.

"No one's ever lived to tell about it" expressed Giterod and the fear was showing in his eyes. "Staying here is crazy. I'm not going to stay. I'll camp closer to the road. I'll meet you in the morning up the road a little way. I'm not about to spend the night here." Giterod grabbed one of the burning sticks from the leprechauns' fire and hurriedly left the camp. He went back out to the road and journeyed down the road a little way to set up his own campsite.

The leprechauns finished their meal and decided to bed down for the night. They took turns at the night watch always keeping an eye out for the quist and for Giterod.

The morning arrived uneventfully. The quist never came out of the water and Giterod's fear of it must have been real enough to have kept away from the leprechaun camp. "I'm sure glad we decided not to take a bath last night realizing now that it was enough to keep Giterod away." Elasti was sitting up and stretching trying to wipe the sleep out of his eyes.

Then to everyone's surprise Bydola sat up and said, "Hi guys. It's sure nice to see you again."

No one could respond. They were all in shock. It was as though they had just seen Bydola return from the dead. They didn't know what to expect from him, but they didn't expect anything quite so normal.

"Wake up," Bydola continued. "I'm not dead. In fact, I'm quite alive. Thanks for taking care of me last night. I felt pretty out of it." The dull orange light still emanated from around him. It didn't seem possible that he could really be their friend Bydola, yet he talked and acted the same.

"Is that really you," stated Elasti. "We thought we had lost you."

"It's me, but at the same time it isn't me. I'm still Bydola but I'm also a lot more. I wish I could explain but that privilege has been forbidden. Perhaps someday we will all understand." Bydola had always been thought of as all muscle and no brains. Now he seemed to emanate a deep-rooted intelligence.

"What are you talking about?" questioned Yanon in an attempt to understand.

"I can't explain any further," replied Bydola. "Trust me that I'm still your friend who has now learned about a much greater strength than that of the body. This greater strength is the strength to love. Please treat me no differently than before, only have faith in my love for you."

"How can we not treat you differently? You've changed so much." Yanon was still unsure of what he was dealing with in this new version of Bydola. "Let's eat breakfast and you can tell us all about what happened to you."

"I'll gladly join you for breakfast," replied Bydola. "But I've been forbidden to tell my story of the last few days."

"By who? Who told you not to tell us?" asked Yanon acting as the group's spokesman.

"This also I cannot tell," was Bydola's only reply.

Breakfast was eaten with everyone deep in thought. Each was wondering what the change in Bydola meant to the expedition. Then Bydola, attempting to break the ice that seemed to be forming between them, asked, "Tell me about Giter. Were your efforts there successful?"

Yanon proceeded to tell the story of their encounter with the king and of their difficulties in convincing him of the dangers that existed. Then he told about Giterod and their experiences and their fears with him. Just then Giterod could be seen coming in the distance. "Can I join you for breakfast?" he yelled.

"Sure. Come on over," returned Yanon. "There's plenty."

"This sudden nice guy image is sickening," whispered Elasti. "Who does he think he's kidding?"

"The evil in him is great, but the good in him is also great," whispered Bydola. "Perhaps he has a misguided good that was turned to evil."

Giterod was now close enough so that no more whispering could be done. This last comment of Bydola left his three companions confused and deep in thought. What had he meant? What new insight had he been given? This comment was so out of character for Bydola that it left all the other leprechauns surprised and giving each other glances of confusion.

"The quist is not supposed to come out of the water during the day," started Giterod but he still made sure that the place where he sat was as far away from the pond as possible.

Bydola remarked, "Fear not the quist unless you fear yourself." Again, Bydola's comment left everyone including Giterod stunned. What was that supposed to mean? No one dared to ask for fear that maybe the answer was something they didn't want to hear.

The travelers finished breakfast quickly. Everyone seemed to be in a hurry to get away from mirror pond, all except Bydola. As the others started to leave Bydola stood facing the pond for a few moments in silent reverence. When he finally turned to follow his companions, he could be seen wiping away tears.

Far above them in a tree that was too far overhead for them to notice, an eagle left its perch and flew southward.

The expedition walked on in silence, Yanon in the lead, followed by Agot and Obydon. Giterod was next, always keeping a lusty eye on the sword at Obydon's side. Bydola brought up the rear as though he really didn't want to leave Mirror Pond behind.

The day was beautiful for traveling. It was sunny but slightly overcast, just enough to keep the sun from making the journey intolerably hot. Often birds could be heard singing in the few scattered trees that they passed by. It was the kind of day that left everyone relaxed and deep in thought.

The journey toward the Tako Ruins would take about two to three days. This part of the journey brought back memories for Elasti. These memories were hard for him to live with. He could see his friends Agot and Broch traveling the road with him. Now their memory haunted him. His thoughts left him quiet and sober.

Elasti was also troubled by the change that had come over Bydola, as were Yanon and Obydon. He wasn't sure how these changes had occurred or what the long-term effect of these changes would be on Bydola. Were the changes for good or for evil? He wondered about the orange ora and what significance it had. He wondered about the staff that Bydola now carried and found it unusual. He wondered if Bydola would change back to the same old personality they all knew before or if this change was permanent. He wondered what role the water quist had played in this transformation and what Bydola meant by his comment "Fear not the quist unless you fear yourself". His comments about Giterod being good and bad also seemed confusing. Elasti wondered what had happened to Bydola's leg injury that had earlier left him limping. Now there seemed to be no sign of a limp. The questions kept coming yet he knew he could not confront Bydola with them because Bydola had already made it clear that he would reveal nothing.

Yanon was also deep in thought. His thoughts centered around the possible danger that Hasko, Hiztin, and Jesves would encounter if they met up with the werewolves. How could he have been so stupid to let them go off on such a dangerous mission? He felt personally responsible for their lives since he was assigned the job of expedition leader. He wished that there was some way of helping or warning them but he feared it may already be too late.

Yanon's thoughts dwelt on the possibility that the four leprechauns would be finishing the journey alone. He feared the possibility that the Gije expedition had been a failure. He was also confident that Giterod would attempt to steal the sword. He mapped out plans in his mind scheming how to make the journey north a success.

Obydon had his own thoughts as well. His concerns centered on the threat the Giterod posed to him personally. He must be extra careful with the sword. If he were to lose it the entire expedition north would be futile. The threat of losing the sword increased with the possibility that Giterod might kill for it. Would the lepelf really be that desperate? Obydon wished he could confront Giterod with the problem and ask him straight out what he thought but Giterod would then deny the whole thing and end up being more cautious because of it. They couldn't just send Giterod home because this would increase the alienation between the leprechauns and the lepelves. The two needed to work together more than ever, especially if a war were to occur.

Obydon also wondered about Bydola and especially about what he had said about Giterod. What did he mean when he said, "The evil in him is great, but the good in him is also great? Perhaps he is misguided good that was turned to evil." The statement pounded through his mind. Was it possible that the evil they saw in Giterod was the result of some other force, and not the fault of Giterod's own wishes? Bydola 's insight left him puzzled. Obydon didn't want to do Giterod any injustice by mistrusting him unduly yet he didn't want to risk the sword unnecessarily either.

Giterod dwelt on his frustrations. He could no longer attempt to delay the expedition. The leprechauns had made it obvious that they would simply leave him behind. He must win their trust if he was going to get a chance to steal the sword. But the time he spent trying to gain their trust caused him to get further and further away from Giter. He should have taken his chances that first night and risked knocking Obydon over the head in order to get the sword. Now it seemed as though the chances of getting the sword had decreased significantly. He must risk everything tonight in an attempt to get the sword or else he might end up at the Kilo Pass. The thought of traveling the Kilo Pass scared him. What if there really were gnomes moving down from the Kabul. He had no intention of encountering them alone while he was trying to escape the leprechaun camp with the sword. He must get that sword tonight.

Bydola was swarming with thoughts of the events that he had encountered during the previous days. It seemed as though the entire episode with the Creator had taken only a few hours but in reality, he had been down there for days.

Bydola was overwhelmed. Why was he selected for such a great honor? Why was he selected to meet with the Creator and then given the great blessing of knowledge and power? Why was he chosen to be instrumental in the Creator's plan for the protection of Small World? What would be expected of him? The questions and thoughts of the past days flooded through his mind. He had never thought of himself as anyone special, in fact, there were plenty of leprechauns who were wiser than he was. Why was he chosen for such a great honor? He felt so unworthy.

He felt detached from his friends. He had a secret that was greater and more beautiful than any he had ever known yet he couldn't share it.

He wanted to scream with excitement; about all he had learned but he acknowledged the wisdom of the Creator. If he did attempt to share his experiences his friends would become leery of him, possibly even become his enemies and consider him insane. It was best to keep all this newfound knowledge inside.

Tears swelled up in his eyes. Never had he felt such an immense love as he felt when he was in the presence of the Creator. He longed for the opportunity to feel that love again. He knew that one day when order had been restored to Small World, he would search out Mirror Pond in hopes that he might once again be able to meet with and talk to the Creator.

Lunch time came and went, with no one really interested in stopping to eat except Giterod. They ate as they continued down the South Road, looking forward to meeting their friends at the Tako Ruins. Occasionally someone made a passing comment but for the most part everyone kept to themselves. They all seemed to enjoy the silence.

It was approaching late afternoon when the travelers arrived at the edge of the Avol River. The pull boat was waiting for them on the east side of the river just the way Elasti had left it when he returned from his encounter with the gnomes. He even recognized the sloppy tying job that he had left in his rush to get back to Amins. Again, memories of Agot and Broch plagued him.

"Let's stay on this side of the river tonight," Giterod suggested. His fear of the unknown was more than he could handle. "I'd feel a lot safer here not worrying about any gnomes lurking about."

Elasti and Obydon agreed but since they had both decided in their minds that Giterod was their enemy they were not about to give in to him when Yanon said, "Let's not hold back, we've got enough daylight to get us across. That way we won't waste valuable daylight tomorrow." His biggest concern was getting to the Tako Ruins to see how the expedition to Gije fared.

Yanon began to load his pack onto the pull boat. Giterod decided not to resist or he would probably be left alone on this side of the river which would be even scarier than being on the other side with the rest of the party.

The boat was small, so it took several trips across before all the travelers and their packs were safely on the other side. Yanon had already made a fire and set up camp when the last load was safely across.

Elasti was saddened by the fact that their camp was in the exact same location as the camp that he and his friends had made earlier. The memories haunted him. He left the camp and found an isolated tree where he slumped down and began to cry.

Obydon watched Elasti and knew what he was feeling. He left him to his mourning realizing that Elasti needed to be able to cry it out. When he saw Yanon moving toward Elasti to comfort him Obydon stopped him explaining that it was better to leave him to himself.

Dinner was quickly prepared, and everyone, including Elasti, sat down to enjoy the final meal of the day. Night watches were scheduled and Yanon realized that if Giterod was not allowed to take a watch, he might get suspicious. Yanon planned it so that his own watch would precede that of Giterod, and this way he could keep an eye on the lepelf during his watch.

Everyone went to sleep under the stars. The warmth of the evening made sleeping outside beautiful. Elasti took the first watch. He was still dwelling on the loss of his friends and was not in the mood for sleeping.

The watches were short, only one and a half hours each, since there were five travelers to keep watch. Elasti took his turn followed by Obydon who wanted to make sure that Elasti felt better. By then Elasti had recovered from his emotional breakdown and fell quickly to sleep. The next watch was Yanon's, followed by Giterod.

Yanon found it difficult to stay awake during Giterod's watch. The day had not been overly laborious, but the warmth had drained him of his strength. He knew he had to keep awake in order to watch Giterod. The first half hour was uneventful. Giterod seemed unconcerned with anything but the fire. Then, when Yanon was finding it hardest to keep awake he noticed Giterod get up from his seat. The lepelf walked quietly over to where Obydon slept. Yanon had a good view of Obydon's bed and was able to watch all of Giterod's actions. Obydon was lying on his side and it appeared as though he had turned off of the sword leaving it exposed and readily available for Giterod to grab. Before Yanon realized what was happening Giterod was running toward the river with the Southern Sword firmly in his grasp.

Yanon jumped out of his sleeping sack suddenly being brought to life by the urgent turn of events. "Get up! Giterod has stolen the Southern Sword!" he yelled waking the entire camp. He took off running down to the edge of the river only to find that Giterod was already over halfway across on the pull boat. Giterod, being the last to cross the river earlier in the evening had left the boat ready for this planned escape.

Yanon hoped to stop the progress of the boat by pulling the towrope against Giterod's progress, but Giterod had even planned for that eventuality. He had cut the towrope off at the east end of the river, and there was no way for the leprechauns to catch him now. They would have to swim the river to cross it and by the time they made it across, Giterod would be well down the South Road on his way back to Giter.

At the east edge of the river Giterod jumped off the boat and started running down the South Road as quickly as he could. He knew that even if a leprechaun ran at full speed, he couldn't catch up with a lepelf's long stride. He hurried on, walking and running and occasionally stumbling. He had distanced himself from the leprechauns by several hours. Soon the light of day made traveling easier. He felt relaxed and successful. He knew he had enough distance that the leprechauns would find it impossible to catch up with him.

Feeling comfortably ahead of the leprechauns his curiosity got the better of him. He had to see what was so great about this Southern Sword that had made it worth stealing. He slowly unraveled the protective wrappings that had been placed around the handle. As he pulled the wrappings off, he was stunned. There in the hilt of the Southern Sword were two sticks, tied together to give the appearance of a sword. The wrappings that had been placed around the sticks had caused them to appear exactly like the Southern Sword.

Giterod sat down at the side of the road, leaned against a tree and began to cry. His victory had turned to disaster. How could he face the king? The king would not accept his failure. And he couldn't return to the leprechauns because he had destroyed any chance of them trusting him in the future.

Yanon was about to jump into the river after Giterod when Obydon grabbed his shoulder. "Let him go," he whispered, "I've still got the sword. All he has is a couple sticks and my hilt."

Yanon looked at Obydon in surprise. Then he smiled in understanding. He watched Giterod disappear along the South Road. Then Yanon turned to Obydon and slapped him on the back. "Good work Obydon. What inspired that little bit of ingenuity?"

"I was getting tired of worrying about whether my life was in danger or not, so I decided to make it easy for him to get what he thought was the sword. I made a sword out of sticks and wrapped them up as if they were the Southern Sword and put them in the hilt. Sure, enough Giterod stole what he thought was the sword just as we anticipated."

Yanon mused, "Looks like we've seen the last of him. He wouldn't dare follow us now for fear that we'll kill him for what he's done. Besides, I think he's truly scared to death of gnomes and he wouldn't dare travel these roads alone."

"You know what?" commented Obydon. "I've been thinking about what Bydola said about Giterod; about him being partially good. I'll bet that king put him up to this like you said. Can you imagine what would happen if he didn't notice the switch until he got back to the king. I feel sorry for the fool."

"Well no sense crying over it now," commented Elasti thoughtfully. "At least none of us got hurt thanks to Obydon's quick thinking. But I would sure feel a lot better if we didn't stay here any longer just in case, he notices the switch sooner then we think."

"I agree," added Yanon. "We're all wide awake now and the sun will be rising soon anyway. Why don't we start traveling a little earlier today to avoid any sudden reappearances of Giterod?"

All were quick to agree, and it wasn't long before they were packed and the fire extinguished. They began traveling but found that the darkness caused them to trip and stumble. Bydola realized their difficulty and reached into his pocket and pulled out a strange glowing orange rock. The rock had the brightness of the fire that they had just left behind and made traveling considerably easier. Yanon, Obydon, and Elasti each mused at the strange rock, wondering about its unnatural origin and wondering how Bydola had come to be in possession of such a rock. They also noticed that the orange light from the rock seemed to be the same type of light as the light of the ora that surrounded Bydola during the day.

"What other little tricks do you have up your sleeve?" asked Elasti looking at the rock light and not really expecting an answer. Bydola made no comment.

They traveled for an hour under the guidance of the orange light before the sun had risen sufficiently to guide their way. Then Bydola returned the orange rock to his pocket. The four traveled for five more hours with each deep in their own thoughts. They were planning and scheming their futures and the possibility of a return visit by Giterod even though such a visit seemed highly unlikely. Finally, they stopped for a rest and lunch.

Lunch was kept short. The nearness of the Tako Ruins drove them onwards. They all felt obsessed with getting as far as possible that day.

Bydola had become less of an oddity by now. Yanon, Elasti, and Obydon had gotten used to his strange orange rock light, his ora, and his staff. They had even grown accustomed to his new intelligence. If they were back home in Amins they could have avoided him. But here they had to deal with him and make him a part of their team. In many ways he had become more valuable. He was now less grumpy and therefore more pleasant to be with then previously.

It was nearing sunset when they encountered the cutoff road north toward the Kilo Pass. They had made it this far in their journey and a feeling of great achievement overcame them. Although it had only been nine days since they had left Amins it had begun to seem as though they had aged years and that arriving at the North Groves had been their lifelong goal.

Elasti was glad that the party had finally turned north. Now he would be able to put aside his remorse. This was a departure from the route he had traveled with his friends. It would now be easier to try to hide the memories of his dead friends, or at least to stop from being constantly reminded of them.

They headed north along the cutoff until they found a clearing large enough for the four of them to make camp and they bedded down for the night. They avoided building a fire because they feared the possibility of gnomes in the area. They also wanted to avoid the remote chance that Giterod would be following them. They used Bydola's light to eat and to set up camp and they drew lots using twigs to determine who took first watch.

The morning was exciting. They knew that they were just a few short hours from the Tako Ruins. Arriving there meant meeting Hasko, Hiztin, and Jesves. Previously back in Amins, these three individuals held no interest in each other. But now all seven of the travelers felt a special bond. They hurried through breakfast and started off as soon as their packs were prepared.

"Does anyone know what these Tako Ruins are all about?" asked Elasti as they set out not really expecting much of an answer.

"They've got something to do with an earlier civilization," started Yanon, "but I don't know much beyond that."

Then Bydola began his explanation. "The Tako Ruins were once the great city of Tako, a community where all cultures lived in peace and trust." Bydola was amazed. It was as if some other voice or some other source of knowledge was speaking through him. Yet he knew that it was indeed his newly acquired knowledge that was being expressed. His fellow companions weren't surprised. There was little about Bydola that would surprise them anymore. He continued, "The culture that lived here was a mixture of elves, lepelves, and leprechauns and was advanced far beyond anything we have today.

"Their downfall was caused by a destructive force that came from the Upperworld. It was a force built upon the accumulation of hate and competitive zeal. At that time numerous cultures lived in Upperworld. But these cultures developed fear and mistrust between themselves. Weapons were developed. These weren't necessarily for war but to be used to threaten each other so that one culture could not control another. However, as cultures emerged, and divisions grew between them not all of them believed that keeping weapons only for their threat potential was adequate. Some decided to use the weapons on each other. Eventually the weapons became weapons of violence and destruction.

"The result was a war in Upperworld leaving only small parts of it inhabitable. Its residents hoarded these limited areas, finding them inadequate for survival.

"This war also affected the physical structure of many of the individuals who lived in Upperworld. It created a mutant population who's physical, mental, and often even spiritual essence was disrupted. The unaffected Upperworld citizens ejected these mutants from what remained of their world and cast them into the wastelands.

"Small World had an entrance that had long been hidden by the frozen wastelands of Upperworld. Unfortunately, many of these frozen areas had been melted down by the war, leaving the entrance exposed. Hoards of mutants found their way to this entrance and started to pour into Small World.

"As these hoards arrived in the northern parts of Small World, they found it very desirable and planned to take control of all of it. They weren't going to let themselves be thrown out of this land the way they were thrown out of their last home in Upperworld. These hoards are what we now refer to as gnomes. These gnomes successfully battled and conquered the North Groves and the Central Ranges, and soon they had found their way to the greatest city of all, Tako. Although many of the mutants had died along the way their numbers were still so great that soon Tako was overpowered and destroyed. The mutants then went on to Gije, but the elves were ready. The elves were successful in overpowering most of the gnomes along the cliffs of the Jove Plateau, and those that made it up the plateau never made it past the well-fortified walls of Gije. Here they were defeated and driven back to what is now called the Kabul where they have now come under the power and the control of Lord Krakus. Sadly, they left the beautiful city of Tako utterly devastated and its people completely destroyed. This invasion and the defeat of the gnomes are now referred to as the Lifefight Wars."

Elasti, Obydon, and Yanon were stunned. They were surprised at this story and amazed at the insight and enlightened discourse from Bydola. His overwhelming new knowledge was quite impressive for they knew that no one in Amins, with the exception of possibly Bananot, had such a detailed knowledge of the earlier events in Small World.

"Bydola, you're amazing," Elasti stated. He was grateful yet mystified by the story he had just heard. He now had a new appreciation for the Tako Ruins and couldn't wait to explore them.

Bydola's story had taken up a considerable amount of time and by the time he had finished they could see the ruins of the great city off in the distance. They moved even faster hoping to explore the ruins and anticipating a reunion with their friends. But as they approached what was left of the outer walls of the city, they were disappointed. Their friends were nowhere to be found. Although the ruins of the city were extensive, and it spread far in all directions it was anticipated that the reunion would occur at the point where the Kilo Pass met the ruins. Their friends were nowhere. The pass gave no sign of any travelers having been there.

"I guess we beat them here," commented Yanon hoping in the back of his mind that their friends would indeed arrive shortly. "I guess we'll have the opportunity to explore the ruins a little before they show up."

The party threw down their packs and began scrambling about on the ruins. Occasionally someone would find a treasure like an old bowl or a painted wall and they would all muse at its purpose and function. Often metal artifacts would be found which were truly a treasure because metal was now the prime basis for geld, the leprechaun form of money.

Yanon had been a little braver than some of the others and had ventured a little further away from the group. He found the ruined remains of an old building that appeared to have some importance because of its elaborately designed stonework and its colorful plastering. He climbed into the center and started kicking away some of the rock pieces that lay loosely on the floor. Most of the plaster and cement that was used in the construction of the buildings had now turned into rubble and by kicking it Yanon was stirring up a cloud of dust.

As he kicked the dust around, his foot suddenly became stuck. The abruptness at which his foot ended its swing and the force with which he had swung his foot caused him severe pain. As he investigated what his foot had hit, he found what appeared to be a slab of stone covering some kind of stone box. As he brushed away the dust and rubble that covered it, he found the stone to be almost perfectly intact. It seemed unaffected by the rest of the destruction that surrounded it. The stone was perfectly squared off at its edges and was circular, about the diameter of half a leprechaun's height. But what had caught Yanon's foot earlier was one of the four metal handles protruding out of the stone.

This puzzled Yanon. Why would this stone have four handles if it wasn't a storage box of some type? "Obydon, Elasti, Bydola, get over here and help me lift this stone!" Yanon's curiosity had gotten the better of him. He had to see what was under the stone.

As the others arrived, he explained his discovery and began giving instructions. They each grabbed a hold of one of the handles and gave the rock a strong tug. Nothing happened. They tried again, and this time Bydola's corner of the rock started to lift. "Why don't you come and help me here on this handle," Bydola instructed Yanon. "Elasti and Obydon, why don't you come up with some sort of wedge to shove under this corner of the stone as we lift it."

Each of the leprechauns quickly took to their newly assigned tasks. Yanon and Bydola attempted to pull the rock up once again. This time they were successful in lifting the stone high enough for two wedges to be placed underneath. Then they were slowly able to pry the stone lid up. Once they had gotten it about a forth a leprechaun up, they placed a rock under it so that they would no longer be forced to hold the wedges.

"Look here," was Yanon's excited comment as he peeked under the stone. "It looks like we've uncovered some kind of library of books. I can see piles of bark scrolls under there." Yanon attempted to reach underneath and pull one of the scrolls out.

He managed to get two of them, and as he unraveled the first, he noticed a familiar writing on it. It was a form of writing quite similar to what he was used to reading in his old military books. The first scroll contained some sort of history of an earlier age.

When he uncovered the second scroll, he found a different writing had been used. Even the symbols used in the writing were different.

"What do you make of this?" Yanon asked Bydola, hoping that in his newfound knowledge, he would be able to shed some light on the scrolls.

"This second scroll was written in the sacred language," Bydola started. "All religious mysteries were written in the language of the religious leaders which only they were permitted to understand." Bydola took the scroll from Yanon and began to look it over. "This scroll tells about some of the festive worship practices of the people of Tako."

"Can you read that stuff?" Yanon asked pointing to the scroll in Bydola's hand.

"Yes," commented Bydola rather matter-of-factly. "Would you like me to read it to you?"

"Maybe later," returned Yanon. He was starting to wonder if there would be anything Bydola didn't know.

Meanwhile Elasti had become disinterested in the scrolls and had found a tall pillar which appeared to have once been the corner of a huge building. The walls to one side of this corner were still partially in place, and he found it easy to scurry up the side of the wall to the top of the pillar. He hoped that by getting to the top he would be able to get a view of all the ruins, and thereby be able to pick out points of interest worth investigating from the ground.

Suddenly and without warning as he was approaching the top of the pillar the entire pillar started to collapse. First it fell slowly and then more rapidly, finishing with one massive crash. Elasti tried to jump off fast enough to avoid being hit by the pillar but his footing was poor, and he slipped. He found himself falling helplessly. When he landed, he was struck by the clutter of the crumbled cement and bricks covering him in a living grave.

"Elasti!" Obydon screamed, seeing the plight of his friend. He started running over in the direction where Elasti had fallen.

Then came the cry from Yanon that sent shivers of horror through all the travelers, "Riposters!" Apparently, the destruction of the pillar had awoken a hoard of the creatures that had made their home in the Tako Ruins. Riposters were an abortion from creation. They had fish bodies, bird's wings, and rat's teeth. They were vicious flesh-eating monstrosities.

The leprechauns had encountered riposters once before when the creatures had attacked their hometown. During this attack their number had been small, only a few dozen and escaping to the inside of a home was easy. But this time the creatures numbered in the hundreds, and there was no safe escape.

Yanon, Obydon, and Bydola dropped the scrolls and drew their swords. They began to battle for their lives. The riposters, with their fish heads and razor-sharp teeth would dive at the intruders. Their winged bodies allowed them flexibility and mobility. They would attack in teams. Defense was difficult. While several of the creatures attacked from the front several more would simultaneously attack from behind. They would attach themselves to the clothing and chew through it until they were able to dig into the flesh.

Yanon wielded his sword with a vengeance. He knew the damage that these creatures could do. A group of about ten swooped down at him and he swung at them viciously hacking and chopping at them with all his might. Killing them was easy. Each stroke of the sword would leave one or more of the creatures falling to the ground. Unfortunately, with each new attack, more pieces of flesh would be torn off the back of his head and off his shoulders. After the fourth attack Yanon was bleeding profusely from his right shoulder and from behind his right ear. The loss of blood was so intense that he was starting to become weak. He feared that soon he would be totally at the mercy of these creatures.

Bydola wasn't faring much better. His strength allowed him to withstand the blows better than Yanon, but his ability with the sword found him swinging senselessly at the air far too often. Soon he found himself with a riposter painfully attached to the back of his left shoulder and even the swats of his sword didn't encourage it to release its hold. It was hard to swing at a creature that was attached to his back. His right shoulder also had several gashes which were oozing with blood.

Obydon was in worse condition. The riposters had attacked him so successfully and in such numbers, that he soon found himself with his shoulders gouged and bleeding. Also, his hands and arms were so chewed up that he could no longer wield the sword. A riposter had even found its way to his cheek and had left a cut so close to his left eye that he feared he would be blinded for life.

Finally, Obydon collapsed. The pain and loss of blood had been too much for him. His sword fell from his hands and he dropped face down into the dust of the ruined city. The riposters were quick to react and swarmed down on the back of this legs and back.

Bydola seeing what happened rushed quickly to his companion's aid. He beat the riposters off Obydon's back and stood, straddling the helpless, seemingly lifeless body. He hacked and battled using all the strength he had left in him to protect his friend. In spite of his efforts a riposter still clung to Bydola's left shoulder.

Then Bydola noticed Yanon waver, stumble, and attempt to recover. He knew that Yanon would soon meet the same fate as Obydon. How could he lose all his fellow travelers so suddenly?

Bydola cried out in a plea for mercy, "Creator, don't let us die like this."

Yanon tripped, stumbled, and fell to the ground.

CHAPTER THIRTEEN

THE TAKO RUINS

The sun was high in the sky before Doctor Erock would allow Jesves to start traveling. Hasko, Hiztin, Gido, and Gijivure were already packed and waiting outside the doctor's door when the time finally came for their departure. They were all overjoyed when Jesves finally came through the door, not because they were now able to depart but because of how healthy she appeared.

They congratulated her on her quick recovery and thanked the doctor for his efforts. Then they threw their packs on their backs and were off. The townspeople cheered them as they walked down the main street toward the gate of the city. The expedition had originally planned to take a mihorse and a wagon in order to make their journey easier but later it was decided that these would force the expedition to stay on the trail. They decided that they would be safer if they had the flexibility to be off the trail in the event of any encounters with the gnomes.

The council and Lord Gimans met them as they neared the gate and gave them well wishes for a safe and quick journey. The party left the city through the gate that just two days earlier had been such a welcome sight. They headed north along the South Road. The farmers working out in the fields cheered them as they passed by and soon, they were out of sight. It took several hours before Gije became nothing more than a small speck in the distance behind them.

As they traveled Gido and Gijivure introduced themselves to Jesves. They explained why they were selected for the journey. Gijivure was selected for his bowman ship and Gido as a representative of the Council. They explained how grateful they were for the risks she had taken on behalf of their city and told her that she would always be welcome in their city.

Jesves was slightly embarrassed by all the attention but she soon came to realize that it was part of the nature of elves to be grateful, sympathetic, and courteous. She respected them for their compassion.

The journey across the plateau was easy, much easier than what they had experienced coming to Gije. They now had a nice trail to follow allowing them to travel at full speed. This trail had obviously received more use than the back roads they had used to travel to the elves initially. Following the doctor's instructions, they didn't push themselves too fast feeling somewhat uncertain about Jesves's health, but they still made good time. The day was cloudy and overcast but there didn't seem to be any threat of rain. The clouds made the temperature a little cooler than it would have otherwise been which also made traveling easier.

"We must journey,
Off the plateau;
The werewolves will come,
If we don't do so," Gido commented. He intended that the travelers should be over the edge of the plateau before nightfall in order to avoid the threat of the werewolves. The werewolves would never journey off the plateau because they feared the unknown of the world below.

"For us to go,
We must go quick;
The trail is slick,
Down below."

Gijivure was expressing his concern that the little party wasn't traveling fast enough. He hadn't become accustomed to the shorter strides of the leprechauns and constantly felt as though he was just crawling along.

The sun was already starting to set when they finally arrived at the trail that would take them to the bottom of the Jove Cliff. In spite of the risk that the darkness posed they decided to press on. They knew it would take at least two hours before they arrived at the bottom. The risk of walking on this slippery trail at night was more desirable than the danger of encountering the werewolves. They continued on cautiously.

It was a slow descent. After two hours of switchback trails, they finally arrived at the valley floor below. At this point they became concerned about the possible threat posed by the gnomes. They would constantly need to be on the lookout for fire or movement on the valley floor below. Fortunately, they saw no sign of activity. This gave them only a mild comfort. They still hesitated to camp too close to the road in case they might be noticed by a gnome scouting party. Fortunately, the valley floor was heavily wooded allowing them to be able to walk only a short ways off the road and into the trees before they were well hidden. They didn't dare make a fire because of the possibility of being noticed so they threw their sleeping sacks on the ground wherever they could find a spot and were soon asleep.

The next day felt a little cooler because of the shade of the trees and because they were now on the valley floor. The leprechauns and elves broke camp quickly and set out on their way toward the Tako Ruins. They decided to stay off to the side of the trail hoping to avoid being noticed. They traveled in the trees keeping a close watch to see if there were any travelers on the road.

Within a few hours they encountered the first Albo Pass cutoff. They had seen no sign of any gnomes. Gimans' scouts had been right. The gnomes had not yet ventured into the Southern Plains.

They traveled a couple hours further before they encountered the second Albo Pass cutoff. There still had been no sign of any gnomes. They were beginning to feel confident that they would make it to the Tako Ruins unnoticed.

They continued traveling off on the side of the main road for a couple more hours avoiding any possible encounters with gnomes. When they still hadn't seen any sign of their enemy Hasko said, "Let's start journeying on the South Road. We'll make much better time. Based on Giman's scouts report and based on what we've seen, I feel sure we will be safe enough."

"With this I agree,
That we should go;
Along a route,
That's not so slow," responded Gido.
"Before we do,
Why don't we eat?
My stomach says,
It wants a treat."

It was close to lunch time, so they all sat down and enjoyed a meal together. After hungrily consuming their food, they set out moving east along the South Road. They were able to move much faster, and they seemed to be able to cover twice as much distance in the same amount of time.

Hasko and Gido had taken on the leadership roles. They would walk out ahead of everyone else, side-by-side, discussing strategies for the trek toward the North Groves. Hasko was fascinated by Gido's rhyming speech and enjoyed conversing with him.

Gijivure was a bit of a loner. Even though he was friendly when anyone addressed him, he wasn't much for starting conversations on his own. He walked behind Hasko and Gido and listened to their scheming. He formed his own opinions of what he thought they should do but never voiced any of them. He felt closer to Gido than to any of the rest mostly because the two were both elves and so he stayed closest to him. Whenever Gido brought Gijivure into the discussion by asking him a question, Gijivure would temporarily return to his jolly old mannerisms. He had never interacted with leprechauns before and he wasn't comfortable with them. He was a minority now and he hadn't gotten used to that. The thought of meeting up with four more leprechauns was something he had not reckoned with.

Hiztin and Jesves brought up the rear. Hiztin stayed close by Jesves under the pretense that he was making sure she was alright but in reality, he hoped to continue the personal conversations that they had started a few days earlier at the other end of the Jove Plateau. He felt a warm feeling when they were talking together, and he wanted more of that. He would ask her questions about her past. She always seemed eager to respond.

Jesves was also feeling a closeness to Hiztin blaming her feelings on the fact that he had shown an interest in her and cared about her. Although her feelings were perhaps not as strong as the feelings that Hiztin had, they still existed, and she appreciated his kindness and enjoyed his company. She felt as though they were companions in this struggle together and at times it was hard to believe that they had only known each other for nine days. It seemed as though they had known each other for a lifetime.

Hiztin wanted to talk to Jesves about his feelings hoping that she felt the same. But every time he felt the opportunity was appropriate, he invented some excuse in his own mind for not starting the discussion. He feared her possible reaction. Would she get angry with him? Then he wouldn't be able to walk with her at all. Or if the feelings weren't mutual what next? Would she think he was strange? Would she tend to avoid him? For now, he decided not to take the risk of asking her. He would just have to go on enjoying being her friend.

The sun had started to set. The travelers decided to make camp slightly off the road to avoid possible detection. The thickness of the trees had subsided a little and so they had to travel deeper into the woods in order to find adequate cover from the road. They again avoided making a fire. They ate a cold dinner and were soon asleep.

No one noticed that an eagle watched from a tree overhead.

The morning was a little warmer. They checked the South Road and saw no sign of any travelers. They packed up their belongings, ate breakfast quickly and were off.

"I really hate making Yanon and the rest of them wait so long for us," Hasko commented to Gido. "They're probably worried sick about us."

"If we hurry,
We'll arrive today;
Then with your friends,
You'll get to stay,'" Gido responded. He continued with;
"I think we're only,
A day away;
We'll soon be ten,
And all is gay."

"I sure hope so," returned Hasko. "I'll feel a lot safer when there are more of us in the expedition."

About two hours into their journey they came across the Avoli River Bridge on the South Road. The sight of the Avoli River fascinated them and caused them to take a few minutes for sightseeing. The canyon created by the river was sharp and magnificently deep. "How could anything so beautiful be so treacherous?" questioned Hasko. "And to think that all this beauty disappears into the great Lamos. What a shame."

The travelers stood on the bridge for a few minutes admiring the beauty but then Gido urged them on,

"We must go on,
If we today;
The Tako Ruins,

Plan to stay."

"Don't rush me," Hasko said jokingly. The closeness that he had developed with Gido in this short time had allowed them some liberty in teasing each other. But he knew Gido was right, and soon they were off. Only a half hour after crossing the bridge the party came to the Kilo Pass cutoff turning northward. "Well, here goes nothing," commented Hasko as he turned north with Gido.

The five didn't delay their travels by stopping for lunch. They decided to eat as they traveled feeling the excitement of meeting up with their friends as they came closer and closer to the ruins. They were certain that their friends' journey had been quicker. They anticipated meeting the other leprechauns there and wanted to get together with them as soon as possible.

The day seemed to drag on slowly as days often do when anticipating something. The afternoon's travel seemed to go on for endless hours. The day was again filled with patchy clouds which in conjunction with the trees helped to keep the sun from beating down on the travelers. The journey was cool, and the weather was comfortable.

It was approaching sunset when a cry went out from Hasko, "Tako Ruins dead ahead!" Then in his excitement he started to run toward the ruins.

The others followed his lead sensing the excitement that he felt. Soon the walls of the crumbled city were clearly within view and Hasko, who was well ahead of the rest, cried out, "Look, I see their packs." He pointed at the hastily dropped packs of the Giter expedition along the side of the road close to the entrance of the ruins. He ran on through the entrance and into the ruins hoping to find his friends. He was struck with horror. There off in the distance lying on the ground and covered with riposters was what appeared to be the lifeless form of Yanon. "Hurry," he screamed back at his friends and ran off toward Yanon.

The others seeing Hasko draw his sword and take off running realized that there must be trouble. Their speed took on a sudden burst of energy as they raced toward the middle of the ruins with swords drawn and ready for battle. The first sight that met their eyes was Hasko frantically battling riposters away from the fallen form of Yanon. Then they saw Obydon, surrounded by a strange orange glow, standing over Bydola. He wobbled and seemed unsteady as if all his energy had been drained out of him. His shirt was soaked with blood.

"Riposters must be fought,
Back-to-back;
Hiztin go to Hasko,
Jesves and I attack," Gido was frantically yelling out instructions. Hiztin hurried over to Hasko and took his position at his back. Jesves and Gido went to relieve the wavering Bydola. He would help take over the guard of Obydon. And Gijivure ran to the back of Bydola to give him badly needed protection. He beat the riposter off of Bydola's left shoulder and helped him divert the hoards attacking his back.

Gido's back-to-back technique was very effective against the riposters. He later explained that the elves had been forced to learn how to battle these creatures because they would occasionally be attacked by them out in the fields. With this back-to-back method the riposters were no longer successful at attacking the travelers from the rear. All attacks had to be from the front. Although occasionally one of the mutants would get through a frantically wielded sword, the creatures were not able to inflict the same amount of damage.

The battle raged until it was nearly dark when almost on request the riposters retreated to some distant place in the Tako Ruins. Ragged and bewildered, with the riposters seemingly taking the night off, the expedition was now able to look after their wounded. Minor injuries had been inflicted on Hasko and Hiztin, but Jesves, Gido, and Gijivure had successfully escaped with only a few scratches.

Serious damage had been inflicted on the others. Bydola was still standing but had lost so much blood that he had lost all sense of direction and coordination. Jesves took his hand and led him as best she could back to the camp outside the wall of the ruins. Here Bydola pulled the orange rock out of his pocket, giving the camp enough light in which to work. Jesves went to work on the injuries, using what medical supplies she was able to find in their packs.

The other four, Hasko, Hiztin, Gido, and Gijivure, lifted and carried Yanon, and later Obydon, to the safety of the camp where their wounds could be treated. As they arrived with Obydon and laid him on the grass he stirred and cried out in a whimper, "Elasti!"

"Elasti, did anyone see Elasti?" asked Hasko frantically. No one could answer. They hadn't seen him anywhere. Had the rescue party left him to the mercy of the riposters?

"Try to revive Obydon so that we can find out where Elasti went," yelled Hiztin. Immediately they went to work on Obydon, but he was too far gone to talk. "Let's try Bydola," Hiztin suggested. They attempted to revive Bydola who after much pleading slowly opened his eyes. "Where's Elasti?" they asked him.

"Under the fallen wall," was all he could say before he slumped back into unconsciousness.

"Come on!" Hasko cried out to Hiztin and the four jumped up quickly to go and retrieve their companion. Jesves stayed back to work on the injuries. The four found it necessary to take the mysterious orange rock with them so they could see leaving Jesves to work by firelight. As they searched around the ruins, they found so many fallen walls that it became difficult to discern which might be the one Elasti was buried under. Then suddenly Hiztin cried out, "Over here. This must be the one. The dust is still pretty loose."

Hasko rushed over and helped Hiztin dig around in the dust. Each of the other searchers also made their way over and started to dig down into the dust and rubble in different places hoping they might encounter Elasti. After some time, the search seemed hopeless. They found nothing. They began to wonder if they had even found the correct "fallen wall". Gido gave up the search and started to look around for another fallen wall as the others continued digging holes.

Finally, Hiztin was successfully clearing away some rubble when he encountered what he guessed was the back of a belt. They rescuers quickly cleared the rubble away and uncovered Elasti finding him lying face down and unconsciousness. They pulled him out of his grave and began an attempt to revive him.

"He's still breathing,'" exclaimed Hasko with glee. "Let's hurry and get him back to camp." Hasko, Hiztin, Gido, and Gijivure carried him back to the camp guided by the strange light.

Back at the camp they checked him further and found that, although he appeared unconscious Elasti had no broken bones. Unfortunately, he had a large number of dirt filled scrapes and bruises that needed immediate attention.

Hasko, Hiztin assisted Jesves with Yanon, Obydon, and Bydola. The loss of blood for each of them had been tremendous and it was this loss of blood, more than their injuries that endangered their lives. Jesves had earlier tried to bind up the most serious of the injuries in order to stop the flow of blood but now all the injuries needed to be given proper attention stitching and taping the cuts so they could heal properly.

Yanon had experienced the most serious of the injuries which covered the entire back side of his body. Although many of these individual wounds were no larger than the size of a thumb, they still needed proper attention. His most serious gash was the one on his head. It was the size of the palm of his hand and clearly revealed his skull cap. It was difficult to bind this injury properly since so much of the skin had been removed and the wound bled profusely. The injury on his right shoulder wasn't as bad as at first feared and could easily be bandaged.

The next most serious injuries belonged to Obydon who also had many of the same thumb sized gashes on his legs, back, shoulders, and arms. He only had about half as many gashes in total as Yanon. The protection that Bydola was able to offer him had saved him from the seriousness of Yanon's injuries. He was inflicted with one of these gashes on his left cheek which was extremely close to his eye. This concerned Jesves greatly because it was hard to tell if any injury had occurred to the eye itself.

Bydola having been the strongest and biggest of the three was able to survive the greatest loss of blood. His most serious injury was on his left shoulder where the riposter had attached itself and dug a deep hole. He also had several thumb sized wounds. But in comparison to Obydon and Yanon he had been very lucky.

Jesves was saddened as she busily worked to save her comrades. Never before had she seen so much blood and pain. She whispered a silent prayer to the God of the rainbow as she hurriedly tried to do her best taking on the role of doctor.

As Hasko, Hiztin, and Jesves attended to the wounds, Gido and Gijivure started constructing a lean-to against the outer wall of the city. This would provide a place where the expedition could hide and protect themselves against the possibility of a repeat attack from the riposters which they knew would occur in the morning. They felled a few smaller trees and used their trunks for the structure of the lean-to. They then used leaf covered branches to close in their new shelter.

The lean-to was built quite long and roomy. The elves felt this was necessary if they were to house nine travelers and still be able to have some comforts. They realized that they would be forced to spend several days in this home waiting for the recovery of their newfound friends.

Hasko saw that Jesves and Hiztin were doing a good job of cleaning and preparing the injuries. He had a problem seeing so much blood, so he proceeded to focus on maintaining the fire. This fire would supply additional light for the elf's construction efforts. He also prepared a meal which everyone hastily ate after which he assisted Gido and Gijivure by bringing them branches that they could use to close in their lean-to structure.

"Can any of you explain this orange light that Bydola's got?" questioned Hiztin.

"I've been wondering about that myself," returned Hasko overhearing the question. "When I arrived at the ruins ahead of the rest of you there was still a little daylight, and I noticed that the same orange light surrounded Bydola as well."

"Yeah," returned Hiztin, "I noticed that. I wonder what it means. Do you think the lepelves have discovered some kind of new light?"

"The light you adore,
Legends explain;
It is the gain,
Of the Creator.
No one has ever seen it,
Doubted it wasn't true;
I see it first with you,
It is a mystery."

Gijivure explained but his explanation seemed to confuse more than explain this light. Hiztin decided that he would just have to wait until Bydola had recovered sufficiently so that he could explain the light himself.

After several hours of working on the injuries and the lean-to structure using the firelight and the light of Bydola's rock, the building of their shelter and the patching of the wounds was finally done. The party slowly and carefully transported the four injured leprechauns into their new home.

"How are your friends?
I hope they're fine;
I'd gladly take,
Their pains as mine," Gido expressed sympathetically. He truly hurt for each of the suffering leprechauns.

"I think they all have a good chance of recovering commented Jesves, "but it will take time."

"This is time I'm willing to spend," commented Hiztin sadly remembering how only a few days earlier it was Jesves who had been suffering. He dreaded seeing anyone in such pain. "Who would have ever expected our reunion to be like this? I would sure like to see these guys back in full spirits again."

Bydola had slightly regained some of his consciousness while being transported but he was still very week and as he lay again on the ground with his eyes closed, he listened to the elves and his leprechaun friends. It caused him to smile. The thought occurred to him that maybe it was possible to have the Creator's love shared by all. The love and compassion that he heard expressed by these dear individuals, some of whom he had not even met, made a tear swell up in his eyes.

Then he was hit with the thought, "Has everything been recovered so that the riposters cannot cause any additional damage? What about those scrolls? Did we recover them? The knowledge within them could be invaluable. But more importantly what about his newly acquired staff. Had anyone retrieved the staff that was given to him by the Creator? And what about the Southern Sword? Was it also lost somewhere out in that rubble? The entire mission to the North required that the sword not be lost." He must warn them. He tried to speak but found that he was just too weak. He strained himself trying to move his hand in an attempt to get their attention, but his efforts drained him of the little strength that he had left, and he dozed off into unconsciousness.

CHAPTER FOURTEEN

THE KILO PASS

It was a busy evening at the tavern in Giter, much busier than normal. The townspeople were filled with curiosity wondering what had happened during Gabrona's trek to find the king and why the king's trusted aid Giterod had returned to Giter ahead of the king. Why had Giterod been so anxious to chase after those leprechauns after they had left town earlier that afternoon? It didn't make sense to any of them.

Gabrona was busily serving tables and was repeatedly stopped to tell his story. He was so much the center of attention that his father was becoming jealous. His father always wanted to be the center of attention and the townspeople were showing too much of it to his son. The tavern owner jumped up onto the bar and barked out for the attention of the crowd. "Quiet down everyone." He stomped his feet several times in an attempt to get their attention. "Listen up!" he yelled.

Slowly the crowd became silent. It wasn't the first time the tavern owner had gotten up on his soapbox to give everyone a lecture. Usually it was his drunkenness speaking and no one was very interested in hearing it. Most of the crowd just assumed that this was another one of those drunken lectures that he was so fond of.

"I want your attention so I can tell all of you at the same time what happened to my son on his trip with those fool foreigners when they went to visit the king." He stomped his foot again. The crowd became quieter. This sounded like something they wanted to hear. Then he continued, "Every one of you keeps interrupting my son and you're not letting him get his work done so I'm gonna tell his story once-and-for-all so that you won't have to bother him anymore. Then leave him alone and let him do his work. Now listen up so I don't have to repeat it.

"Gabrona was paid to take those leprechauns to the king. They told the king some fool story about an attack from the Kabul. Well, the king didn't believe it, so the leprechauns were crazy enough to show him the Southern Sword that they were carrying. The king sent Giterod after them in order to get it before those fools lost it. The king wants to secure it for the Southern Plains. He believes it belongs to the city of Giter. Those fool leprechauns were going to take it to the North Groves where the dwarfs would surely have stolen it and then we'd never see it again. Anyway, that's all there is to the story now do any of you have any questions before I get back to work?"

"Yes, I do," a skinny tall lepelf spoke up. "Why do these leprechauns think that we're getting attacked anyway?"

"How should I know?" returned Gabrona's father. "They were probably just trying to rip off the king and get some of his jewels to help them in their make-believe war. They would have probably taken them to the North Groves too. Who knows what kinds of tricks they had up their sleeves."

"Why not let Gabrona tell that part of the story?" a large woman, sitting near the door of the tavern yelled out. "He told me all about the meeting with the king when he explained it to me."

Gabrona's father was furious. Instead of stopping the interest in his son he had now sparked an even deeper interest in him. "He can't be interrupted from his duties. He has to get his job done."

"Let him up there to talk to us. We all have a right to know." It was the first lepelf blurting out the request, followed by several murmurs in the crowd supporting his idea.

"Get up here Gabrona," yelled the tavern owner to his son, "but make it quick."

Gabrona climbed up on the tavern bar and began telling his version of the story. "The leprechauns arrived here four days ago, and it took them that long just to get a chance to see the king. On the first day the king told them he was too busy, and he would see them on the second day. Then when they returned on the second day the king had left for a goose hunt so they asked my father if he knew of anyone who could take them to the king and my father volunteered me for a price.

"The following morning, I went north with them to find the king's camp and we arrived there at nightfall. I went to the king and requested an audience for them. The king allowed it even though he wasn't very happy about it. They told their story to him. Their story goes like this. About two weeks ago one of those three leprechauns that were here to see the king had also been sent to the North Groves about one week ago in order to find out why the dwarfs weren't trading with them anymore. This leprechaun and two other leprechauns came through here asking if there were any lepelves that wanted to go North with them. They were turned them down."

"I remember that," one of the lepelves in the audience yelled out. "I was by the palace when they came through here and I went over to hear what they were doing. It sounded like a pretty fool idea, going up there to meet those dwarfs and all. They were laughed out of town."

"That's right," Gabrona continued his story. "They went on through town and headed for the Albo Pass. They had just crossed over the Avoli River Bridge on the pass when they were attacked by gnomes and two of the leprechauns were killed. The third one that was here a couple days ago barely escaped with his life.

"That third leprechaun made it back to Amins and reported the news to his council. They in turn decided that it was now even more important to contact the dwarfs because they held the Northern Sword. The two swords would have to be crossed in order to wake the Wizard of Havinis. They think that without the help of the wizard we don't stand a chance against the Kabul."

Someone in the crowd started to laugh and soon several more started to laugh. Then someone from the crowd blurted out. "Wake the Wizard of Havinis? That's the dumbest thing I ever heard. There's no such thing as a Wizard of Havinis, let alone believing that a couple swords are going to awake him."

"Maybe they're going to slap him with the sword," someone else joked. "That would wake him for sure!"

"They were serious," Gabrona yelled out at the crowd in frustration.

"So am I," returned the second jokester. The crowd started laughing even harder.

Gabrona could see his father laughing at him and this hurt him greatly. Gabrona's face started to turn red more out of anger than embarrassment. He yelled out, "They even brought the Southern Sword with to show the king that they were serious."

"All that proves is that they're a bunch of fools." This time the comment came from Gabrona's father which made it hurt even worse.

Gabrona started to get down off of the bar. Before he could get very far someone in the crowd yelled out, "Hold it! I want to hear the rest of the story."

Gabrona wasn't in a mood to continue his story but one look from his father told him he had better return to the top of the bar and continue. His father felt in charge of the crowd again and everyone laughed at his joke. He was now using his son to boost his popularity.

Gabrona went on, "The leprechauns requested that the king plan to protect Giter. They also requested that the king send an ambassador along with them to the North Groves to demonstrate the true unity of the South. The king told them to return the next morning and he would give them an answer. But the next morning when we went back the king had departed for one of his morning goose escapades."

"Be respectful when you talk about our king!" a palace guard in the crowd barked out. The entire audience fell silent waiting to see if a conflict between Gabrona and the guard would flare up.

Gabrona ignored the guard's comment and the guard didn't push the issue. "When the king finally returned to the camp," Gabrona continued, "he sent Giterod to join the leprechauns and that is why he returned here to Giter earlier today."

"Yea that's right," the guard spoke up again. "He told me that the king had sent him to steal the Southern Sword so that he could protect it. That's why he was trying to stall the leprechauns in Giter, and why he went after them this evening."

"I think they're really serious about us being attacked." Gabrona was defensive. "They even sent a party to Gije to get help from the elves."

"And those fool elves are dumb enough to help the leprechauns too," someone yelled out. Gabrona saw that trying to convince his townspeople was a hopeless task. He became too frustrated and embarrassed to continue trying. He climbed down from the bar and ran off to his room where he slammed the door, jumped on his bed and started crying.

Soon his father entered his room and scolded him, "That's about enough of that. It's time you got back to work. You can't just lie around here all evening when I need your help out there. Now get going."

Gabrona was hesitant but he saw that he had no choice. He got up and slowly walked out into the tavern. As he entered the tavern, he noticed that many of the patrons had already left for the evening. The ones that were still there were pretty drunk by now and as they saw him enter, they started laughing at him once again. He did his best to ignore them and started clearing tables.

Gabrona's work lasted for another three hours. It was now the wee early hours of the morning when the last drunk finally left the bar to stumble homeward. Gabrona returned to his room. Without getting undressed he jumped on his bed and lay there. He thought about the humiliation he had suffered. What angered him the most was the lack of interest that the townspeople had in the danger that existed. "They won't believe it until it slaps them in the face," he thought out loud.

He also felt embarrassed that the only lepelf that was going along on this expedition was a thief. He felt utterly humiliated to think that all his life he had considered Giterod to be a hero and now he learned that he was nothing more than the king's private crook. "*Those leprechauns must really think we lepelves are stupid*," he thought.

Thoughts continued to turn around in his mind until he dozed off into unconsciousness.

When Gabrona awoke in the morning he found himself still in his work clothes. He had been so wrapped up in his thoughts and frustrations that he had fallen asleep without changing.

It was already late morning by the time he awoke. He had experienced a late night and now he knew he would be in trouble for having gotten up so late and for not having gotten his morning chores completed. He rushed outside to get wood for the fire and returned with his arms loaded down.

As he entered the tavern his father was alone sitting at a table eating his breakfast. "It's about time you got up," his father barked. "You realize you were quite an embarrassment to me last night don't you. You and your stories about leprechauns were ridiculous. You darn near got yourself thrown in prison for making the king look bad, and then what would I do for help around the tavern? You watch your tongue in the future, you hear."

Gabrona nodded his head. He knew better than to talk back to his father. He continued his chores and kept himself as busy as possible. It was all he could do to keep from screaming out with irritation whenever someone came into the tavern and harassed him about his leprechaun story. He just wanted to avoid the whole issue but the lepelves wouldn't leave his thoughts.

After another long day he returned once again to his room. His mind had been rolling all day and by this time he had made a decision. He wasn't going to lie around in his bed until he fell asleep with his clothes on. He was going to leave. During the day he had slipped food into his room and now he bundled up some clothes and the food and tied them together into a sack.

He couldn't handle another day of ridicule like the one he had already experienced. He decided that if Giter wouldn't help itself then he was going to have to be the one who helped all of them. In spite of his frustration and irritation it was still his home and he was going save it. He would show them.

He slung the sack over his shoulder and snuck out the back door of the tavern. He cut north of town avoiding anyone that might recognize him. That way he avoided the South Road. He hurried along in the fields until he was past the western edge of town. Then he turned south in order to meet the South Road and continue his journey along that route.

Once on the South Road he headed west. He had decided that he was personally going to be the lepelf representative on the expedition to the North Groves with or without the king's permission. He was determined in what he was about to do. As he walked along, he remembered his humiliation. He thought about his home, and he started crying.

Giterod was crushed. The leprechauns had once again been successful in tricking him. He could never appear before the king with his story of failure. He would be the laughingstock of Giter. He thought of inventing some other story about how the leprechauns tricked him and robbed him but then the king would just get mad at him and consider him a fool. He would be better off going back and following the leprechauns. Maybe he would still be able to find an opportunity to accomplish his mission.

The leprechauns would never trust him now. He would have to sneak behind them without them knowing that he was following. When they were asleep, he would have to again try to steal the sword. How foolish of him to have let himself get tricked the way he did.

Chills ran down his back as he thought about venturing alone into unknown areas that were possibly infested with gnomes. The thought of the dangers that lay ahead were more than he could bear. He decided to quit thinking about them. He wiped the tears out of his eyes, stood up and started walking at a fast pace west along the South Road hoping that it wouldn't be long before he was able to catch them.

He crossed the Avol River by wading and swimming across pulling the rope from the pull boat back to the other side. He then fastened the rope to a tree. He would need that boat later when he once again tried to make his escape from the leprechauns. He continued his journey west. He traveled as quickly as he could all day long and just as night approached he could see the Kilo Pass cutoff in the distance. He climbed up into a cluster of trees and made himself a bed. Soon he was asleep. Even his fear of gnomes couldn't keep him awake after the quick pace he had maintained all day long. He also suffered from having had a short night's sleep the previous night, which made him even more tired.

In the morning he got up, ate breakfast and took off again following the leprechauns. It was shortly after noon when he was finally able to see the Tako Ruins off in the distance. He noticed the packs of his traveling partners lying just outside of the walls of the ruins. He quickly ducked behind some bushes hoping that he hadn't been spotted. He heard the leprechauns talking just on the other side of the wall and guessed that they must be exploring the ruined remains of the city.

He stayed in hiding for the rest of the day watching the events that took place. He heard a loud crash from inside the walls of the city and guessed that some old structure must have broken down. He saw the arrival of the party from Gije off in the distance and watched their hurried entrance within the walls of the city. He heard them shouting but was not able to determine what all the excitement was focused on. Later he noticed several of the leprechauns being carried out of the ruins and guessed that they must have injured themselves somehow in the ruins. He watched them build a lean-to, wondering why the elves and lepelves insisted on going through so much trouble. Why not just use their tents?

As the leprechauns and the elves bedded down for the night, he realized that he wouldn't get a chance to steal the sword that night. The lean-to had made it too difficult to get anywhere near the sword without being noticed. He decided to bed down for the night but as he did so the thought occurred to him, *"What if those fools left the sword behind in the ruins when they carried out those injured leprechauns?"* He decided he had better check in the morning before they wake up. He dozed off to sleep.

It was barely sunlight when Giterod was already up and sneaking over toward the ruins. He couldn't hear anyone in the lean-to. He guessed that they were still asleep and that he was safe. He entered the area of the ruins and started to scout around for a sign of anything that the leprechauns may have left behind.

Then he noticed one of the swords. Surely if they left this sword behind, perhaps they also left others behind. Maybe they were scared off. Or maybe they had just become too lazy to carry their heavy swords. He looked around walking in various directions hoping to find other treasures that the leprechauns may have left behind. After some time, he went back and took a closer look at the sword that had been laying there and he realized that this was indeed the Southern Sword. He had been successful in acquiring the sword and the King would be so proud of him. He picked up the sword and waved it toward the sky. He would be a hero back home.

Then he heard a ruffling sound that sounded like feathers of a large number of birds. That sound was followed by a screeching sound.

"We must hurry up,
We must get back-to-back.
That's the only way, to avoid another attack," Gido recommended. The party of seven leprechauns and two elves heard the riposte beginning their attack on the lean-to shelter.

Luckily Gido had noticed the attack before any of the creatures had managed to work their way through the shelter but it wouldn't be long before they would have broken in. Gido realized that the back-to-back strategy wasn't necessary since no riposters had broken through yet. He grabbed his sword and swiftly wacked the head off of the riposter he had first noticed and who was nearly through the wall of the shelter. Then he proceeded to beat off many of the other creatures as they struggled for entry into the protective enclosure.

The travelers distributed the riposter holes into the shelter so that each could protect their share. This made defending the shelter easy. They would wait until a riposter started to make a slight entry into their shelter and then they would quickly kill the creature with their swords before it could get through.

"What a way to wake a guy up in the morning," complained Hasko as he swatted the head off another creature. "Isn't it bad enough that I have to defend you guys. Do you really have to wake me up by stomping on my face? I'm pretty lucky. I ended up with only a few bites. If I rolled over on one of them, I'd sure feel it." Then he wondered, "Do you think we're going to have to keep up fighting with the riposters all day?"

"I sure hope not," returned Hiztin. "I'm getting hungry. I'd like to get a bite to eat before too long."

"Riposters make,
A delightful meal;
Their meat will feel,
Good in your belly," Gijivure commented thinking that the process of killing riposters could be turned to their gain.

"Yuck," returned Hiztin. "I couldn't bear to think of eating a creature that has some of my blood or hide sitting in its stomach. No way am I going to eat one of those creatures."

Hasko laughed. He remembered how squeamish Hiztin had been when they encountered the Quali Swamps. However, Gijivure was slightly disappointed. He thought his idea of eating the riposters was a good one.

"Look we don't all have to keep up this defense," commented Jesves "Why don't we close up some of these holes with the branches we've been sleeping on, and we ought to be able to free up one or two of us so that we can take turns eating. Besides I'd like to check the bandages and injuries of Yanon, Elasti, Bydola, and Obydon."

"Good idea," returned Hasko who had taken up a position next to her. "Hiztin and I will guard your holes while you try to close a few of them up." Hiztin was located on the other side of Jesves, and he and Hasko were now sharing the load of Jesves' area, keeping the riposters out. Jesves scrambled around in an attempt to locate branches that could be inserted into some of the existing holes thus shutting the riposters out.

"Don't cover up all the holes;
Always leave open a few;
The creatures will pick the easiest route,
Makes our jobs easier to do," Gido suggested.

Jesves understood Gido's idea and she intentionally left several open holes that were easy to get at with a sword. Suddenly, as she was filling in a hole near the floor, a riposter attempted to break through right above her head. It was too close to Jesves for Hasko to take a good swing at without the risk of hitting her. Before he could warn Jesves the riposter had broken through the protective covering. It was now flying around inside the shelter.

At first it appeared as though the creature was more frightened than the leprechauns or the elves. It fluttered around confused and trying to decide where to strike. It seemed lost. It did not have the protection of a larger number of riposters that it had grown accustomed to. Then it noticed Obydon lying helplessly on the ground and it made a dive for him. By now Jesves had realized what had happened and had recovered her sword. Just as she saw the creature approach Obydon she quickly swung her sword and sliced the creature in half causing the pieces to fly through the air on top of Bydola's sleeping face.

"What happened?" blurted Bydola as he jumped up. He brushed the creature off of his face and looked around. "What's going on? Where are we?"

Everyone was surprised to see Bydola's sudden recovery. "We're in a lean-to that our friends the elves built for us. And we're in the midst of fighting off a riposter attack," explained Jesves. "Don't worry. Everything will be alright."

"How can I help?" asked Bydola attempting to get up.

"By staying where you are!" insisted Jesves. "We're doing just fine. We just let one of the critters slip through."

"But I feel fine. Give me a sword. I can help too," Bydola demanded.

"Nothing doing," returned Hasko still thinking he was badly injured. "You stay right where you are."

Bydola looked around. He noticed that the battle was indeed under control. The riposters appeared to be flying to their slaughter and the elves and leprechauns seemed to have the invasion contained.

Jesves continued closing up some of the holes that were harder to protect. Soon the job of protecting the lean-to had become an assignment that three individuals could easily handle. Hiztin volunteered to prepare breakfast and Jesves went back to work checking on the injured.

She approached Bydola first since he was already awake. She had him roll over and took the bandages off of his left shoulder, the one that had been injured most severely. As she finished unwrapping the wound, she was shocked. She sat down and stared at what she saw with her mouth gaped wide open. After a couple moments, when she had recovered from her shock, she called out, "Hiztin, come here."

Hiztin hurried over to see what had caused her sudden urgency. When he saw the reason, he was also amazed. In the spot where the night before there had been a large gaping hole, a gash so deep that it surely must have hit the bone, there was now nothing. The injury had healed over entirely. There wasn't even a scar. There wasn't any sign that there had ever been an injury. Jesves and Hiztin stared at each other in amazement. They feared that what they would say would sound stupid.

Finally, Hiztin broke the silence. "Let's check his other shoulder."

Slowly they removed the bandages off of his right shoulder. Even though the injuries on this shoulder had been minor in comparison, they had also disappeared as completely as the one from his left shoulder.

"Let's check the others," Jesves whispered trying to prevent Bydola or anyone else from becoming curious about their discoveries. They moved over to Yanon who had suffered the severest of the injuries and checked one of the minor gashes on his back. Although the bleeding had stopped the dried hard blood still identified the location of the sore. In his case the skin around the hole was still frayed and broken much the way it had been the previous night. They went over to Obydon and found that his injuries were still there as were those of Elasti.

"Alright. That does it," Hiztin broke out. He couldn't stand the mystery any longer. "What's going on here Bydola?" Bydola rolled over and curiously looked at Hiztin as if he had no understanding of what he meant. Hiztin had managed to gain the attention of the elves and Hasko as well with his outburst. "First we see you with some strange orange ora around you just like you are right now," Hiztin pointed at the dull orange light that emanated from Bydola's body. "Then you come up with this glowing rock. And now your injuries disappear. What's happened to you? Are you possessed by something?" Hiztin hoped for some explanation. The comment about Bydola being possessed was intended as an exaggerated joke.

"I guess you could say in a way that I am possessed," Bydola started his explanation. The others were stunned. What had happened to their friend? He continued, "Unfortunately I have been forbidden from telling the story of what happened to me. All I can say is that I can distinguish good and evil and I have been given other powers of which I still know very little about. I'm still learning them. For example, I didn't know anything about this healing power. It must not be complete since I still feel weak from the loss of blood. But apparently, I have the ability to heal quickly, faster than most other individuals." Bydola paused for a moment and looked at his inquisitors. Then he asked, "Now you must answer an urgent question for me. Did any of you retrieve the Southern Sword when you so bravely saved us from the riposters?"

The expeditioners all looked at each other. They had all forgotten about the Southern Sword in their haste to help their injured friends. They realized that their first priority today after sunset when the riposters went back to their homes would be to find and retrieve the Southern

Sword as well as any other items left behind like the Protee staff and their travel sacks.

The leprechauns and elves passed the time by relating their respecttive travel stories with each other. The day drug on slowly waiting for the riposters to end their siege on the expedition's shelter. Hasko started by telling the story of their travels across the Southern back road. He discussed the muidivengers and the swamp rats. He over dramatized the stories and thereby made it extra exciting for his listeners.

Then it was Bydola's turn and he related the experience with Giterod explaining how the lepelf had attempted to steal the sword. This surprised everyone. "I noticed you didn't have any lepelves with you," commented Hasko, "but I figured it was because they just didn't want to go along. But now you tell me that they even went so far as to try to disrupt our expedition to the North. It amazes me how stupid those fools can really be." They hoped that Giterod had not been able to find his way back to their camp last night and had not been able to look for the sword during the night.

Bydola continued, "We also found several scrolls out there. Did any of you see them?" No one answered and Gijivure shook his head no. "How about my staff? I have a wooden staff which is slightly taller than I am. Did any of you see it?" Again, no answer. "Hopefully by tonight I will feel strong enough to help you go out there and search. We'll experience a great loss toward the success of this mission if we lose these items."

Bydola laid back down returning to his prone position. He wanted to recover as much as possible so he could conduct a search that evening. Meanwhile he left the others stunned with his comments. They didn't know what to say. Not only had he not answered any of their questions about the changes that had happened to him. Instead he had left them with more to think about and worry about.

"This knowledge of good and evil,
And the orange light rock;
This is all Creator talk,
Somehow, he was influenced by the Creator.
Legend talks of such things,
But it says his presence won't be here;
Until the time when life may disappear,
In Small World," Gijivure's comment only added more confusion to an already frustrating situation.

"You know what?" thought Hiztin out loud, "Gijivure's right. When we came out of the Quali Swamp we had lost the trail and some mud creatures that called themselves muidivengers suddenly appeared to help us out. They were strange little creatures. They were real slimy and you couldn't tell which side was front. Anyways this one led us down a shortcut back to our trail using a series of tunnels. Based on what we saw there must have been a whole civilization of muidivengers. There were a large number of tunnels we saw down there. Along the walls of these tunnels were these same orange rocks, exactly like this one that Bydola has except a little smaller. When one of the muidivengers saw us looking at the light he said, 'Creator make'. Somehow Bydola must have encountered these same creatures along the South Road," then he turned to Bydola and asked, "Isn't that right Bydola?"

Bydola had rolled over in amazement at Hiztin's comment and was now staring at him with his mouth gaping wide open. Questions rolled around in Bydola's mind. Was the Creator involved with the success of the entire expedition? Has he personally been chosen to be the source of unusual power giving the Gije expedition special powers as well? Was Hiztin's team in the same tunnels that he was or do the muidivenger tunnels stretch all over the Southern Plains? "Yes, I guess so," responded Bydola. His curiosity got the better of him and he had to ask. "Did you see the Creator?"

"No." It was Hasko that decided to answer the question. "I was never sure if there even was such a thing as a creator or if they were just making the whole thing up. Actually, we were glad to get out of those tunnels when we did. We were getting worried that we were going to be stuck down there forever."

"There is a creator!" Bydola responded, "But I don't dare say any more than that. I've probably already said too much." The others were stunned. They wished they could open up his mind and learn all his secrets. What had happened to Bydola? Perhaps they would never know.

Over time, fending off the riposters had become easier. Only occasionally would one attempt to venture through one of the small openings. This made it more relaxing for the expedition members, allowing them to enjoy the meal that Hiztin had prepared.

Jesves had become the doctor of the party. She had given a thorough cleaning and rebinding of the wounds on Yanon, Obydon, and Elasti. Elasti was regaining consciousness and even though he was too stiff and sore to move he was able to converse with the other members of the expedition. He was very interested in hearing everyone's story of what had happened since he had missed out on most of the excitement after he had been buried under the collapsed wall. He was interested and concerned about the riposters. He was especially curious about the strange healing experience that Bydola had gone through. He was also happy to hear the successful arrival of the Gije party in spite of all their difficulties. But he was extremely worried about the injuries of Yanon and Obydon and blamed himself for being stupid enough to climb the wall that crashed down and caused the riposters to attack.

Elasti had severe back and neck pains from his wounds when the wall fell on him. It felt as though he had sprained his back. It hurt to move. No broken bones could be found and there were only a few open scratches. But his body was also filled with large bruises many of which were the size of the palm of his hand. There wasn't much Jesves could do to help him. The best thing that he could do was to rest. At least there didn't seem to be anything life threatening.

Yanon however brought her great concern. His skull injury still exposed the skull cap and she wondered if he would ever be able to heal back to normal. Feeling sad and worried she said, "I'm afraid that Yanon

will always be missing this hunk of his scalp. I wish I could do something to help him."

"Buy him a hat," joked Hiztin, trying to cheer her up.

"That's an awful comment," Jesves returned.

"I'm sorry. I was just trying to cheer you up," returned Hiztin, feeling rather stupid at his attempt to make her smile.

Obydon's injuries seemed to be recovering as nicely as they could in one night. The injury on his cheek still worried Jesves, but it didn't appear to be as bad as at first. Occasionally he would groan and turn his head. This also gave the indication that he was recovering but again it was apparent that his recovery would take quite a bit of time.

Hasko, Hiztin, Gido, and Gijivure took turns guarding against the riposters while Jesves continued tending the injuries. The day went slow and was almost boring with the entire party being packed together in the small lean-to. The thought that they would have to spend even more days cramped together started to wear on their nerves. Hasko was the first to express his frustration. "I think that tonight I'll increase the size of this lean-to before I go nuts being squashed up in here."

"Increase the size,
We should not do;
We'll have a lot,
More work to do.
The riposters will,
Have much more room;
With which to try,
To cause our doom.
I know it's hard,
To be so tight;
But while we are,
There'll be less to fight," Gido felt safer having less of an area to defend. He didn't want to make the job of protecting the lean-to harder than necessary.

The day drug on. Each person in the party shared their stories. Bydola expressing excitement about the scrolls that the group had found. Elasti worried about the Southern Sword and if Giterod might have come back to look for it. The Gije expedition told of all their trials and frustrations during their travels. Then they discussed next steps. But soon there was little left to discuss.

As evening approached, the setting of the sun was noticeable. It no longer beat down on their lean-to. The approaching darkness could be seen through the riposter holes. The party ate dinner and as they were finishing their meal the attack of the riposters stopped.

"Looks like it's safe for us to leave this tunnel," commented Hasko. "Is it possible for us to move out of range of these riposters so we won't have to spend another day cooped up in here?"

"No way," Jesves insisted. "I won't let you move Yanon. The danger of his wounds reopening is too great. He's lost too much blood already. I'm also not sure that Elasti can be moved. The pain we would inflict on him during the move would be immense. We're just stuck waiting it out here for at least one more day. Then we'll see how everyone is doing."

"Well at least I'm going to get a little freedom now." Hasko pushed one of the end enclosures of the lean-to out of his way and started to exit the shelter. Once outside he confirmed that the darkness was upon them and the riposters were gone. He poked his head back inside the enclosure. "You don't happen to have two of those orange stones do you Bydola? It's awfully dark out there."

"No, I don't," he sadly replied. Then remembering the missing belongings that still lay amongst the ruins he suggested, "Maybe we should venture out into the ruins and search for the sword, my staff, and the scrolls. But I'll need to take the stone with me. Would anyone like to go?" All but Elasti and Obydon, who still couldn't move, wanted to enjoy a little freedom so they left the shelter guided by Bydola and his strange orange light.

They stayed close together more out of a fear of the unknown around them, than out of a lack of light. The orange stone emitted a light like that of a great bonfire and illuminated quite a large section of the surrounding area.

They entered the ruins and started to look around. Bydola, still a little weak from the loss of blood slowly went off in the direction of the scroll library where he had previously dropped his staff. He found everything exactly as he had so hastily left it earlier. He picked up his staff and found it unharmed. Then he picked up the two scrolls that he had left lying on the ground earlier and rolled them up. He reached into the scroll tunnel and pulled out two more scrolls. He planned to read them when he returned to the lean-to.

"Oh God help!" came the panicked cry of Jesves. She had found the Southern Sword but what she found with it horrified her. The others came quickly running over to her side.

Gabrona had spent the night along the side of the South Road, making himself as comfortable as he could in the grass. It was now early afternoon and he was scared. He realized the risk that he may never be able to catch up with the North Grove expedition. The group may have already gone quite a ways up the Kilo Pass and he may not be able to catch up with them. He felt it would be impossible to battle gnomes by himself.

But since he was going to be in trouble with his father anyway, he decided to push on as quickly as he could. He would at least try to catch up with the party. Later if he got to the point where catching up with them seemed hopeless, he would simply have to turn around and return home. But he would not give up yet. He would try to catch up.

He thought about a strange feeling that had come over him. It was something that he couldn't quite identify. He knew it had something to do with the Southern Sword because ever since he held it, he was over-whelmed with the urge to venture out to search for worlds beyond Giter. This was an unusual feeling for a lepelf to have. Most lepelves wanted to stay at home in their own little lepelf world. However, he suddenly felt the need to achieve some greater purpose. The feeling confused him. It was unexplainable and this bothered him. But he decided to follow his urge to chase after the expedition.

At the Avol River he pulled the pull boat across to his side and then quickly used it to go back across the river. He hurried along the trail hoping he would get as far as the Kilo Pass before nightfall but the evening caught up with him too quickly and he found that he would be forced to spend another night along the South Road.

The following morning, he got up early and took off quickly, racing to catch up with the party. He became fascinated by the scenery. He had never seen this part of Small World before, and its beauty excited him.

He continued along realizing that if he didn't push himself further, he would end up spending still another night along the South Road. But just as the sun was about to set, he noticed a cutoff to the North, some distance ahead of him. The excitement of finally making it to what must surely be the Kilo Pass came over him and he started running.

He turned north and shortly thereafter passed by what appeared to have been the earlier campsite of the leprechaun expedition. Finding no one there he tried to hurry onward but soon it became too dark for him to travel any further. However, finding the campsite increased his hope of catching up with the expedition. The travelers couldn't be more than a couple days ahead. The campsite wasn't that old.

Being too dark to travel he made a bed for himself in the grasses and soon dozed off to sleep.

"What was it," asked Hasko as he joined Jesves, looking down at a glob that was destroyed beyond recognition. He wanted to see what all the excitement was about. When he arrived at her side, he looked down at what he initially thought might be a gnome. The two of them stared at a mess of blood and bones, destroyed by the riposters. A hand reached out from the gore trying desperately to cling to the Southern Sword.

"Let's turn it over what we can," commented Hiztin, who by now had also arrived along with the others. He drew his sword and attempted to wedge it under the remains of a carcass. Gido quickly did the same in an attempt to assist him. The body was stiff, but the damage done by the riposters had left it destroyed to the point where it started to fall apart when they tried to flip it. Its arms fell from the body remaining attached only by the fabric of the shirtsleeves.

As the body flipped over, Bydola, the last of the party to come to the scene recognized the face. "Oh, how ugly," he exclaimed. "It's Giterod, or what's left of him anyway. I wouldn't have wished a death like this even on him. What a cruel way to die. He apparently came back for the sword."

"He ended up paying for his evil intentions with his life," Hiztin stated.

"How ugly is life,
How cruel it can be;
When even the devil,
Must suffer like me," Gido expressed a mellow scriptural passage from the Elfin Book of Learning.

"Let's hurry up and bury him," Jesves was getting squeamish. "I can't stand looking at him anymore."

"I know a grave that's readymade for us to use," added Hasko as he pointed to the trench from which they had earlier dug out Elasti. "It isn't anything special, but it will do the job."

The job of transferring the bloody mess that was once Giterod to the grave that Elasti had once occupied was an ugly job and Hasko and Hiztin had volunteered for the assignment. They soon found themselves smeared with blood. It took them several trips to transfer the body because the body parts kept falling off. Then Giterod's remains were covered over with rubble from the Tako Ruins.

Gido felt it appropriate to say a few words of respect even for a thieving lepelf. He proceeded with another scriptural reference:
"The day grows dark, and all must die,
We all will soon return;
To that kind place, from whence we came,
Where all gain what they earn.
We came down here, to pay the price,
For mistakes we made above;
If we improve, while we are here,
We'll know the gains of love.
For he who sent us, from above,
Wants us to soon come back;
So do your best and you'll move up,
You'll ever be on track."

Everyone bowed their head in respect then silently broke up the small ceremony and started walking back toward their lean-to. Once back in the lean-to everyone felt safe and comfortable. Seeing what the riposters had done to Giterod had increased their fear and hesitation about being outside. Jesves again inspected the injuries of Yanon and Obydon. Unfortunately, the healing process seemed to be progressing slowly. "It looks like it's going to take several days before these two are going to be able to travel," she explained to the rest of her friends. "And Elasti could probably benefit from additional rest as well." Although Elasti had regained consciousness, it was still extremely painful for him to move.

"That's too bad," responded Hiztin, "but we better wait until they are ready, or we may cause them even more harm." Hiztin stayed close by Jesves and tried to give her whatever help he could. Jesves enjoyed his closeness and felt comfortable with his presence. The two had become dependent on each other for companionship.

Hiztin, Giterod and Hasko decided to get to sleep since they had endured a busy day fighting off the riposters and there was probably another attack in store for them in the morning. However, Bydola couldn't go to sleep. He was too fascinated with the scrolls he had retrieved from the ruins. He went right to work translating and reading each of them carefully. One of the scrolls was written in the language of his own people. It described a history of the migrations to Small World. It discussed a great city built in the depths of Hitl Lake, a lake that had no rivers flowing into or out of it. It explained how decedents of these people later migrated to the Central Ranges and then down to the Southern Plains where they formed the great city of Tako.

The second scroll was also written in the language of the ancient people. It discussed the development of technology in Tako. It explained how machines were created that could be taken to the top of a high hill, and then by using this machine someone could actually fly in the air. This amazed and fascinated Bydola. He doubted if this was an event that truly took place. He suspected that this was just one of those stories that were used to explain the unexplainable and to keep children from straying too far out of line. He reasoned that this "flying" probably was used to suggest that someone was watching from above and could be used to encourage children to be good.

The other two scrolls were written in the sacred Protee language which was not commonly available to the average citizen. Only a select group of religious leaders possessed the Protee. These were the only ones allowed to understand and learn this language. Knowledge of this language had been miraculously given to Bydola during his stay with the Creator. He read the scrolls with ease and couldn't resist learning the truths that they explained.

The first of the religious scrolls described the ritualistic worship practices that were used by the inhabitants of Tako, such as the practice of drowning sacrifice offerings to the God of the Rainbow.

The second of the sacred scrolls was by far the most interesting to Bydola. It was an index of the scrolls describing the contents of the various scrolls. From this list he could find listings on ceremonies, buildings, festivals, clothing and many other elements of religious life. But one entry caught his eye. It listed as its contents the Protee procedure for healing. His heart started to thump with excitement. Perhaps this scroll was exactly what the expedition needed if they were going to proceed with their journey northward.

Bydola looked around him at the other members and found that all of them, even Jesves and Hiztin, had already fallen asleep. This made him wonder how long he had been reading the scrolls. He realized that he had lost all track of time. He knew that if he was going to find the scroll on healing, he would have to do it that night. He didn't want to delay helping his friends if he had the power to heal them.

He snuck out of the enclosure taking his orange rock with him for light. He also took the scrolls with him since he felt somehow that keeping them close was a necessary way to reverence them. He felt unworthy to be in possession of them and he planned to return them to the box from which he had retrieved them. As he arrived at the box he decided to sit down and ask for help. "Creator," he prayed, "please help me find the healing scroll. Also please help me to be able to return here someday so that I will be able to read all these scrolls." As he prayed, he knew he was going to get help. He could feel it and so as he concluded his prayer he said, "Thank you."

He laid himself on the ground and reached through the crack under the rock and started retrieving scrolls looking at each of them as he pulled them out. He was starting to become discouraged, but on about his tenth try he was successful. He had found the scroll on the healing procedures.

He placed the other scrolls back into the box feeling that they would be safer there. He wouldn't be able to take them on his travels. But he planned to return someday and pull all the scrolls out. He sat down to read his newfound discovery. He was too excited to wait until he returned to the lean-to. He wanted to read it right away. As he read, he was excited by the explanations that were within. It discussed how the injured or sick individual would need to be taken to a sacred pool of water. It explained that any pool of water could be made sacred just by saying the appropriate words over it. It then explained that the individual who represented the Protee had the power to take the injured individual into the water and then using the Staff of Protee he had to invoke the secret name. After this procedure the healing process would begin. Depending on the seriousness of the injuries and the personal power of the Protee wielder the healing process would take anywhere from a few seconds to a day.

Everything discussed in the scroll seemed to be within the powers Bydola possessed. There wasn't anything that was difficult except for the secret name. What was this secret name that was referred to in the scroll? Bydola thought back to his encounter with the Creator but he couldn't remember any instance where the Creator had called him by anything other than Bydola.

He read the sacred words of the scroll once again so that he would be sure to remember them when the time was appropriate to use them. Then he returned the scroll back to the box. He proceeded to kick the wedge out from under the lid allowing the stone lid to fall into place. He knew that someday curiosity would draw him back to this location. He would never forget about these scrolls. Someday he would again want to investigate the contents of the library and read the rest of the scrolls. Information like what he just learned about healing may transform life in Small World forever.

He returned to the lean-to and realizing that he wouldn't be able to do much to help his friends without the water and the secret name, he lay himself down on his bed in frustration and fell asleep.

In his sleep he was impressed to review the dreams that he had experienced on the slab in the Creator's tunnel. He didn't know why reviewing these dreams seemed so important to him, but he felt that he had to do it. He revisited all the events that occurred to him one at a time until he finally started to relive the experience in the labyrinth. He remembered being lost and then encountering the strange light that led him to some being off in the distance.

"That being," he spoke out loud in his sleep, "he referred to me as Abogidyide. Is that my secret name? It must be. I don't know any other name." He continued to reflect on the incident in his dream. He felt as though he had reached some great insight or understanding.

"Wow!" expressed Bydola in the midst of his dream. "Thanks, Creator. Now please help me find a pool of water."

But his dream didn't stop. It continued going off in a different direction. It now centered on the orange rock light which seemed to be the private creation and possession of the Creator. But somehow it was the light that belonged to the Creator and not the rock itself. This didn't seem to make sense. The rock seemed somehow separate from the light. In his vision he was instructed that the staff was associated with both the orange light and the rock. Then the dream abruptly ended. He started to snore loudly.

"Help!" was the cry that startled Gido and Gijivure. "Please help!" It was early morning and the elves were more sensitive to the cries then the leprechauns.

The elves jumped up quickly and looked around them. The cry came from outside of the shelter, but they didn't see anyone missing. No one else in the lean-to seemed to hear the cry. The elves could also hear the riposters starting another attack.

"Remember the lepelf,
The way he suffered;
Quick wake up Hasko,
He'll keep us covered."

Gido's thoughts of Giterod left him with no choice but to rescue whoever it was that was in trouble outside.

Hasko was quickly awaken and placed in charge of protecting the shelter. Then Gido and Gijivure slowly opened one of the ends of the protective covering and attempted to sneak out. The voice outside had already gone silent and the elves feared the worst.

Their exit through the doorway was too slow and before they could get out two riposters had flown into the shelter. Hasko immediately swung his sword at the creatures and it wasn't too long before he had sliced them both. But as he successfully conquered the first two riposters another one worked its way through one of the holes in the shelter and was now flying around within its covering. Hasko immediately attempted to strike it down, but during one of the swings of his sword, he lost his balance and stepped on Hiztin's face.

"Owwww!" Hiztin yelled waking Jesves as well. "Why'd you do that? Can't you be more careful?" Then he noticed Hasko's plight and immediately jumped up to help him. Jesves also came to the rescue and it wasn't long before the attack of the riposters had been quelled with no new damage to any of the members of the expedition.

They heard someone kicking at the door of their protective covering. "It's Gido. Hurry up and open the door," yelled Hasko to Hiztin who was closest to the covering. Hiztin quickly opened the enclosure and let Gido and Gijivure enter carrying with them a lepelf that showed obvious signs of having been attacked by riposters. Each elf also had a riposter attached to them, Gido on the shoulder and Gijivure on his back. Hasko and Hiztin quickly sliced each of the attackers in half.

"Who's that," questioned Jesves, "another lepelf trying to steal the Southern Sword?" They laid the intruder down on Hasko's bedding and Jesves immediately went to work on the lepelf's injuries. Although he had lost a lot of blood his injuries were mostly the thumb sized bites that the others had received. None of the injuries were very deep. The loss of blood wasn't as intense as it had been with Yanon or Obydon.

Gido and Gijivure immediately started to help Hasko and Hiztin in their efforts to battle the riposters who had renewed their attack on the shelter.

"You got to him just in time by the looks of it," commented Jesves as she finalized the last few bandages. Then she proceeded to patch the bites Gido and Gijivure had received during the rescue effort.

In all the excitement Bydola and Elasti had also awaken and Bydola had now joined the rescuers. "Who's this?" he asked.

"We have no idea," replied Hasko. "It's probably someone that was sent to help Giterod."

"What's that?" asked Elasti, unable to move from his bed because of the intense pain that it caused him in his legs and back. "Did I hear you say that we have another lepelf visitor?"

"That's right," returned Bydola, "but I can't identify him. I wasn't in Giter long enough to have met any of the lepelves."

"Is there any way I can see him?" asked Elasti.

"Let's prop him up a little," instructed Jesves hoping to have the lepelf identified.

"That's Gabrona," explained Elasti when the lepelf had been raised enough to be visible. "He's the tavern owner's son who helped us with the king. Why is he following us?" They lowered Gabrona back down to his reclining position and as they did so he started to groan and squirm. Apparently Gabrona had passed out more from fear than from physical injury but he had never been totally unconsciousness. As he started to recover, he was startled and confused about where he was.

"Don't worry. No one's going to harm you. You are in a shelter and the riposters are outside," Jesves tried to be reassuring realizing that Gabrona was awakening from a terrible nightmare. Then looking at Elasti she said, "He's just a kid. Why'd he come all the way out here alone?"

"Help me!" came a groaning and pleading cry from the lips of the lepelf. Then his eyes suddenly popped wide open. He looked around as if he had awakened from a bad dream. "Where am I? Where are those dreadful creatures? How'd I get here?" He could still hear the riposters outside attacking the shelter and it scared him.

"Calm down," returned Jesves, "you're safe now. The riposters attacked you but you're out of danger."

"Who are you?" he asked.

"I'm Jesves. I'm part of the expedition heading to the North Groves along with my friends that you see here." She pointed to her companions.

"Where's Yanon, Elasti, Obydon, and Giterod?" he asked.

"I'm over here," Elasti responded. "We were all attacked by the riposters just like you only you got off a little luckier than we did."

"Boy I am glad to see you guys! I came to warn you. Giterod was sent by the king to steal the Southern Sword. Where is Giterod?" he asked realizing that he hadn't noticed him anywhere.

"So, the king was behind it after all," responded Elasti. Then he proceeded to tell the story of Giterod's attempt to steal the sword at the Avol River and how Obydon had foiled the attempt. He also related the tragic story of Giterod's death and expressed his regrets at the ugliness of the occurrence.

"That's terrible," commented Gabrona. In the back of his mind he wondered if Giterod's fate had truly been accidental or if the leprechauns had discovered Giterod's intentions to steal the sword and had killed him. Gabrona had been told all his life about how sneaky leprechauns were but he found it hard to believe that these individuals could actually commit coldblooded murder. Nevertheless, all his early indoctrination left doubt plaguing his mind.

"I find it hard to believe that you came all the way out here just to tell us about Giterod. Do you plan to return to Giter?" questioned Elasti. "Are you going back to report on our expedition? Is there more to your story that you haven't told me yet?"

"I don't want to go back to Giter. I want to go with you," replied Gabrona.

"But aren't you a little too young?" questioned Jesves. "Will your father allow this?"

"I can't go back," responded Gabrona softly bowing his head. Then he proceeded to tell the story of his humiliation and rejection.

"But that's no reason for you to risk your life by going with us to the North Groves," Hiztin pleaded. "You nearly lost your life already. You're not prepared for such a journey. You don't have the necessary clothing or weapons or training."

"I won't go back!" Gabrona was furious with Hiztin's remark. "I want to go with you guys." He realized that the story of being rejected by his own people was just an excuse. He couldn't explain his strong desire to make this journey. He had the lust to venture out and explore. He knew he must go to the North Groves with the leprechauns and the elves.

"At this point he's in less danger coming with us than if we were to send him back." Elasti was concerned about gnomes or the riposters catching up with Gabrona. He had learned to like the lepelf. He felt a need to keep him safe from danger. He also felt that sending him back to Giter could be cruel. Elasti suggested, "I'd spend the whole time worrying about him if we send him back now."

"Well it looks like we're going to be sitting here for a few more days anyway," commented Jesves still concerned about Gabrona's safety. "Maybe one of us should help him get as far back as possible. Maybe even across the Avol River."

"I'm not going back! I'm going with you guys," Gabrona was emphatic. "If you take me back, I'll just follow after you again."

"We may not have to wait around here any longer," Bydola's comment surprised everyone. "Last night while all of you were sleeping, I was reading through those scrolls at the Taco ruins library that we found yesterday, and I learned something interesting. One of the scrolls described a method of healing and I think I'm capable of performing the process."

"Why didn't you tell us about it last night?" questioned Elasti. "I would have gladly been awakened to learn about a way to end this misery."

"I wasn't sure how to use the information that I received from the scrolls until I had a dream last night," Bydola explained. "But what I experienced was more than just a dream. It was as if I was actually there in person seeing all the events that happened to me. It confuses me because I don't know whether to believe what I dreamed or if it was just my imagination playing tricks on my mind. Anyway, if you're willing, we can try the healing process tonight."

"Why not right now?" asked Elasti with excitement.

"Because I need a large pool of water in order to perform the healing and we'll have to find one," explained Bydola.

Gabrona looked at Bydola closely listening to his explanations in amazement. This was the first time he had gotten a good look at him and he noticed the orange ora. "What's with the orange light?" he asked.

The others were stunned. First, they were surprised at Bydola's comment about healing and then Gabrona's frank and youthful question. They had all resisted asking too many questions earlier for fear of offending Bydola, but Gabrona didn't seem to have any such inhibitions.

Elasti was feeling uncomfortable about Gabrona's question. He attempted to change the conversation back to a discussion about Bydola's healing ability as quickly as possible. "That's great, Bydola? I can't wait till we get a chance to try the healing process."

"Unfortunately, we can't do it now," responded Bydola, "Like I said, I need that pool of water. But if we venture out tonight toward the North maybe we can find enough water and I can attempt to perform the healing. It may save us as much as a week's time in waiting around here for everyone to improve. And it will be a lot less painful." Then he turned to Gabrona and said, "In answer to your question about the orange light, it represents a sacred power. As the elves have already correctly guessed it is associated with the powers of the Creator.

Unfortunately, I cannot explain how it works or why it works because I don't know the answers. The Creator caused the lights and that's all I know."

Responding to the need to go to water in order to be healed, Elasti announced, "Well I for one am willing to suffer a little pain by being moved if it means being healed quicker. Let's try it tonight. I'll gladly volunteer for the experiment."

The day drug on slowly with everyone cooped up in the shelter. Everyone went through introductions and then had idle conversations about the Gije expedition. They reviewed their plans to meet with the dwarfs. Gabrona immediately felt as though he was a part of the expedition. He was excited about accomplishing something as critically important as the journey north and the crossing of the swords. It seemed as though Bydola's comments regarding healing had eliminated the pressure about having him return to Giter. Now he would be the youngest individual on the expedition. He would also be the only lepelf. These two facts made him feel proud even if the other lepelves of his city would never appreciate his efforts.

Night seemed to approach quickly, much quicker than on the previous day. The party looked forward to the evening. The excitement surrounding the arrival of Gabrona and the stories that Bydola told about the scrolls made for interesting conversation. Obydon would stir occasionally as though he were about to regain consciousness at any time but Yanon continued to lie as still as a rock.

With the night came another end to the daily riposter attack. Bydola left the shelter for a few minutes in order to experiment with making a few more of the strange orange rocks. The hope was that each of the travelers could have one. Bydola explained, "I'm going to try to make more orange rocks but I need to take this rock with me so I can see what I'm doing. Does anyone want to come with me, or do you want to stay here?" He asked the group in general.

"I'll go," returned Hasko. "I look forward to getting out of here in the evening."

Soon Hasko, Hiztin, Jesves, Gabrona, Gido, and Gijivure were all outside of the enclosure tagging after Bydola with his light and his staff. The staff bearer went over to the ruins where he searched for nine rocks, all a little smaller in size then the one he currently possessed. He laid the stones out next to each other. Then he stood up. Using his staff, he touched the first stone saying, "By the power of Protee and in the name of Abogidyide I turn this stone to light." However, when he was trying to say the name Abogidyide no sound came out of his mouth. As he finished his prayer a flash of orange light moved down his staff striking the stone. Just as he had anticipated the flash suddenly turned the stone into an orange light. Then he proceeded to do the same to each of the other stones, one at a time each time saying the same words as he touched each one. After some time, he finished his prayer on each stone and a new orange light was seen emanating from each one.

Bydola was confused. He had invoked the secret name Abogidyide just as his dream and the scrolls had instructed him to do but each time, he said the name it was as though his voice failed him? The name itself never seemed to pass his lips. He never intentionally tried to prevent it from doing so. "*Perhaps this is the way the name is kept secret,*" he thought to himself, "*I am prevented from saying it at all times because it is secret.*"

In an attempt to understand the secret name further Bydola asked Hasko, "What did I say over each of the rocks?"

Hasko shrugged his shoulders and said, "By the power of Protee, I turn this stone to light."

"It's true," thought Bydola, "they were not allowed to hear the secret name. How interesting."

Now that he had successfully completed the transformation of all the rocks, he felt much more confident that the healings would also work. He proceeded to hand out the new orange stones and said, "I'm going north on the Kilo Pass in an attempt to find a pool of water. Now that you each have your own light you no longer need to stay close to me. You can either go back to the shelter or come with me. But I would suggest that no one do any more exploring around these ruins after all the mishaps we've had so far."

Gido, Hasko, and Gijivure followed Bydola while Jesves and Hiztin decided to return to the shelter to check on the injured travelers. Bydola handed the remainder of the undistributed stones over to Jesves and headed north.

"We have a legend,
In our books of old;
That tells of the temple,
Of which you told;
The temple still stands,
Our legends say;
Close to this pass,
On which we stray," Gido had enjoyed hearing Bydola's discussion earlier about the contents of the scrolls. He wanted to share some elf legends as well.

"Really," commented Bydola. "I sure hope we get to see it. That temple would really be something worth exploring."

"No! Don't explore the temple,
Many persons already have died;
The temple has dangers inside,
To enter means certain death.
These legends of which Gido speaks,
Tell of the shadow warriors who defend;
So only the sacred can attend,
The holy places within.
Even the gnomes in the Lifefight War,
Attempted to enter the building;
Shadow warriors started their killing;
And the gnomes never went close to it again."

Gijivure expressed concern at the thought of exploring the temple and had no desire to violate anything sacred much less to battle with the shadow warriors.

But Bydola's thoughts drifted off in another direction. Would he be allowed to enter the temple? After all, he now had the power of the Protee. Does this power mean that he was considered one of the "sacred" ones that would be allowed admittance? Exploring the temple had to be something that waited until he returned some day in the future. Between the temple and the scrolls he now felt an urgency to return soon after the expedition was completed.

Before Bydola could worry about temples and scrolls he would first need to find a pool of water that would allow him to perform the necessary healings. The healings would allow the expedition to move forward with fewer delays. But he couldn't help but wonder how many more interesting things he would find before this expedition was finished. The Protee had given him an entirely new perspective. Now he was allowed to see things that previously he would not have recognized as significant. An entirely new world had been opened to him.

The little party traveled North along the trail and in the dark, wondering if they would even see a body of water because of the darkness. The city stretched on and on. After some time, they were becoming discouraged and feeling that there was little chance that they would find the necessary pool of water close enough. Fortunately, luck was on their side and soon they found what appeared to be a water pond. It looked like a cistern or part of the water system of the city because it was tucked inside the confines of what was still part of the Tako Ruins. The pond looked as though it may once have been an enormous fountain of some type that was now partially filled with rubble. A small part of the fountain was obstructed by clutter. Bydola investigated the cleared part of the fountain. He found it to be about a third of a leprechaun deep and long enough for about two leprechauns to lie down in it. It was filled with rainwater. The water was a little stagnant and green. Bydola didn't recall reading that the water had to be pure, so he decided to give it a try.

"Hasko, I want you to go back to the shelter and get Elasti and bring him here so we can give this healing process a try." Then he turned to the elves, "Gido and Gijivure, why don't you see what our journey is going to be like past the Tako Ruins to the North. Maybe we can make a camp up in that direction without having to travel back to where we just came from. I'm going to stay here and prepare this water."

The three nodded their heads in acknowledgement and departed. Bydola proceeded to scrape some of the algae off the top of the water. He cleaned it as best he could. Then he decided to invoke the prayer that was mentioned in the scroll. He wanted to prepare the water for healing. He clutched his staff and touching the water with it he said, "By the power of Protee, I Abogidyide declare this water sacred." A bolt of orange light flashed down the staff and surged over the top of the water for several minutes. When the process had finished the water was suddenly clear and pure showing no signs of its previous contamination.

Again, as on the previous occasion when he uttered the sacred name it was as though his voice had ceased to exist. He was baffled but pleased with the success he had achieved. He now felt even more confident that the healing process would work.

Realizing that it would still be a few minutes before Elasti arrived, Bydola decided to walk around in the ruins ignoring his own instructions about not exploring the ruins any further. He wanted to see what he could discover. He was convinced that there were more treasures in this ancient city, just like the scrolls he had already discovered. As he walked around the back side of a large pile of rubble he looked up and saw what he knew must be the temple off in the distance. It was as if the moon was shining specifically on this structure, which gave it an eerie significance. The temple was a large four-sided pyramid that was at least two hundred leprechauns tall. He had been standing only a hundred leprechauns away from it but the rubble he had just walked around had prevented him from seeing it. Bydola stared at it in amazement. He wondered what was inside. He wanted to go and investigate further but he realized that it was still too far away for him to go to it quickly. As he stood there in fascination, he heard his name being called.

"Bydola, where are you?" It was the voice of Hasko.

"He must have returned with Elasti," thought Bydola as he turned and started to return to the pool of water.

As he approached, he saw that Jesves, Hasko, Hiztin, Elasti, and Gabrona had all arrived. "I wanted to come too just in case you were successful," responded Gabrona.

Elasti was obviously in a great deal of pain and was being helped on either side by Hiztin and Hasko. "We're going to have to lay you down in the pool of water," Bydola commented.

"In that murky mess?" asked Hasko not yet noticing how clean it had become.

"I'll do anything," commented Elasti as he tried to walk over to the pool under the support of his aids.

"Wow! What happened to the water?" questioned Hasko realizing that the water had been purified. Bydola didn't answer because he felt that he didn't need to answer. The power of the purification process would have been performed similar to the creating of the glowing rocks.

Hasko, Hiztin, and Bydola lifted Elasti and placed him in the water. He laid down in it and his body was completely covered, all but his head which Hasko supported by holding his hands under it. Bydola touched Elasti with his staff. Then he said the healing words, "By the power of Protee, I ------ command thy body to heal itself of all infirmities." The orange light flashed down the staff and wrapped itself around Elasti. At first it scared everyone. They thought that the light might somehow burn Elasti. But then they realized Elasti wasn't feeling any discomfort. Hasko, who was holding Elasti's head, received a sudden surge of power which made him jump and drop the leprechaun's head. Elasti's head fell under the water.

The entire process took about a minute. After it was finished Elasti sat up in the pond and exclaimed, "I'm healed!" He stood up and started to feel his body to check where the sores had once been. "I'm completely cured!" he declared.

"That's impossible," declared Bydola. "The scrolls said that the healing process might take as much as a day."

"Well I don't know what to tell you about what the scrolls said," responded Elasti, "All I know is that I'm healed."

Just then Gido and Gijivure returned and they were also excited by the success of Bydola's newfound healing ability. "I wonder what other powers you have that you don't even know about?" Jesves questioned Bydola. "This is amazing. You're sure going to be a great help on this trip."

Bydola continued to do healings for the other members of the team who had bites and sores. He also instructed the members of the expedition, "Gido, Gijivure, Hasko, Hiztin, and Elasti, which of you is going to go back and get Yanon and Obydon while Jesves helps me work on Gabrona?"

"All of us and with pleasure," returned Elasti. "I can't wait until all my friends are back to normal health."

They departed for the lean-to while Jesves and Bydola helped Gabrona enter the water. This time no one held up his head in the water. He was left to do the best he could on his own dunking his head at the appropriate time. Again, Bydola uttered the sacred words and again a complete recovery occurred.

Unfortunately, Yanon was extremely difficult to help. He had to be carried all the way from the shelter to the pool of water and this turned out to be a slow and strenuous process. A stretcher had to be created using parts of the lean-to and then he was laid out on it. Eventually he arrived and was placed into the water. A rock was used as a pillow supporting his head and allowing him to breathe.

As soon as Yanon was in the water they left him for Bydola and Jesves to take care of and they returned to the lean-to in order to retrieve Obydon. Bydola proceeded with the healing process by using his staff and the same sacred words that he had used previously. Just like before they saw the flash of orange light move down the shaft and surround Yanon's body. Yanon didn't recover consciousness immediately as hoped. It took him a little longer than the other travelers. Jesves became concerned that the healing had not worked. She jumped into the water and unwrapped a couple of the bandages around his skull. She found that some healing had occurred but that the most serious wounds around the skull had not healed completely.

Bydola was stunned and disappointed. Yanon needed the healing more than anyone. In examining the process that he had gone through he immediately realized the problem "Only that part of his skull that was submerged under water was healed. We're going to have to risk dunking him completely under water in order to see if we can get the rest of his damaged skull healed. He expressed these thoughts to Jesves, "We will need to submerge him completely and redo the healing process. You will need to get in the water with him and be his pillow."

Jesves agreed and sloshed to Yanon's head to take on her role. Bydola proceeded as quickly as possible so that Yanon wouldn't be left under the water long. Jesves cradled Yanon's head above the water and just as Bydola started to utter the healing words she dropped Yanon's head. The orange light engulfed Yanon violently as he performed the healing ritual. Then the light suddenly stopped. The two were breathless with excitement. Jesves had just started to reach into the water to lift Yanon's head out when he suddenly sat up coughing, choking and spitting out water. "Were you trying to drown me?" he asked. He didn't understand what happened. Jesves quickly explained the situation to him. She told him about the riposter attack and how he had been unconscious ever since. She also explained about the scrolls and how Bydola had received some special healing powers from the Creator. Then she checked his head wounds. All his wounds had been totally healed.

As the three waited for Obydon to be carried from the lean-to to the pool, Jesves brought Yanon up to date with the details of all the events that had transpired since the riposter attack. Obydon finally arrived being carried on the stretcher. Bydola sent all the healthy members except Jesves back to the lean-to to retrieve everyone's belongings. "There's not much sense waiting around in that lean to another day when we could be making progress in our journey up the Kilo Pass," Bydola stressed and all agreed. They had lost too much time already because of the injuries caused by the riposters and no one wanted to spend any more time in the cramped lean-to. They wanted to get away from this area tonight.

The healing process on Obydon was performed and Bydola had by now become a master at the healing technique. As the three sat and waited for the team to return with their belongings, they discussed all their experiences and reviewed what they still planned to accomplish that same evening.

As the remainder of the expedition returned to the fountain it felt as though a big family had just experienced a joyous reunion of all its members. The experience of a speedy and healthy recovery for everyone on the team brought excitement and left them even more baffled about the newfound powers of Bydola.

Obydon thanked Bydola for all the help that he had given him even though he didn't really understand what had caused the healing that had occurred. He was thrilled to be back at full strength. Soon Elasti and Yanon were showering him with their gratefulness as well. They also weren't sure what had happened, but they were overwhelmingly grateful that it had occurred.

Bydola insisted that he had not done the healing himself. He had simply followed the procedure that was explained on the scroll. He explained that it was the power of the Protee. Through the power of the Creator who had given him the Protee he had actually done the healing. The Protee and the staff generated the orange light that signified the instrumentality through which all this had worked. The travelers were confused but grateful for what had happened.

They collected their packs and anxiously headed north hoping to get as far away from Tako as possible before daybreak thereby averting any more attacks from the riposters. Gabrona was given Giterod's sword and knife so that he would have his own set of weapons for protection.

As they began their journey Bydola asked the elves if they knew anything about the trail northward out of the city.

"The trail north of Tako,
Will be difficult to conquer;
The forest gets thicker,
And the undergrowth gets denser.
We won't make as good time,
As we've done in the past;
But we must do our best,
And we must do it fast," Gido responded.

As they arrived at the northern edge of the city, they found Gido was right. The forest undergrowth had almost completely taken over the trail. The expedition would have to fight their way through brush and ferns.

Hasko being an outdoorsman and therefore ingenious with cords developed a technique allowing him to tie up his new orange glowing rock and hang it around his neck. He turned it into a necklace. This made traveling a lot easier since it left his hands free to push brush out of his path. The others, seeing his ingenuity convinced him to create a similar necklace for each of them. Soon the entire party used their orange necklaces to guide them through the brush at night.

The light from the necklaces was so bright that it appeared as if the expedition was traveling in the sun. Most of the traveling was done in single file. They took turns as leader blazing the trail before them. Now that his health was restored Yanon resumed his role as expedition leader. He recognized the importance of each of the expedition participants and saw no need to be a domineering leader. He tried to stay open to suggestions and recommendations thereby preventing resentment developing amongst the other travelers. Gido, Obydon, and Hasko became his aids and he regularly consulted with them when decisions needed to be made.

Yanon was the military leader from Amins. Hasko was the young scout from Amins. Gido was the elfin council member. Obydon was the carrier of the Southern Sword and the future head of the Amins council. Each of them shared the details of their separate experiences during their trips to the Tako Ruins. They discussed the strange transformation that had come over Bydola and admitted that in spite of his strange behavior they were glad of his new healing powers and his orange lights. They were concerned about how little they understood his transformation, but they were thankful for his help. They were uncertain how it would affect the expedition but so far it had been extremely helpful.

The four leaders also discussed alternatives for the future. They developed schemes, planning how they would handle any threats from the Kabul. Yanon expressed his gratitude for having ten members in the expedition where at one time he feared that he would have as few as three.

Gijivure, the elfin warrior found a new friend in Gabrona the inn-keeper's son from Giter. Their connection was not because they were of the same personality or because they had the same interests but because they both felt like minorities. They felt isolated in the throng of leprechauns. They talked about their homes and their personal lives and it wasn't long before Gabrona became extremely excited about someday seeing Gije. It sounded like an ideal place to him. He became convinced that it must be a little bit of heaven on earth where people worked together and shared and helped one another. He had always felt that people were meant to live that way. However, growing up in Giter was very different from that.

Hiztin the bowman from Amins was finally able to get Jesves alone and to himself once again. He now had the opportunity to walk with her and get all of her attention. Jesves enjoyed the attention as well. It was something she had never before experienced in her life and now she felt as though she had met someone who really cared about her. The two discussed their shared experiences and their future plans and continued to grow closer together by the minute.

Elasti the hero from the first expedition up the Albo Pass walked with Bydola, the strongman from Amins who now had the strange power of the Protee. It wasn't that he wanted any special favors from Bydola. It was just that he didn't enjoy walking with anyone else. He found that he had the most in common with Bydola and enjoyed talking with him. Bydola tended to spend most of his time in thought and Elasti also enjoyed the silence. Both had a lot to think about. Elasti was concerned about the dangers and the near-death experiences he had encountered and was concerned about returning to his future bride back home.

Bydola's thoughts were wrapped up in the scrolls he had read back at the Tako Ruins. He found that he was able to recount perfectly word-for-word everything that each of the scrolls said. He read them over and over again in his mind searching for hidden meanings or ideas. He became quite excited about returning to the library of scrolls and reading more of them. He was also enticed by the temple desiring to investigate it. Many of the things he learned when he was with the Creator seemed to tie directly to what he read in the scrolls and this made him wonder what role the Creator had played in the beliefs and religions of the great city of Tako. He was also absorbed by the comment that "the presence of the Creator will not be here until life may disappear in Small World". He wondered what role he was going to play and how his ability to recognize evil would be used toward the destruction of evil.

They traveled on becoming chilled by the dampness of the forest undergrowth. As daylight approached, they welcomed the warmth of the sun. But now they had another concern. The travelers became worried about any dangers they may be in. Would the riposters be able to find them and attack them again? They hoped that they had traveled far enough to be out of reach of those creatures. They pushed ahead, moving a little quicker, fearing the thought that the riposters might be right behind them.

Chapter Fifteen

The Kabul

It was late in the morning when weariness overcame Gabrona and he finally started to complain. He had suffered the greatest of any of the expedition from a lack of sleep. He had gotten up early the previous morning in his attempt to catch up with the travelers and he hadn't received any sleep since.

"Can't we take a break?" Gabrona complained, "My legs are starting to shake from weariness." He wasn't used to such long hiking expeditions and, like most other lepelves, he treasured his rest.

"I'll go for that," agreed Elasti. His pains had kept him from getting a comfortable sleep the previous night, and he looked forward to a good rest.

"I suppose it would be alright," returned Yanon. "If the riposters were going to attack us they would have done so by now. I'm not feeling too tired. How about we continue traveling for a few more hours just to make sure?"

"You've been sleeping for the last two days Yanon," interjected Hasko sarcastically feeling overworked. "It's no wonder you're not as tired as the rest of us. But some of us have been battling riposters by day and scouting around at night and we're extremely exhausted."

Just then a shadow flashed over the top of the North Grove expedition causing some of them to jump. They were still a bit nervous about the possibility of riposters attacking. But Elasti had experienced a similar shadow once before and he looked skyward, "Look, up there!" he yelled pointing to the sky. "It's an eagle. I'll bet it's the same eagle that followed me on my return trip from the Albo Pass. Eagles are rare in the Southern Plains. Why would an eagle be following us?"

"An eagle was following you on the Albo trip?" questioned Yanon. Elasti had not included the eagle in the story he told previously because he hadn't considered it to be relevant. The eagle seemed more coincidental than real.

"Yes, and I think it's the same one we see now," responded Elasti. Everyone looked skyward and watched the eagle as it landed in a tree high above their heads. They were confused by it. No one had any explanation to offer.

"Why don't we take,
A rest from our travels;
The feet feel like gravels,
They need to recline," responded Gijivure. Surprisingly Gijivure was interested in taking a break which surprised the rest of the travelers since elves had a longer stride and didn't get weary as quickly.

"I see evil intentions in that eagle," commented Bydola looking skyward, "But there's also a small trace of good. I wonder what its purpose is." This comment left everyone as confused as his previous similar comment about Giterod.

"Alright. This is as good a place as any to rest," responded Yanon as he pointed off the road to a small patch of grass next to the path. There weren't many such patches since most of the forest bottom was heavily overgrown.

The expedition made themselves comfortable in the grassy field. Several of them lay out in the grass. It wasn't long before they began dozing off.

The camp was quiet. Yanon and Obydon, who couldn't sleep, whispered to each other about the eagle while trying to keep from waking any of the others. The remainder of the expedition had fallen asleep all except for Gijivure. He got up and stretched and made motions to Yanon that he was going to go off into the bushes. Then he slipped away through the bushes until he was out of sight of the camp. He continued on a little further until he was sure that no one in the expedition could hear him. Then he sat down on a small patch of grass, crossed his legs, folded his arms, closed his eyes, bowed his head, and began to hum.

"Hummmmm ummmmm ummmmm," went Gijivure's chant for several minutes. Then quietly the eagle flew down swooping close by him and landed on a bush in front of him. "How's it going Gijivure?" asked the eagle.

Gijivure opened his eyes, looked up and smiled.

Yanon found it curious that Gijivure who had been so insistent about stopping to rest, was the only one left awake. By now even Obydon had dozed off and Gijivure still hadn't returned from his little walk in the woods. The expedition leader looked up in the direction where the elf had wandered and still did not notice any sign of his return. He became suspicious and decided to keep a close watch on Gijivure in the future. But he has also become tired and decided to lay his head down and rest.

No sooner had he become comfortable, when he noticed the sound of someone breaking through the bushes. He raised his head to look and noticed that Gijivure was finally returning. He laid his head back down satisfied that Gijivure was safe, and quickly joined the rest of his friends in sleep.

It was early afternoon before some of the party finally started to awaken. Yanon and Bydola had been among the first to do so. The two had started preparing a meal for the other members of the quest. None of the travelers had enjoyed a warm meal for at least two days and this was a golden opportunity to prepare one for them. As they woke up, they each took part in the feast that had been prepared. Soon only Elasti, Gijivure, and Gabrona were still asleep.

Yanon was eager to continue the expedition north, and he spoke up, "I think we ought to wake those three up so they can eat while the food is hot. Maybe we can still hike for a while before it gets dark today." Gido agreed and was given the task of waking up the last sleepers.

The meal was enjoyable and very relaxed. Soon everyone was packed and ready to resume their travels. They continued heading north with Yanon taking the initial lead position hacking away at the brush when necessary. As they rounded a bend in the trail, they could see a straight stretch where the trail continued on in the same direction for what appeared to be one thousand strides. Then the trail seemed to end abruptly into what appeared to be a wall.

The travelers stopped and peered at the strange sight, "What is it?" questioned Hiztin.

"It appears to be a wall of mist," returned Yanon.

"The Kabul is said to contain,
A traveling cloud;
That brings a chill to all,
Whose minds aren't sound,"
Gido responded.

"Another one of those darn scriptures that don't make any sense," complained Obydon. "What's a sound mind?"

"A mind that's sound,
Will have no fear;
Will have no stress,
Can always hear.
A mind that's sound,
Is your best friend;
Will comfort you,
When at wits end.
So never fear,
What lies ahead;
A mind that's sound,
Will prevent dread," Gido responded.

Gido would have continued on with his quotation of scripture but Obydon began to feel as though he was going around in circles, so he interrupted, "That's enough Gido! I get the idea! We're going to enter the Kabul and we're going to have to pass through some thick cloud." But he didn't really understand. He just hoped that his mind was sound enough to withstand any test that might come up.

"I see evil in that cloud," commented Bydola, "lots of evil. It worries me to think that we are entering it."

"I don't see any choice but to enter," returned Yanon. "That's where the trail goes, and we have to follow it."

"What do you mean you 'see evil'?" questioned Obydon. "How do you see evil?"

"I'm not sure why I see it except that I was told that I would be able to see it. It looks like an overpowering darkness that destroys life. I can see it in that cloud," responded Bydola.

Obydon was starting to get irritated, "You two drive me nuts with your 'mind that's sound' and you're 'seeing evil'. What the heck are you two talking about? Is there a real danger that threatens us in that cloud, or can we make it through safely? That's all I want to know."

"A mind that's sound,
Has little danger;
A mind that's weak,
Will find disaster,"
suggested Gido.

"Well how do I know if I have a sound mind or a weak mind?" pleaded Obydon.

"A mind that's sound,
Knows deep inside;
That love and truth,
Can never hide," responded Gido.

"I give up!" Obydon threw his hands up in the air in total frustration.

"All evil can be defeated by good," Bydola continued to try to explain. "The evil I see can be defeated if we strive for the good and persist in it. That is what Gido keeps referring to as a 'sound mind'. It is persistence towards doing and being good. It's not something you can hold in your hand and say, 'This is a sound mind'. A sound mind is one that persists, works, and strives. It never gives up in working toward the good. Whether your mind is sound or not depends on your moods, impressions, feelings, reactions, lusts, goals, and many other things. Are these things striving for perfection and for good, or are they just coasting? Only you know your intentions and only your intentions will determine if your mind is 'sound'."

"Got it," thanked Obydon. "That helped a lot. What you're saying is that if I keep good thoughts in my mind, I'll overcome the evil in that mist."

"That's a good start," replied Bydola. "You also can't let fear or hesitation control you. You must have confidence and faith in what you are doing and that it is right. Do not foster doubt about yourself and your actions or you will encourage destruction."

By now all the members of the party were listening intently. Gido nodded his head in agreement with all that Bydola said. Gijivure was also in agreement and pointing toward the cloud he said,

"That place works like a mirror,
The good will see loving;
And the bad will see suffering;

And all emotions are then magnified.
The jealous will be envious,
The greedy will want more;
The haters will abhor,
And the lover will love more.
We must be very careful,
And keep our feelings pure;
For safety to be sure,
And exit guaranteed," Gijivure added this warning from the Elfin Book of Learning.

The expedition stared at the wall as if paralyzed, and then Yanon said, "Well let's get it over with. I don't want to put this off any longer." And he started to lead the party towards the Kabul and the unknown dangers that lay ahead.

Yanon was determined yet concerned. He was determined not to let the Kabul, or its lord conquer him. He was obsessed with the need to win this conflict and protect his homeland. Yet he was concerned with the danger into which he was dragging his friends. Being the leader of the expedition, he felt responsible for Giterod's death even though he was in no position to prevent it. And the thought that the riposters nearly took the lives of three additional members of the expedition as well as himself caused him even more concern. He must be more careful with those entrusted to his care. Yet now he was dragging them into some unknown danger, a danger which might destroy them all. He felt the urgency to push forward or their arrival at the North Groves might be too late to save Small World.

Gido walked next to Yanon in silence. He was hesitant to enter the borders of the Kabul. Why had Krakus braved leaving the borders of the Kabul unless he felt he was strong enough to defeat and control the whole of Small World? What power did he have that made him feel so confident of this victory? The elves had defeated the gnome hoards earlier and in much larger numbers. The Kabul hoards couldn't possibly have grown back to those same numbers so quickly. Why did they feel they had the power to defeat the elves? When they were defeated in the Lifefight War there were three times as many gnomes as there were elves, yet their lack of skill could not be compensated for by their large numbers. Was Krakus somehow able to improve the abilities of these creatures making them strong enough to attack and succeed? He wished he knew what new dangers lay ahead for him and the rest of the members of this expedition.

Hasko, having acclaimed himself as one of the leaders in the expedition, walked close to Yanon. He was feeling successful and all powerful. His team had saved the Giter expedition from total devastation and he felt proud. His team had also successfully journeyed to Gije and had gained the support of the community with fewer team members than Yanon took to Giter. He felt as though he could conquer anything especially a little fog. How could that possibly be a threat to his abilities?

Obydon, the last of the expedition leaders, felt humbled. He had previously felt jealous at not having been selected to be the leader of this expedition. Now he saw how foolish his jealousy really was. The only reason he still possessed the Southern Sword for safekeeping was because the riposters had decided to attack Giterod. In his stupidity he could have lost the sword for good. He now walked along carrying the sword wrapped up in some of his clothes as if it wasn't good enough to have its own sheath. He didn't find the sheath with Giterod and was uncertain what had happened to it. But in the end, it was the sword, not the sheath that would call the wizard. However not having the sheath was humiliating. Since he had done such a poor job of taking care of the sword, what right did he have to think that he could do better than Yanon in caring for the entire expedition? He felt grateful that a strong figure like Yanon was assigned to this task and he felt as if he could learn a lot by watching him closely. He was also grateful for Bydola and his amazing healing powers. It was difficult to imagine what effect the new Bydola would have on the overall success of the mission. He knew it could only be good.

Gabrona, following behind the four leaders of this quest, felt insecure. He was troubled by the death of Giterod. If the leprechauns wanted to kill the lepelf warrior, why didn't they just do it with a sword? Why did they have to torture him with riposters? Or perhaps when they were attacked by the creatures, they just didn't think Giterod was worth saving. Would they feel that way about him when they were all in danger again? As he thought more about this dilemma, he felt a little stupid. All his life he had been raised with doubts about what his people back home called 'foreigners'. Now he had to identify whether these ideas were false feelings or whether there was truly some threat to his safety. He enjoyed the company of the leprechauns in many ways more so than he enjoyed his own people. But he felt he had to be careful not to be fooled by false friendships.

Gabrona also felt a little childish. He had insisted on going on the expedition but was completely unprepared for the dangerous journey. No wonder they wanted to send him back to Giter. He had no pack in which to stow his belongings. And the weapons he carried were not even his own. He wished he could be a key part of this expedition, but he realized he would have to first prove himself worthy of the honor.

Gijivure who walked and talked with Gabrona was excited. He knew the eagle and had received its message, but he felt torn. He wanted badly to share its message with the others because he felt proud to be the bearer of such news. He felt proud to be in his new position of strength. But he knew that his message was not meant for the ears of his companions. He would have to hold it inside of him as he had been commanded to do and maybe someday in the future the time would be right to share what he knew.

Elasti followed behind Gijivure and Gabrona. His thoughts once again turned to Jizeel. He felt a little foolish to have turned his bride away in order to go on this expedition. Would she wait for him or would she be frustrated by his foolish sense of duty and reject him? She must be filled with hurt, maybe even anger and he had no way to comfort her. Had his lust for revenge for the deaths of Agot and Broch blinded him to the possibility of a greater loss which was the loss of his beloved Jizeel? How would he ever be able to forgive himself if he came home to find out that she had rejected him? His only hope was that perhaps if he returned a hero his efforts would not have been in vain. However, if the expedition didn't successfully get to the North Groves, he may lose everything; his pride, Jizeel, and the opportunity to avenge the deaths of his friends. He wasn't sure he would be able to live with such a defeat. His whole life would become meaningless. He had to succeed in this mission even if he had to finish it alone. No cloud or mist nor the Kabul Lord was going to stop him.

Bydola stepped forward and began walking next to Elasti toward the mist. He was filled with an internal turmoil that caused confusion and frustration. He knew there was evil ahead. He could see it and sense it somehow. But he didn't know what it was. He felt strangely responsible for the danger they were in as though he was expected to somehow remove this threat. But he didn't understand how. What should he do? The Creator hadn't told him enough. He hadn't told him how to tap this vast new base of knowledge that he had been blessed with.

He recalled how earlier as the expedition approached the Tako Ruins he was filled with information about the city of Tako. This information came to him as though someone was talking through him. It didn't seem as though he had actually said those words. It was a knowledge he had in him, but he hadn't yet learned how to tap into it on his own. He had also somehow guessed at how to convert those rocks into orange lights. This knowledge seemed to pop into his head from the dream he had experienced as if someone else was thinking through him but at the same time he felt as though this was knowledge he had always had, and that he had simply recalled it and used it. The words of the Creator, "I give you little knowledge you don't already have. I only open your eyes to it," played over and over again in his mind. What did that statement mean? Did he already know about healing and about orange lights somewhere in the back of his mind?

His ability to read and memorize the scrolls also amazed him. But he felt comfortable with that knowledge because he could recall that knowledge in his mind and review it. He felt proud, having learned the knowledge of healing, and felt pleasure in having been able to help his friends. But the tools he possessed in order to counter the evil ahead of him, if indeed he possessed these tools, were beyond his grasp. He felt helpless. What would he do if they found themselves in trouble?

Jesves was also in the processional march toward the Kabul, feeling proud in her new role as doctor of the expedition. She had always been a little squeamish about blood trying to avoid the sight of it whenever possible. But when she saw the pain that her friends were in after the riposter attack she felt as though she was left with no alternative but to forget her fears and try to help them as quickly as possible. Somehow during the planning of the Amins Council, they had forgotten that the expedition may need medical help and no one with any medical training

was sent along. She enjoyed the thought that she may have saved the lives of Yanon and Obydon when they were losing blood so rapidly. She felt that when the expedition was completed, she would take up a study of doctoring so that she would be able to help more people in that same way.

Jesves also felt a strong new friendship in Hiztin. At first his constant and persistent presence was a nuisance to her. She was used to being alone and sometimes it felt that he was invading her privacy. But lately there were many times when she appreciated his nearness. She enjoyed being able to talk to someone who seemed to really care about her feelings. She discussed her interests in being a doctor with him and he was excited at the idea telling her how wonderful she would be as a doctor. He praised her for how gentle and lovingly she had taken care of the injured expedition members. Hearing those words from Hiztin made her feel proud. It was the kind of encouragement she needed. She had always thought of herself as not being very good around other people. Now she felt as though other people needed her and she had found a deeper meaning in her life. Hiztin had become a part of that deeper meaning.

Hiztin was starting to feel more like himself. He wasn't spending large portions of the night lying around worrying about what Jesves thought of him and how he could approach her with his feelings. He had given all that nonsense up. He had decided that he would just be the best friend he possibly could to her, and that by being her friend maybe someday she would feel the same way about him.

When he reflected on his life in Amins it seemed empty as though it really didn't have much purpose. He now felt as though the true purpose of his life could be found in Jesves, but he was worried. He didn't want to place pressure on her by being too pushy. He might scare her away before he had a chance to really develop a close relationship with her. He had to be careful. He had to back off and be more conscious of her desires and not just his own. He had to learn how to truly care for her by listening to her needs. He felt successful when she discussed her interest in doctoring and he knew that maybe by helping her achieve her goal he could show her that he truly cared for her.

Hiztin was at first confused by Jesves's religious attitudes but now he had learned to respect her for it. She prayed often to the God of the Rainbow. She prayed for help when she was taking care of the injured. She prayed each night before she went to sleep. She often encouraged Hiztin to join her. At first this offended him. He felt that she thought that he needed to straighten out his life. Soon he realized that if it was important to her and if he wanted to get closer, to her then he had better make it important to himself also. He had never done much praying before, only during ceremonial times, so praying regularly seemed strange to him. Eventually he had worked up enough courage to accept her invitation to pray with her one evening and he found that it wasn't so strange after all. He even found it to be fulfilling. It seemed to help him build closeness between him and Jesves. It was a common tie that they could share. Considering how he was starting to feel about her anything that would make them closer was worth it.

The expedition approached the mist wall getting closer and closer. It looked like a huge wall through which nothing could penetrate. It was straight up and down and flat as if a window had been set up against which the cloud pressed but through which the cloud could not pass. It was a light, smoky gray mixed with dark lines of turbulence. It also churned violently and appeared dangerous. It seemed as if someone were to enter it, they would immediately be torn apart limb-by-limb.

Yanon walked up to the wall of mist and reached out as if to touch it. Although it appeared to be thick enough to allow his hand to rest on it similar to the surface of a door, instead his hand passed through easily as though it were passing through thin air. As he pulled it back it felt strangely cold. While in the cloud his hand he felt no wind or turbulent pressure against it.

"I'm going to tie the end of a rope around my waist and enter into that stuff to see what it's like," Yanon explained. "If you feel a tug on the rope, pull me out quickly." He had already started to pull a rope out of his pack which he quickly tied around himself. Then he instructed, "Don't hesitate to pull me out if you sense any danger. I'll come back out and let you know what I learned."

Yanon hesitated briefly as he stepped into the cold wall. He could see nothing. It wasn't dark but the thickness of the mist prevented him from being able to see his own hands, even when he held them close to his face. He reached into this pocket and pulled out the rock light that Bydola had so mysteriously provided everyone, but it didn't help. He could see the orange hue of the light, but it wasn't strong enough to penetrate the mist. He returned the rock to his pocket and pressed on.

Walking was difficult. He would occasionally stumble on the irregular surface of the trail. He strangely noticed that there didn't seem to be any more bushes or undergrowth beneath his feet. He felt as though he were walking on hard dry ground.

He stumbled on in a straight line hoping that the trail stayed on course. He felt as though he was walking downhill. He kept his arms out in front of him as though he expected to encounter a tree or some other object at any moment. But he felt nothing. He wondered how the expedition team would avoid getting lost. He was discouraged at the hopelessness of the situation and began thinking of alternative schemes. They could camp in front of the wall of mist and try to wait it out hoping it would dissipate. But somehow this wall didn't seem to be a natural phenomenon that would eventually go away. There seemed to be some unnatural purpose. It possessed something he did not yet understand. Unfortunately, Bydola with all his newfound knowledge hadn't been any help in understanding this threat.

Suddenly as if to stop a bad dream the wall of mist ended, or at least its thickness ended. Yanon walked out into what seemed to be a new world. There was still a slight layer of foggy mist in the air, but it wasn't nearly as thick as it had been previously. The tall trees that he had been walking amongst on the other side of the wall had totally disappeared.

He was now surrounded by small bushy trees that were only about two leprechauns high. They were beautiful trees covered with blossoms. There was a grassy meadow filled with flowers. A small brook could be seen off in the distance trickling through the field. The Kilo Pass trail was plainly visible as it meandered through the grasses. It was as though he had entered some type of paradise. This land was too beautiful to be real.

"Is this supposed to be the Kabul?" Yanon asked himself in disbelief. "Why do legends call this a place of desolation? It's beautiful here."

He was excited. He couldn't wait to get back to his friends in order to tell them about his discovery.

Obydon and Gido nodded in agreement when Yanon instructed them to watch the rope. They picked up their end of it and watched as Yanon slowly walked toward the mist and then entered it. Instantly, he disappeared lost in the density of the cloud. Their rope kept slowly feeding into the cloud with no indication of any trouble.

"How are we supposed to be able to keep on the trail once we get in there?" Hasko asked. "I wonder if it wouldn't be better to just wait until this cloud goes away."

"This doesn't seem like the kind of cloud that is eventually going to go away," responded Obydon. "I think Yanon's right. We're going to have to brave it because it's our only choice."

Just then Yanon returned from out of the mist. "This mist is strange,'" he explained. "It is extremely thick for about twenty strides as though it is separating two worlds. Then it suddenly thins out into a world totally different from the one we see on this side of the wall."

"Will we be able to find our way once we've passed through this wall?" asked Hasko.

"Quite easily," responded Yanon. "It's still cloudy and misty once you've passed through the wall and get to the other side. But it's not so bad that we won't be able to see where we're going. You'll be utterly amazed at what you see on the other side." Yanon had decided to keep his discovery a secret allowing his companions to discover for themselves what lay on the other side. "We should tie ourselves together with ropes so that we won't get separated from one another and then I'll lead us through."

The ropes were quickly tied and Yanon slowly entered into the mist. He remembered approximately how many steps he had taken previously in order to get through the cloud of mist but this time it seemed to be taking much longer. He also remembered that the walk through the cloud had been a downward walk but this time he felt as though he were climbing. This confused him. His senses must have been deceived.

He walked on for what he was sure must have been at least twice as far as he had previously traveled. Suddenly and unexplainably, just like before, he was out of the thick mist. He looked behind and saw that all his companions had also escaped the mist at the same instant he had. This surprised him. He thought that the thick mist was like a wall that could be passed through, but apparently the mist enclosed him and then lifted itself.

He was amazed as he looked around and saw desolation and destruction. There were tall trees, just like in the hills they had just left but these trees were barren. Their tops were hidden by this mist that seemed to get thicker the higher up it went.

This time the ground was dry and parched and showed no signs of ever having supported vegetation. The brook he had seen previously had disappeared totally. Fortunately, the trail was still recognizable, but it looked as though it had been pounded into the earth by the passing of millions of feet. "What's going on?" he asked himself. "Is this place really the Kabul? And if it is where did I end up the last time I came through that foggy mess?"

Most of the members of the expedition had now caught up with Yanon and were circled around him. "This is about what I expected the Kabul to look like," commented Hasko. "It's ugly."

Yanon decided not to tell the story of what he had seen the first time he passed through the wall. He wondered if he had somehow been deceived by the evil that Bydola had claimed was in the mist. He reflected on the possibility that this type of trickery was what was in store for all of them as they passed through this region of the Kabul.

"Please, let's hurry," Bydola commented, "I sense evil everywhere and it frightens me. We must try to get through this land as quickly as possible."

No one argued or hesitated. They continued wearing the rope that tied them together, just in case they were to arrive at another wall of mist similar to the one they had just passed through. They traveled on as quickly as they could.

Travel was much faster than it had been outside of the Kabul on the Kilo Pass. The travelers no longer had the brush and ferns to contend with. They moved on at a pace that nearly forced the short-legged leprechauns to run, but no one complained. They all wanted to get through this desolate land as quickly as possible.

Eventually it became dark. The thick mist overhead hid any sign of the sun so they could only guess that the sun had set. "I guess it's about time to make camp," commented Yanon.

"Don't do it on my account," returned Obydon, "I'd rather keep traveling using those rocks that Bydola supplied us with. That way we can get further down the trail."

Yanon asked the others how they felt about stopping realizing that they had spent most of the previous night hiking to get away from the Tako Ruins. A quick vote was taken and all but Gabrona agreed to continue on for at least two more hours before they camped. They decided to eat as they walked so that they would not have to stop for dinner.

Bydola's orange lights were very effective in allowing the expedition to journey ahead. At the end of the additional two hours it seemed as though the expedition would still have to travel many more hours before they finally escaped the mists. A camp was quickly made, and everyone retired for the night having already eaten their fill along the way.

It was late into the night and everyone was asleep except Hiztin. He lay there looking at Jesves. He could barely make her out in the light of Bydola's orange rock, but he enjoyed watching her, so he lay there and stared. Suddenly he jumped up out of his sack. He wasn't sure why he had risen up. It was as though some hidden power had taken control of his body. He didn't feel in control of his movements. He felt as though he could see what he was doing but he couldn't restrain himself. He thought that this must be what it felt like to be hypnotized. He felt as though he was watching the actions of someone else.

He walked over to where Jesves had made her bed and laid himself down next to her. He kissed her on the cheek and laid his head down next to hers. He watched her for a few minutes feeling rattled and frightened inside. He feared that at any time she might wake up and be extremely angry with him. He wanted to jump up and run back over to his bed and pretend that none of this had really happened, but he couldn't. He had lost all control of his body.

Jesves was startled. She lay in her bed realizing that someone had just lain down next to her and then she felt the kiss on her cheek, but she couldn't react. She was frozen with fear. She was afraid and then confused. She couldn't even get her eyes open so she could see who had kissed her. Was it Hiztin? She hoped so but she couldn't find out for sure. She was afraid that it probably wasn't him because she doubted, he would ever have enough courage to do a thing like this. She wanted to scream for fear her mouth wouldn't move.

She lay there for several minutes wrapped in her frustration. Then she heard the sound of snoring. Whoever it was that had laid down next to her had begun snoring. How strange.

Finally, her eyes popped open. She couldn't understand why they opened now when all this time she had tried to open them but couldn't. Maybe because this individual had fallen asleep, she now felt braver. She discovered that it was Hiztin next to her and she was shocked. How could he do a thing like that? How sneaky of him to come over to her bed in the middle of the night and kiss her. Didn't he have enough courage to do it during the day? What was the matter with him? She wanted to shake him and yell at him, but she couldn't force herself to move. Then she was forced by some unknown power that was beyond her own to lean over and kiss his cheek.

Jesves was now the one that was out of control of her actions. She got up out of her sleeping sack went over to her pack and pulled a long cord out of it. Her mind was reeling wondering what her body was doing. She wanted badly to stop the uncontrolled process but could do nothing.

She went and tied a clump of hair from each of the sleeping members of the team to the cord keeping the cord tight so that if any of her companions would awaken and sit the cord would immediately cause the others to also wake up by pulling their hair out. Having completed her deed, she snuck back into her sleeping sack next to Hiztin and gave him another kiss. She rolled over and tried to sleep.

Her mind kept reeling. It would be funny to see the faces of the members of the expedition when they all woke up at the same time. They would be sure to find out it was her that did the deed since her cord would be the only cord that was missing. The realization that she had now laid down next to Hiztin as if to approve of what he'd done left her flabbergasted.

She heard someone cry out loudly, but she couldn't force herself to look. Drowsiness and some unknown power had over-powered her and she uncontrollably put her arm around Hiztin in a loving embrace and fell asleep.

Obydon missed his wife. He was angry at everyone around him for having made him go on this expedition and leave her. He wanted to go home, and this made him cry. He was also mad at the lepelves. The trick that Giterod had tried to pull on him in order to steal the sword made him angry. Was Gabrona just another lepelf up to the same tricks? Probably. In irritation he suddenly sat up feeling a sharp yank on his hair as he did so.

"Ouch," yelled Elasti, waking up from the sudden jerk, "who's pulling my hair?"

"You pulled my hair!" yelled Obydon angrily as he arose out of his bed. He noticed the cord tied to his hair and pulled it off quickly. He walked over to where Elasti was laying and kicked him in the side. "What's the big idea pulling my hair?"

Elasti was angered by Obydon's unjustified rebuff and grabbed his leg and pulled him over. Elasti also became obsessed with a confused anger and yelled out, "You fools think that because I was with Agot and Broch when they were killed that you can just kick me around? Their deaths weren't my fault!" As Obydon was trying to pull himself off the ground Elasti had jumped out of his sack and was now clambering on top of him kicking and beating on him as if the two of them had been mortal enemies all their lives.

Yanon was also awaken by the pull of the cord. He got up quickly when he saw the two fighting and pulled Elasti off yelling, "Look you two jerks. If you don't like the way I'm running this expedition you run it. I'm sick and tired of all this childish behavior?"

Bydola was another individual irritated at having his hair pulled out. He sat up and looked around. What he saw was utter confusion. Hiztin and Jesves locked in a loving embrace. Elasti and Obydon who were soon to become brothers-in-law were scrapping on the ground like children. And now Yanon acting as though he was obsessed was accusing everyone of wanting to take his leadership position away from him.

Suddenly Hasko jumped up and screamed. Of all the members in the expedition only Bydola seemed to notice. "I've been deserted," Hasko yelled, "I've been replaced by Jesves and now Hiztin hates me." Bydola was about to get up to comfort him when suddenly Hasko jumped up and started running in circles yelling, "I can't take this anymore." Then he took off running away from the camp.

Bydola jumped up and started to run after him but it was too late. Bydola gave him chase for several minutes but Hasko had gotten too much of a head start on him. Bydola could find very little in the mist that would help him locate the fleeing leprechaun. He returned to camp hoping that somehow Hasko would find his way back.

As Bydola returned he was just in time to see Gabrona sneaking behind Gido who was now sitting and watching the ruckus between the leprechauns. Gabrona was about to hit Gido with his pack as Bydola yelled out, "Lookout Gido!" Gido jumped up quickly out of the way of the flying pack. Gabrona and the pack came crashing to the ground.
"What's the big idea?
You twerp lepelf boy,
You looking for a fight,
I'll make you scream for joy," yelled Gido.

Gido grabbed Gabrona by the back of the collar, lifted him and gave him a hard pull forward. He sent him flying until he finally fell face first to the ground. The lepelf rolled over and yelled, "You killed Giterod and now you're going to kill me, well I'm not going to give you the chance." He rolled back over again, his face towards the ground and started crying.

Gido sat down on the ground and laughed. "How foolish," he thought, "a lepelf child that thinks he's a hero."

Gijivure lay there watching the excitement with his head propped up on his arm and laughed. He laughed so hard that it seemed as though he were going to cry. He realized the foolishness of what he was seeing. He realized that these fools that were on the expedition with him were being trapped by the "call of the mist", a mysterious force that makes lusts, desires, and suspicions come to the surface to the point where the individual cannot control himself any longer. He knew he would not be affected. The eagle had promised him that. But he realized he would have to stop this ruckus before someone was seriously hurt.

Bydola watched and reviewed the events he was seeing. He saw the passion in Hiztin and Jesves and the frustrations of Hasko, Obydon, Elasti, Gido, and Gabrona. The emotions of each were exposed. He noticed Gabrona in the midst of his sobbing suddenly fall back asleep right where he lay in the dirt. Gido soon laid down in his sleeping sack as well. Yanon, Obydon and Elasti wore themselves out fighting with each other and soon they all fell back into the dirt, huffing and puffing with exhaustion. Suddenly as if someone had blown out a candle all three of them were asleep. The entire commotion only lasted about twenty minutes and it seemed to end as quickly as it had started. Hiztin and Jesves hadn't moved the whole time this was going on. The two of them were still lying next to each other, Jesves with her arm around Hiztin.

But Gijivure wasn't acting at all like the rest of the party. He seemed to have some kind of immunity against this strange force. He still lay on the ground and laughed at the antics of his friends. Bydola stood back and watched the actions of this elf from a distance. The leprechaun saw the same image of evil permeate from Gijivure and he wondered what it meant. He questioned if perhaps Gijivure was the only one in the expedition that had a "mind that's sound". He was frustrated by the thought that someone who exhibited evil could be of a "sound mind".

Bydola wasn't sure why he personally hadn't been affected by the strange possession that had overcome the rest of his friends. He was glad that up to now it had spared him. Perhaps his turn was yet to come. He hoped that his fate would not be the same as that of Hasko who went running blindly into the darkness. He hoped that perhaps through his contact with the Creator he had received some special immunity from the evil that persisted here in the Kabul.

Bydola wondered about Hasko and hoped that his friend was just a little way outside of the camp perhaps even watching them. He hoped that Hasko had also mysteriously dropped to the ground and fallen asleep just as the rest of his companions had and that he would return to them in the morning. Bydola felt frustrated. He wasn't sure what else to expect from the Kabul so he decided that the best thing he could do was to stay alert by getting a good rest. There seemed to be very little he could do to help anyway now that they were all asleep. He returned to his bed. He crawled in, rolled over onto his side, forgot about Gijivure's mysterious laughing and fell asleep.

As daylight broke and the campers started to get up, they found their campsite in a disaster. "What happened here last night?" asked Yanon. "Were we attacked?"

"Don't you remember what happened?" asked Bydola.

"No! Should I?"

"You, Elasti, and Obydon were wrestling and fighting with each other like crazy. Why do you think you were asleep out there in the middle of the dirt?"

"I thought someone drug me out there," was Yanon's reply.

"How about you, Elasti and Obydon, do you remember your little encounter?" Bydola wanted to see if any of them remembered the previous night's events.

"I don't remember anything, but I sure feel sore and bruised. I didn't get that by sleeping," responded Elasti.

"I don't remember anything either," commented Obydon. "Tell us what happened."

Without answering Obydon's question Bydola turned to Gido and asked him, "How about you, do you remember anything?"

"I remember,
Not a thing;
But I feel,
A pain within," was Gido's reply.

"How about you, Gabrona," Bydola continued his questioning.

"I hurt bad. My face feels as though it was smashed in. But I can't remember how it happened," Gabrona replied.

Then testing Gijivure in order to see his reaction, he asked, "How about you Gijivure?"

Gijivure hesitated at first as if he wasn't sure how he should answer the question and then he said;

"Last night many things must have happened,

But I can't remember any;

I'm not sure there were many,

That were able to remember what happened."

"That leaves you two," Bydola turned to Hiztin and Jesves, who were both blushing as if they had been caught doing something sneaky. "Do you remember anything?"

"Well yes, I do," returned Hiztin. "But I don't remember anything about what happened to any of the rest of you. I only remember what happened to myself. I thought everyone else was asleep." Then he relayed the story about how he had lost control of his body and how he was forced to lay down next to Jesves. He left out some of the details, like kissing her.

"You've got to be kidding," teased Elasti. "You're going to try to convince me that you were forced to lie down next to Jesves. I'll bet you've been sneaking over next to her every night but tonight was just the first time you got caught at it!"

The rest of the members of the expedition all laughed except Jesves who spoke up quickly, "It's true. It happened to me too." She told about her tying everyone's hair together and then about laying down with Hiztin and putting her arm around him.

Again, everyone laughed causing Hiztin and Jesves to turn red. "It's alright, we don't mind," Elasti continued to tease them. "Now you won't have to hide the fact that you're lovey-dovey anymore. We'll just try to look the other way whenever you two are together." Another hearty laugh followed.

"Sorry about all this," Hiztin whispered to Jesves in a sheepish embarrassed voice.

"I'm not," Jesves replied as she turned away from him trying to avoid eye contact. This comment startled Hiztin and for a few seconds he didn't know what to say.

"What do you mean?" he asked but Jesves was already getting up and moving away from him, trying to avoid any further embarrassment.

"Stop it you jokers. When you get done teasing Jesves and Hiztin perhaps you'll notice that one of us is missing." Bydola was sarcastic but serious. He was concerned that Hasko had not returned and feared that the leprechaun would be lost somewhere out in the mist. His concern increased even more when he realized that Hasko would also most likely not remember anything that had occurred.

"Hasko," Hiztin yelled out fearing that something dreadful had happened to his lifelong friend. "Where is he?" he turned to Bydola with a questioning look.

"I don't know," returned Bydola. "He took off running out of here as though all of the Kabul was after him. By the time I got out of my sack and started after him he was so far gone that I had no chance of catching up. I had hoped that he would somehow make his way back to camp by this morning, but it looks like that didn't happen."

"Where did he go?" asked Hiztin in exasperation. "I'm going to go after him."

"It's no use," returned Bydola. "He didn't run off in one direction, he ran every-which-way running one way for a while then turning and running in a completely different direction. You'll have no hope of finding him in this fog."

"But I've got to try!" Hiztin insisted. "I can't just leave him out there alone."

"Bydola's right," interjected Yanon trying to assure Hiztin. "Hasko is a good scout. He's not lost. He has a much better chance of finding us than we have of finding him. The best thing we can do is press on. We'll leave him a note here with his pack telling him that we decided it was best to go ahead, and that he should hurry and catch up with us a quickly as he can."

"The smartest thing for us to do," he continued, "is to get out of the Kabul before anything else happens. We shouldn't risk another night here unless we have to. We should get out of here as quickly as possible, and then once we are outside, we can wait for Hasko."

Hiztin bowed his head in dejection. His friend needed him and there was no way he could help him. He felt frustrated but he knew that Bydola and Yanon were right. His friend was a good scout and would be better at finding the quest than Hiztin would be at trying to find him.

"Tell us about last night?" asked Elasti who was still curious about his bruises. "That must have been a strange night."

Bydola was caught in a dilemma. If no one remembered anything about the previous night, then wouldn't it be better just to leave all those hostilities alone? He decided that it wouldn't be a good idea to build up unnecessary tensions between the members of the expedition by exposing their deepest thoughts. "You guys just decided to have a jolly wrestling match in the middle of the night. I thought you were all crazy. You goofed around until you were all so worn out that you fell asleep right where you lay. I've never seen anything like it in my life." Then whispering he said, "and I hope I never see anything like it again."

Hasko ran blindly into the darkness that surrounded him. He had lost all sense of direction and all sense of time. He wasn't sure who he was, and he didn't seem to care. He ran for hours without stopping pushing his body far beyond the limit of endurance. He had lost control of his senses and his mind. He was moving at the will of some unknown force, totally oblivious to its powers.

He ran through the trees, having long ago left the path that his friends would be traveling along. The hardness of the earth would keep his companions from being able to recognize any tracks that he might have made therefore making it impossible to follow him. But at the moment he didn't seem to care if they ever found him or not. He seemed to have forgotten why he was running. He only knew that he must keep on running until he escaped.

He eventually came back upon the mist wall that marked the edge of the Kabul, but he didn't seem to recognize it either. He charged forward at full speed directly into the wall of mist as if it wasn't there. Once within the mist he continued running but only for a few minutes when suddenly the wall disappeared, and he found himself in a land beyond description.

He had run into what seemed to be a new world far more beautiful than any he had ever experienced. The nighttime that he had left behind him in the Kabul had now turned to daylight that was so bright that it seemed like the middle of the day even though he knew it was the middle of the night. There were small bushy trees all around, each only about two leprechauns high surrounded by the same thin mist that had existed in the Kabul. Beautiful blossoms covered the trees and the ground was a grassy meadow filled with flowers. A small brook could be seen off in the distance trickling through the field. A trail was plainly visible as it meandered through the grasses, but this trail surely couldn't be the Kilo Pass trail that he had left just a few hours ago.

Unfortunately, Hasko was oblivious to it all. His mind was in a haze. He felt nothing as though nothing really mattered, and nothing even existed. He ran on for another twenty minutes. Finally, he tripped and fell flat on his face in the grass. He looked up and found himself surrounded by what appeared to be a giant ribcage of what must have been an enormous animal at one time. The skeleton was gigantic, and he found himself in the middle of the creature's chest staring through prison bars made up of the animal's ribs. But Hasko was still oblivious to it all. He rolled over with his face to the ground. His head and body appeared to be smothered in the grass and flowers. He was quickly lost in a deep sleep.

Hiztin wrote a note for Hasko and attached it to his friend's pack. He left the pack near the Kilo Pass trail so that if Hasko followed the trail he would be sure to find it. Then he and all the other members of the team packed up their belongings, ate a quick breakfast, and prepared to continue north on the path.

They departed and although Hiztin was hesitant to leave the spot where Hasko may be returning he also felt the urgency of leaving the Kabul. They hurried on making good time on the dry dirt trail.

They had traveled about an hour when Bydola began to sense an evil that seemed to permeate from the ground. He looked around in all directions and noticed that this evil seemed to be everywhere. At first, he didn't take much notice of it guessing that it was probably the Kabul itself that he was sensing. He didn't mention it to his friends since they probably wouldn't take him seriously anyway. But then this sensation of evil grew stronger and stronger. He looked around and there seemed to be no direction of escape. The sensation became so strong that he felt as though at any moment this unknown force would pounce on him and his companions.

"Help!" he suddenly screamed out. He couldn't contain the sensation any longer. "Run," he screamed, "run for your lives!"

At first his friends gave him a questioning look wondering about his sanity but when they saw the urgency in his eyes and the fear in his expression, they realized he was serious. Bydola began running down the Kilo Pass and his friends quickly followed his lead.

Suddenly as if somehow triggered by Bydola's scream, small snake like creatures began popping out of the dry, parched earth. It was as if the hardness of the ground had no effect on them as they broke through its surface. They were small, only about the length of a hand, but they were too fat to be worms.

Hundreds of the creatures started to appear. Soon there were thousands, and then tens of thousands. There seemed to be no end to them as they continued to appear. It wasn't long before the entire surface of the ground was covered with them.

The expedition continued running along over the top of the creatures. They didn't recognize them and questioned if they were really a threat to the safety of the quest. Bydola had no doubt about their evil intent. These creatures emanated evil so strongly that he was left with no choice but to run for his life. It was difficult to avoid stepping on the little creatures and many of them would find their deaths under the feet of one of the travelers.

At first the little creatures gave no sign of their intent. They climbed out of their hard dirt holes and stationed themselves as guards at the top of each hole. But suddenly, as if triggered by some silent signal, they simultaneously attacked. They started surrounding and chasing after the members of the quest. The creatures would cling onto the shoes of the expedition members and hang on tightly, but fortunately they were easily kicked off as the travelers continued running wildly.

Then the travelers realized something frightful. They could no longer see the Kilo Pass trail. There were now so many of the creatures, all thronging together in an attempt to get at the travelers, that the trail was no longer visible. They no longer knew which way to run. But they realized that they must continue running.

"Ow,'" yelled Gabrona, "those little buggers hurt!" Since he had not properly prepared himself for the expedition, he had also forgotten to wear appropriate boots. The shoes that he wore were low cut, and one of the creatures had successfully worked its way up the side of the shoe far enough to where it was now taking a solid grip on Gabrona's leg. Gabrona kicked the creature off and continued running after his friends.

Bydola still held the lead. He ran along blindly hoping that he was heading in the direction of the Kilo Pass. All of his friends frantically followed him trying desperately not to get separated from each other. Then they noticed something else that was frightening. There was something that instilled more fear in the North Groves expedition than anything they had up to now encountered. Off in the distance they saw that the snake creatures were piling themselves up on top of each other. They were actually building a wall, one snake at a time and this wall was growing on all sides.

Bydola's pace slowed, as if he was unsure what to do. Yanon, Giji-vure, and Gabrona were able to catch up with him. "What do we do now?" yelled Yanon.

"I'm not sure," responded Bydola, as if it had now become his responsibility to find a way for his friends to escape. But Gijivure held no hesitation,

"There's only one choice,
We must fight;
With all our might,
If we are to escape."

Gijivure was already pulling forth his sword, preparing himself for the battle of his life.

"I wish I felt,
The way you do;
I feel there's better,
Things to do.
But I don't know,
How to be rid;
Of this new evil,
That's so horrid,"

Gido was hoping that Bydola would be able to come up with a better method of warding off the creatures but the leprechaun volunteered no suggestion.

"I guess we fight," responded Yanon as he also drew his sword.

During all this, the snake walls continued to pile higher and higher. In some places the wall was already higher than their heads. Then they noticed something even more freighting. They noticed this living wall start to encircle and close in on them. The wall was no longer growing taller by the addition of more of these creatures. Its height seemed to increase by the merging and pushing together of the large ring. As the snake-wall circle closed in the creatures making up the wall would merge and mingle together flowing amongst one another as if they were liquid. The ever-decreasing circle wall caused the wall to continually growing higher.

Yanon grew desperate. The snakes were still nipping at his shoes as he continually kicked them off. He selected an area of the wall that seemed to be the lowest, and with his sword held forward, he charged. His friends quickly picked up on the attack and followed him.

Obydon was irritated. The wrappings that he used as a scabbard for his sword wouldn't come off quickly. He was in a hurry to use his sword, but he couldn't free it. Eventually he was successful but not until everyone else was already beating on the wall of snakes with their weapons. They were having limited success. Each blow of their sword would end the lives of many of the small snake creatures but more of them always seemed to be available to take the place of those that were killed.

Obydon approached the wall feeling the same sense of hopelessness that his companions were experiencing and wondering if there was any hope for their escape. He reeled the Southern Sword over the top of his head and with all his might forced a hard blow upon the snakes. As the sword struck flesh, a flash of yellow light surged from the point of impact. The sword seemed to flow through the creatures as if they were water. The momentum he had placed behind the force, and the ease at which it cut through the snakes, caused him to stumble forward and crumble to the ground, falling amongst the creatures that he had hoped to annihilate.

He quickly jumped up beating off several of the creatures that had successfully attached themselves to various parts of his body like leeches. On occasion small pieces of his flesh were ripped off as he pulled off the creatures. The sores were small and didn't affect his enthusiasm to strike again.

After several thrusts he finally had a chance to look at the damage that his sword had done to the wall. Burned snake flesh could be seen lying on the ground in all directions. His sword had successfully sliced a gash into the living wall and even though the snakes were desperately working to correct the damage Obydon now realized that he had found the means necessary to defeat this new enemy.

He raised his sword and once again leveled it on the snakes. As before the same yellow light flashed and the air was filled with the scent of burning flesh. Again, and again he pounded at the wall slicing it down lower and lower because of the reduced numbers of the creatures that were available to refill the opening. It took many swift strokes but soon the snake wall was no more than knee high. Obydon took several more swift strokes in rapid succession and opened up a wedge large enough for someone to pass through. He yelled at Jesves who was standing next to him, "Hurry up and run through!"

Jesves didn't hesitate. She safely found herself on the other side of the snake wall. This process was repeated several times. Each time Obydon would open a hole and each time one of the travelers would scurry through. Eventually only Obydon, Yanon, and Gabrona remained within the confines of the living wall circle. Obydon was about to strike against the wall once again in an attempt to widen the hole when suddenly, as if on cue, the snake wall disbanded itself and within seconds all the snakes scurried down into the holes from which they had previously come. They totally disappeared. Their sudden departure was as shocking as their arrival had been. Without any warning they had mysteriously taken refuge back into the earth.

With swords still in hand the remaining party crossed over the area where the wall had been and meandered toward one another in disbelief. They seemed unsure that the attack was really over. They wondered if there would be another sudden attack. They looked at each other in amazed surprise unable to find the words that would properly express what they felt.

Elasti finally broke the silence, "I'll sure be glad when we get out of the Kabul." No one responded to this remark, but they all felt the same.

"I hope we're done with those buggers," commented Yanon. "If it wouldn't have been for Obydon and the Southern Sword we would all be suffering a slow cruel death." Again, the comment left everyone silent.

Bydola reassuringly spoke in his prophetic tone, "The evil departs. It grows fainter and fainter all the time. I don't see any sign of another attack. At least no attack in the immediate future."

"Then let's get a move on and get out of here!" suggested Yanon with a level of urgency.

The travelers trusted Bydola's remark and started putting away their weapons. Gido stooped down to the ground and inspected some of the dead creatures that had nearly taken his life.

"These things aren't snakes,
They're lizard shaped;
Their legs are missing,
Their backs are flaked.
Their mouths and eyes,
Are all not right;
Their noses are pointed,
Their head is affright.
Their teeth are many,
And sharp as well;
The Kabul is,
A living hell."

"I'm sure glad that they didn't take more out of my hide than they did," commented Obydon who had suffered the most from the bites. He inspected his wounds and found only four that needed attention. He knew Bydola could heal him whenever the opportunity existed.

"I wonder why they gave up the attack," questioned Obydon. "They must have felt that defeating us was hopeless."

"I think you're right," returned Bydola, "but there's something that worries me more. I wonder why they attacked us to begin with. It was almost as if they were sent after us the way they came out so suddenly and in unison. And if they were sent to attack us who sent them and why? Does Krakus already know about our expedition and is he sending forces after us? The thought of him knowing about us scares me." Bydola was sharing his thoughts and didn't really expect anyone to answer.

Yanon had already begun searching around hoping to again spot the Kilo Pass trail, "I think I see the path off to the north of us," he commented. "We're not as far off the trail as I feared."

"I see it," added Jesves. "That's definitely the trail."

The North Groves expedition having survived another trial ventured forth toward the trail and once again resumed their journey hoping to save their homeland from devastation.

They traveled for twenty minutes satisfied that their attackers had given up their pursuit. Suddenly the trail started climbing sharply. It went up steeply as if they had encountered the edge of a high mountain. This climbing continued for the next three hours and they were becoming extremely weary. The climb forced them to rest often.

Suddenly Yanon yelled out, "Look ahead! We've found the mist wall." The expedition had once again encountered the dense mist that marked their entrance to the Kabul and now, they hoped it would mean their exit from this dreaded place.

"Yipeeeeee!" yelled Elasti. He cheered for all, since they were all grateful to see the end of their trials.

"Let's connect ourselves again with a rope so that we will be able to stay together," Yanon recommended and the rope was quickly connected.

Slowly Yanon again started to lead the party through the mists taking each step carefully as he moved. He ventured on for what seemed to be an eternity. It was much further than he had gone either of the two previous times that he had entered the mist. Suddenly he and all his companions were again exposed to the mountains of the Central Ranges with its beautiful tall trees. They also encountered something that left them stunned. This was something they had never experienced before. It was something they had not prepared themselves for and that they now had to face head on. It was snowing. It wasn't a heavy snow, just a light mild snow, but based on the depth of the snow on the ground, it had been falling for quite some time. It was thick enough to make traveling extremely difficult.

Luckily, the trail was identifiable since it was cleared of trees which were thick on either side of the trail. The rest of the forest was heavily wooded. However, an occasional bush did break through the snow, even along the trail.

"What the heck is this stuff?" asked Obydon teasingly.

"I'd forgotten about the snow up here," responded Elasti. "When I traveled through the Albo Pass with the dwarfs the weather had been good but even then, I could see that there was snow on the ground at the highest points of the trail."

"What the heck do we do now?" inquired Hiztin.

"We go on," responded Yanon. "I'm not interested in returning to the Kabul. We'll have to try and make it to the first Kilo Pass tunnel before nightfall. We're not well enough equipped to last very long in this stuff."

"We can survive," returned Elasti. "The dwarfs taught me how. But I don't want to try it if we don't have to. There's always a risk that goes with it."

"But what about Hasko?" protested Hiztin. His concern for his friend was becoming intense.

"He's smart enough to know that we wouldn't have tried to spend the night in this stuff," said Yanon comfortingly. "He'll do his best to catch up with us."

"But what if he has to spend the night in this stuff and he doesn't know how to do it. Then what?" continued Hiztin.

Hiztin had made a good point, a point for which no one had any answers. How indeed would Hasko be able to care for himself in this snow?

Hiztin insisted that he stay behind and wait for his boyhood friend. He wasn't going to let his friend die in the snow. Yanon and Obydon pleaded with him to give up his foolishness. Surely Hasko would know how to get himself out of this mess.

Jesves was concerned about losing the best friend she had ever had. She came up with an alternative idea in an attempt to appease Hiztin. "What if we cut a long pole, say about three leprechauns high, and stick it right in the middle of the trail. Then we'll attach a note to it explaining to Hasko what he needs to do to survive a night in the snow. We'll tell him to hurry and catch up with us in the first tunnel. That way he'll get the information he needs and none of us will need to unnecessarily risk our life."

"That's a great idea," commented Hiztin.

"Fabulous," added Obydon. "I'm glad we've found a solution."

Hiztin was pleased. He didn't want to spend his time concerned about deserting his friend. He was glad that his persistence had forced Jesves to come up with an idea that would allow him to continue on with the rest of the expedition.

A thin tree was found and quickly cut down by Hiztin and Yanon. Elasti wrote out instructions for the construction of a snow tunnel. Then the note was attached to the end of the pole, and it was stuck deep into the snow. The snow was deep enough to hold the stick up. For additional support they rolled large balls of snow around it to assure that it wouldn't fall over in a wind.

The expedition pressed on moving as quickly as they could in hopes that they would soon arrive at the first Kilo Pass tunnel.

CHAPTER SIXTEEN

THE FIRST TUNNEL

Travel was slow. The snow made it difficult to walk. The expedition's feet sank deeply into the soft whiteness that covered the earth.

"This stuff is cold," complained Obydon, "I'm sure glad we don't get any of it in Amins."

"We'd sure have to wear different clothes if we did," returned Yanon. "We aren't very prepared for this type of weather."

They had only traveled two hours and already the members of the expedition were suffering from the cold. They tried to tuck their hands into their pockets in order to keep them warm, but this only helped slightly. Every time someone would slip in the snow their hands came out of their pockets and ended up touching the snow.

"We will stop to make a fire,
And get everybody warm;
From freezing or numbness,
So, no one will have harm;
Then when we're dried,
And we have all gotten warm;
We'll provide clothes for our bodies,
and socks for our hands,
Which should prevent harm," suggested Gido

Gijivure and Gido were more familiar with the snow. Up on the Jove Plateau they would occasionally get enough to remind them what it was like. They knew that they must get better prepared for the cold weather or they would never make it to the first tunnel. The first step in getting them prepared was to get them a warm fire where they could get dried off and properly clothed.

Gijivure and Gido were the only two members of the expedition who had gloves and they set to work collecting wood and preparing a fire that the others could stand next to, watching and shivering. It was difficult to. find enough dry twigs to get the fire started. Once it was going, its warmth dried off enough wood to allow the fire to become quite large

The travelers enjoyed the fire quickly warming themselves up. It was a necessary disruption to their travels. Then they pulled extra layers of pants and shirts out of their packs and put them on in order to get the extra protection they needed. They also pulled extra socks out of their packs and proceeded to use them for gloves as well as adding to the protection of their feet. These socks would keep their hands warmer than by trying to use their pockets.

"This was a great idea Gijivure," thanked Elasti, "I'm not sure how much further I could have continued in this snow before my fingers would have started falling off. I guess the Amins Council doesn't know much about the weather in the Lamos Ranges or they would have warned us to dress better."

"We can't blame them. We didn't know any better either." Yanon considered it his role to defend the Council.

"I was beginning to wonder if we shouldn't have stayed in the Kabul longer in spite of its dangers until it stops snowing," returned Elasti.

"It will take months,
To remove the snow;
We haven't the time,
We have to go," responded Gido.

"Well, Gido, it sure would have been nicer without it," responded Elasti. "But at the same time, I'm glad to get out of the Kabul. I sure didn't like the games it played with our minds."

Suddenly up out of the snow popped a creature that was so white it was difficult to distinguish from the snow itself. It shot straight out of the snow not making any tracks other than the hole that it had come out of and it landed in Jesves' lap. Jesves had been sitting on a log close to the fire and now she jumped up and tried to knock the intruder off her lap. The creature disappeared back into the snow where it had come from. Jesves wanted desperately to cry out in fear, but she bit her lip resisting the temptation. She didn't want to look like a fool.

She looked up at Bydola as if he held all explanations and asked, "What the heck was that?"

"Beats the heck out of me," was his meaningless response. "All I can say is that I saw no evil in it. I haven't seen it or anything like it before."

Suddenly and just as surprisingly as before the creature again popped out of the snow this time landing in Hiztin's lap. Hiztin's reaction was much the same. He jumped up and started flapping his arms around frantically as if the movement would create enough wind to blow the creature away. The creature wasn't able to cling to him and it fell off once again disappearing under the snow.

"Did you see the size of that thing?" yelled Hiztin. "It's huge!"

Yanon, seeing Hiztin's frantic actions, couldn't control himself and he burst out laughing. Soon Elasti and Obydon were laughing too.

"What's so funny?" complained Hiztin.

Just then the creature popped out of the snow again, this time landing on the lap of Elasti. Elasti jumped. The humor of the situation had suddenly faded for him. Realizing that he was now opening himself to teasing he tried to remain calm. He stayed seated watching this thing that had made itself comfortable at his expense.

He held his arms away from it hoping it wouldn't bite his arms or legs, "What is this thing?"

No one had an answer for him. Bydola, having the least fear of the creature because he saw no evil in it, approached it and began inspecting it. As he did so the creature squirmed causing Elasti again to jump. Hiztin, taking advantage of this opportunity for revenge burst out laughing. "What's the matter Elasti? Why aren't you as brave now as you were when that thing was on my lap?" Elasti didn't answer. He remained tense.

Bydola continued inspecting the creature, and soon he was accompanied by Gabrona. "What do you think it is?" questioned the lepelf.

"I have no idea," responded Bydola. "It seems friendly enough. I think it's just looking for a little warmth just like we are."

Bydola continued inspecting the creature. At first, he avoided getting too close because of his concern about how the creature might react. The creature looked like a series of interwoven bubbles without any indication of what was front or back or top or bottom. Bydola reached out to touch the animal. As his hand came close to the creature it started to squirm causing Elasti to become fearful that he might be bitten. When Bydola's hand came into contact with the creature it squirmed even more but made no sign of wanting to escape.

"It feels like a cold rock. It's very smooth and slippery," explained Bydola. He placed both of his hands on the creature and tried to turn it over but as he rolled the bubbles over the bottom appeared the same as the top, which was also the same as any of the sides. Actually, he wasn't sure he had even turned the creature over, and he wondered if perhaps the slipperiness of the creature's skin made it only seem like it was being turned over.

"This creature looks the same from all sides," explained Bydola. "It feels like a half a dozen large, slippery boulders that are somehow interconnected with each other. I can't tell where the front is."

"It doesn't feel heavy enough to be boulders," commented Elasti. "It feels pretty light for its size." Elasti felt much better hearing that the creature looked the same on the bottom. This gave him confidence that perhaps the creature couldn't bite him. He started to run his hands over the creature as well, inspecting its cold, marble-like surface.

The creature seemed to become comfortable with being touched. It didn't squirm as much when Bydola and Elasti ran their hands over it. It just seemed to want to rest in the comfortable, warm lap of Elasti. Soon others in the expedition came over and touched it as well wondering what the purpose of the curious creature was.

"I don't understand this critter," commented Yanon. "It doesn't seem to have any way of movement, yet it travels through snow at very high speeds. It can't seem to see yet it has no trouble finding our laps. It doesn't seem to have any way to eat yet it lives and is quite lively. It definitely isn't as afraid of us as we are of it."

"Maybe it's just too stupid to be afraid," responded Hiztin sarcastically, still not appreciating the strange new intruder.

"What are we going to do with it?" questioned Elasti, who was by now getting tired of providing it with a resting place.

"I guess we throw it back into the snow where it came from," responded Yanon as he started to throw snow on the fire. "It's time for us to get going anyway if we plan to make it to the first tunnel before nightfall."

Elasti carefully pushed the creature off his lap hoping that it wouldn't retaliate. The animal slipped off into the snow as if it didn't exist, leaving a hole in the snow as it disappeared. Elasti stood up inspecting himself for damage caused by the creature but he found no sign that the creature had ever been there. He wasn't even wet from the snow that the creature should have carried with it.

It was difficult to get the expedition to continue with their travels once they had become so comfortable around the fire. They all knew that they must get moving if they were to achieve their destination. They arose slowly, grabbed their packs, and continued on.

Traveling was again extremely slow. The snowfall had let up, but the softness of the fallen snow still hindered rapid progress. Often the depth of the snow came up to the waists of the leprechauns which caused them a lot of strain as they tried to push their way through.

Travel for the elves and the lepelf wasn't quite as bad. Their advantage in height allowed them to step through the snow more easily than the leprechauns. But still their steps had to be high and carefully made and this caused an abnormal strain on their bodies. The taller individuals usually took the lead blazing a bit of a trail for the leprechauns.

The travelers remained quiet pushing ahead in silence as each concentrated on the hope that they would soon encounter the first tunnel. The energy exerted in walking through the snow forced them to burn so much energy that they were too exhausted to talk.

Gido stopped. He was in the lead and now in silence he pointed to something off in the distance. As everyone caught up with him, they were able to see what he was directing their attention to. Ahead of them they could see the smoke of a fire.

"What is it?" questioned Gabrona.

"It's probably a gnome camp," whispered Yanon. "I can't think of anyone else who would be out here in this snow."

"Oh rats!" responded Elasti. "I was hoping we would avoid any more of those killers. I thought this trail would be safer than the Albo Pass."

"We're lucky that it has been snowing," added Obydon. "The snow blotted out our fire. Otherwise, we would probably be crawling with gnomes already."

Yanon interjected, "And the snow is probably keeping all the gnomes together in their camp by their nice warm fire or else we might have already encountered a scouting party. I guess we should be thankful that the snow is falling instead of complaining about it."

"How can we be thankful about encountering a bunch of gnomes?" questioned Elasti sarcastically. "They're probably guarding the entrance to the tunnel that we've been searching for."

"You're probably right," returned Yanon. "The first thing we better do is get off the road. We don't want to be seen out here in the open. Then we better work out some kind of plan."

Several of the party nodded their heads in acknowledgement of what Yanon had said and started to move to the south side of the trail into the trees. They didn't have to go far before they were well hidden by the trees and the snow. The party huddled together; partly so that they could hear each other talk without having to be too loud, and also in hopes that their closeness would keep them warm.

"I hope they don't come up the trail and notice our footsteps."

"They'll notice the bright colors of our clothes before they notice our trails," commented Yanon. "If the snow keeps falling for a little while yet our trail will be covered up and they won't be able to spot it. I doubt that any of them will be interested in venturing down this pass in the snow unless we give them a reason to. All we have to do is keep out of sight."

"What are we going to do?" questioned Elasti. "We can't stand around in this snow forever."

"Gijivure and I will go ahead and scout,
To see if the tunnel is there;
If it's not there, we go around,
Otherwise we must beware.
Maybe we'll go around the tunnel,
And skip it entirely;
That way we will avoid the gnomes,
And continue ahead safely," commented Gido.

"Gido," objected Elasti, "I know your intentions are good, but there's no way I'm going to survive in this snow especially if we have to climb any mountains in order to get around that tunnel. I'll freeze to death. We've got to figure out some way of getting into that tunnel."

"I agree with Elasti," responded Obydon. "We must get into that tunnel. My fingers feel like they are almost frozen off already. First let's be certain that the gnomes are at the tunnel's entrance. Gido, why don't you and Gijivure do what you said? You should go and scout out what the gnomes are up to."

Gido looked at Yanon to verify that the leader of expedition was in agreement. Yanon nodded his head in approval. Gido and Gijivure dropped their packs and carefully slipped toward the camp they had seen from a distance. Their longer legs allowed them to move through the snow easier than any of the others. Their thinner bodies seemed to give them the ability to move gracefully anywhere, even on the side of a snow-covered mountain.

The remainder of the expedition stood in silence waiting for the return of the elves. It was as if they were afraid to disturb the silent beauty of the snow that was softly falling around them. The forest looked majestic with its tall snow-covered trees.

But standing under the trees also had its dangers. Occasionally a clump of snow would come crashing down off one of the branches hitting one of the weary travelers over the head and covering them with snow. Although they were irritated when this happened, no one complained. They knew that they must keep as silent as possible. Even though they were covered with the double set of clothes and they wore socks on their hands, cold still penetrated their clothing.

The two elves crept closer and closer toward the campfire. They knew that the falling snow would dampen some of the noise that they would make in moving through the snow and that the crackling of the campfire would disguise their presence even more. It wasn't long before the camp was in full view. It was indeed occupied by gnomes, about two dozen of them, all comfortably huddling close to the fire. In the distance past the camp laid the entrance to the first Kilo Pass tunnel. Even if they waited till nightfall, the entrance would still be plainly visible to the gnome party because of the fire. Discouraged, the elves quickly made their way back toward the location of their friends.

"I'm afraid, we have bad news,
It's gnomes that keep the fire;
There's only twelve, which may be good,
If war this will require," reported Gido.

"That is bad news Gido," said Yanon. "Why aren't the gnomes in the tunnel where it's warmer? Maybe they're afraid of the tunnels. Or maybe there's a greater danger inside. Hopefully, they're just afraid which means that if we can get inside the tunnel unnoticed, we may be free of their threat and they won't come in after us."

Elasti added, "I'm surprised there are only twelve guards on this pass. There were many more than that on the Albo Pass. The gnomes must not consider this route a very serious threat. You're probably right, Yanon. This may be the last we see of the gnomes if we can get through here safely."

But Gijivure objected,
"The tunnel is close to the campfire,
Entrance to the tunnel, will be hard;
Even at night, there will be a guard,
We can't enter without detection.
But avoiding detection is important,
There's no way for entrance;
Gido's suggestion about avoidance,
Maybe the smartest thing for us to do."

"We've got to get into that tunnel," pleaded Obydon, "I'm just not built for this kind of weather. I'd much rather face the gnomes and any dangers that may lie inside that tunnel than to face camping overnight in snow tunnels and spending several more days in this cold."

"Why don't we come up with some kind of diversion," suggested Hiztin, "something that will throw the gnomes off guard. Something that will take them away from the entrance of the tunnel so that we can enter safely and unnoticed."

"That's a great idea," responded Obydon. "Maybe a forest fire would chase them away."

"How about an arrow in one of the gnomes, shot from the opposite side of the road," added Hiztin. "Then the gnomes will go running off in one direction while all of us sneak into the tunnel from the other side of the trail."

"Both of those schemes could get out of control," mused Yanon thoughtfully. "I like the idea of a diversion, but a forest fire would be hard to start in this snow, and then we would damage these beautiful trees. The trees are our friends and that would be a cruel abuse of them if we so deliberately misuse them." He recalled his experience in the Amins Groves and now he had a new respect for the trees. "I don't feel comfortable with the idea of one of us risking our lives shooting a gnome either. Besides, that will make our presence known. We've got to come up with something that will allow us to scare them off and still not give away our presence."

"What if we start an avalanche?" asked Jesves.

Yanon looked at her confused and asked, "What do you mean by an avalanche?"

"If we could find a build-up of snow near the ridge of one of these mountains perhaps we could cause it to come crashing down. Hopefully the noise from its fall would cause the gnomes to run off to investigate its cause leaving the entrance to the tunnel unprotected."

"That's a great idea Jesves," commented Hiztin who was always her first and best supporter.

"How do we set off the avalanche? And how do we get out of its way?" questioned Obydon skeptically.

"If we can find an appropriate snowpack, we'll build a tunnel under it and then set a small fire in the tunnel. Eventually as the tunnel warms the fire will trigger the slide."

"How are we going to get out of the way before the slide comes down on us?" asked Obydon.

Gijivure supported the idea;
"If we tie a rope around the tunnel digger,
And stand prepared in the event of a slide;
Three or four of us will stay to the side,
And pull him out as quickly as possible.
The technique is risky but will work,
We'll have to do it with care;
There'll be a lot to prepare,
We must hurry and see if there's a place."

"I like it." Yanon appeared excited. "I hope we can find an appropriate hill. Gido, perhaps you and Gijivure could do us the favor of scouting for a hill that would be appropriate for our avalanche"

Gido and Gijivure nodded in agreement and each took off in a different direction looking for the ideal location. Gijivure crossed the road and sought a hill on the opposite side of the road while Gido scouted out the side they were already on.

After the elves had departed, Elasti complained, "I sure hope this works. I won't be able to survive this cold much longer." His fingers had started to ache immensely, and he longed for the cover of the tunnel, hoping that he would be able to get warm once they had entered it.

It wasn't long before Gido returned;
"I found a hillside,
Without any trees;
It's perfect because,
Stuff will slide with ease.
There's a good snow build-up,
Above and below;
When the avalanche falls,
It will make quite a show."
"Good," thanked Jesves, "Let's get going."

Gijivure crossed the Kilo Pass and started to circle around the far side of the gnome camp looking for an appropriate hillside. He was happy to get away from the rest of the party even if it was only for a few minutes. He hadn't made contact with the eagle for a long time. He knew that he had to stay in touch. He climbed around the side of a small hill trying to stay far enough out of sight so that if anyone were to follow him, they wouldn't be able to spot him easily. He found a flat spot where he could sit down. He sat cross-legged in the snow folding his arms and closing his eyes.

"Hummmmm ummmmm ummmmm," he started his chant which lasted for several minutes. Down through the falling snow flew an eagle swooping between the trees and landing in front of him.

"How's it going Gijivure?" asked the eagle.

Gijivure opened his eyes and smiled.

Gabrona stayed behind to await Gijivure's return while the rest of the party started out toward the hill Gido had found. It took quite a while to get to the location he had identified. It was steep but eventually they arrived at the edge of the snowbank.

"This is perfect," Yanon congratulated Gido as he crossed the edge. "We should be able to trigger a large avalanche here."

The spot was well out of sight of the gnome camp, but the smoke of their fire could still be seen off in the distance. Bydola volunteered for the role of snow tunnel builder and tied a rope around himself. He crawled out over the snow and underneath the embankment. He immediately went to work digging the tunnel with his sock covered hands realizing that speed was very important to his friends who all wanted to get into the Kilo Pass Tunnel as quickly as possible. It took a half hour before he had a tunnel dug that was large enough for him to stand up in with a depth of about twice his height.

He left the tunnel and rejoined his friends who had been preparing a pile of twigs and branches that would be used to kindle the fire. He carried the wood into the tunnel and piled it, ready to be lit.

Just as they were nearing the completion of their work Gijivure and Gabrona arrived. "You guys sure timed that right," was Elasti' sarcastic remark.

Gijivure responded,
"I'm sorry I was so late,
I looked hard in hopes to find;
A place that would match the mind,
Of our desires."

Bydola using his newly acquired sense of good and evil had feelings that Gijivure had evil embedded in him, but he convinced himself that he was wrong. How could Gijivure be accused of evil? After all, wasn't he a part of the expedition to save the South? But the indication of evil persisted. It was stronger in Gijivure than it had been in Giterod. Bydola felt torn. If he accused Gijivure of evil the other members of the expedition would demand an explanation and maybe even accuse Bydola of being crazy. He decided he must keep a careful watch on Gijivure and make sure that nothing out of the ordinary occurred. He didn't want anything to happen that would affect the outcome of this important mission.

The final preparations in the tunnel were quickly finished. "Why don't all of us shorter travelers get moving over to the other side of the Kilo Pass in preparation for this avalanche? The elves start the fire. They can catch up with us much easier," Yanon suggested.

The elves agreed and the rope was taken off of Bydola and tied around Gijivure. The leprechauns and the lepelf started back down the side of the incline while the elves waited for them to get out of sight.

The elves waited ten minutes when they were sure that the party was safe. Then Gijivure began his trek across the snowbank toward the tunnel. He was almost at the entrance of the snow tunnel when suddenly he heard a loud crash. The tunnel that Bydola had so carefully built had collapsed, and the avalanche had begun without even starting the fire. Fear raged through Gijivure's. Could he escape or would he be buried alive in the snow?

The snow started to break apart slowly in large moving chunks. As Gido saw this movement, he quickly started to rescue his friend. He hoped he could do it in time. Gijivure had also started to run towards safety as he watched the mound of snow slowly move toward him. The avalanche had begun without the fire and it was now all he could do to avoid being trapped under it.

Gijivure ran but it was difficult to move swiftly in the snow. He trip-ped falling face down in it. Gido saw his plight and pulled with all his might on the rope, as he watched the first traces of the avalanche move over the top of his companion.

The layer of snow that had covered Gijivure wasn't very deep. He was able to push his way through it. He stood up and once again began running. He no longer headed directly toward Gido because that route had now been blocked by the advancing snow. He now started running down the hill and to the side trying to stay ahead of the first traces of the snow slide.

It took a desperate amount of effort, but he made it. He was safely off to the side of the approaching avalanche as Gido ran up to him and gave him a relieved embrace. Just then the avalanche took full force and burst down the side of the mountain rumbling and crashing as it fell.

The elves knew that they had to hurry if they were to take advantage of the diversion. They rushed down the side of the hill following the trail that their leprechaun companions had left and crossed over to the other side of the Kilo Pass where they were safely out of sight of the gnome camp.

As they approached the gnome camp from the far side of the road, they noticed that the gnomes and their expedition friends were gone. They continued following the paths that their companions had left and found that they had already entered the First Kilo Pass Tunnel. The diversion had been a success, but it had almost cost the life of Gijivure. The elves soon followed the rest of their companions into the tunnels.

The leprechauns and Gabrona were all suffering enormously from the cold and all looked forward to the shelter and rest that they would get in the First Kilo Pass Tunnel. They worked their way down the hillside and moved back up along the side of the road away from the gnome camp until they were sure that they would not be seen. They moved around to the far side of the trail away from the gnome camp hiding as well as they could.

Luckily, the gnomes were intensely involved in their conversation and with their fire and never looked outside their little circle. The travelers were not yet in position when suddenly they heard a loud CRASHHHHH! The avalanche had already started. They waited, concerned that they would not have enough time to get into the tunnel.

The gnomes jumped up quickly looking in the direction of the crash with fear and trepidation. At first, they hesitated, and it looked as though the planned diversion had been a failure because the gnomes did not appear to be interested in investigating the cause of the noise. But then one of the gnomes, the only one that was wearing a hat, barked out a series of commands that set the entire group running towards the diversion.

As soon as the gnomes were out of sight Yanon, who was closest to the tunnel, moved out of his hiding position and started running through the snow towards the entrance to the tunnel. Immediately upon seeing

Yanon's departure the rest of the party followed and soon they were all entering what they hoped would be warmth and safety.

Once inside the tunnel Yanon took a quick head count of the members of the expedition. He suggested that they all take their orange glowing rocks out of their pockets and hang them around their necks. Then they waited for what seemed like an eternity before the arrival of their elfin friends. When the elves burst through the entrance of the tunnel everyone was relieved that the travelers were once again reunited. They all started moving rapidly down into the tunnel hoping to avoid detection by the gnomes. Lower and lower they went hoping to get far enough away so that the gnomes would not be able to hear the echoes of their running feet.

CRASHHHH! Everyone stopped and turned quickly. Elasti, who was trailing the rest of the party had tripped and was now lying on the ground. "Be careful!" scolded Yanon. "What's the matter with you? Do you want the gnomes to hear us?"

"Help!" cried Elasti letting the expedition know that he was hurt. Bydola who was traveling closest to Elasti noticed a root wrapping itself around Elasti's leg. Bydola quickly drew his sword and chopped at the root until it fell harmlessly off Elasti's leg.

"That thing hurt. It was starting to get a real tight grip on me. What the heck was it anyway?" complained Elasti.

"It's a retant. It's the living root of the Karkat tree," explained Bydola. "It crushes its victims and then sucks the blood from them thereby elevating the Karkat tree to a higher level of life above that of any other tree that exists. Some Karkat trees are even known to be able to communicate."

"I've heard of that tree before, but I never knew that they got their special powers by sucking the blood out of other living creatures," shivered Elasti. "I sure don't want to become one of its victims."

"Nor do any of us," added Obydon. "Watch out for them. We'll need to watch out for each other if someone else gets attacked."

"I guess that explains why the gnomes had no interest in coming into this tunnel," added Yanon. "They'd rather suffer the cold than put up with the retants. I guess I can't blame them for that."

"Ouch," complained Jesves. Hiztin quickly drew his sword and hacked off a retant that was coming out of the side of the tunnel and had grabbed onto her arm. "That thing felt like it had skin. It felt like a hand," she exclaimed.

"Let's get a move on before they come at us from all directions." Yanon wanted the party to continue its journey in hopes that they would soon be able to find a large cavern free from retants where they would be able to spend the night.

They journeyed on. Lower and lower they went. Deeper and deeper they traveled into the depths of the mountain. The tunnel was wide enough for two to walk side-by-side but because of the retants reaching out for them travel was more comfortable walking in a single file. This made it harder for the roots to reach out and grab the travelers. Occasionally a retant would even reach down from the ceiling and grab for them. Often the expedition members would have to sidestep one of the roots that was reaching out. The roots seemed to be able to sense the presence of the Southerners.

After they had traveled for an hour the path leveled out and become wider. The ceiling also became a little higher, allowing them to move safely without as much disturbance from the retants. Since it was now more comfortable to walk, they continued on for another two hours. Tired and worn out they pushed ahead but no one complained. They hoped for a safe place to spend the night in a spot that wasn't accessible to the retants.

It was cool in the tunnels but significantly warmer than the snow they had been traveling through. The numbness had finally started to depart from their legs and hands. They were grateful that they had escaped the cold snow when they did. They weren't sure how much longer they would have survived in the frigid weather.

They were becoming extremely worn out. It had been a long hard day of travel. Then suddenly as if on request they encountered a side tunnel. Yanon decided to investigate the tunnel and found himself in a large chamber about 100 leprechauns across and 20 leprechauns high. "Yipeee!" he yelled. "Now we can get some rest!"

They had dismissed the thought that the gnomes were going to follow them. They assumed that their diversion had been a success and that the gnomes had no idea that the quest team had entered the tunnel. All the members quickly entered Yanon's newfound sanctuary. They were sure the retants would never be able to reach them now from either the ceiling or the walls.

They huddled in the center of the tunnel and Elasti suggested a fire.

"Where do you propose to get the wood for it?" questioned Yanon.

"You go over to the wall and attract retants, and I'll whack them off," responded Elasti. "It won't take long till we have plenty of roots for a nice fire."

Yanon liked the idea and helped Elasti collect chunks of retant roots. Obydon piled up the retants and started the fire. "Let's not build it too big," suggested Bydola, "or else the smoke will drive us out of here."

Yanon and Elasti responded by not throwing any more retants on the fire. Instead they built up a pile of the dead roots next to the fire adding them only when necessary.

"I'll bet those retant creatures are afraid of fire," commented Obydon. "Let's try putting some against them and see." He took a burning retant stick and held it against a retant that was reaching out toward him. The creature retreated quickly from the flame. "If we build four or five small fires around us then the retants wouldn't dare attack us," he concluded.

"Great idea," added Hiztin. "But let's not make the fires too big like Bydola suggested so we don't get smoked out." The draft of air through the tunnel allowed some of the smoke to be blown away, but too much smoke could still be a danger.

"I think we'll also need to take turns tonight. We need to post a watch

just in case the gnomes or the retants are trickier than we thought. It's always better to be safe than to be sorry later." Yanon was concerned about the safety of his companions. "We'll also need someone to keep the small fires going."

The travelers drew lots for the watch. Since there was nine of them, they would not all be required to keep watch, and only four were selected for that duty. Hiztin was selected for the first watch. After everyone had warmed up and had eaten the rest of the travelers quickly slipped inside their sacks and fell asleep.

Hiztin enjoyed the opportunity to be able to watch Jesves for about an hour. He worked up enough courage to walk over to where she was sleeping, kneel down beside her and kiss her lightly on the cheek. He had wanted to do that for a long time, ever since he had been forced to do it in the Kabul. This time it was his choice to do it. He had enjoyed it then and he enjoyed it even more now. Jesves stirred but didn't awake.

Gijivure had the second watch. Bydola was uncomfortable at the thought of the elf having one of the watches remembering the evil that seemed to surround him. Bydola decided he would try to keep an eye on his activities. This became difficult. Since he was very tired, he would often doze off. But he was successful in keeping track of Gijivure's activities during most of his watch and he noticed nothing peculiar.

Suddenly there was a scream! "Owwwwww!" Obydon was squirming frantically in his sleep. Gabrona, who was on the third watch, went running to his side. Soon Gabrona and Bydola were also both kneeling at his side. They couldn't identify the cause of his anguish, until Gabrona threw back the covers of his sack. They noticed a retant was wrapped firmly around the left arm of the leprechaun. It had slipped into the sack, coming up from the floor, and had twisted itself tightly around his arm. The arm looked twisted and strangely deformed as if all life had been crushed out of it.

Quickly Gabrona grabbed Giterod's knife that he had been carrying and started hacking at the retant. He chopped at the point where it came up out of the ground. Brutally he beat at it until he had severed it. Then he pulled it off of Obydon's lifeless arm causing blood to ooze from the arm. Somehow the root had tapped into Obydon's life blood and was draining it out of him. Obydon lay unconscious.

Several of the other members of the expedition had also been awakened by the cry. As Yanon got up he found that he had also acquired a retant visitor but fortunately it had not yet overpowered him, and he was quickly able to repel its intrusion. Cutting it off and throwing it into the fire he investigated the rest of his companions for additional attackers but found none. Obydon had been the only one that had been attacked so severely.

Earlier, Jesves had also awakened and she was now at the side of Obydon doing what she could to stop the flow of blood. "Can't you help him Bydola?" she asked pleadingly remembering how Bydola was able to restore life to Obydon earlier when the riposters had so brutally attacked him.

"I'm sorry," responded Bydola with his head bowed in dejection. "I can't do anything without a pool of water large enough to submerge him. The only one who can help him now is you." Jesves wrapped the wounds as best she could to stop the flow of blood. She prepared a splint for the crushed arm. There was very little else she could do. She feared that the arm would never function normally again. But her main concern was the fear that Obydon had lost too much blood to recover. She had no indication of how much blood had been drained from his body. The retant had been very effective in making sure that all the captured blood was transferred directly to the life of the tree.

All the members of the camp were awake now and all were leery of going back to sleep for fear that they might meet the same fate as Obydon. "It seems like every night for the last few nights we have had some kind of excitement to deal with," complained Elasti. "First were the riposters. Then there was the struggle with the Kabul deranging our minds. Then we had the snake creatures forming a wall. And now the attacks of the retants. Won't this ever end?" There was no answer.

The travelers broke camp, they were all awake anyway, and prepared to travel further into the tunnels. Several of the members grabbed burning sticks with which to ward off any future attackers. Slowly and wearily they started moving on down the trail. They decided that it was better to keep moving. They all hoped that perhaps they would be able to find a pool of water that would allow Bydola to perform his special miracle and heal Obydon.

"I'll carry Obydon," suggested Bydola since he was the strongest of the party. If someone will help carry my pack, his pack, and my staff." Quickly the contents were distributed amongst Gido, Gijivure, and Gabrona who were the strongest of the remaining members. And they were off with Obydon being carried on Bydola's shoulder like a sack.

They were thankful that there had been no gnomes to deal with as well. Hopefully, their entrance had not been noticed and there would be no further gnome encounters as the team traveled on toward the North Groves. They returned to the main tunnel that they had originally been traveling through and as they journeyed on, they began to encounter many side chambers as if they were traveling along the main thorough-fare of what used to be a city.

"I'll bet those retants chased these previous inhabitants right out of here," commented Elasti.

They traveled for several hours and had still not encountered a pool of water. The path was wide and high. The torches that had been brought with in order to ward off the retants had long ago burned out and they traveled once again by the light of their orange rocks. They had their swords ready to strike any attacker.

After traveling about seven hours they started hearing a noise. It sounded like a whistling sound. It sounded like wind blowing through the trees. "We must be getting close to the exit," suggested Elasti. "Perhaps it's still dark outside and we can't see the tunnel exit."

"It can't be nighttime anymore," responded Yanon. "We traveled long enough for it to be getting close to noon by now."

"What's that noise then?" questioned Hiztin.

"I have a feeling we'll find out soon enough," responded Jesves fearfully. "I only hope it's not as dreadful as these retants are."

"Or the riposters. Or the Kabul," added Hiztin.

They traveled on for another hour with the whistling sound getting louder and louder. Soon it became unbearably loud, and the travelers shuffled on with their hands covering their ears. This was difficult for Bydola who had his arms wrapped around Obydon and could not use them for protecting his ears. Just then they encountered a tile-like floor. It surprised them that the dirt surface they had been traveling on would suddenly change to a hard tile surface. What was even stranger was that the tiles, which at first were about the size of the palm of their hand, seemed to grow larger as they continued on. There were no more side tunnels leaving the tiles as the only thing that they could walk on.

Not only did the tiles grow larger in size, but the cracks between them also grew until the members of the expedition were forced to jump from one tile to another. After traveling for another fifteen minutes each tile had grown to about the size of a leprechaun and the cracks between the tiles were about an arm's length across. Most of the travelers were able to cross these cracks with little difficulty but Bydola, who had to jump with Obydon on his back found them to be more and more diffi-cult.

The travelers didn't attempt to talk to one another. The whistling was still too loud for any of them to hear. Elasti signaled to Yanon that he was going to throw something into one of the cracks to see how deep it was. Yanon nodded his approval and Elasti pulled a clump of dirt off one of the side walls and tossed it into the crevice. There was no sound above the whistling of the wind. He tried again this time he dropped a much larger clump of dirt. Again, he heard nothing that indicated that the clump had struck anything.

Bydola seeing what Elasti and Yanon were attempting, and knowing they couldn't hear him above the whistling, went over to the dirt wall and scratched an explanation on it, "Lamos", and pointed down the crack.

Yanon and Elasti were astonished and gave Bydola a questioning look as if to ask, "Are you sure?"

Bydola gave a positive nod, as if there was no doubt in his mind. Elasti wanted to ask, "What's holding up the tiles," but he knew he would have to wait until later.

Travel now became difficult, not because the tiles were any more dangerous or because the cracks were any larger but because the fear of falling all the way down into the Lamos brought chills to all the travelers. What had earlier seemed like an easy jump now seemed like an enormous leap. They hesitated every time they had to jump between the tiles and cringed at the thought that each jump might be their last.

Suddenly when Elasti was making what appeared to be an easy jump he landed on the corner of a tile and it chipped and broke off. Elasti began to fall but because of the forward momentum from his jump he was able to grab on to the edge of the tile. "Help!" he screamed, as if he thought anyone could hear him over the whistling noise. But Bydola saw what had happened. Quickly and gently he put Obydon down and leapt over to the tile to where Elasti was clinging. He grabbed Elasti's arm and yanked him to safety. The face of Elasti was filled with gratefulness. He had to sit down and rest. His hands and feet were shaking so badly that he was no longer able to support himself. The fear of falling into the Lamos had almost become a reality.

Elasti's companions surrounded him and attempted to comfort him by placing their hands on his shoulders. They even tried hugging him in an attempt to calm him. He sat there for about fifteen minutes before he attempted to get up and venture across the cracks once again. It took several successful jumps before he finally regained some confidence.

Soon the tiles started to become smaller once again and correspondingly the cracks became narrower. But the cavern was also becoming narrower and the ceiling was becoming lower much the way it had been when they had entered the tunnel originally. This gave the travelers a double danger; the possibility of falling off into the Lamos and the danger of being captured by the retants. The biggest fear soon became a fear of being tripped by a retant thus causing someone to fall into the crevice.

They traveled on with great care watching for retants and protecting each other from them. They moved on for another half hour before they successfully passed the last of the tiles. Now they were left with only the retants to deal with. The whistling sound also began to die down as they moved further and further away from the tiles.

"Boy that noise was terrible!" commented Elasti. "What was that anyways?"

"Those were the Erates," explained Bydola, as if he had been selected as the one to answer such questions, "floating tiles with cracks that fall all the way to the Lamos."

"I'm sure glad to get away from them. To think that I nearly got to see the Lamos up close gives me the chills." Elasti felt as though he had plenty to be thankful for. Now if only Obydon could be healed, he would truly be grateful all around.

They traveled on exhausted and weary always hoping that they would soon be rid of the retants and be able to rest. But luck was not with them. The retants became their persistent tormentors.

After several more hours the whistling of the wind had totally died down and the trail had begun an upward climb.

"It looks like we're finally coming to the end of this tunnel," speculated Yanon. "I'll be glad to get away from the retants but I'm not so sure I'm ready to return to the snow."

Bydola was still carrying Obydon but somehow it seemed to affect him less and less. He didn't seem to be disappointed at not having found any water in which he could heal the leprechaun. He just felt the urgency to push ahead.

The climb upward was steep and tiring for the travelers. They hadn't had a full night's sleep for several days. But they pushed ahead since the thought of stopping raised too high a risk of a retant attack.

Side tunnels started to appear once again suggesting that the earlier citizens of this tunnel had avoided the area of the retants. They traveled on climbing more and more in anticipation that they would soon be back in the snow. "I wonder how late it is?" questioned Yanon. "We must have been down here for at least a night and a day. It's probably dark again outside." If it was dark, it would be easier to avoid any gnomes that were out there, but it would also make it harder for them to travel. They wouldn't be able to use their orange lights for fear they might be noticed.

Suddenly as they were passing one of the side tunnels Yanon came to a halt and stepped back quickly. He put his finger over his lips indicating that no one should make a sound. Everyone froze in place and fell silent.

"What is it?" whispered Elasti.

"Gnomes," responded Yanon. "They must have been sent down here after us. They're huddled around a campfire."

"That means that there is probably a gnome camp at the entrance to this tunnel waiting for us right now!" declared Elasti fearfully.

"You're probably right," responded Yanon.

Gido had slipped past Yanon and had peered into the tunnel at the gnomes. He quietly suggested,

"With arrows we can make quick work,
Of these seven gnomes we found;
Gijivure and I and maybe Hiztin to,
Will shoot them to the ground."

Yanon nodded in approval. Gido, Gijivure, and Hiztin took positions at the entrance of the tunnel and prepared their arrows. When all three were ready Gido gave the signal and they let their arrows fly. Three of the gnomes immediately fell to the ground. The other four gnomes, seeing what had happened to their companions quickly jumped up pulled their swords out of their belts and started charging.

Before the gnomes could get within striking distance three more arrows flew dropping two of the gnomes in mid stride. The third arrow hit one of the two remaining gnomes in the shoulder, but it did not stop him. Two gnomes with their swords raised high continued advancing toward the three bowmen.

By now the gnomes were too close to shoot a third volley of arrows. The bowmen had to step out of their way quickly in order to avoid the attack of the gnome swords. They jumped to the side of the cavern entrance and the gnomes came crashing through with swords flying. Yanon, Elasti, Gabrona, and Bydola, who had temporarily left Obydon lying on the floor, were waiting for them with their swords drawn for battle.

Jesves had decided to stay out of the battle. They didn't need her when there were only two gnomes left. She would probably just be in the way. But she stood ready with her sword in her hand in the event that they needed reinforcements. She didn't want a retant to grab hold of Obydon, so she stayed close to protect him. She kept busy hitting, poking and cutting the roots as they reached out for the unconscious leprechaun.

During the battle between the gnomes and the quest members a second battle also raged. The three bowmen had moved too close to the side walls of the tunnel, and Hiztin suddenly found himself entangled with retants. "Help!" he yelled and Gido and Gijivure quickly came to his rescue severing the retants before they were able to do him serious damage. But his yelling had managed to distract Elasti temporarily allowing one of the gnomes to successfully strike him and leave him with a large gash in his arm. Elasti retreated leaving his three sword wielding companions to take over the battle. Jesves quickly pulled Elasti to her side and tended to his arm by stopping the flow of blood.

The gnomes were larger than the other travelers but in the smallness of the tunnel this had become a disadvantage. The quest members were able to move easily and were able to strike several blows at the gnomes for every one that was wielded against them. Soon the gnomes were bleeding from their many wounds and they were becoming very weary. Finally, one of the gnomes fell dead to the ground, and shortly thereafter, the second gnome fell also. It wasn't long before the riposters had found their victims and were entangling the gnomes in their roots.

"Boy that was close," commented Elasti rubbing the arm that Jesves had carefully bandaged for him. "I could have lost my head in that little bit of excitement."

Bydola returned to where he had left Obydon laying. He quickly lifted him back onto his shoulder. The only additional injury suffered by the quest members was the arm wound of Elasti and a few scratches on Bydola. They were all eager to continue on.

"I was concerned that we might encounter other gnomes in these tunnels," relayed Yanon to his companions, "but I'm sure that if there were any others they would have heard the noise we made and would've come running. I'd guess we are rid of the gnomes for a little while anyway."

"You can bet that we're going to find more gnomes at the exit of the tunnel!" added Hiztin. "I only hope there aren't too many of them."

"Somehow they must have found out about us entering the tunnel. They were obviously sent in here after us or they wouldn't have stayed down here." Elasti wondered how they were discovered. "If someone saw us enter the tunnel, I would have expected them to come after us right away. I'd guess they must have found our footprints in the snow or else figured out that our avalanche wasn't natural and so they decided to get us when we came out at the other end."

"In order to do that they would've had to move over the Lamos mountains quickly. Or sent a message to the other side. But how would they have accomplished that?" Yanon was also puzzled by the actions of the gnomes. "They must have some way of communication that we don't know about. There must have been some gnomes stationed close to the back end of this tunnel that were warned to attack us. I don't see how else they got the message that quickly."

"Maybe that eagle we keep seeing has something to do with it," responded Elasti.

"I doubt it," returned Yanon, "or else that first group of gnomes would have been ready for us and we wouldn't have stood a chance. They would have ambushed us along the trail. No, I don't think the eagle has anything to do with these gnomes coming after us." The discussion about the eagle left Gijivure uncomfortable but attentive.

"Are we even sure that these gnomes were coming after us?" questioned Hiztin. "It's possible that they came in here on their own in order to get out of the snow."

"I doubt that," returned Yanon, "or the other gnomes would have attempted to venture into these tunnels as well at the other end of the tunnel. I believe that the gnomes knew about the dangers in these tunnels like the retants and they knew that they would have to come in on the back side of the tunnel in order to get us. I'm sure they must have something such as an eagle that allows them to communicate with each other, and that somehow the gnomes at the other end of this tunnel were warned about our arrival. But I just don't know how."

"This could sure make our journey a lot riskier not knowing what powers the enemy has over us," commented Elasti.

Gijivure walked along listening to the analysis that his fellow expedition members were going through and he smiled to himself. He considered it humorous that they were guessing at the purpose of the eagle when only he knew the truth.

The travelers were weary. The battle with the gnomes had worn them out completely. They trudged along slowly. They traveled much slower than they had moved earlier but they didn't dare stop for fear that the retants would quickly be upon them. So, they pushed ahead.

The tunnel continued to climb. It rose higher and higher adding to the strain that was placed on each of their weary bodies. Suddenly as if in mid stride Yanon who had once again taken up the lead of the expedition stopped and pointed ahead.

"What is it this time?" whispered Elasti.

Yanon, not making any effort to remain quite, responded, "It looks like some of the gnomes didn't make it down into the tunnel." There in front of him, pinned to the wall of the tunnel were two gnomes crushed by retants. The life blood had been drained from their bodies. It was a grotesque sight to see anyone meet death in this horrid way even for the members of the quest who hated the gnomes. They shivered to think that it might have been one of the expedition members that had suffered a similar fate.

"Let's get going," demanded Jesves. "I can't stand looking at them. This is horrible."

The travelers moved on. It had now been at least two hours since the last battle with the gnomes and traveling became harder. The tunnel was becoming narrower and narrower barely offering them enough room to pass comfortably and requiring them to be more cautious because of the retants. The travelers were convinced that they were finally getting near the exit of the tunnel.

Abruptly Gido who had now taken the lead in Yanon's weariness came to a halt and quickly tucked his orange stone in his pocket. He turned around and waved his companions toward him and pointed down the tunnel passage to what must surely be the exit.

Gido recommended;
"I see the light at the end of the tunnel,
But the light isn't the light of the sun;
We must hide our lights, so we aren't noticed,
Or our exit will not be much fun."

Then Gijivure added;
"That light is the light of a fire,
That means gnomes are waiting for us there;
What are we going to do to prepare,
For the battle that lies ahead?"

"It's going to be hard to set up a diversion from inside the tunnel," added Yanon. "It's also going to be dangerous to travel through this tunnel without the use of our lights when all these retants are reaching out to grab us."

"I know what we could use for a diversion," suggested Hiztin.

"Out with it," demanded Yanon, "what's your idea?"

"These retants even after they are cut off still squirm quite a bit. We could cut a bunch of them off and when we're ready to exit the tunnel we could throw them at the gnomes."

"But they'll see us," protested Jesves.

"They already know we're here," responded Hiztin defensively.

"I'd just as soon do battle with the gnomes and get it over with," suggested Gabrona. He felt successful after the last battle with the gnomes. "Why throw retants at them when they'll be waving swords at us?"

"That's true," responded Elasti.

"I like both ideas," responded Yanon. "I think we should use the retants the way Hiztin suggested in order to give them an initial scare and then we should be prepared to do battle."

"Good enough," responded Elasti who was anxious to move forward, "let's do it."

Quick work was made of cutting off retants. They were then collected together. They squirmed around in the arms of the quest members and gave them an eerie feeling. The roots felt like arms squirming to get free.

The orange rock lights were tucked away into their pockets and they slowly proceeded to walk toward the exit. Arriving at the door of the tunnel they were pleased to see that there were only five gnomes sitting around the campfire desperately trying to keep warm. There were at least ten more gnomes sleeping in sacks around the perimeter of the fire. On Yanon's signal they scrambled out of the tunnel and threw the retants at the gnomes. The gnomes jumped up in fright, frantically trying to rid themselves of the wiggling creatures. They yelled and started to run away from the campfire. However, two of the gnomes weren't so easily scared and almost immediately turned around and came forward to attack the group.

Immediately Hiztin, Gijivure, and Gido went to work with their bows and the two gnomes fell into the snow in midstride. The expedition began running up the trail. No snow was currently falling and the snow on the ground wasn't quite as thick on this end of the tunnel. It had only reached about knee high to a leprechaun. The leprechauns were able to take full strides and move quickly. But unfortunately, they were not able to move as quickly as the gnomes. The three gnomes that had been frightened by the retants returned to their camp and quickly roused their remaining companions. Soon the expedition was being chased by a dozen gnomes. Bydola was having difficulty. His size caused him to move slower and carrying Obydon slowed him down even more.

The three archers of the expedition realized Bydola's plight and stood ground. They quickly felled three of the leading gnomes. This halted the rest of the gnomes temporarily and allowed Bydola to get off the trail into the shelter of the trees. The rest of the party had also taken refuge in the trees and the archers, taking advantage of the hesitation of the gnomes, quickly followed.

Hiding in the trees made it easy for Hiztin, Gido, and Gijivure to selectively shoot at the gnomes using the trees for shelter. They were able to make every shot count. Soon they had dropped three more of the enemy. The remaining gnomes retreated running back to camp to tell their few remaining companions about their plight. The gnomes would use this opportunity to regroup and strike again.

As soon as the gnomes were comfortably out of earshot Yanon quietly called out to the members of the expedition in order to gather them together. Luckily, they had all left the trail in about the same area and were quickly reunited. "We're going to have to stay off the trail because you can bet those gnomes will be coming after us again," Yanon instructed. "We also won't be able to use our orange rocks or else we'll give away our locations. That will make travel more difficult the further we get from the gnomes campfire. We'll be left out in the dark with only the moonlight guiding us."

He continued "Let's try to follow each other's path so that the trail through the snow will be easier to travel. Gido, why don't you, Gijivure, and Hiztin, stay to the back of the party? You can keep the gnomes at a distance. Gabrona can lead the way for us and blaze a nice path in the snow."

With these instructions the expedition set off once again working its way through the snow by moving parallel to the Kilo Pass as best they could in the dark. Luck was with them once again. The gnomes didn't attack. Eight of their number had already been killed. Apparently, they were planning to wait until the daylight offered them a better chance at spotting the expedition members.

But Hiztin, Gijivure, and Gido had their own plan. They let their arrows fly in rapid succession. Before the gnomes knew what was happening, and had a chance to react, the remaining gnomes had fallen to the ground. But was this all the gnomes at this camp, or were there others out scouting the area?

The travelers continued on their way moving slowly and carefully through the snow. After another hour's journey daylight began to break and they increased their pace. But the risk of another gnome attack also increased. The expedition avoided the trail suspecting the possibility of an ambush by the gnomes. The cold of the snow had removed some of their weariness, but their muscles still ached as they pushed ahead toward the Second Kilo Pass Tunnel.

They had traveled for about another hour when they started to hear a noise behind them. Everyone stopped fearful of making any noise in case they were being attacked. The archers quickly positioned themselves behind a tree anticipating an attack by gnomes. The rest of the travelers also hid themselves as best they could and Yanon directed Elasti to climb a tree to investigate.

They waited listening as the noises drew closer and closer. "Gnomes," Elasti whispered as loudly as he dared. He was pointing over toward the trail indicating that gnomes were on the Kilo Pass. Just then the sounds drawing up behind them became louder.

"Dis trail dem fools left us is easy to follow," could be heard from the gnomes. "Dem little critters sure is dummies."

It was gnomes all right. Now the expeditions only concern was to figure out how many there were. They waited as the voices became louder and louder. The gnomes on the trail beside them had now passed by and could be heard slightly toward the front of them but still on the trail.

Three whistling sounds could be heard, followed by a loud groan. Hiztin, Gijivure, and Gido had let their arrows fly and two of the gnomes fell to the ground. Hiztin and Gijivure had shot the same gnome, and Gido had successfully stuck an arrow into the throat of a second gnome.

"Help," yelled one of the three remaining gnomes and the gnomes off to the side could be heard running back towards the cry. It was difficult to tell how many gnomes were on their way back, but it sounded like an entire army. Three more whistling sounds were made, and two more gnomes fell to the ground leaving only one in the original party. Unfortunately, he was not visible to the three archers.

"We're bein tacked by undred leprechauns!" yelled the remaining gnome. The stomping of feet along the Kilo Pass trail intensified. When these gnomes were opposite the voice of the crying gnome several of them raced into the bush to find him. But there was at least one other gnome who could be heard running down the Kilo Pass toward the second tunnel.

Why did they send a single gnome off to the second tunnel? They must have reinforcements there. That's why the expedition members weren't pursued during the night. There were gnomes guarding the second tunnel as well. This made the expedition team feel hopeless. But then Yanon was hit with a thought that chilled him even more. Perhaps the gnome that was sent ahead was told to obstruct the entrance to the second tunnel. What if he was told to cave-in the entrance? Would his companions be able to endure the difficulty and hardship of having to hike around the tunnel in the cold snow? Suddenly the thought of gnome reinforcements didn't seem so bad and he hoped that more gnomes was indeed the worst threat he would have to encounter.

Yelling could be heard from the gnomes and five of them charged toward the expedition. Three more arrows were sent singing their way through the cold mountain air and three more gnomes fell to the ground dead. But the remaining two gnomes broke through the line of archers and once again Yanon, Gabrona, Bydola, along with Elasti who had quickly scurried down from his tree, were prepared to meet them with swords.

The gnomes were taller and stronger than any of the heroes but none of them were as skilled as Yanon. He was able to stab the first gnome quickly laying him down in the soft white snow. The second gnome wasn't so easy. He battled viciously with the four travelers. The archers watched for an opportunity to fire at the gnome. They feared that if they shot, they might cause one of their own companions to be hit by a stray arrow. Therefore, the work of the battle was left to the swordsmen.

The battle raged with no one seeming to get the advantage over the other. The four swordsmen tended to get into each other's way and so the battle was turned over to Yanon. When opportunity arose Yanon was able to slip his sword between the gnome's ribs. The gnome fell with a thud his red life smeared the crisp white snow.

With the gnome down the urgency to get to the second tunnel returned. "Let's get a move on," yelled Yanon, "before those other gnome reinforcements get back. I think one of the gnomes was sent to the second tunnel to get help."

Bydola lifted Obydon back on to his shoulder and they were off. Luckily no one had suffered any injuries in the most recent conflict and the travelers were all able to move at the full speed. Occasionally Elasti or Hiztin would climb a tree to scout the Kilo Pass. The danger of an ambush always existed now that the gnomes knew they were here.

Gido suggested;
"We would be safer,
If we did mass;
Along the opposite,
Side of this pass."

Gido felt that the gnomes would anticipate their being on this west side of the pass where they had been traveling. They would be better off moving to the east side of the trail hopefully throwing the gnomes off guard. Yanon agreed with this logic and Gijivure, who was bringing up the rear of the expedition, was told to use a branch to cover up their trail as they crossed over the Kilo Pass. They crossed the trail and once on the other side they continued to push ahead staying far enough in the trees to avoid detection.

They traveled for several more hours, wondering why the anticipated gnomes never appeared. They felt sure that the gnomes were waiting in ambush on the other side of the road and the expedition tried to stay as quiet as possible hoping to avoid detection as they went. But the gnomes were never sighted, and the ambush never occurred.

It was now early afternoon. The party had been eating food out of their packs. They hungered for a warm meal and the opportunity to get their hands and feet near a fire again. But the urgency to stay ahead of the gnomes caused them to push ahead without complaining. They realized that they wouldn't be able to last the night in the snow. They hoped that the next tunnel would finally offer them a comfortable night's rest.

Elasti and Hiztin would occasionally check the area around them by climbing a tree and scoping out the area. One time while Hiztin was taking his turn in the tree he waved to his companions below and signaled for their silence. He had spotted something. He scurried down the tree in order to offer everyone an explanation.

"There's a gnome campfire up ahead and I could see the entrance to the tunnel. But there were only two gnomes sitting by the fire. It was a pretty big fire for only two gnomes. There's probably more but they must be hiding somewhere waiting to ambush us. I'll bet the two gnomes that are by the fire are just bait to make us think that it'll be easy for us to get by them, and thereby draw us out into the open."

"You're probably right." Yanon had anticipated all along that there would be some attempt at an ambush. He was pleased to hear that the entrance to the tunnel had not been tampered with. His fears of the gnomes closing off the entrance had been avoided. He suggested, "Gijivure why don't you go ahead and scout out the gnome camp while we wait here. Let us know what you find." Elves were smoother, quieter, and swifter at surveillance.

The remainder of the expedition waited patiently until Gijivure returned. When he finally arrived, about a half hour later he explained;
"The gnomes are up above the tunnel,
They're waiting there with arrows;
They'll catch us in the narrow,
If we go straight to the entrance."
"What do you suggest," Yanon questioned Gijivure.
"There must be ten above the tunnel,
And two upon the ground;
We must go up and around,
Behind them for our attack."
That's what I was thinking," agreed Yanon. "Gido, Gijivure, and Hiztin, circle behind the gnomes and get into position with your bows. Bydola, Elasti, Gabrona and I will follow you with our swords. Jesves, you stay here and take care of Obydon."

Everyone was quick to move forward in their assignments. The archers worked slowly and carefully up the side of the mountain and circled around above and behind the tunnel entrance followed by the swordsmen. They were slightly above the gnomes but were still far from being in a good position for an attack when a loud groan of pain could be heard back in the direction of Jesves. The gnomes along the ridge perked up. The two gnomes by the fire stood up and started to move toward the location of Jesves. Hiztin panicked. He couldn't let the two gnomes attack his beloved Jesves. He quickly fired off a shot that felled one of the gnomes, but the second gnome escaped.

Hiztin had sacrificed his location in his attempt to save Jesves. Now all the gnomes along the ridge knew where he was, and they were quick to react. Several of the gnomes let arrows fly off in the direction of Hiztin. Luckily Hiztin was hidden behind a tree, and none of the arrows were aimed well. They all fell worthlessly to the ground. Gijivure and Gido had better targets to shoot at. They had been watching the gnomes as the two elves attempted to creep around behind them and they now took the opportunity to shoot two of the enemy to the ground. They carefully selected which gnomes to shoot first. By shooting the two gnomes that were hiding behind the last trees they avoided detection by the other gnomes who were focusing their attention in the opposite direction.

The remaining gnomes decided to be more careful. They waited and didn't shoot until they had a clear shot. Gijivure and Gido, who were positioned higher up the side of the mountain than Hiztin continued to move further up the side of the incline. They managed to circle into a position where they would be able to strike at more of the gnomes. They could see the remaining eight gnomes each lurking behind a tree waiting for the expedition members to reveal themselves. Carefully they selected the next two gnomes that were the furthest back and fired arrows into their throats. The thuds of their bodies hitting the snowpack was the only sound that could be heard.

The next two gnomes from behind also met the same fate. Unfortunately one of these gnomes was able to let out a grunt of pain before he fell in the snow. The gnome leader turned and stepped out from his hiding place to see what had caused the noise. This became his fatal mistake as he found himself with an arrow in his neck. Hiztin had remained at his original post and was finally able to take a shot at someone. He had used the opportunity to lay the leader in the snow.

The three remaining gnomes didn't know how to react. They had all seen the death of their leader and in a panic, they wildly let their arrows fly in Hiztin's direction. Gijivure and Gido were now given enough time to prepare another round of arrows. As Gido let his arrow fly one of the gnomes heard it and quickly retaliated by sending his own arrow in the direction of the elves. Gijivure, who was just about to shoot, received the gnome arrow in his shoulder. In pain Gijivure proceeded to fire his arrow which successfully caused his target to plant himself face first in the snow. Gido's arrow had also been successful, leaving only one remaining gnome on the hilltop.

This last gnome was frantic. He didn't know which way to run. He charged down the side of the hill firing arrows randomly. Yanon, seeing this action, got ready to meet him and as the gnome ran close by the tree where Yanon was hiding the gnome found the leprechauns sword planted firmly in his side.

Jesves was starting to get irritated by the fact that she had been the one chosen to be left behind. "Don't they have any respect for what I can do?" she complained to herself. She sat down next to Obydon and waited for her companions to return. Then suddenly to her dismay a white marble skinned creature similar to the one that had caused them so much excitement at the earlier campfire popped out of the snow and landed right on Obydon's stomach causing Obydon to let out a loud, painful groan.

Jesves jumped up quickly, "What's the matter with you?" she scolded quietly. She wasn't sure whether to be irritated at the snow creature or at Obydon. "You picked the dandiest time to decide to come back to life," she scolded Obydon. Jesves knew she must act quickly. Surely the gnomes would have heard the noise and would be coming after her now. She brushed the snow creature off Obydon so that it wouldn't cause him to make any more noise. Then she moved away from his resting place and hid herself behind a tree. It wasn't long before she could see a gnome charging through the trees straight for Obydon. When the gnome arrived, he held his sword at Obydon's chest and looked him over. He snickered when he realized that Obydon was no threat to him and looked around to see if he could spot any of the other members of the expedition.

The gnome had his back turned to Jesves. She had slipped behind a tree and now she silently stepped away from the tree and lowered her sword swiftly on the gnome's head. The gnome fell with a crash right over the top of Obydon his sword finding its way into the leprechaun's damaged left shoulder as he fell.

Jesves was repulsed by the blood that came pouring out of the gnome's head onto the snow. The blood of her companions had not affected her like that. This was the first blood that she had caused to be spilt. The cruelty of it chilled her. She was thankful that she didn't have to do much fighting.

She tried to pull the dead gnome off Obydon, but he was just too heavy for her to move. She tried to inspect the damage done to Obydon's shoulder. She realized that the gnome's sword had nearly severed the arm completely. It was all she could do to try and stop the bleeding. She tied the wound tightly, stopping most of the flow of blood. In despair, she felt that the only hope Obydon had left was for her to pray. She knelt down and held a silent vigil with the God of the Rainbow asking him for help.

No sooner was she done with her private thoughts, when Elasti, Gijivure, and Bydola returned. "We must hurry," Bydola insisted not realizing the damage that had been done to Obydon. "Gijivure has been seriously injured by a gnome arrow." Then he noticed the gnome. "What caused the noise that brought this gnome over here?" he asked.

"Obydon cried out," was Jesves' reply, "but I'm afraid the gnome's sword may have rendered our friend's arm worthless. It almost severed the arm completely."

"I see what you mean," responded Bydola using his special powers to inspect the damage. "I see no life in his arm at all. I feel that it may be hopelessly lost."

"You mean you won't be able to fix it?" questioned Jesves.

"I'll try but it doesn't look good," was the reply.

Jesves started to feel guilty. If she hadn't hit the gnome right, then maybe the sword wouldn't have ended up in Obydon's shoulder. She comforted herself with the thought that if she hadn't hit the gnome, he might have killed Obydon.

Gijivure was carried to Jesves and laid down on the ground close to Obydon. Bydola proceeded to cut the skin around the arrow. After a large enough wound had been opened the leprechaun proceeded to pull the arrow out of the elf's shoulder. Gijivure's pain was apparent as he ground his teeth. When Bydola was done Jesves was ready with the torn shreds of clothing that she used for bandages and she quickly wrapped the wound and stopped the bleeding.

Bydola and Elasti drug the gnome off Obydon. Bydola carefully put the injured companion over his shoulder. "We must hurry and get into the tunnel before any more gnomes show up," Bydola urgently pleaded. "Let's get going!"

Jesves and Elasti quickly collected all the packs of their companions and took off toward the tunnel. It was all Gijivure could do to follow them with pain surging through his body at every step.

To their disappointment there were still more gnomes. As Gido, Yanon, Hiztin, and Gabrona approached the entrance to the tunnel in order to inspect it they encountered three more gnomes rushing at them from the bushes. Quickly, Yanon and Gabrona drew their swords and waited to fend off the attack. Hiztin and Gido were still carrying their bows and they each quickly prepared an arrow and let it fly. One of the gnomes fell dead but because of the hastiness with which he had fired his arrow Gido had missed his mark.

The two remaining gnomes bore down on the heroes with a vengeance. Hiztin and Gido found that they had to take flight quickly since they were not prepared to fend off a sword. Yanon and Gabrona found themselves in mortal combat again each fighting a gnome that was much stronger and bigger than themselves.

But they weren't alone for long. Gido and Hiztin had thrown their bows to the side and with their swords drawn came to the aid of their friends. Just as Gido arrived to help Gabrona, the lepelf was struck on the head by a gnome sword and fell to the ground as if dead. Gido was left to fight the gnome by himself hoping that he would not meet the fate of his friend. Luck was on his side. Just then Gijivure and Elasti came running to his aid, and the three of them successfully conquered the gnome. Hiztin and Yanon were also successful although the task took them a little longer.

As the last gnome dropped, Yanon yelled out, "Let's get in the tunnel quickly before any more gnomes show up!" This they did running into the tunnel as fast as they could. Gido had picked up the fallen lepelf and carried him into the tunnel hoping that there would still be life in the young boy's body.

CHAPTER SEVENTEEN

THE SECOND TUNNEL

They made it into the second tunnel. Now they would discover if this would be a blessing or a curse. They had killed all the gnomes that were outside of the tunnel, or at least they thought they had. This gave them hope that there wouldn't be any gnomes left to follow them. But Yanon remembered the strange way in which the gnomes at the exit to the first tunnel had learned about their presence. Somehow there had been a communication system established between the gnomes that allowed them to know about the expedition's activities. He had no idea what that system could be, but he feared that there might be other gnomes already on their way toward the exit to this second tunnel.

This worried Yanon, but he had long ago decided that the northward expedition could only be handled one step at a time. The immediate dangers that lay ahead in this second tunnel were all that he was able to concentrate on now. Would they encounter retants again? Would his weary friends be able to get a night's sleep in these tunnels? Would there be water available where his friends could be cured? These problems concerned him more than the gnomes. Later he would concern himself about what lie in store for them at the end of the tunnel.

"Gido, you and I will take the front guard and Hiztin and Jesves take up the rear," ordered Yanon. He had learned to take every step cautiously. Every step seemed to contain dangers that he had never before encountered.

Suddenly the expedition was startled by a loud command. "Halt!" ordered a voice which seemed to emanate from all directions at once. The voice barked out, "Who are you?"

"We are leprechauns from Amins, elves from Gije, and a lepelf from Giter," responded Yanon, who had stepped into the lead uncertain what this new danger meant. "Who are you?" he questioned in return.

"Who I am doesn't concern you," returned the commanding voice. "What is that orange light that you possess?" The orange lights had once

again, been slung around the necks of each of the travelers allowing them to be guided by the creator's light.

"It is the light of the Creator," responded Yanon trying to impress his questioner with what he assumed to be true. "It was given to us through a representative of his who is amongst us. We are on a special assignment to the North Groves."

"Why do you come through here and disturb us?" continued the voice. "Why don't you take the Albo Pass?"

"The Albo Pass has been taken over by the Kabul." Yanon was a little surprised that these creatures didn't know the gnomes were guarding the entrance and exit to their tunnels. He wondered if this wasn't just some trick of the Kabul in order to find out their purpose. "For the sake of our mission I cannot tell you anymore until I learn whether you are friend or foe. Step out and make yourself known," Yanon commanded. "If you are a friend please help us. We have many injured amongst us."

"Wait where you are," returned the voice. "I will let you know shortly what is to be done with you."

The expedition waited for several minutes causing Elasti to become anxious. "What's the matter with these guys?" he asked no one in particular. "What do they hope to gain by making us stand around like this?"

Just then they heard a second voice, "Look what we've found?" The voice seemed to be coming from in front of the expedition, but it was still too dark to see the source. "This is the first time I've seen anyone from the Southern Plains. You guys are just as ugly as I figured." Yanon couldn't decide if the voice was joking or not.

What appeared to be an older gentleman came forward into the orange light and approached Yanon. He was a strange looking individual with arms but no legs. His body simply ended below his stomach. His arms were long enough so that they acted as legs thereby allowing the creature to move forward.

"We're Worlepreeks," explained the legless creature, "ancient ancestors to the leprechauns, who came down into these tunnels because we didn't like all the dangers of the war outside. We lost our legs over time because of a lack of use. My name is Oply. I'm the Council Lord of the Worlepreeks. What is your name?" The elderly Worlepreeks sat down on his lower body and held out his hand to Yanon in greeting.

"I've heard about Worlepreeks, but I always thought they were just a legend," Yanon commented.

Laughter could be heard originating from deep down in the tunnel. Oply smiled and commented, "I've been called a living legend before if that's what you mean."

Yanon could see that Oply was joking and this made him feel more comfortable. Greetings were exchanged and introductions made. No other Worlepreeks had made their presence known and this worried Yanon somewhat but Oply seemed friendly enough and Yanon was thankful for his openness.

"Follow me," directed Oply as he started to shuffle with his arms down into the tunnel. "You're going to have to tell me more about this mission of yours and about this strange orange light you are all carrying around your necks. You realize that it's that light that saved your hides, don't you? The sentries are commanded to shoot any intruders, but they were curious about your lights."

Yanon and the others were quick to follow. They hadn't had a friendly invitation for quite some time and they looked forward to whatever Oply had to offer. Yanon decided to make an appeal for help. "The members of our expedition haven't slept for days and they haven't had any warm food for nearly as long. They're very tired and hungry. We also need a pool of water to take care of our injured."

"What are you going to do?" questioned Oply lacking any understanding of how a pool of water would help the injured, "Put them out of their misery by drowning them?"

"Our friend that represents the Creator has learned a method of healing that requires water, and we would appreciate your help."

"You guys are weird!" responded Oply not believing what he was being told. "But don't worry. I'll take good care of you."

Oply turned a corner into a side tunnel and the expedition found itself in a large open chamber with a very high ceiling. The room had plastered walls that were painted white. The floor was elaborately covered with beautiful tiles. A few candles gave light to the chamber. There was barely enough light for one person. When the expedition's orange rocks entered the room, it was lit up immensely.

In the center of the tunnel stood an extremely low circular table beautifully carved in wood with what appeared to be a hundred legless chairs situated around it. The walls were extensively decorated with carvings and statues of what must have been Worlepreeks of historical fame.

"We have to limit the number of candles we use for light," explained Oply. "Our eyes have become adapted to the dark, and we whitewash as many walls as possible. This allows the light to be reflected. That is why we are so fascinated with your orange light. A light like that would allow us to have light without smoke thereby not discoloring our walls or ruining our air. I am interested in an exchange. I will give you food, beds for resting, a pool of water for bathing or for your healing, protection while you're here, and anything else you need, in exchange for just one of your orange lights."

Yanon, hesitating to give up something that wasn't rightly his eagerly turned to Bydola for the answer. Bydola was the Creator of the rocks and only he had the right to say how they should be used but he hoped that Bydola would buy the expedition this opportunity for rest.

"I cannot allow you to have any of these rocks in exchange for what you offer," Bydola stated, leaving the rest of the members of the expedition astonished. Oply's offer had been so generous. They felt they didn't need all the rocks anyway. Besides, couldn't Bydola create a few more if need be?

Oply showed the disappointment on his face. The rock would have been so valuable to him. He looked up at Yanon and said, "Maybe you can talk him out of it. It would mean so much to our people. Nevertheless, you are still my welcome guests. My people are already preparing a feast for you and they will be arriving with it shortly. This is our dining and meeting chamber, and this is where we will be served."

Bydola was still carrying Obydon on his shoulders and he now laid him down on the ground. Then he turned to Oply, "I had to know if you were friend or foe before I gave you any gift belonging to the Creator. I see no evil in you. As I said, I will not give you our rocks. However, I will make you similar stones of your own as many as you like. I will do it out of friendship and not in exchange for anything you have to offer."

Oply was worried, "I didn't mean to insult you. Your friendship is much more important to me than any gift. It is just that the stones would give us light after we have been in the dark for so many generations. I couldn't pass up this opportunity to ask you for one of them."

Bydola interrupted what he thought might turn out to be a long lecture and pleaded, "Please, get me to a pool of water as quickly as possible so that I can help my injured friends."

"Of course, immediately. Ordo!" Oply yelled out, and a Worlepreeks entered the chamber through a door on the opposite side of the chamber, "Bring our leprechaun friends to the tubs immediately and go fetch Doc Opopp to assist them."

"Right away sir," responded Ordo as he shuffled around the table and across the room toward Bydola.

"I'll go too," added Jesves. She was involved in all the previous healings and wanted to be a participant in these as well.

Bydola once again lifted Obydon on his shoulders. They were joined by Gido carrying Gabrona followed by Elasti, and Gijivure. They left the chamber leaving Yanon, Hiztin, and Oply in the eating chamber.

"What are these tubs that Oply mentioned?" asked Bydola with concern. "Will they be big enough to contain an elf completely submerged?"

Ordo was surprised at the question, "Are they going to be taking a bath?"

"No," answered Bydola. "I need to submerge them completely if they are to be healed. Otherwise, the healing won't work."

"I'm not sure what we can do," responded Ordo with concern. "The tubs are all Worlepreeks size which is smaller than any of you. Let's ask the people at the baths if there is anything bigger."

Ordo led the members of the expedition down the main tunnel for only a few moments before he turned into what seemed to be a dead end. Amazingly as if on command the wall opened for him. Walking through the door he entered another larger tunnel. As the party traveled down this tunnel, they passed many side tunnels. "These are the homes of my people," Ordo explained.

"Do you have any trouble with the retants?" questioned Jesves.

"For many years my people have worked on a way to defeat the retants. We used to live in the other tunnel along this pass. You must have passed through that tunnel on your way to this one. My ancestors left that tunnel many years ago long before I was born because the retants had become so treacherous. My people had not yet found a way to stop them. They were forced out of that tunnel by the retants and they migrated here to this one where the retants weren't as bad.

"Here my people continued working to find something that would keep the retants away and eventually they succeeded. They found that the sap of dead retants repulsed the creatures. Today, we use it to coat our walls. Everywhere that you travel down here is coated with this sap except for one of the tunnels that we left untouched. We use it to capture retants that we need to recoat our walls. The coating process occurs once every fifty days. We smear all our ceilings and walls. The tiles you see on the floors also keep the retants away because they make it too difficult for the roots to break through."

"Why did your people stay down in these tunnels? Why didn't they return to the surface?" Jesves continued questioning.

Ordo turned a corner at the intersection of two tunnels and continued his explanation, "My people moved into these tunnels during the Life-fight Wars because they wanted to avoid the killing and torture. They found that the gnomes were afraid of the dark and the retants and hesitated to come into the tunnels. My ancestors also learned that by building secret portals in the walls and ceilings, these tunnels were extremely easy to defend with bow and arrow.

"After we had made homes for ourselves hiding out down in these tunnels, we found out that the water and vegetation down here was purer than above. So, we never moved out after the war was over. We had become quite comfortable down here. And now, because of the evolutionary transformations that have occurred to our bodies it is no longer desirable for us to return to the surface."

"How did you lose the use of your legs?"

"Most of our work in the tunnels had to be done on our bellies. Eventually we became very good at crawling and moving without our legs. By not using our legs we were able to stay low in the tunnels requiring them to be only half as tall. Low tunnels were also a very good defensive measure against the gnomes. It wasn't until later that we got around to increasing the size of our tunnels to the point that you see them now. By then several generations had passed away and our legs were gone." Ordo stopped shuffling forward and waited in front of one of the cavern entrances but continued his explanation. "We don't miss our legs. We've gotten used to living without them. We're quite happy the way we are." Then he explained his sudden stop. "This is where Doctor Opopp works. Wait here for a minute and I'll go get him. Then we'll go on to the baths." He disappeared through the entrance of the cavern.

It was only a couple minutes before Ordo returned. Next to him was an elderly gentleman about the age of Oply. "How can I help?" asked the elderly doctor kindly.

"My name is Bydola and this is Obydon who I am carrying. He is near death. We need a pool of water so that I can perform a healing ritual," responded Bydola.

"A healing ritual, did you say?" asked the doctor. "I'm not too sure what good that will do but if you want, I'll be glad to see what I can do for your injured friends if you'll bring them into my chambers."

"The healing ritual has worked before," interjected Jesves defensively. "Please help him with what he needs," she pleaded.

"Such foolishness," insisted the doctor. "Let's not waste time on superstitious nonsense when we could actually be helping your friends. Bring them in quickly so that I can get to work."

"We are quite sure that you can do an excellent job," returned Bydola not wanting to offend the doctor. "But the Creator gave me the gift and powers to perform the healing ritual and it has been extremely effective. Please help us identify a pool of water that is large enough for us to submerge his entire body."

"The Creator," grumped Opopp, "more foolishness. What type of gift has he given you anyway?"

"He has given him this staff," interjected Jesves holding up the staff she was carrying for Bydola. She was becoming irritated at the doctor's disbelief. "This staff helps him heal."

"Sure, it does," retorted the doctor sarcastically. "All right. You go and play with your staff. When you're done with your magic act bring the patients back to me so that I can heal them."

The doctor was about to go back inside when Ordo cried out, "Please come with Doctor Opopp. Lord Oply wants you to join us."

Opopp hesitated then responded, "Well, all right. Wait here while I get my bag."

The doctor entered his chamber and quickly returned carrying his medical bag. "Where do we go?" he asked.

"We need a place where we can dunk the injured person completely under water," responded Ordo. "Do you know of such a place?"

"Dunk them under water?" questioned the doctor. "What are you trying to do? Drown them too? What foolishness. All you're going to do is cause them to lose more blood. Please don't endanger them with such nonsense."

Bydola, acting as if he didn't hear the doctor's question repeated Ordo's question, "Where is a place where we can dunk the injured under water?"

In frustration the doctor said, "How about the fountain?"

"Excellent idea," returned Ordo. "Let's go," and he led the way through the tunnels toward the fountain.

"How'd all your friends get hurt?" asked the physician as he traveled beside Jesves.

"We had a battle with gnomes," responded Jesves. "Even though we won we suffered many injuries." Again, the doctor had a skeptical look.

Ordo rounded a corner in the caverns and entered a large chamber which was much larger than the dining chamber that the expedition had been in with Oply. In the middle of the chamber was a large fountain with children playing in it. As the group entered the area it suddenly became bright with light from the orange rocks. The Worlepreeks that were in the area covered their eyes as if to prevent some harm that the lights may cause.

"This is our town center," explained Ordo. Looking around it was possible to see many exit tunnels branching out from the central area. It looked like streets radiating out from this central point. The outside perimeter of the cavern was filled with little shops where vendors were doing business of every sort. There were food vendors, fabric and jewelry vendors, and many others.

"This is quite a large town," commented Bydola, impressed by the large number of people that he saw. "It must be every bit as large as Amins."

"Once we solved the problem of the retants our rate of population growth was much faster," explained Ordo.

"How do you seat everyone at the banquet table?" asked Jesves.

Ordo continued "We don't. That's just used for special occasions."

They walked over to the center fountain and Opopp and Ordo quickly chased the children out of the water. It wasn't long before a crowd had gathered to see what was going on. They were becoming used to the orange lights and this was the first time most of them had seen creatures walking on legs. They were amazed at the sight. Comments could be heard like, "I've always heard that the existence of leprechauns with legs was a legend. I didn't believe that legend. They look so strange."

Bydola was nervous. He hadn't anticipated such a large audience. He proceeded to lay Obydon on the ground and took the staff from Jesves. Opopp immediately bent down to look at Obydon and sighed. "This arm is beyond hope. It's already turning green. The best thing we can do is cut the arm off, so the green disease doesn't infect the rest of his body and eventually kill him."

Bydola acted as though he hadn't heard the comment and proceeded to bless and sanctify the water. He spoke the words which none of the other participants heard, "By the power of Protee, I, Abogidyide, declare this water sacred." An orange light flashed down his staff and struck the water. The water, which had been dirty from the activities of the children, suddenly became pure and clean. Bydola was relieved when he saw the flash. He had been a little nervous about using his new powers. He feared that he might do something wrong and the healings wouldn't work.

"Wow!" several of the Worlepreeks reacted in surprise when the saw the flash of light.

By now Opopp had given up on Bydola and was inspecting Gabrona's head wound. "He's still alive," he reported. "But he's in a coma and I don't know how long he'll last like that."

Bydola continued to ignore the doctor and lifted Obydon into the water. Jesves moved immediately to her station in the water by Obydon's head propping it up until Bydola was ready. Bydola lifted his staff and placed it on Obydon signaled for Jesves to drop the head she was holding. Then he spoke the healing words, "By the power of Protee I, Abogidyide, command thy body to heal itself of all infirmities." The orange light again flashed down the staff and covered the entire body of Obydon except for his left arm.

Opopp was aghast at the sight of Obydon's head falling under the water. He started to jump up to rescue Obydon but when he saw the unexpected orange light surrounding the body he hesitated. He no longer knew what to think. Then in amazement he watched as Obydon sat up in the fountain sputtering and coughing water out of his lungs.

"What happened?" was Obydon's first comment but no one answered. Everyone looked at his left shoulder in shock. Obydon looked too and was aghast. His left arm was missing completely and the shoulder was cleanly healed as if there had never been an arm there. "Where's my left arm?" he screamed in anguish?

Bydola, feeling the hurt of the loss of his friend's arm attempted to explain, "The retants destroyed your arm and later a gnome severed it completely from your shoulder. I had hoped that I would be able to restore it, but unfortunately I cannot restore something that is already dead." Obydon looked into the water and saw his arm laying there beside him withered and dried.

Obydon started to cry. He hadn't anticipated something like this would happening. He had thought that he might lose his life, but he never considered being deformed. He felt that death would've been better than this. After a few moments of listening to his friends console him he recognized his foolishness and stood up and started to climb out of the fountain.

"Thank you for trying," he thanked Bydola, knowing that his friend had indeed done his best to help him. Bydola hugged Obydon in an attempt to show his sympathy and love. Bydola then went over to Gabrona lifting him and putting him in the fountain.

Opopp was dumbfounded. He had never seen such an amazing recovery. He didn't know what to think of it. He decided he would watch the next healing to see if he could learn any new tricks. The procedure was the same. Bydola lowered Gabrona into the water, touched him with the staff, and said, "By the power of Protee, I, Abogidyide, command thy body to heal itself of all infirmities." Even the orange light was the same.

Gabrona sat up in the water and looked fully recovered. He looked at Bydola and knew immediately what had happened. "That gnome got me, didn't he?" Bydola nodded. "Thanks for the help Bydola."

Bydola was about to start the procedure for Elasti and Gijivure when Opopp suddenly ran away from the fountain. Obydon and Gabrona were updated about all that had happened since each of them was knocked unconscious. They were told about the battles with the gnomes, about entering the second tunnel, and about finding their distant relatives the Worlepreeks. The two were glad to hear that the team had found the Worlepreeks and that they were now able to help the expedition in their most desperate hour of need. The opportunity to rest and recover was critical to the expedition members.

Bydola made quick work of Elasti's injured arm and was just finishing his work on Gijivure when Opopp reappeared bringing a female Worlepreek who appeared to be in a great deal of pain. The doctor guided her toward the fountain. As he arrived Bydola saw the seriousness in the doctor's eyes. The doctor's feelings showed a mixture of both love and fear. Opopp looked up at Bydola and made his request, "Bydola, this is my wife who has been stricken with a disease for which

I have no cure." Opopp hesitated temporarily because his voice was cracking. He had turned his head down to the ground in an attempt to hide the tears that were swelling up in his eyes. After a few moments he continued, "I greatly fear for her life." He tried to look up again but was unable. He looked toward the ground and continued, "Would you be so kind as to try and help her? I would gladly give you everything I own for her sake." He could no longer hold back the tears in his eyes. The love he felt for her was overwhelming. It was apparent that he would truly sacrifice anything including his own life for her sake. Opopp started to turn away from Bydola feeling embarrassment and fearing the possibility of rejection, especially after he had made so many sarcastic remarks.

Bydola, recognizing the doctor's embarrassment responded quickly, "I would never use any gift of the Creator for a price, but I would gladly give it to you freely." Opopp could not hold his feelings back any longer. He burst into tears placing his hands over his eyes.

Jesves was touched. Her heart ached for the old woman that was so deeply loved. She hoped that Bydola could indeed help her. Bydola walked over and took the doctor's wife by the hand and led her to the pool of water. He gently lifted her in and explained what he was going to do. He told her to put her head under the water when he started to say the sacred words and that after the orange light had left her body, she would be able to sit up once again. Having her in position he proceeded with his sacred prayer, "By the power of Protee I, Abogidyide, command thy body to heal itself of all infirmities." The flash of orange light followed and surrounded her body.

After the flash Opopp's wife sat up in the water and immediately began to get out on her own. It was as though the bent and crippled old women that had entered the water had totally disappeared. She stood up straight and beautiful. She was still old but no longer bent and withered. She appeared strong and healthy. Her husband by this time was so emotionally shaken that he had fallen to his elbows and was sobbing.

The scene was beautiful and touched everyone present. It was filled with love and emotion. The Worlepreeks that watched the incident were awestricken. They were silent. They couldn't believe what they had just witnessed. Seeing the healings of the strangers was curious enough but to see one of their own healed right before their eyes was more than any of them could comprehend.

Soon the Worlepreeks were shuffling around frantically grabbing their sick and any loved ones that had an ailment. A line began to form. Everyone was hoping to take advantage of Bydola's power. He was glad to share it with everyone, but he worried about how long all this would take since he was exhausted. He was tempted to put a little more ritual and mysticism around the healing process thereby keeping the onlookers enticed. In his heart he felt that this would be an abuse of powers that weren't really his and that perhaps if he added ceremony, he would just end up bringing the wrath of the Creator upon his head. It would be better if he didn't feel as though he had something better than everyone else. Rather, he had something that belonged to everyone else and that it was his duty to make it available to everyone.

Bydola was about to start the healing process on the first of these people when Opopp's wife came before him fell to her elbows and began to thank him. Bydola was astonished and quickly reached down and lifted her. "I have no right to accept your thanks. Give your thanks to the Creator who gave me this gift to share with everyone. Please don't thank me for something that he did."

She understood or at least she acted like she understood and then she said, "Well, thank you for coming and being available to help me. I will always hold your Creator in sacred esteem and consider him my Creator."

Opopp followed right behind her, "I know you won't accept any gift from me. If there is ever anything, I can do for you I would be overjoyed to do it. Please call on me." Bydola nodded in recognition.

By now the throng of Worlepreeks had increased substantially. Sick and elderly where closing in on Bydola from every side. "Opopp!" he called out and the doctor quickly turned around. "Maybe there is something you can help me with?"

"Anything!" replied the doctor excitedly. "What is it?"

"There are so many Worlepreeks coming for aid. It would take hours to heal them all. I feel that tonight I can only heal those that are near death. In the morning after I have had a chance to eat and rest, I can help the others. I am very weary. Perhaps you can help me manage the multitude."

"Absolutely!" Opopp responded in understanding. He quickly climbed up on the edge of the fountain so that he could be heard and seen by all his friends. "My people, you have all seen what has been done here tonight and for that I am grateful beyond belief. We must also keep the health of our visitor in mind. Tonight, he will help only those that are near death. The rest of you will have to wait till morning when he will graciously help all the rest of you as well. Please, only bring forth those of you that are seriously ill tonight and return in the morning with the others."

Then Opopp climbed down from the fountain and turned to the leprechaun and said, "Perhaps, if you teach me how to do what you do I can help you and you won't have to do it all by yourself."

"I truly wish I could," responded Bydola, "but there are several problems. One is that we only have one staff. Another is that the power of the Protee was given me by the Creator and I have no way to give it to you. And a third problem is that you haven't been given your own personal and sacred name that will invoke the power."

"The staff I can understand but the name and the Protee don't make sense to me. All you did was touch the sick with the staff and say; 'By the power of Protee, I command thy body to heal itself of all infirmities.' Right?"

"Not exactly. You are missing the name which cannot be uttered. The name which invokes the power. I say it but no one else can hear it. But I see that you will not be convinced until I let you try so here is the staff. Go ahead and try." Bydola handed the staff to Opopp and the doctor called over a small boy with a badly deformed arm. He had the boy get into the water and instructed him on what needed to be done. The boy followed his directions eagerly.

Opopp touched the boy with the staff and signaled him to put his head under the water. Then he said the words, "By the power of Protee I command thy body to heal itself of all infirmities." Nothing happened. There was no orange light and the boy had to sit up because he could no longer hold his breath. He sat in the pool gasping for air.

The doctor turned to Bydola and said, "I see that this is something only you were meant to do." He handed back the staff and Bydola walked over to the pool of water. He signaled the boy to once again submerge himself.

Then Bydola said, "By the power of Protee I, Abogidyide, command thy body to heal itself of all infirmities." The orange light came down the staff and shortly thereafter the boy sat up with his arm totally healed. Bydola turned to Opopp and said, "My having this power requires that I must help everyone who needs it."

The doctor nodded, seeming to understand. Then he concluded, "As you already know I seriously doubted your sanity when you wanted to submerge your injured in this fountain. But now I see that maybe I wasn't as smart as I thought I was. It brings to my mind an old psalm that is in our scriptures. The psalm hasn't meant much to me in the past but seeing what I have just seen today makes me realize its true meaning. I now know that although scientifically this shouldn't work, that there is much more out there for us to learn. The psalm goes like this:

Truth is truth wherever it's found;
Whether on Worlepreeks or heathen ground."

Opopp turned away from Bydola toward the crowd and started to assist the leprechaun by directing the healing activities.

After the injured had left the eating chamber Oply turned to Yanon and asked, "Tell me about this important mission that you say you are on. Also, about the gnomes that you have encountered. And about Bydola and his Creator."

Yanon turning to one of the chairs stationed around the banquet table asked, "May I sit down?"

"Of course!" Oply waived him toward the chairs. They had no legs, only a cushioned seat and a back to lean against.

Yanon went over to one of the chairs. His legs were tired, and he needed to rest. He sat down stretching his legs under the table. Hiztin quickly followed his example and Oply joined them as well. Yanon turned to Hiztin and said, "Tell our host about the first expedition which triggered all this."

Hiztin proceeded to explain Elasti's journey to the Albo Pass with Agot and Broch. He explained the deaths of the two leprechaun friends. Then he told of the decision of the council including how a committee composed of leprechauns, elves, and lepelves was formed. He relayed their adventures in the Tako Ruins and the Kabul and explained the loss of Hasko.

Suddenly Oply interrupted. "Now you've found a way I can help you," he started. "You need help locating your friend. I'll send some Worlepreeks to the first tunnel and they'll watch for him, protect him, and bring him here if they find him. Most of my people are afraid of travelling between the caves because they don't have legs, but after all you've done for us, my people are eager and willing to risk it."

"That would be great," interjected Hiztin who hadn't stopped worrying about his dear boyhood friend. "I would really appreciate that. He means a lot to me. But you have to be cautious because there are gnomes out there."

"I'll send someone out tonight while it's dark," responded Oply. Then he turned again to Hiztin and said, "Now, please continue your story. I still haven't heard about the gnomes."

Hiztin continued, explaining their exit from the Kabul and their encounter with gnomes at the first tunnel. Oply laughed when he heard how they had tricked the gnomes with the avalanche. Yanon told of the retants, the erates, and the gnomes that were waiting for them at the exit of the first tunnel. He discussed Obydon's injuries, and their long arduous journey to the second tunnel including the battle they fought to get into the tunnel He told about Gijivure and Gabrona's injuries and how Bydola had the ability to heal them.

Oply was a little skeptical of Hiztin's story assuming that some of it was a little stretched, especially the business about the healings and the Kabul. He tried to reassure himself by telling himself, "*I suppose if they can have the light, they might magically be able to heal also.*"

The explanations took a long time. Yanon outlined the purpose of meeting with the dwarfs and how the expedition planned to conquer the Kabul. This intrigued Oply and made him wish he could be involved in their expedition, but he realized that he would never be able to help them without legs.

A Worlepreek lady with long beautiful dark hair entered the room and announced that the meal had been prepared and was now ready to be served. "Get someone who can run as a messenger and fetch the rest of our guests," instructed Oply. The girl bowed and left the room.

Moments later another boy about Ordo's age entered the room and Oply instructed him to go to the baths and return with the rest of the party. "I'll go with," Hiztin requested. "I'd enjoy seeing more of this place."

"Of course," replied Oply and he waved the youngster over to Hiztin. The two were off in search of their friends.

They went to the baths as instructed but when they found no one there they were confused. They asked someone "Haven't you heard?" questioned the passerby in surprise. "They're healing Worlepreeks in the town fountain."

This surprised both Hiztin and his guide so they journeyed toward the town square. When they arrived, they encountered a throng of people that was so great it looked as though it would be impossible to get to the center of it all where Bydola and the others must surely be. They forced their way through and after several minutes arrived at the fountain.

"What the heck's going on here?" Hiztin asked Jesves who was the first familiar face he encountered.

"The whole community wants Bydola to heal them," was her response. "He's already cured about fifty Worlepreeks and the line keeps growing. Look at all these people." She waved her hands over the top of them.

"We're supposed to go eat now," reported Hiztin to Jesves. "Do you think we can pull Bydola away from all this?"

"He's getting awfully tired," she responded. "Why don't you come with me?" She led Hiztin over to the doctor and said, "We have got to let Bydola eat and rest. Would you help us so that he can get him away from here?"

"Of course!" replied the doctor, and he climbed up on the edge of the fountain. Then he yelled out to the crowd, "We must stop the healings for today. Bydola has agreed to return to us in the morning and do some more then."

Jesves anticipated groans of disappointment at this announcement but instead she heard cheers and applause of gratitude. The Worlepreeks were grateful for the healings that were done. "How strange," she thought. "In Amins it would have been just the opposite. These are truly beautiful people."

The guests were led out of the town center by Opopp. He and Ordo guided them back to the eating chambers. At their arrival they saw that food was already being placed on the table and everyone quickly took a seat around it.

Yanon looked at the previously injured companions and exclaimed, "How good to see all of you back to health. That is truly a divine gift you have Bydola. I'm glad the Creator decided to give it to you at a time like this. It's already saved us many days and several lives. How about your injuries Bydola? Have they healed yet?"

Jesves was awestruck. She felt it as her responsibility to look after the health of the members of the expedition but now she realized that she had forgotten about Bydola's injuries mostly because other injuries were so much more serious and because he didn't complain about his own injuries. She went over to him and investigated his bandages. As she removed them, she noted that once again, Bydola had somehow healed himself, and there was no sign of his previous injuries.

Then Yanon noticed the missing arm of Obydon, "Your arm, Obydon, what happened to it?"

"It was already dead and could not be brought back to life," explained Bydola. His head was bowed in sorrow.

"Don't be sad," comforted Obydon. "None of us is lying in a grave at the Tako Ruins next to Giterod. I'm grateful to still be alive. When I look around and see the Worlepreeks I realize that if they have the strength to adapt so well without legs than who am I to complain. I can handle the small challenge of missing one arm. Don't be sad for me. I'm thankful I'm alive." All were comforted and proud of Obydon's courageous attitude.

Oply was fascinated by the amazing healings. He decided that he would have to learn more about them from Opopp later. In an attempt to change the topic of conversation away from the lost arms and healings Oply asked, "Show me this Southern Sword that I've heard so much about. I'd sure like to see it."

Obydon eagerly pulled the sword out of its protective wrappings. He found it challenging to try to unwrap the weapon with the aid of only one hand, but he refused the offers of aid that he received from his companions. He needed to learn how to work with only one arm. As the sword was freed from its coverings, its yellow light appeared, and the green jewel shone brilliantly.

Oply was awestricken. He reached out for the sword and held it as if it were power itself. "Have you nothing better in which to keep this sword other than those poor wrappings?" he asked.

Obydon relayed the story of Giterod leaving out any derogatory remarks about lepelves. Oply returned the sword and Obydon once again wrapped the sword in its sad coverings. He joined the others at the table preparing himself for the feast.

Sitting around the table with their legs out of sight underneath it made the leprechauns look like Worlepreeks. Once everyone was seated the food trays were uncovered. The guests were astonished and hesitant. Before them lay a feast of roasted ants, spiders, lizards, and what looked like boiled snails. There were also fried roots which looked much like the retants that they had done battle within the last tunnel.

Elasti thought to himself, *"I'd prefer another cold meal to this stuff,"* but he knew, as did the rest, that if he refused to eat he would insult their hosts and so he decided to grin and tolerate it.

Plates full of what the Worlepreeks considered gourmet food were dished out to each of the guests and they each hesitantly sampled everything. Surprisingly they found they enjoyed the fried ants, and the lizard tails weren't bad either. Their hunger overtook them, and they soon found themselves gulping down the food as if it were their favorite meal.

After the meal had gone on for some time Opopp started to explain his version of the healing that Bydola had done for the people of the city. He explained to Oply and the others who weren't present in the town center how the healings worked and how Bydola had helped a large number of the town's population.

Oply was amazed. He had never heard of such a power before. Nowhere in their historical writings or scriptures was there any knowledge of such a healing power. After Opopp's explanation was completed Bydola turned to Oply and said, "You mentioned a need for our orange rocks. Tomorrow I will do more healings at the fountain and, if you wish, I can create several of the rocks for you at the same time. But I will need you to bring several rocks to me so that I can change them. Perhaps you can have someone do that before morning."

"Oh, thank you for your kindness," responded Oply, "I'm not sure we will ever be able to repay you."

"As I said before, repayment would be an insult to the Creator. It would be as if I were getting the benefit of his gift. I will not accept any payment." Bydola was insistent.

Oply turned to Yanon, "Can I encourage you to spend the day with us tomorrow? I would like you to speak before the council and tell them your story. Also, I would like to declare it a day of celebration in honor of our guests. Please don't cheat us of this opportunity."

Yanon could see in Oply's eyes how much this would mean to him and so he accepted. "Taking a day to rest would do us good," Yanon stressed. "We have suffered from a hard and difficult journey. Thank you for your invitation. We accept. But the very next morning we must be off again at sunrise."

"Agreed," responded Oply. "I will delay you no longer than that." Then he turned to Gido and requested, "Tell me about the elfin city of Gijc. I have often wondered how the Lifefight Wars left it."

"The city of Gije,
Is a beautiful town;
But these new Kabul dangers,
Have made it frown.
Its people live well,
And are building protection;
The Jove Plateau,
Will prevent destruction."

Gido was proud of his home and enjoyed telling the Worlepreeks about it. Then Hiztin added, "He's right, their city is the finest place I've ever seen. You'll have to go see it some time."

The travelers were wrapping up their meals and as they concluded Oply suggested, "Now allow me to escort you to the bath chambers and to the sleeping chambers we have prepared for you so that you can enjoy a good night's rest. You've got a heavy day of celebrating ahead of you tomorrow."

"With pleasure," resounded Elasti and with that everyone got up from the table.

Yanon lay in his sleeping chamber. It was a small room with only a few decorations on the walls. The only furniture was a table, a chair, and four small beds, two of which had to be placed end-to-end for the leperchaun to be able to lay on it comfortably. In the other pair of beds next to him lay Bydola.

It was dark in the chamber. The teams' orange lights had been stored away in their packs. Bydola was still awake and Yanon wondered how he was able to tolerate so much. He had carried Obydon for two days straight and had taken on much more than his share of the chores, yet he looked as though he wasn't a bit tired. Yanon felt thankful that the expedition was blessed with the powers given to Bydola. They had all benefited greatly.

Yanon was also thankful for the Worlepreeks and for the kindness extended by Oply. It was a stroke of luck that allowed them to find these friends in what was probably their greatest time of need. He felt as though someone was taking care of him and his expedition. He was grateful for their success with the gnomes and hoped that the problem would not reoccur when they left this last tunnel.

He looked forward to his departure, not because he disliked the hospitality of the Worlepreeks, but because he was concerned about the safety of the South. He had no way of knowing if the gnomes had already attacked the South. He hoped that the two swords would be joined in time to prevent a slaughter of his people. The urgency of the situation made him wish that he wouldn't lose a day's travel. But he had already promised his attendance at the council on the following day and maybe there would be some way that these Worlepreeks could help the expedition after all. He also realized that even though Obydon and Gabrona were healed they had not yet fully recovered their strength and the extra day would do them, and everyone else on the expedition, a lot of good.

Bydola was lying across from Yanon in the same sleeping chamber. The heavy wooden door to the chamber had been closed making it quite dark inside without the aid of the orange lights. He was worried that these Worlepreeks did not understand the true significance of his healing powers. It wasn't something he wanted any praise for. He wished he could instill in them the true understanding of who the Creator really was. Unfortunately, he wasn't sure himself. He was glad that the elves revealed that the lights and Bydola's powers were from the Creator.

He felt concerned about his duty. The Creator had sent him on a mission to dispel an evil that threatened the whole land. Yet he had encountered very little evil at all. The only evil he had encountered so far came from Giterod, Gijivure, the eagle, and the Kabul, but he didn't fully understand how any of these threatened the total safety of Small World. He was especially confused about the Creator's statement that the destructive evil was a protection for the South? He was left mystified and uncertain about how it would all be connected. He hoped he had not made some grave mistake in his efforts to discover, remove and destroy this evil.

He also worried about Gijivure. He could not understand the evil that emanated from him. He had kept a close watch on the elf and other than the incident in the Kabul, he noticed nothing out of the ordinary. It seemed hard to believe that someone who had been such an asset to the expedition could actually possess evil within him. But never-the-less the evil within Gijivure shone stronger than the evil in Giterod and it could not be denied. He would have to continue keeping a close watch on the elf and on the eagle as well. Perhaps he would be able to discover their true purpose.

In the neighboring sleeping chamber lay Gido and Gijivure. For them, even two Worlepreeks beds put end-to-end were too short. They pulled up their legs a little and made themselves as comfortable as possible. Gido felt a little discouraged. He didn't think it was wise to trust the Worlepreeks so fully especially since they had just met them. He didn't trust Oply as completely as Yanon did. He thought that maybe Oply was only after the orange rocks and maybe now that the little guy had seen the Southern Sword he would be after it as well. Gido reflected on Yanon's trust of Giterod and how it had almost cost the expedition the sword. He didn't want that mistrust repeated. Yet when he tried to discuss his concern with Yanon, the leprechaun passed over it lightly.

He was also a little jealous of Yanon's dominance over the expedition. At first it didn't bother him as much because Yanon treated him with respect and carefully considered his suggestions. But lately Yanon just did what he pleased without any regard for Gido's experience. The elf resented this but hoped that maybe Yanon's manner was the temporary result of stress and a lack of rest. Perhaps the best thing to do was to have patience and to wait it out. Hopefully Yanon's attitude would change.

Gido had also become concerned about Gijivure. The younger elf had always been very talkative and sociable but lately he seemed reposed. He seemed intent on some unknown activity or idea. *"Perhaps he has just had too much of these talkative leprechauns,"* thought Gido. *"Maybe that's why we don't hear much from him. I tend to get my fill of them too. Gijivure will probably return to normal when we meet with the dwarfs."* He looked forward to the successful completion of the mission to the North.

Gijivure lay on his bed in the dark room. He stared at the ceiling wondering how he would once again communicate with the eagle. He needed to be out in the open. At least this would be the last of the tunnels. He knew that soon he would be able to go forth on his own personal assigned mission. He looked forward to the future when he would be rid of all these fool companions of his including Gido who only wanted to be boss over Yanon. He resented leprechauns telling him what to do.

The next sleeping chamber contained Elasti and Obydon. Elasti laid thinking about Jizeel and how badly he missed her. He thought about his family and how he wished he could somehow let them know that he was alright. He knew that they would be worried about him.

He also thought of Obydon. "I'm awfully sorry about your arm," he said sympathetically.

"Please don't worry," replied Obydon. "I'm really glad to be alive. I've had two narrow escapes, and I sure don't want any more." But Obydon was concerned. He wondered how his father and more importantly his wife would feel about this loss. He hoped he wouldn't be thought of as handicapped or incapacitated. Tolerating the stares, the whispers, and the persistent help of do-gooders, would be the hardest part of his new challenge. He hoped that he could still be Obydon and not "Obydon the cripple".

Obydon had another concern. He was worried about the Southern Sword. He had been entrusted with this prized possession, yet he had almost lost control of it four times. Three times were at the hand of Giterod and once at the hand of the gnomes. He felt truly unworthy to be trusted with such a prized possession. Now with the loss of his left arm he felt even more inadequate. Why should the expedition entrust him any longer? He must turn over his possession to someone more capable of performing the job of protecting the sword.

Across the hall from Obydon rested Gabrona and Hiztin. Gabrona had experienced much. He had never expected the journey north to be so dangerous and although he missed his home terribly, he was glad he had run away to join the expedition. He had eliminated his former suspicions about the intentions of the leprechauns and had given up on the thought that they might have actually killed Giterod. He now proudly wielded the sword and knife of Giterod as a representative of the great city of Giter and hoped to regain the respect of the elves and leprechaun by his actions.

He knew that his father and his friends would be furious with him for what he had done. They would think he was crazy and had no business being on such a dangerous and long journey. If he had stayed in Giter he would constantly be worrying about Giterod and wondering if the lepelf would jeopardize the expedition by intercepting the Southern Sword. Gabrona knew this expedition was much more important than attending to his father's tavern.

Hiztin lay across from Gabrona filled with conflict being both de-lighted and concerned. He was happy to be in the Worlepreeks tunnels under the protection of Oply yet at the same time he was concerned about Hasko. He worried about the safety of his friend. He would never forgive himself if anything happened to him. He hoped that somehow his boyhood buddy would be able to catch up with the expedition during their stay here in the Worlepreeks tunnels. He looked forward to the reunion when the two would once again be together.

Hiztin had become very close to Jesves. The two shared many secret wishes and dreams. It delighted Hiztin to have found someone that would share so much with him. But somehow even this didn't seem like enough. There had to be a next step in their relationship. He wanted something that would allow him to be in the next room with her and not stranded here with Gabrona. The only thing that crossed his mind was marriage and yet the thought of marriage frightened him. He wasn't sure he was ready for anything quite that dramatic.

In the next sleeping chamber Jesves was grateful to be. This was one occasion when she was glad to be female because it gave her an excuse for more privacy. She was down on her knees talking to her God of the Rainbow and thanking him for directing them to the Worlepreeks. She also thanked him for the healings and blessings that everyone was receiving at the hand of Bydola. She prayed that no further dangers would be encountered. Her last prayer, one she felt personally and deeply, was for Hiztin and her newfound relationship with him. She asked for their love to grow and blossom into something real and beautiful. She had never felt this excited, this entranced, this infatuated, with anyone. She prayed that Hiztin would feel the same about her.

As Jesves finished her prayer she got off her knees and lay down on her bed. She was confused by this Creator that Bydola referred to often. The elves had also referred to a Creator and she felt sure that they were talking about the same individual. Bydola claims to have spoken with or met this Creator. "Was this Creator a God?" she wondered to herself. "Is the God of the Rainbow the Creator they are referring to?" She knew that the God of the Rainbow was real. He had answered her prayers in too many amazing ways not to be real. But this other Creator must be real too. Should she be praying to both of these beings? She knew she wouldn't find any answers in the empty dark chamber where she now lay but she hoped that someday she could learn more about both of these Godly beings. She rolled over on her side allowing weariness to overcome her. She closed her eyes and fell asleep.

It was late morning before the members of the expedition finally awoke. There was no light in their chambers to awaken them, and so they slept on as though the nighttime never ended. Eventually they did get up and as they did, they took their rocks out of their pockets and released the orange light to illuminate their tiny chambers. They found breakfast waiting for them on a small table in each of their rooms. They ate quickly and one at a time the expedition members exited their rooms only to find Worlepreeks waiting outside to greet them.

As Yanon came out of his chamber he found Oply standing by, "Good morning my fine Worlepreeks host," the leprechaun exclaimed.

"Good morning to you my friend," was the reply. "Would you still like to join me at the council meeting?"

"Most definitely," replied Yanon and the two hurried off together.

After several turns and tunnel changes the two arrived at the location where they had previously been. The area was filled with Worlepreeks who gave a rousing cheer when they saw the host and his guest enter the area. Oply led Yanon directly to the center of the room where a raised platform stood. They climbed to the top where a throne and several chairs were situated. Oply made himself comfortable on the throne and Yanon took a seat next to him.

He leaned over to Yanon and whispered, "Everyone has heard about your expedition. You're the first people that they've seen here that walk on legs and they're excited about that. And they're also excited about the healings. We're a little late so we'll start right away." Oply waved his hand as a signal and a loud ringing could be heard bringing all the Worlepreeks to silence and attention.

Oply raised his head and started talking in a loud voice so all could hear. "As you know, we are hosting honored guests from the Southern Plains. We have leprechauns who are our long-lost ancestors, elves and lepelves." Oply proceeded to introduce Yanon and to explain the purpose of the expedition to everyone. He asked the Worlepreek community for suggestions that would help towards the successful completion of the mission.

Then Oply stopped talking and sat down. The entire chamber fell silent. Yanon was confused by this action for a few minutes and didn't know if there was something that he should be doing. Then someone in the crowd spoke up, "Tell us what it's like outside in the Southern Plains. We've only heard about it but have never seen it."

Yanon was surprised by the question, but gladly explained as best he could what life was like on the outside. After this question there were many more questions about the expedition, the Kabul, and in general what it was like to live in the outside world with legs. Yanon answered questions about whatever else the Worlepreeks were curious about. Then as the questions diminished Oply asked the crowd, "I heard that there was trouble of some kind last night. What happened?"

"Gnomes tried to break into the tunnel," someone responded. "I was part of the front line of defense that had to repel the attacking gnomes and even though they were no match for us this time I wonder if they will attack again perhaps next time in bigger numbers."

Then someone else spoke up, "Hopefully they'll think that our guests met the same fate as the gnomes, and they will leave us alone."

Then there was a third voice. "We could convince the gnomes that the expedition met the same fate if we were able to get the quest out of here unnoticed. Then they wouldn't be looking for them anymore. Maybe the gnomes don't know about our secret northern exit, and that perhaps this is the route we should use to get the southerners out of here."

"Excellent idea," spoke up another.

Yanon looked at Oply and asked, "Is there a secret exit that the gnomes don't know about?"

"It appears so," replied Oply. "I've never been much interested in getting out of here so I don't know but it appears you may be in luck."

Another Worlepreek yelled out, "We should offer our shelter, food, and medicine to anyone who is ever in the area and in need."

"They have no need for our medicine," another Worlepreek yelled.

Then Oply spoke up, "Do we have any word from the scouts that we sent after the missing leprechaun?"

Someone yelled out, "They made it safely to the other tunnel but haven't found any sign of the leprechaun. It's difficult for us because we have no way to get across the Erates, and the leprechaun may be on the other side of them, so we'll just have to wait for him to come across."

Oply feeling that he owed Yanon an explanation turned to him and said, "During the Lifefight Wars our people built the Kilo Pass and these two tunnels. We hid the Albo Pass. We used these tunnels to trap the invaders. Many traps were built into the tunnels, but two of the best traps were natural, one was the Worlepreeks, and the other was the Erates. We would throw a false cover over the Erates cracks using branches. That would disguise them, and when someone walked over the branches, they would fall off into the Lamos. As time went on and we lost the use of our legs, we found it impossible to jump over the Erates cracks. That is what is hampering our rescue party from wandering further into the tunnels."

Someone else yelled out, "We have made gifts for the leprechauns, as a thank you for their visit." Then a sheathe was brought forward and handed to Yanon. "We noticed that the Southern Sword was covered with rags and we felt that it deserved better. Please accept this as our gift to your expedition."

Then another Worlepreek brought a backpack and laid it at Yanon's feet. "We also noticed the sad pack that your lepelf friend is using and we felt that he needed better so this is for him." Gabrona was still forced to carry the rag-wrapped pack he had used to escape from Giter. He had intended to take Giterod's, but in the hasty departure from the Tako Ruins he had forgotten to take the better pack.

Yanon stood up, "I don't know how to thank you enough for all you've done for us already. Your help has been perfectly timed. Thank you." A loud cheer went up. As the crowd started to quiet down Yanon was about to continue his speech, but Oply cut him off.

"Great," Oply bellowed out, "now it's time to celebrate." Then he turned to Yanon and whispered, "I can't let you give them too many thank yous or it will go to their head. Besides, I want to party."

Oply led Yanon back off the platform and by the time they reached the bottom, the party was already in full swing.

As Bydola left his sleeping chambers, he found that Opopp was waiting for him. "The council has just ended, and I was wondering if you are still interested in healing some of our sick?"

"Of course," replied Bydola, "lead the way."

Opopp guided him along with the rest of the expedition members to the center of town where an unbelievable throng was now waiting for him. "There must be twice as many Worlepreeks here as yesterday," commented Bydola looking around him.

"Word gets around quickly," was Opopp's reply.

"Let's start with the sickest first in case we run out time," suggested Bydola.

"Of course," responded Opopp. "I'll handle the crowd, so you won't be bothered with it. We also have the rocks here next to the fountain just the way you requested."

Bydola was surprised to find over 50 stones laid out for him to convert. He realized that this day would be a busy one, but he was proud to be able to share his gift with a people that were so grateful. He began with the rocks, converting them one at a time using the words, "By the power of Protee I, Abogidyide turn this stone to light."

Then he blessed the water as before and proceeded to heal the seemingly endless line of people. The job seemed hopelessly large but after several hours the line had decreased significantly.

Bydola's friends who had followed him to the town square were now deeply involved with the Worlepreeks. The small tunnel-dwellers were extremely interested in learning about the "outside world", a place they feared they would never be able to see. They bombarded their guests with questions and stuffed them with food and drink.

In the council chamber, a band had begun to play music and many of the Worlepreeks began to dance. The band was composed of five members who played wind instruments carved out of wood. They also beat on skin-covered drums. The music sounded more like a shrieking and grinding noise to the travelers but the Worlepreeks seemed to enjoy it as they shook, bounced, and rolled around on the floor in their own peculiar dance.

The party continued well into the afternoon. Yanon and his friends had to keep asking what time it was because they had lost all sense of time in the tunnels. The travelers wandered amongst their hosts receiving greetings and well wishes.

Yanon went up to Obydon and said, "Here," as he held up the newly crafted sheathe for the Southern Sword, "look what they made for you."

"It's beautiful," was Obydon's response. "The Southern Sword will be well protected in it. However, it is not for me?"

Yanon was surprised by this remark and asked, "What do you mean?"

"I have decided to turn the Southern Sword over to someone else who can take better care of it. I've nearly lost it four times and now I've lost much of my capability to defend myself."

"Nonsense!" blurted Yanon. "The fact that you nearly lost it but didn't lose it proves that you are the best for this assignment. In spite of all your difficulties and problems you still have possession of it. And as far as defending it goes, how many arms do you need to wield a sword anyway? You're probably better off with your other arm out of the way." Yanon's comment was made jokingly with a smile.

"I just don't feel right about keeping the sword," Obydon insisted.

"Don't try to shirk off your responsibility,'" scolded Yanon. "You were given a duty on this expedition and just like everyone else I expect you to live up to it just the way I expect everyone else to live up to theirs. Now quit this nonsense and accept this sheathe and enjoy the party."

Obydon took the sheathe. He didn't know what else to say. He was still concerned about his abilities, but he was gratified that Yanon had confidence in him.

The orange lights that Bydola had created started appearing in the various meeting places bringing cheers from the crowds. They helped illuminate the rooms better than the small candles had previously.

The elves had found themselves a new friend in Ordo. They had become enticed by the psalm that Opopp had quoted on the previous day and they had talked Ordo into showing them the Worlepreek Book of Psalms. The elves and Ordo spent most of the day in an elaborate

library studying the writings of the Worlepreek ancestors and enjoying their poetic content.

Gabrona had also found many friends amongst his hosts. He was invited to join in with the excitement and gaiety. He felt important as the center of attention. He wanted to impress his audience so when he was asked if he would like a drink he immediately agreed. He had often tasted ale in his father's tavern and found it easy to tolerate. But he had never experienced Worlepreek wine. As he gulped his first helping of the retant root extract he was amazed at how quickly his head responded causing his senses to be slightly fuzzed. But he was too wrapped up in being important to let a little fuzziness stop him and so when he was asked if he would like another he immediately accepted. It wasn't long before Gabrona's thought process had slowed down to the point where he seemed to review everything after it happened. When asked a question he would answer immediately then consider his response. When asked to dance he went out on the dance floor and started to put on a display of waving his hands and feet to the extent that he forced many of the Worlepreeks to leave the dance floor in fear of their safety. An hour later he found himself sprawled out on the dance floor. Several of the Worlepreeks realizing what had happened carried him back to his bedchamber and put him to bed for the night.

As the afternoon drifted on, the celebrants began to tire, and the festivities seemed to slow down. Yanon, who was still escorted by Oply, turned to him and asked, "Is there a room where I can collect all the members of the expedition together so we can practice a little sword play. They haven't received much training and could use a short practice session in the event we encounter anymore gnomes. Also, it would be good for us to regroup and talk strategy."

"Of course," responded Oply. "I'll send messengers to collect all your friends together into one of our larger chambers.

"Please have the messengers remind each of them to fetch their swords."

Oply proceeded to send messengers for all of Yanon's friends, and then led Yanon off down to one of the tunnels.

It had taken about a half hour before all the members of the expedition were once again reunited. Gabrona wasn't there and his fate was quickly explained. The members shared their pleasure at the excitement of the day, the greatest of which seemed to be the help that Bydola had given to countless Worlepreeks.

Then Yanon proceeded, with the help of the elves, to teach the remaining members of the expedition some basic sword maneuvers. He avoided the use of the Southern Sword in these training exercises remembering how he had been knocked out by it in the fields north of Giter.

The practice lasted for several hours and was willingly needed by all the travelers. They realized the importance of the training that they received during these few hours and that it might be enough to save their lives at their next encounter.

After the training session they discussed their plans to leave the tunnel the next day through a secret passage and that hopefully would be their last challenge before arriving at the Northern Plains. Then it was time for bed. The travelers were tired, not so much from their activities of the day but because they had not yet fully recovered their strength from their previous trials. They also wanted to get an early start the following morning and take advantage of as much of the daylight as possible.

They enjoyed a final evening feast surrounded by many of their new friends and then retreated to their sleeping chambers.

CHAPTER EIGHTEEN

THE HILE GROVES

Yanonidine was awakened by a tug on his shoulder which made him jump up with a start. "What's the matter?" he asked as he recognized Oply standing beside his bed.

"You wanted me to wake you so you could get an early start today."

"Oh, thanks a lot," Yanon responded with a slight sarcastic overtone. "I probably would have slept half the day away if you hadn't helped me."

Oply and Yanon proceeded to wake the other companions. Everyone quickly gathered their things together, all except for Gabrona who was still having difficulty pulling himself together.

Yanon teased Gabrona with a smile, "The party's over. Get up and get dressed. We're going."

"He looks like he had a little too much to drink last night," suggested Oply. "We have a cure for his condition. If you'd like me to use it I will, but I warn you he probably won't like it."

"What is it?" questioned Elasti.

"It's a special recipe," confided Oply, "but I'll guarantee you that it works."

"Go ahead and give it a try," responded Yanon. "What have we got to lose?"

Oply waved to Ordo and instructed him to get some of their secret potion for curing hangovers. Ordo ran off with a slight snicker on his face which left Yanon and Elasti wondering what this potion was, but they were curious enough to see its results, so they didn't question him any further.

Gabrona sat on his bed rubbing his head groaning and swearing that he never wanted to see another drop of Worlepreek wine for the rest of his life. He mentioned that he could throw up any minute.

"Well Bydola," observed Yanon, "it looks like you may have to do another healing today if this Worlepreek potion doesn't work."

Just then Ordo, still wearing that peculiar smile on his face returned carrying a bucket on his head. He took the bucket and entered Gabrona's

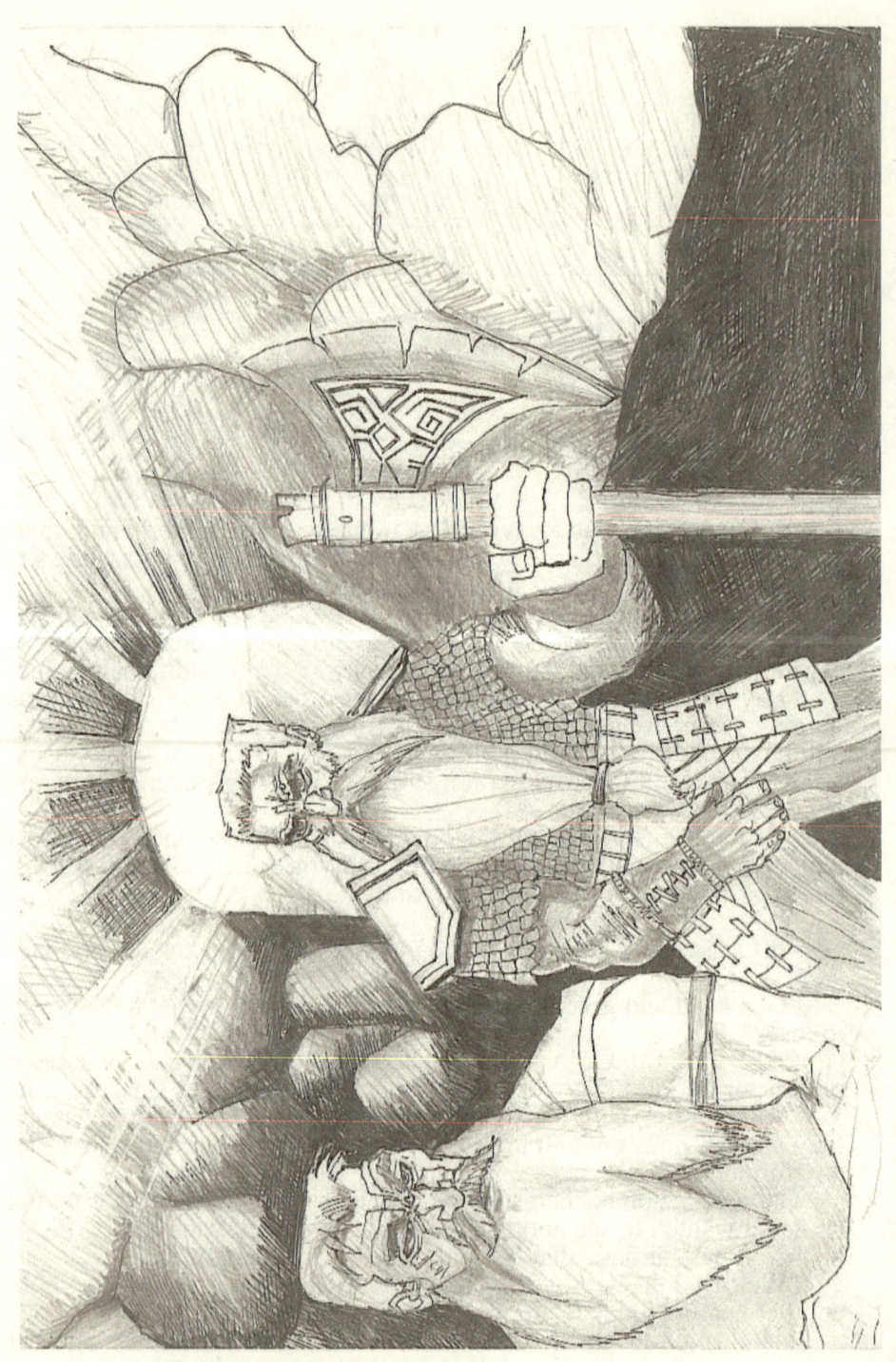

chamber. "Are you ready for our cure?" he questioned. Gabrona slowly moved his head upwards to look at the Worlepreek hesitating as he did as if the motion increased his pain. Oply took the bucket from Ordo and suddenly released the entire bucket full of liquid sending the entire contents pouring over Gabrona's face.

Gabrona jumped up as if stung by a bee. "What the heck kind of a cure is that?" he yelled out in irritation.

"It's the best cure," responded Oply his snicker turning into a laugh. "It gets you moving and lets you forget about your headache. Now you've got something else to worry about."

Ordo was standing in the doorway with Elasti and Yanon and when he saw the lepelf jump up in irritation he burst into an uncontrollable laughter. Elasti and Yanon, seeing that a joke had been played on their lepelf friend also laughed hardily.

Gabrona was the only one that didn't think it was funny at all. He was furious. "Get out of here!" he commanded his spectators. They slowly departed still laughing as Gabrona slammed the door behind them.

After the door was shut Yanon remembered his idea. He yelled out to Gabrona, "Hey! Before you change out of your wet clothes maybe you should have Bydola cure you of your headache."

At this Gabrona immediately opened the door and growled, "All right, let's get with it."

Bydola and Gabrona were guided by Ordo and taken to the pond in the town square. Bydola performed the ritual of cleansing the water and instructed Gabrona to step into the water. The appropriate words were said, and the orange light flashed. Then Gabrona got out of the water as expected but after stepping out on the dry surface he commented with irritation, "I don't feel any better. What's the matter Bydola? Why didn't I get healed?"

Bydola was stunned. This was the first time the healing procedure had not worked. "I'm not sure what's wrong," he observed in response to Gabrona's question. "Everything seemed to go correctly." But then he recalled something about intentionally inflicted injuries. He recalled the contents of the healing scroll in his mind and read down the scroll until he arrived at the information that he had been searching for. It said, "The Protee powers will not support evil. It will only oppose it. And if it is used for evil it will have no effect. It will only work for the purposes of good. Injury and sickness that are the result of self-inflicted evil cannot be cured."

Bydola explained that passage to Gabrona who was irritated at the fact that he would have to suffer the consequences of the wine. He was even more irritated at himself for having been stupid enough to allow himself to drink so much. "*But what the heck,*" he tried to console himself. "*I had fun last night anyway.*"

As the disappointed lepelf returned to the sleeping chambers with his escorts he found that his friends were ready to depart. They had prepared Gabrona's belongings and had packed them into his new backpack. "Wow," he exclaimed at the sight of his gift. "That's really neat."

Oply then proceeded to escort the expedition out to eat their final meal with the Worlepreeks. They found this meal a little tastier than previous meals had been. Apparently, someone had learned what type of food each of the leprechauns, elves, and lepelves liked, because they each had their favorite dish sitting before them. Although they had already become used to eating ants, spiders, and lizards, they were very grateful to see their own favorite foods.

Oply informed the travelers that there had been another attack by the gnomes during the night. The battle had been fierce and about thirty gnomes had been killed. It got so bad that the bodies of the dead gnomes were piled up and used to dam up the tunnel thereby preventing other gnomes from getting in. Finally, the gnomes gave up and retreated. The bodies of the dead gnomes still lay where they had fallen because the Worlepreeks didn't want to retrieve them and risk being attacked.

Oply also reported that there had still been no word about Hasko. But it was possible that no word was sent because of the large numbers of gnomes that were trying to get into the tunnel. Oply promised that his people would take good care of Hasko when he finally showed up and that if his health was good, he would be sent to the Hile Groves to meet them.

Gido expressed his appreciation;
"Thank you for letting us,
Learn from your people;
Your psalm books of old,
Are filled with good council.
We enjoyed the chance,
To be here with you;
We look forward to when,
We'll come back here too."

Gido reflected on the pleasure he had gained from studying the Worlepreek books. He had learned a new appreciation for the great intelligence that the Worlepreeks possessed.

Thanks, were given all around. The Worlepreeks and the travelers had become close friends in the short time they had been together. The departure would be a sad one.

Finally, one of the Worlepreeks guided them toward the secret exit. Many of their newfound friends followed along behind the party to see them off.

It was several hours of easy walking often downhill and with many diversions switching from one tunnel to another before they finally arrived at the secret exit. It was just becoming light outside. They had timed their arrival perfectly to make maximum use of the daylight hours. They were careful to stay sufficiently far away from the exit so as to avoid being overheard or seen by any gnomes that might be waiting outside. The Worlepreeks and their guests gave each other many farewell hugs and thank yous and then the quest members departed.

The travelers approached the exit carefully with swords drawn and bows strung. At the exit they peered out but saw and heard no one. "It may be an ambush, so we'll have to be careful," whispered Yanon.

"What shall we do?" asked Elasti. "How are we going to draw them out if they're there waiting for us?"

"We'll have to send someone out there as bait in order to draw their attention," responded Yanon. "It probably should be me because I'm the best with the sword."

But Gabrona had different plans. He had been irritated about feeling like a useless bystander, and now was his chance to demonstrate that lepelves had courage too. He dashed off before anyone had a chance to stop him.

"Look," whispered Hiztin as loud as he dared. "Gabrona has run out of the tunnel. He must still be full of wine." Quickly everyone prepared themselves to go out and ward off any attack by the gnomes.

Gabrona was running down the secret pass toward the Kilo Pass trail at full speed. He was running in an irregular pattern in case there were attackers. He knew that arrows could best be avoided by not running in a straight line. After he had run quite a ways down the path he stopped. No attempt had been made on his life. No shots had been fired and no gnomes could be seen. He looked carefully in all directions but could see no one. He walked off the trail to climb a tree in order to scout out the area. Still he saw no one.

When his companions in the tunnel saw that there had been no attempt on Gabrona's life Yanon instructed, "Three more of us will walk out of this tunnel in a manner that indicates that we are not worried about any threat. If there are any gnomes, they will think that we are the rest of the expedition and begin their attack. I'll be one of them. Are there any other volunteers?"

Elasti stepped forward quickly and so did Obydon. The three left the tunnel acting confidently as Yanon had suggested. Nothing happened.

By this time Gabrona was already climbing down the tree. The path descended down out of the mountains. The trees had gotten pretty thin and Gabrona had been able to see out in many directions. He felt confident that they were safe. He could see all the way to the Kilo Pass and there were no gnomes anywhere.

The secret trail wasn't a very good trail. It was overgrown with bushes and trees, which helped to keep it secret. So Gabrona didn't expect to find gnomes on this trail. But he did expect to find gnomes along the Kilo Pass, and there were none. He also looked for campfires and there was nothing. The area seemed completely deserted.

The four leading the expedition continued walking. At this lower elevation in the mountains the travelers were starting to come out of the forest, and they found only traces of snow in the shady areas. The air was brisk but not so cold that they wouldn't be able to tolerate it easily. There was very little underbrush and the pass was easy to travel. They journeyed on, always keeping a watch for any possible attacks.

Back in the tunnel, Gido, Yanon's second in command, instructed the remaining members of the quest;

"When they are far ahead of us,
But not so far that we can't see;
We'll follow quickly after them,
But stay hid in the trees."

Yanon and his companions were just about out of sight at this point and the five slowly and carefully followed after them. They stayed off to the side of the road in the trees.

Travel was easy. The trail had less snow and the forest was thinner. They were well rested and fed. The team felt as though they could walk for days. They regrouped and journeyed forward to the Kilo Pass, always cautious about finding gnomes. There was nothing. It was as if the gnomes had given up on them. After several hours of journeying along the pass the forest had become so thin that there were hardly any more trees for them to stay hidden in. This meant that there were also none for any gnomes to hide behind. The expedition members decided that trying to hide any longer was foolish and they started to travel down the main roadway walking as quickly as they could.

It was approaching noon when the expedition suddenly lost sight of their trail. It was as if someone was purposefully trying to hide the path. "Jesves," yelled Yanon, "we need your help. We need your direction sense. Can you get us back on the right trail?"

"I hope so," was her reply. She headed due north in the same direction that the trail had been leading them earlier. She had found no indication that the trail would go in any other direction. After an hour's travel the expedition arrived at the intersection of several trails. Yanon stopped and looked at Elasti as if to ask, "What now?"

Elasti had never been in this area before. His previous journey to the North Grove had been via the Albo Pass which caused him to come out at a completely different location. "This trail heading south must be the original Kilo Pass trail. It must have died out somewhere and then started up once again and we missed it somehow. As for these other trails heading north, I would suggest that we take the one that goes in the northernmost direction. We should eventually hit the Hile Groves."

"They sure kept the second exit well hidden," commented Yanon. "We'd never be able to find it if we didn't know exactly where to look."

"That's why the gnomes didn't know about it," added Obydon.

Yanon waved to Jesves to continue leading the way and she started down the trail suggested by Elasti. They traveled for only an hour when the trail began to fade out again this time due to the thick grass overgrowth. They were entering the North Groves. Jesves was undaunted by the knee-high grass. She continued heading north hoping that eventually they would encounter the Hile Groves.

It was several more hours before there was any change in the scenery. Elasti was the first to notice and yelled out, "Look ahead! It's the Hile Groves. We have made it to the home of the dwarfs. Surely now we will be able to cross the swords of power and call on the Wizard of Havinis. Now we will be able to defeat the evil of the Kabul!"

A cheer went up amongst the travelers. Leprechaun, lepelf, and elf all felt the excitement of having completed their mission. Elasti began running through the high grasses toward the groves. It had seemed like an eternity to get this far and now the pounding of his heart made his head throb just to be amongst the beautiful dwarfen trees once again. He ran on, harder and harder, faster and faster.

His friends getting caught up in his excitement started running too. They frolicked and jumped in the grass as if they were children at play. The last part of their journey had been quiet. They had not encountered any evil elements. They now had no reason to expect any new evil to appear once they were within the protective confines of the dwarf's domain. They ran on, faster and faster, until they all had entered the Hile Groves. They were inside. They were safe.

They all looked at Elasti as if to say, "Now where do we go?"

Elasti pointed toward the northeast. And as the sun settled gently in the west, the expedition of six leprechauns, two elves, and one lepelf, began marching toward the home of the dwarfs.

High above them, sitting in a tree, unnoticed by anyone but Gijivure, sat an eagle, and he smiled.

Here ends the The Siege of The Small World.

First book of the History of Small World.

THUS ENDS THE FIRST BOOK

IN THE HISTORY OF SMALL WORLD

GLOSSARY

Abogidyide - the secret name of Bydola

Agot - Leprechaun from Amins - brave, young friend of Elasti chosen for the first expedition

Algo - Leprechaun from Amins - the old "Wise Elder" of the council

Amaz - Leprechaun from Amins - Head of the Council of Amins and a "Wise Elder"

Amber - Southern Sword's light

Amins - the Southern Plains city of the leprechauns where the Small World saga begins

Avre - Leprechaun from Amins - a wise member of the council and a furniture maker

Balbot - Leprechaun from Amins - outspoken, aggressive council member

Balkwood - a favorite climbing tree

Bananot - Leprechaun from Amins - the old wise foreseer

Broch - Leprechaun from Amins - brave, young friend of Elasti chosen for the first expedition

Bydola – Leprechaun from Amins - the strong rock-mine worker

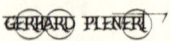

Creator -builder of all things

Dwarfs – small but strong and heavily built inhabitants of Small World, dwelling in the North Groves

Elasti - Leprechaun from Amins - the fearful son of a carpenter who was forced on the first expedition and then volunteered for the second

Egione - leader of the dwarf council

Elfin Book of Learning - elfin scriptures

Elf – the pretty inhabitants of Small World living in the south-west corner of the Southern Plains

Erates - tiles with cracks that fall to the Lamos

Erock – Elf from Gije - doctor

Gabrona – Lepelf from Giter - innkeeper's son who joined the expedition

Gamotz - the Central Ranges city of the gnomes

Gath – Elf from Gije - last to travel on the Back Road before this expedition

Geday – Elf from Gije - farmer

Geld - money, coinage

Gibbon - small cat-like creature

Gido – Elf from Gije - council member and representative on the expedition

Gije - the city of the elves, the "pretty" residents of Small World's Southern Plains

Gijivure –Elf from Gije - warrior and bowman representing Gije on the expedition

Gilbon – Lepelf from Giter - Yanon's military friend

Gimans – Elf from Gije - the Lord of Gije

Gingoras – the North Groves city of the shy giants

Gione – Elf from Gije - farmer

Giter - the Southern Plains city of the lazy and apathetic lepelves

Giterod – Lepelf from Giter - representative on the expedition and king's assistant

Giterquake - earthquakes centered around Giter

Gnomes – deformed and mutant creatures created by the holocaust that occurred in Upperworld

God of the Rainbow – Leprechauns' God

Gorbot – Lepelf from Giter - King

Hasko - Leprechaun from Amins - the scout

Hastle - nickname for Hiztin

Hilebin - the North Groves royal city of the dwarfs

Hilebon - the North Groves commercial city of the dwarfs

Hitl Lake – lake in the Hile Groves that once contained a great city in its depths. No rivers flow into or out of the lake.

Hiztin - Leprechaun from Amins - the bowman

Hopls - One-legged noisy birds

Jesves - Leprechaun from Amins - the fearless girl that never gets lost but keeps getting into trouble

Jizeel - Leprechaun from Amins - the daughter of Amaz, engaged to Elasti

Kabul - The Central Ranges land ruled by Krakus

Karkat - tree with extremely hard wood and living roots

Krakus - mutant Wizard and Emperor / Lord of the Kabul

Lepelves - Residents of Giter that are the result of a union of elves and leprechauns

Leprechauns – the smallest inhabitants of Small World living the furthest south in the Southern Plains

Lifefight Wars - the original invasion Small World by the gnomes from Upperworld who afterward made their home in the Kabul

Magotites – Magotites were magot-eaten dead animals brought back to life by the Kabul Lord so that he could use them for his evil designs. They lived in the northern part of the Kabul

Mihorse - small domesticated horse used in farming

Mirror Pond -a large pond west of Giter which contains a water quist and was sometimes used to get to the Creator.

Morgos - the Central Ranges city of the magotites

Muidivengers - mud caretakers of the Creator that are deaf

Northern Sword - magical sword given to the dwarfs after the Lifefight Wars

Obydon - Leprechaun from Amins - the son of Amaz, sword carrier on the expedition

Oply – Worlepreek from Second Tunnel - Council Lord

Opopp - Worlepreek from Second Tunnel - Doctor

Orange - Creator's light

Ordo - Worlepreek from Second Tunnel - Oply's assistant

Pollo Weed -narcotic weed

Protee - an organization of power against evil directed by the Creator. The organization uses a staff and a secret name to invoke its power, the presence of which was expressed by an orange light. They also have their own language for com-munication.

Pull boat - a boat used to cross the Avol River that had a rope tied at each shore

Purple - Raker's color

Quali Swamp Rats - rats controlling the Quali Swamps

Raker – mysterious swamp creature

Retants - living roots from the Karkat tree

Riposters - mutant bird-fish from the Kabul

Shadow Warriors - protectors of the Tako Temple

Southern Sword - magical sword given to the leprechauns after the Lifefight Wars

Staff of Protee - staff given to Bydola by the Creator

Temple at Tako - pyramid temple structure built and ruled over by the Protee in the demolished city of Tako

Tragis - the Central Ranges city of the trolls

Trolls – monstrous, slow moving and slightly backwards for-est dwellers

Small World - a world within the world

Upperworld - the outside world of Small World

Werewolves - humans turned into wolves

Water Quist - creature living in Mirror Pond

Wizard of Havinis - the helpful "Great Wizard" who was a human but was transferred into Small World during the Life-fight Wars by the power of the crossed swords

Worlepreeks - leprechauns without legs that live in the northernmost tunnel of the Kilo Pass

Worlepreeks Book of Psalms - Worlepreeks scriptures

Yanon - Leprechaun from Amins - the military leader who becomes expedition leader

Yellow - Southern Sword's light

About the Author

Dr. Gerhard Plenert

Gerhard, obsessed with the world of fantasy is an internationally recognized author having written and published books for organizations like the United Nations, and for various universities in the United States, Japan, and Europe. This will be his sixteenth book. He also has 150+ articles published in journals and magazines around the world. His publications have been endorsed by companies like Black and Decker, AT&T, and FedEx and by internationally recognized bestselling authors like Stephen R. Covey. He travels internationally and works as a business consultant.

Other Books By

Dr. Gerhard Plenert

The History of The Small World Series

- *The Siege of the Small World* - Dr. Gerhard Plenert
- *The Uniting of the Small World* - Dr. Gerhard Plenert

The New Templars Series

- *Dawn of the New Templars* - Gerhard Plenert
- *Activating the New Templars* - Gerhard Plenert

Other Fiction Titles

- *The Dragon Pit* - Gerhard Plenert

Non-fiction Business Titles

- *Discover Excellence: An Overview of the Shingo Model and Its Principles* - Edited by Gerhard Plenert
- *Driving Strategy to Execution Using Lean Six Sigma: A Framework for Creating High Performance Organizations* - Gerhard Plenert | Tom Cluley

- *Finite Capacity Scheduling: Optimizing A Constrained Supply Chain* - Bill Kirchmier | Gerhard Plenert | Gregory Quinn
- *International Management and Production* - Gerhard Johannes Plenert, Ph.D.
- *International Operations Management* - Gerhard Plenert
- *Lean Management Principles for Information Technology* - Gerhard J. Plenert
- *Making Innovation Happen - Concept Management Through Integration* - Gerhard Plenert | Shozo Hibino
- *Module 17 Operations Management* - Gerhard Plenert
- *Reinventing Lean: Introducing Lean Management Into The Supply Chain* - Gerhard Plenert
- *Strategic Continuous Process Improvement: Which Quality Tools to Use, and When to Use Them* - Gerhard Plenert
- *Strategic Continuous Process Improvement: Which Quality Tools to Use, and When to Use Them* - Gerhard Plenert, Ph.D., CPIM
- *Strategic Excellence in the Architecture, Engineering, and Construction Industries* - Gerhard Plenert | Joshua Plenert
- *Supply Chain Optimization through Segmentation and Analytics* - Gerhard Plenert
- *The eManager: Value Chain Management in an eCommerce World* - Gerhard Plenert
- *The Plant Operations Handbook: A Tactical Guide to Everyday Management* - Gerhard J. Plenert
- *Toyota's Global Marketing Strategy: Innovation through Breakthrough Thinking and Kaizen* - Shozo Hibino | Kolchiro Noguchi | Gerhard Plenert
- *World Class Manager* - Gerhard Plenert, Ph.D.

VISIT THE AUTHOR

SOCIAL AND OTHER MEDIA

PUBLISHER:

DonnaInk Publications:
www.donnaink.com

SOCIAL MEDIA:

Facebook:
https://www.facebook.com/authorgerhardplenert

LinkedIn:
www.linkedin.com/pub/gerhard-plenert/1/b0/75b

Twitter:
http://www.twitter.com/AuthorGPlenert
https://twitter.com/GPlenert

WORDPRESS BLOG:

http://authorgerdplet.wordpress.com
http://gerhard338.wordpress.com

WEBSITE:

www.gerhardplenert.com

Special Offers

In 2020 onward, Gerhard Plenert will feature a suite of merchandise and perhaps a newsletter regarding fantasy fiction – you can visit his WordPress blog and join the followers he has there as well.

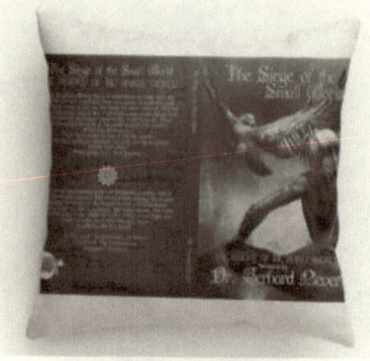

Donnalnk Publications, L.L.C.

Publisher
www.donnaink.com

For bulk orders, special orders, etc.
Special Markets Division
Donnalnk Publications, L.L.C.
601 McReynolds Street
Carthage, North Carolina 28327
Email:contact@donnainkpublications.com

For Promotions:
Promotions Division
ZenCon Art of Zen Consultancy
601 McReynolds Street
Carthage, North Carolina 28327
Email: verylittlebookstore@gmail.com

ZENCON ART OF
ZEN CONSULTANCY
PR & Marketing

Thunderforge Pubs

Donnalnk Publications, L.L.C.

www.ingramcontent.com/pod-product-compliance
Lightning Source LLC
Chambersburg PA
CBHW051327250626
47155CB00007B/2485